THE STARS IN THE BRIGHT SKY

Alan Warner is the author of five previous novels: *Morvern Callar*, *These Demented Lands*, *The Sopranos*, *The Man Who Walks* and *The Worms Can Carry Me To Heaven*. In 2003 he was chosen as one of *Granta*'s twenty Best of Young British Novelists.

ALAN WARNER

The Stars in the Bright Sky

VINTAGE BOOKS
London

Published by Vintage 2011

2 4 6 8 10 9 7 5 3 1

First published in Great Britain in 2010 by Jonathan Cape

Vintage
Random House, 20 Vauxhall Bridge Road,
London SW1V 2SA

www.vintage-books.co.uk

Addresses for companies within The Random House Group Limited
can be found at: www.randomhouse.co.uk/offices.htm

The Random House Group Limited Reg. No. 954009

A CIP catalogue record for this book is available from the British Library

ISBN 9780099461821

The Random House Group Limited supports The Forest Stewardship
Council (FSC), the leading international forest certification
organisation. All our titles that are printed on Greenpeace approved
FSC certified paper carry the FSC logo. Our paper procurement
policy can be found at www.randomhouse.co.uk/environment

Mixed Sources
Product group from well-managed
forests and other controlled sources
www.fsc.org Cert no. TT-COC-002139
© 1996 Forest Stewardship Council

FSC

Printed and bound in Great Britain by CPI Bookmarque, Croydon, CR0 4TD

. . . K was haunted by the feeling that he was losing himself or wandering into a strange country . . . a country so strange that not even the air had anything in common with his native air, where one might die of strangeness, and yet whose enchantment was such that one could only go on and lose oneself further . . .

Franz Kafka, *The Castle*

The Friday Evening

1

With caution, the four young women had silently observed the illuminated hotel signs placed upon the flat roofs along the vague night skylines – even as the bus repeatedly spun on disorient-ating, curved turnpikes and flyovers: the Renaissance, the Thistle, Holiday Inn, the Ramada, the Meridian, the Skylane. The Flight Deck Hotel sign had been elevated, just above or even slightly among the rich, ink-black hangings of oak and ash, those very lush English trees with their branches moving in an obscurely prophetic way, like languid windsocks.

Suspicious Manda, calm Kay, fascinated Kylah and timid Chell sat alongside one another on the staunchly commandeered back seat of the Hotel Hoppa minibus; other passengers seated in front of them were also looking out, glancing upward at the circular, elevated traffic lanes.

Among all this gloom, the minibus windows seemed dirty, perhaps even tinted, yet the outside entire – those night airs – was dusted with a particular light above each sodium lamp and just below every car park floodlight; a spectral grittiness haloed vehicle tail lamps on the limited feeder lanes where cars and mysterious white vans appeared with an unbound continuity.

Manda called out, 'Here we are. Look, see . . .' She arose as if it were an emergency, ducking her now-blonde hair under the skylight in the bus aisle, then she stumbled forward as if she alone would miss the stop, clutching out onto a seat back with fragile acrylic nails, knuckles ridged with her golden multi-rings. Stooping even further, Manda peered out and up from the side windows. Eye-aching blue roof neon rose above them as they came closer:

The physical appearance of the hotel now faced them with a strange novelty: its long strips of brown frontage, its black glass along three floors, the haphazard patches of grassy shapes in the car park, enclosed within curves of kerbing and the zoological movements of slight, distant figures against the white interior of the glass lobby.

Halted adjacent to Flight Deck Hotel's illuminated, hexagonally inspired glass lobby, the Hotel Hoppa passengers stood up from their seats. The bus driver stepped down through the pneumatic front door and there were almost immediate muffled bumpings as he opened the luggage panniers below the low flooring.

Moving importantly, Manda was first off after the front travellers. Behind her, holding their metallic vanity cases, came Kylah and Chell, free thumbs immediately firing up the lime or purple faces of their mobile phones, checking again for an unlikely inflow of urgent texts from home. With the laptop computer case strap slung across her front like a bandolier, Kay Clarke followed.

High above them, in the nightsome heavens, the rotational movements of the aeroplanes were utterly obscured. Those suspended, gargantuan airborne noises approached, then slowly became an underfoot, chthonic presence. The absorbent buffs of clouds above sealing in some new acoustic against this concrete land.

Since they had arrived by train forty minutes earlier, the young women had repeatedly glanced upwards towards the taking-off noise, glaring at the edges of buildings, convinced these structures were obscuring the aircraft above, but no; as they squinted, almost vertically, nothing showed of the phantasmic aircraft – just aural fury, close in, then a slow diminishing, leaving this oppressive sense of some overwhelming outer world, towards which all this noise was excitedly speeding.

Apart from Kay, the other three young women, rapidly but independently, began lighting up cigarettes as they stood back from the minor scrummage at the side of the minibus where the bus driver was horizontally swishing out suitcases then popping them up vertically. The other passengers cautiously recoiled back then enthusiastically moved in to seize their luggage: a Japanese-looking gentleman and two younger Indian-seeming gentlemen and a couple of right old fogeys were snapping out the telescopic handles and slowly wheeling away their wee cases towards the cosy-looking lobby. Kay had turned to survey the lobby interior – the others knew fine she was looking for Finn and her new best friend, who were coming down from London to rendezvous.

Smoking intently, the other young women shamelessly stared after the fellow hotel guests, one by one, until an aircraft climbed out overhead – seemingly directly above – with a sound of such profundity it was inconceivable that the machine wasn't visible.

It was that earliest of philosophers, old Heraclitus of Ephesus, who postulated that the heavens above us are formed out of vast bowls, their hollow sides turned towards earth. These aircraft engines above seemed to echo out of the very concave dishes of the Ephesian. The young women experienced an inclination to hunch over, as if their very scalps were straying – ever so slightly – into a zone commandeered by air traffic control.

'A nice quiet spot,' Chell sneered, propelling out angry-seeming smoke through her small burgundy lips.

'My wee Sean would love all . . . this,' Manda yelled, both excited and daunted – looking to the others – demanding a response.

'Aye. The wee pet,' Kylah obediently shouted among that rioting riddle of noise.

Chell and Kylah stood next to each other. Since they had begun sharing their small flat back in the town, Chell and Kylah constantly leaned together in devious but wordless conference, communicating with looks and a few barely contacting touches, silently passing cigarettes, offering lighters back and forth in a nicotine telepathy.

Meanwhile, the bus driver had come upon the vast extent of *equipage* accompanying this small party. For just four girls there were seven suitcases, laid out flat in the luggage compartment and six of them were very large, fully packed and stickered with HEAVY warning labels.

'Emigrating?' The driver bent in deeper to manhandle the suit-cases out one by one, heaving them erect upon the pavement.

Smoking her second already, Manda drawled, 'We don't know where we're headed, do we? Down here getting one of these last-minute package deal things on her laptop computer.' Manda pointed aggressively at Kay. 'You don't know what to pack when you don't know what place you'll end up. We could be away some place boiling hot, like Magaluf where I want to go, or end up some daft freezing place they all want to go to. There's so bloody many of them, aren't there? All the places? Wherever places we go, I don't care, cos I've had my bikini wax.'

'Don't go telling him too, Manda.'

'Aye. Leave the mannie alone.'

He grunted and looked at the luggage again, astonished. 'And is that the Scotch accent I hear?'

'Aye, mister.'

Chell told him, 'My uncle says windscreen wiper settings should be: Slow, Medium, Fast, and Scotland.'

The bus driver managed a rum chuckle, all the deeper as he was straining at Chell's very own case.

'Och aye the noooo. I've been to Glasgow,' he winked, obscurely. He looked down at the line of cases, breathing heavily. 'I have two daughters about your age, girls. They pack like this even when they know where they're going.'

The other girls hesitated. Manda had a severely resentful look. 'Actually, I think your daughters'd be impressed how much I got in there.' She softly kicked one of her big sister's two, illicitly borrowed, pink Samsonites.

The driver had reboarded his bus. Before he had even closed the door, Manda turned on the others. 'Hear that? Even the bus drivers are snooty down here. Making out his daughter hoors'd have more good clothes than us. And just a wee totey bus he drives too. No even a red London double decker thing.' She swivelled then dropped her cigarette butt, pulverising it with the back of her yellow three-inch heel.

Chell and Kylah roused uneasily and stubbed out cigarettes

with grudging foot scrapes then began making small adjustments to the positions of their wheeled suitcases; as much as they could, they all held their fragile acrylic nails high in the air and well away from the fatal handles and cumbersome edges.

Kay just had one smaller, distressingly hollow-looking suitcase but the other girls now tried to manoeuvre two cases each. Kylah and Chell also balanced their vanity cases on the tops of their suitcases – in a very precarious way, dragging the pull-out handles and making towards the automatic sliding doors which eventually sealed the group within the hotel lobby, shutting out the kerosene scent but only some of the aviation noise.

Time was now to be qualified by the subtle shake, the subconscious intake of breath at an aircraft taking off, every three or four minutes.

There was a long queue at the hotel reception desk. Chell's vanity case crashed down jarringly to the fake marble floor and people turned to stare. Manda laughed then scowled at the queue for the check-in desk.

The girls drew up into an intimidating, unpredictable phalanx behind and to the side of the orderly queue. People were coming and going past them. There were two colour monitors buried into the walls, showing the departures and arrivals of continual flights in arithmetical columns. An exoticism arose from every surface and object which they looked at.

'Yous watch ma cases. I'll do all the talking.' Manda stepped forward to take a place in the queue, and as she did so, her mobile phone trilled into ringtone: a bad approximation of 'Funky Town' by Lipps Inc. Manda fumbled her shoulder bag aside and drew a mobile from within. She more or less shouted everything: 'Hi. Oh, *Dad*. Aye. Just in the airport now. Aye, girls is fine. It was dark when we got in to London bus station so's on the train here we couldn't see England at all. I thought it was meant to be dead big and all that. How's wee Sean; is he asking for his mummy? Oh, bless.' Then she lowered the voice – 'Did Catriona say anything about the cases? *I* have to get our hotel rooms sorted and all that stuff, then book the plane seats. Let him sleep and I'll phone later. Aye, *Dad*. I've got to go now. I'll phone later. Not too late, no. Bye-bye.'

A man in a business suit was in the queue behind Manda, but she leaned around him and bawled back to the others, 'That's wee Sean sleeping,' and she nodded with a confirmed determination.

Slowly Manda in the queue was drawn away from the girls who stood by the suitcase park.

'I can't take much more of Manda and we're not even on the plane yet.' Chell used a smile as a mask.

'She's nipping my head. And that's official.' Kylah looked at Chell.

'She's worse than two busloads of English pensioners. Arriving in tourist info at the same time,' claimed Chell.

Kay went, 'Manda thinks attention deficit disorder means when people are not giving her enough attention.'

'She's knackering to be with for longer than ten minutes. Who's going to have to share with her the night then?' Kylah rested her head on her own shoulder and gave a grim smile.

'Oh God. What a thought. Let's draw lots.'

'What with?'

'We've no matches. We could get straws over there? That looks like the bar.'

'How's about the coloured condoms from Boots?'

'They're all in the suitcases.'

'We're on holiday. I've mine right here.'

'Dirty besom. Get them out quick.'

'Not for the last time, I hope.'

'Will be if I end up in Turkey again.'

Kylah opened her vanity case while it balanced atop her vertical, resting suitcase and she excavated; in her palm were

three condoms, tight little packets, metallic: two dark blue –
Large-sized – and one bright red – Medium-sized.

'I can't believe they've started selling them by size. I mean,
how does a guy go in Boots to buy them any more?'

'All guys must surely go in and say, "Extra Large for me and
some Small ones for my wee brother please."'

'What sizes did you get?'

'A pack of each. Ever hopeful.'

They sensed Manda across in the queue, snapping around
sharply, scrutinising them.

Kylah whispered towards Kay, 'You mix them up without
looking, then me and Chell draw, an if you're left with the red
it's you, if one us draws the red then it's us shares with her. Fair
enough?'

Kay qualified, 'Yes, okay, but only for tonight. Not when we
get to the hotel in wherever.'

Chell said, 'Oh aye. That'll need a new draw altogether. I
suppose Finn'll be sharing with her pal-thing though.'

Kylah dropped the three little packets in Kay's tracksuit side
pocket.

Kay nodded, grinding the contraceptives around in the pocket.
She removed her hand and flexed her fingers leaving the coloured
packets in the pocket. With her back positioned to the reception desk, Chell reached outward and into Kay's tracksuit – you
could see the rib-like presence of the small fingers moving and
choosing within there, through the fabric; with intense specu-
lation on Chell's small forehead, she removed her hand from
Kay's pocket and she formed a fist. Keeping the hand low but
bent at the wrist, Chell then opened up her hand, revealing a
blue one, foil corners packed tightly inwards.

'Oh no.' Kylah gritted her teeth. She reached into the pocket,
took and discarded several times within, withdrew her clenched
fist and opened. Red.

Without thought, as if it were a hot cinder, Kylah threw the
red foil to the ground with a yelp, but just then two old fogeys,
arm in arm, appeared at Kylah's side, slowly making their way
forth. The prophylactic hit the fake marble floor just in front of

9

the old lady's flat, comfy shoe, which halted. Kylah and the girls stiffened. Slowly, the old lady unbound her linked arm from her husband's; she bent forwards, the bare arm so old and mottled it resembled the grey skin of a turbot, but those shaky finger tips seized upon that Durex.

The girls grimaced in unison.

The old dame came all the way slowly back up, turned towards them and held out the condom to Kylah. 'You dropped your sweetie, my dear.' The lady smiled and moved on, looping arms again with the old fellow who led forward, in uxorious devotion.

'Oh, thank you so very much,' Kylah whispered to the couple's back.

As soon as they politely could, they all burst out laughing.

'My God, she was ancient as old Rose in *Titanic*,' Kylah whispered.

Kay said, 'Hey, watch, here goes Manda now. The booking is in my name but she's too damn pigheaded to admit it. She'll go and give her own name cos she can't delegate control to anyone.'

They watched as Manda reached the top of the queue for reception.

'Right. That's us here then,' Manda told the receptionist.

The receptionist wasn't very receptive; he dropped his head down to his screen. 'Name?' He had a foreign accent – not some unfathomable region of England but foreign. French-sounding. Manda stared at him hard, suspiciously, as if he was utterly inscrutable.

'Amanda Tassy.'

'That's Tass–double "e"?'

'A–m–a–n–d–a.'

'Yes. But surname?'

'T–a–s–s–y.'

The receptionist frowned. He did not click away on his computer but stated, 'We have no reservation under such a name.'

'What do you mean under? What's above it?'

'Pardon me?'

'Maybe our reservation's above it?'

'Above what?'

'Whatever's not under it.'

Manda's accent was unfamiliar to him and English was not the receptionist's first language. 'Are you a party?' he tried.

'Why? Is there one?'

'One what?' He pushed a finger over towards the lurking girls. 'Are you all together?'

'Oh. Them. The whispering Jennies. Aye, we are all together in a manner of speaking and two more still coming – supposedly.' Manda raised her eyes, inviting him to join her in being contemptuous of her entourage.

'Perhaps the booking was made in another name within your party?'

'Eh? Aye. Wait. Kay,' she bawled out suddenly, so the receptionist jumped as her breasts bounced once, sharply upwards. 'Might need your wee credit card thingmyjig over here. The now. Here a minute.' Manda impatiently gestured Kay to immediately advance, using a swishing, crooked forearm.

Kay crossed the foyer to the desk. 'Sorry. I made the reservation using this card in the name of Clarke.' Held in her fingers, Kay sliced forward her father's supplementary gold-coloured credit card, in her own name, and she gave Manda a look, adopting a temporary power over her. 'All three rooms can be charged to this card.'

The receptionist took the card while meeting the eyes of Manda. Solemnly he said, 'That is Clark with an "e" and this is a reservation for . . . three twin rooms; one night only. All smoking.'

'Yes. Two more people are still to come down from London this evening.'

'He knows all that.'

'If the rooms are on this credit card I'll only need your signature, but could you write down the names of all the party on the registration card please.'

'We don't know the name of one,' Manda shook her head frantically, 'Fionnula's English-pal-thing. Don't know her name at all. Do we?'

In a measured way, Kay stated, 'Her name is Ava.'

Manda frowned, ignoring the existence of the receptionist. 'Aye. But you don't know her second name, do you? It'll be one of them posh English ones: Ava Farley Rusks or something.'

'What?'

'Or more like Ava Tendencies, eh, Kay?' Manda snorted a rumple of mirth. 'Ava Tendencies I cannot control.' Then she muttered, trying the word out contemptuously, 'Phil-o-sophy.' Now Manda turned violently to the receptionist and unburdened herself. 'They're students.' She nodded. 'We're all away tomorrow but it's one of these last-minute things on her laptop computer and we're even still deciding where we're going, from among all of the places. It's going to be classic. It's going to be brilliant,' Manda insisted.

'Yes.' The receptionist slid the credit card back towards Kay with the registration form. 'Checkout time is at eleven.' He crisply added, 'Eleven in the morning, that is.'

Kay accepted the pen and began to write in her exasperatingly perfect hand.

Manda pushed in against Kay's arm. 'Write me next. Write me next.'

Kay wrote the names of their party.

Kay Clarke
Kylah Campbell
Amanda Tassy
Rachel McDougall
Fionnula McConnel
Ava —

Manda suddenly snatched up the pen and leaned over, nimbly adding to the registration form:

Kay Clarke	Gemini
Kylah Campbell	Leo
Amanda Tassy	Scorpio
Rachel McDougall	Sagittarius
Fionnula McConnel	Gemini
Ava –	what goes with Gemini

The receptionist looked on, tolerating this with a sort of astonished fascination. Kylah and Chell had also come forward to the reception desk, to nose in on all this action, but wary of the thieving potential in any place which was not home, they adamantly dragged their own large suitcases with them, forcing aside other queuing guests. Again, one of the metallic vanity cases crashed down.

'Fuck sake.'

'It's no check-in, girls, you daft hoors. You don't weigh in your cases *here* for the plane.' Manda turned round and guffawed, 'Chell works in the tourist information but hasn't never been on planes before.' She looked across the whole lobby for a response.

Kylah had a yellow disposable camera in her hands. 'I'm taking a photo. Us checking in to the hotel,' she announced to everyone.

The businessman in the queue behind had a sort of stunned expression as all the girls backed up against the counter in a pose.

Manda pointed at the businessman. 'Hoi. Mister, mister, going to take a photo please so Kylah can get in too?'

Kylah turned to the man and smiled.

'Give it to me,' the man in the suit sighed. Kylah stepped into the line and the businessman lifted the disposable camera, pointed it at the girls along the counter and clicked it.

'Hey, I think my eyes were shut.'

'Please.' The businessman held out the camera.

'Make him take another.'

'No, no. I only have thirty-six photos in it.' Kylah stepped forward. 'Thanks, mister.' She grabbed the camera off him but immediately turned her back because the impatient receptionist was talking.

'These are your key cards and here are your room numbers. You are on the first floor in rooms next to one another. You must use this card inside the door to operate the lights in your room.'

Suddenly serious and utterly absorbed by every detail, Manda nodded a response to each statement. The receptionist surveyed above their hairstyles and pointed in a rote manner. 'To reach the lifts for the first floor, go past the bar and they are on the left.' Every girl except Kay turned round to look, as if there were a good chance of becoming hopelessly disorientated forever, somewhere far across that hotel lobby.

Kay smiled, handing over a key card. 'There you are, Manda, now that's not a Boots Advantage card so don't try and get credit on it.'

They began to relinquish control of the reception counter, most of the length of which they had all leaned against. The frustrated businessman in the queue behind finally pushed forward impatiently, stepping over the charge of suitcases which wheeled round and away from the desk.

'That reception guy was more *gay* than Brian from *Big Brother*,' Manda snarled loudly, without looking back, aggressively heading straight for her two suitcases.

They began the making of their way across the lobby, arms dragged back, umbilical, to those double suitcases. Chell had decided to resort to walking backwards, pulling her two cases behind, head twisting round to view her way. She craned inwards at the hotel bar as they passed its noisy archway. The ceiling in there was low and refurbished from the eighties or perhaps even the seventies. The whole hotel had the ambience of some structure on a flood plain, always prepared to be winched up a few feet at short notice and towed away by monster trucks.

'Everyone's ancient here. Hello, grandads. What did yous do in the war?' Chell frowned in at the bar.

They all halted and peered at the clientele, who were not satisfactory. Tracksuited, beer-bellied divorcees with shaved craniums, all clustered in sporty packs tipping lager pints at their faces; some even went so far as to have the stubby rod of a rolled-up tabloid placed snug under an arm. They were bringing the excitement level down and they evinced zero exoticism about jetting off anywhere tomorrow.

Kylah let out an audible groan.

The tracksuited men turned obediently when sport came up on Sky News screens. Near the archway, an urbane, middle-aged couple faced each other around a fake pine table with a teapot between them, looking mildly startled. There *were* two young people: a handsome couple – he with the proprietary arm slung over her prematurely bare shoulders; they sat erect in the booth, drinks hardly touched, looking hopelessly consumed in each other and the prospects of a fortnight together as well as the available bed upstairs.

Chell got in first, stating, 'Exciting place but who knows where else to go round here?'

Glumly the others conceded and moved ahead to the two sets of polished brass elevator doors.

In single file they approached rooms 1103, 1104, 1105, halfway down the corridor's length. There was something strange about this corridor. Something alien to it that these country girls immediately felt uneasy about. There was no natural light. There were no windows. All through the years it could be any time of day or night in this long airport hotel corridor, where sun never reached.

Manda pushed to the front with her key card.

'Other way round.'

She inserted it and a small green light manifested above the door handle. She squealed with excitement, moving quickly in to a completely darkened room, 'That's amazing. I need one of these at home to stop Dad and Catriona nosing round my bedroom. Have to put this in somewhere for the lights?' And as the lights lit up the girls, even Kay, prowled into room 1103, colluding, slightly purring, Chell and Kylah throwing themselves horizontally onto the two beds.

'It's bigger than my room at home, ya bass. Bigger than Mum and Dad's room.'

'A telly. Smart.'

'Internet access here,' Kay pointed in a businesslike way.

They were opening the wardrobe doors and the cupboards, sliding out drawers; Chell hoisted a kettle and let out a hoot.

'Are all the rooms the same? Are all the rooms the same? Is any one better than the other?'

But Manda was ignored while Kay opened a door and gestured. 'One iron.'

'An iron? I packed my mum's good steam iron from up the house. She'll go mental. The Old Man's shirts'll no be done for his work for a week.'

Kay turned to Kylah. 'You brought an iron?'

'Aye. What's the matter with that?'

'Most hotels have them.'

'No in Turkey they bloody didn't; should of seen the state my tops got in there. I'm no going through all that again.'

'I thought we weren't going to Turkey anyways?'

'Yous can go if yous want. I'm no going back there. Ever.'

'I thought you knew Kylah was bringing the iron. Didn't *you* bring hair straighteners or curling irons as well then, Kay?' Manda smiled.

'No.'

'Did you just think you could borrow ours?'

'I don't use them, Manda.' Kay smiled.

'Oh aye. The *natural* look.' Manda sneered out towards the ceiling and began a speech. 'Well, Kylah and Chell each own curling tongs, so's since I have access to the salon, I took two sets of straighteners. So now we have two sets of curling tongs and two sets of straighteners for us and we can all share them. So I thought that was pretty thoughtful of me, to organise all that, and if you do need them, we'll let you borrow them.'

Kay stated, 'Thank you very much.'

Kylah suddenly stood stock-still and queried, 'You brought straighteners, Manda?'

'Aye, two straighteners.'

Chell said, 'We own straighteners, Manda. You made us buy them. Not curlers. Kylah and I brought two sets of straighteners.'

Manda stared at them. 'Straighteners? Yous are bloody jesting me? *I* brought the straighteners. I thought yous just owned curling tongs?'

'Nut.'

'So we now have four sets of straighteners and no curling tongs?'

'Aye.'

Kay had to turn aside to cover her smirk.

Manda bored a look into the back of Kay's head. 'Och. How did that go and happen?' Manda now gave Kylah a vinegary glance.

'Minibar,' Kylah called.

'Oh yessss.'

'Not free, you know. The prices are *insanely* high. Look at the prices in the room-service menu or they might be there, by the fridge. It's a fiver for a Coke . . . and things.'

'Ach, calm down, Kay, we're only joking.'

'Room-service menu? Couldn't get that at yon hotel complex in Turkey. Wasn't even phones in the rooms,' Kylah mumbled darkly.

'What room do you want then, Manda?' Kay smiled without implication.

Straight away, Manda replied, 'The one in the middle, so's I can hear what's happening in both other rooms. We'll have Kay on one side and Finn and her Ava Tendencies girlfriend on the other side.' Now Manda paused her look upon Kay.

'She's not her girlfriend-girlfriend,' Chell coldly said.

'Aye, I've heard all that before. Who's wanting to share with me?'

Too quickly, Kylah held a voluntary finger up towards the ceiling. 'I will then.'

Manda looked around the three of them. 'So that's what all the whisperings and giggles was about down there.'

'What on earth do you mean?'

'What on earth . . . what on earth . . . come off it. Claiming yous just decided the now Kylah's gonna share with me and no fight about it. Fuck off, ya hoors. That's easier decision-making from you lot than if you'd a whole football team to choose from.' She turned her head slightly to Kay. 'Or a hockey team.'

'Well, who do you want to share with then? If it's such an issue?'

'Oh, Kylah is just great. Me and Kylah will be fine. Won't we, Kyles?'

'Aye.'

'What about getting us online and booked up for tomorrow then?'

Quietly Kay said, 'Well, we need to wait on Finn and her friend, to make any decisions.'

'C'mon, Kylah,' Manda clipped abruptly, implicating Kylah in some faction which didn't exist.

'Back here in five,' said Kylah, hopefully.

'Are yous changing to go down to this mingy bar joint?' Manda turned suddenly, suspiciously enquiring.

'Nah,' Chell shrugged.

Manda commenced banging outwards from the room, grunting, cursing as she struggled, turning and pulling her own suitcases and Kylah followed with her baggage, looking back to Chell and Kay hopelessly. The door swung shut. Out in the corridor they heard: 'Watch my nails. Watch my fucking nails.'

Chell immediately leaned in to Kay's ear and said, 'Let's get changed just to wind her up.'

Kay nodded quickly. She had her laptop up on the desk by the mirror, unzipping it from its black case.

Chell shook off her three-inch heels then threw herself backwards on the single bed furthest from the window; she used the thumb of one hand to check her mobile phone again for texts which were not there, so she placed the mobile on the bedside cabinet. 'Jesus. My head's bursting with Manda. Four sets of hair straighteners. Practice Manageress. That'll be right. She didn't shut up for a single moment all day and night.'

'Except for when she was snoring.'

'And farting. What a niff. I tell you, on that bus to London when we stopped at that service station in the middle of God knows where, I was thinking of asking the driver to get down into my suitcase, cos I packed a pair of those nose clip things for the swimming pool.'

Kay did a bright laugh.

'Aye. Poor Kylah.' Chell dragged out a cigarette and lit it, staring up and blowing smoke towards the ceiling.

Kay unfurled the Internet connection wire.

'I mean, she's our friend since primary and that, but I wanted to batter her twice before we were even on the bus in Glasgow. Two years of it we've had on account of wee Sean, and her single-mother-martyr thing.'

Kay said, voice concentrating on booting up the computer, 'Yes. That's what it is: single-mother martyrdom.'

Chell said, 'Her Old Man and Nana and Catriona do everything for her. Everything. It's them bringing up the wee boy, no her. I tell you.' Chell now hoisted the remote control for the television and began stabbing it pointlessly towards the screen. 'Look at the number of cable stations. Jesus, there's thousands. It's a nice hotel here though, eh?'

'Yes.'

'Thanks for putting tonight all on your credit card thing for the now, Kay. That's appreciated. Appreciated by us at least,' she added.

'It's no problem.'

'Aye. Don't let Manda take advantage. You just tell her when to get off the horse.'

'Don't worry.'

'You're cool. You don't let her wind you up. She drives me to distraction but she's my pal and I can't go off on her. Or not at the start of a holiday with her anyways.' Chell went momentarily quiet. 'Hey, Kay?'

'What?'

'Honest injuns, I tried to feel which condoms were the bigger ones in your pocket when we were choosing.'

'Really?'

'Aye. I feel a wee bit guilty. I might have been able to tell and swindled Kylah.'

'Well, you're a fine judge of a condom then and you deserve to be the winner.'

2

Next door in 1104, Manda had breenged into the bathroom, holding the courtesy soaps and toiletries up to her eyes doubtfully. There weren't many. The body wash, shampoo and conditioner were to be dispensed from containers firmly affixed to the wall tiles inside the shower and bath. She bawled out, 'Don't be using *these* shampoos in here, Kylah, they'll frizz your hair for a bloody month. I've brought great shampoo from the salon and I'll let you use it. Tonight,' she added by way of a subclause.

'Okay.' Kylah's oppressed voice came from through in the bedroom.

Manda sauntered back to her. 'Kay's acting a bit uppity but she seems a wee fraction more relaxed than per-usual. Eh?'

'Dunno. She is on holiday from her uni now.'

'Suppose,' Manda grudgingly conceded. Restlessly she moved to the window, cupped saluting hands to her eyebrows to shield out the interior room light, jetting a froth from her excited nostrils which momentarily curdled upon the black glass. 'I'd of thought you'd have pulled the curtains, Kylah. There might be some English pervo out here watching me.' With an anticipatory gulp she viewed the beyond: a vast car park, illuminated by fantastically high lights suspended out on orbital frames at the top of elevated, tapering silver poles. All the differing parked vehicles had a look of abandonment, the cars awkward in their stillness, yet their temporary irrelevance contradicted by the forensics of the strident, dramatic downlights. Not a living soul stirred anywhere. Beyond was the roof-marker light of a Best Western Hotel sign and blotches of unpunctured darkness. 'England eh. It's so . . . organised. And flat.' Manda sharply pulled the curtains closed and recrossed the room. She kneeled suddenly and jerked open the minibar; all the miniature bottles and cans clunked in unison on their fitments in the back of the door. 'Oh. Check this. Voddy, KitKats, Coke and yeuch stuff and stuff and . . . gin. Fancy a wee voddy and Coke?'

'Kay says. About how pricey the minibar is.'

'Ach, Kay says this, Kay says that. And her with Daddy's credit card. After all, like you say, we *are* on our holidays.' Manda looked up cheekily at Kylah then hoisted out two vodka miniatures and a ridiculously small Coke can. She shoogled them.

Thump thump thump: there was an intrusive, repetitive banging on the bedroom wall, just above Chell's head from behind a graphic, framed painting, and a hysterical but profoundly muffled squeal came from the next room. Chell yelled, 'Is that you putting in your tampon, Manda? Good news, at least for this month.'

Chell had identical suitcases, each numbered on a flank '1' and '2', and in her vanity case she conveyed an accurate inventory of which items were contained within each suitcase. Using assistance from Kay to protect her nails, she'd heaved one of her suitcases up onto her bed and after sitting upon it, had slowly unbound the zip around her. She clambered off to reveal a confused layering of shoes – each wrapped individually within differing superstore carrier bags. She fished in beneath.

Sitting at the desk, with her back to her, Kay said in a patient voice, 'Don't unpack too much, Chell, you'll just have to repack it all in the morning.'

Chell looked at the back of Kay's tall neck, at the pale skin, the quiet earrings. At how her brown hair swirled from the parted roots there, slightly more to the left than the right. Kay hadn't tied it up proper. She was fair easy on the eye, even in a tracksuit. Kay the Lay, boys had once called her when they were at school back in the old town, but only because she was so aloof to them. Finn and Kay. Two beautiful girls in their posse would bring sure benefits of attention when they all hit the clubs, where-bloody-ever. Chell mumbled thoughtfully, 'I'm looking for the silver scarf. Going to wear it with the wee Kookai dress.'

Kay suddenly turned from the computer screen where she appeared to be checking emails, and trying to show more interest said, 'Oh, I know that silver scarf – the one you wore at Easter?'

'Aye. But *that* night I wore it loose; I'm not going to do that again, am I? Now I'm going to knot it and put it over my back so it hangs down.'

'Oh, right. Sorry.'

There were three tentative knocks at the door.

'Shit. The monster's back and I haven't changed.' Chell leaped up; the silver scarf was draped over her arm and her Kookai dress bunched to her stomach as she dashed for the bathroom and shut its door behind her.

Kay stood and walked to the corridor door. Frustrated, but under her breath, she said, 'So I suppose I'm entertaining Manda.' Stomping by the bathroom door, Kay yanked open the main door. Fionnula McConnel stood there with longer hair and a tall, very pretty brunette somewhere just over her left shoulder. Finn screamed and jumped at Kay, grabbing her in close.

'Kay,' Finn said, suddenly and in the manner of a surprised, desperate yelp.

'Hey. Finn,' Kay said flatly and chuckled; her head kind of projected forward, over Finn's right shoulder so Kay's face was stranded, facing the dark-eyed girl in the corridor. 'Ah, hi.' Kay couldn't put her arms all the way around Finn because a big hiking pack hung from Finn's back, so Kay's palms patted at buckles as she continued to helplessly observe the smiling stranger: Ava. She was beautiful.

Now Finn put both her hands on Kay's shoulders and took a step back to look at her. 'This is the sane one, Ava. The others are completely nuts.'

Kay laughed, flattered, looked round the side of Finn's face, which seemed a little flushed. Was Finn embarrassed or had she been drinking? 'Hi, Ava.'

'Hello. Nice to meet you, Kay.'

English accent of course, very posh but maybe mixed with country tones. Kay noticed Ava had a backpack on as well.

'Come in. Come in, quick. Chell's here. Chell, quick. It's

Fionnula, already.' Kay knocked quietly on the bathroom door then retreated a little way down the short corridor, watching as Finn advanced inwards. The bathroom door split open an inch, disgorging intense white light from within. A ration of Chell's face, featuring a mascaraed eye, appeared.

'Finn.' Chell yanked the door open full, standing barefoot, only in matching underwear – a bluish bra with maybe yellow piping – she put out bare arms, drew Finn inwards to the bathroom but Finn's backpack would barely allow her entry round and through the door frame. 'Chell. Baby.' They hugged away. They both just laughed while hugging.

Kay cringed as, unexpectedly, came a heated flush of irrational possessiveness at the pale arms and painted fingernails of Chell, draped innocently on the green plasticity of the backpack. Kay had to blink to reprogramme herself.

'This is Ava from uni. So this one is Kay and this is Chell.'

Ava had to bend her head around the door frame to look in at Chell and she said, 'Hi there.'

Now Chell quickly held the Kookai dress up to cover her bra area and said, 'Hiya, Ava. Sorry I'm in the scud. I'm just quickly changing, to piss off our pal Manda who I told we weren't changing. She's a right one. You'll meet her in a minute. Just ignore her and her jibes.' Chell turned to address Finn. 'She's up to high-doh as per usual.' Chell raised her eyes to the ceiling and pushed the door near but not fully shut and you saw her lower her head, stepping into the dress.

Finn looked at Kay and there was a sort of understanding smile between them. So Kay stood back to allow Finn and Ava to fully enter the hotel bedroom until they all stood, somewhat solidly under the burden of their backpacks.

'How the hell are you?' Finn asked once again. Perhaps nervously.

'I'm good, I'm good. How's third year?'

'Great. But I shouldn't be jinking off. And you?'

'It's brilliant. Heavy going like you, but brill.'

'Is it Edinburgh you're attending, Kay?' Ava asked politely.

'Yes. Architecture. I don't know how I got through the first years. I thought it'd be like building doll's houses and it was pure mathematics.' Kay suddenly said, 'I wanted to take a back-pack too but I was vetoed by the fashion police here and had to bring my mum's old suitcase.' She pointed over to it in the far corner.

Finn was laughing. 'Aye, I knew it'd be controversial. I'll get a slagging but I don't have a bloody suitcase.'

'Look at this.' Kay indicated Chell's opened case on the bed. 'They've brought two suitcases each. Huge packed ones, and about ten pairs of shoes each. They even brought irons and hairdryers and hair straighteners. Four hair straighteners. They managed to forget curling tongs.'

'Oh, I've plenty shoes here on my back,' Finn stated, jerking her thumb over her shoulder. 'I just collected my best pair from the cobbler's this morning with the strap fixed. Aye, there are good things in life, but there is no happiness like stepping out the cobbler's with your favourite heels fixed.'

And they all laughed again in recognition of this.

'Where's Kylah and Manda?'

'In a middle room next us right here. We drew lots to see who would suffer bunking up with Manda and poor Kylah's on the job.'

Finn laughed a deep and surprisingly dirty chortle. She turned to Ava and said, 'See. That's how popular our Manda is.' Finn laughed again but Ava seemed to think it was politic just to smile.

Kay said, 'You two's room is the next one after. Here's the key card. One, one, oh, five. Manda said she wanted to be in the middle room so she could hear everything. I'm surprised she's not heard you and come nosing through yet.'

'How's her wee baby?'

Chell had emerged from the bathroom pulling at the hem of her dress and said, 'He looks like a turnip with an earring.' Chell stepped back into the Russell & Bromley heels.

The others all laughed sharply but again, Ava cautiously restricted her involvements to a smile.

'How's Kylah then?'

'Same us ever,' shrugged Chell.

'Good,' Finn nodded sharply, in a final way.

25

Kay went on, 'Hadn't seen everyone since I was home at Easter but we're all fine. Just the same.'

'How's working in the tourist info, Chell?' Finn turned to Ava. 'Chell works in the tourist information office at home.'

'You wouldn't believe some of it.'

'So's you and Kylah are sharing now, in Albyn Terrace?'

'Aye, and it's brilliant to be away from my folks, but I miss Selwyn.' Chell turned to Ava and politely explained, 'My dog.' Then she turned back to Finn. 'Apart from Kylah's weird music going all the time.'

'Exciting though, isn't it? Not knowing where we'll go,' said Ava suddenly, out of the blue.

'Yes,' Kay replied, looking at her, and she wondered for a moment if Ava was a bit gorgeous-looking but dim. Yet studying French and Philosophy?

Voices were heard in the corridor.

'Here's Manda at the door now and you're no even changed,' Chell snapped at Kay, but it was a warm authority.

'I'll go change. With pleasure.' There was a vicious hammering on the door, so immediate, so loud and so demanding, Finn jumped. Chell tutted but just persisted putting on lippy. Kay picked up her small suitcase and squeezed past the three of them, entered the bathroom and shut the door. This time there was the firm click of a lock.

Finn swung her backpack off and hefted it down between the side of the bed and the wall. 'Just put your stuff down there if you want for now, Ava,' Finn pointed. The hammering at the door came again as Ava unburdened herself of her backpack.

Chell had not shifted from the mirror and said, 'Aye, Finn, will you go hit her with a cattle prod or something?'

Finn strode to the vibrating door and jerked it open, yelling, in game-show-host voice, 'And it's Miss Manda Tassy!'

In the corridor Manda let out her usual theatrical scream. Kylah was behind her but Manda pushed herself possessively into Finn, cuddling, forcing Finn backwards, and Manda was simultaneously gazing over Finn's shoulder, into the room, trying to get a sighting of Ava.

'Fionnula. You're here.'

'And you're blonde.' Finn ruffled her hand through Manda's dyed, shorter hair.

'Do you like it?'

'Aye. How's wee Sean?'

'He's just great. I'll show you the photos. Just brought them special for you. There's a new club in the town. Rascals. You've really missed yourself. There's a new bar too called the Event.'

'Oh, and what happens there then?'

'Eh, nothing much.'

Kylah had followed in and said, 'How're the philosophers then? What's the meaning to life? Have they told you yet?' Kylah shoogled her curls, put both her hands out at waist level and she shook her body in that movement of traditional greeting.

Manda had loosely parted from Finn and stepped impatiently on down the room corridor where she could see Chell leaning in towards the bureau mirror.

Kylah stepped and kissed Finn on the cheek. Manda heard Kylah say, 'You're looking gorgeous. Your hair is dead long.'

Manda had by now noticed Chell's replaced dress. Manda turned her head sharply to the right. Ava stood there and she smiled helplessly. Manda looked directly at Ava then gave her an old up-and-down, took it all in and between her teeth managed a dead, 'Hey,' before immediately turning her complete attention back to Chell.

'Chell. Changed after all, I see.'

After a concentrated pause, Chell turned away from the mirror and looked directly at Ava then back at Manda. 'Manda, this is Ava, Finn's pal.'

'Aye.'

'Hello.'

'Where's Kay?'

'Changing in the bog.'

'As well. I'd better go back and change too then. Hey, Chell,' she lowered her voice, 'Kyles and *I* were drinking out the minibar; we slaughtered all the voddy.'

'Oh. Just miniatures?'

'Aye, but we did it dead quick. Like shots.'

'Don't forget all this is on Kay's credit card. We'll have to pay her back.'

Manda turned to Ava, held her look and raised her eyes to the ceiling in criticism of Chell. Ava's passivity gave Manda considerable encouragement. 'So, it's great you're with us, Ava. You must be dead excited.'

'I'm sure it'll be something else,' Ava cleverly suggested.

Missing nothing, Manda nodded contemptuously towards the floor and said, 'I see yous have both brought –' and she sneered the word in pity '– *backpacks*. Do you have a credit card too?'

'Yes. I've taken one.'

Comprehendingly, Manda slowly nodded, and said, 'I'm away to change then.' But she didn't budge.

Kylah and Finn were now at the end of the small corridor.

'Kylah, this is Ava who's doing the same course as me at uni; Ava this is Kylah, from home, who I've told you all about.'

'Hi, Ava.' Kylah came willingly forward and reached up a little to kiss Ava on a cheek.

'Finn told me you're a beautiful singer.'

'Nah.'

'She should gone in for *Popstars*. We all told her. She could be in Hear'Say, easy-peasy, right now if she'd gone for it. Couldn't she, Chell?' Manda butted her head sharply at each word.

'Nah. I'm nothing special.

'Listen to it. It's a disgrace.'

'So here we all are then,' Finn announced anticlimactically.

'*Your* Miss Clarke is in the bog.' Manda jerked a hitcher's thumb rudely.

'I already saw her,' Finn said tightly to Manda's face.

Kylah turned to Finn. 'Are yous coming now or are you going to have a wee freshen-up? We were just headed down the stair to the grotty-looking pub.'

'Yous are in the big country now, girls, get that hay out from behind your ears,' smiled Finn.

'Or between the ass crack, in Chell's case,' Manda contributed.

They continued to ignore her.

'Will we just head now and have a wee powwow in this pub?'

'I've to get changed,' Manda snarled.

'Get changed then,' Chell said coldly.

'All right, all right, bossy boots. Back in two minutes.' Manda stepped past them and moved to the door which she swung open aggressively and she was gone; a breath's pause and the room door swung shut.

'Phew,' mocked Finn, pretending to wipe a sweated brow. 'Now you get it?' She looked at Ava.

'Formidable,' Ava stated.

'She's been like that since yesterday afternoon.'

'She's been like that since she was five year old.'

A soft voice came from behind them. 'Is that Manda gone?' It was Kay speaking out of the space in the bathroom door.

'Aye. It's safe to come out. She didn't fart once.'

Kylah said, 'To be honest, Ava, she's been a bit like that since our pal Orla passed away.'

'Oh yes. Terrible. Finn told me about that.'

Chell tried to explain. 'We were all a right wee gang at school, you know, in the choir and all that, and after our pal died of a disease, even though this was donkey's ages ago, more than three years back now, Manda seemed to have took it worse than any of us.'

'It's not that,' Finn interrupted. 'She just used Orla as an excuse to get angrier than she already was and she's actually forgot now what it was that started her anger and then she got up the duff by this ridiculous idiot at home, and worse, she had the baby. She's angry at how shit she's made her life.'

Kylah shifted a little uncomfortably.

'Okay. Sorry. Right, that's a debate. We are at variance.' She cocked her clever-clever look at Ava.

Yet all of this utterance from each was completely directed towards a bamboozled Ava, who stood there blinking, barely nodding. Ava's eyelids were very pale and with her dark eyes, it made her long blinks marks of punctuation.

Kay now squeezed into the main room past them. She had

changed into black high-waisted trousers which smoothly defined her figure.

'Cor. You look nice.'

Kay put her ass down at the end of the bed and began pulling on her brown knee-high boots under the trouser legs.

'Let's go to Jericho then and get some drinks.'

'Are we not going to have a quick peek on the computer?' asked Kay.

'Later.'

'Pub, pub, pub,' went Chell.

Looking at Kay on the bed edge, Finn suddenly said out loud, 'How is the old love life, girls?'

'Phoaar,' went Chell.

'Phewwww,' called Kay.

'Yaay haay,' Kylah echoed.

'Cobwebs all round,' sneered Chell, deflated, and they all laughed.

'Know what Manda went and did?' Kylah nodded to the hotel wall, indicating the next room. 'After she bust up with that old hippy guy, Tolson. Know him?'

Finn went, 'Tolson? He's ancient. Like, didn't he used to walk a cat on a lead when we were little?'

'That was his foxy, hippy girlfriend in them days' cat. He's a nice old guy and must of thought his birthdays had come all at once to get his hands on her tits, but Manda soon breaks up with him and she persuades Chell to break up with the guy she was seeing too. Just sort of, "I'm breaking up with my boyfriend so you have to break up with *yours* too." So that Manda has something to talk about: breaking up. Which is all she did talk about, for three months.'

Finn turned to Chell. 'Is that true?'

Chell was at the mirror messing with her lip gloss perfection again. She nodded shyly. 'Aye. She moaned at me so much and give me such a hard time, I broke up with mine just for an easy life. I mean, it wasn't Johnny Depp I was going out with or anything.'

'That's mental.'

'Come on then, Finn,' goes Chell. 'Spill the beans on the latest in London. Are you knee-deep in gorgeous guys, with all the clubs and that?'

Each head now turned to Finn.

Finn retracted. 'That'll be right. I'm like old Sister Condron. I tell yous. All I do is read books and guzzle coffee.'

Chell paused for dramatic effect. 'Suppose Finn is dealing with another fundamental fault in men now? They're all English.'

Everyone roared out in the hysterics while they each deftly noted that Ava joined in.

'Ah, but yous're getting into deep waters, girls. Ava's half French.'

'Ah. You know what we mean then?'

'Ava, speaking French is not to be overlooked as a good reason for a wee holiday in France. Paris?' Finn raised her eyebrows temptingly.

'Aye. Moulin Rouge. Fucking brilliant. Seen the movie? Christina, Mya, Pink and Missy Elliot.'

'Do you speak the lingo good then, Ava?' Kylah yelled over the others.

'Dad does but I'm a bit rusty.'

Finn growled, 'Is she fuck. She's fluent. She dreams in French. I hear her mumbling at night. You'd think it was a radio tuned across the English Channel.'

'All the French that we'll need to know, girls,' Kylah shouted but then sang, really strikingly, that voice just coming out her pretty face:

> 'Giuchie Giuchie ya ya dada,
> Mocha chocalata ya ya,
> Voulez-vous coucher avec moi, ce soir.'

All the girls joined in, taking up singing of just the chorus. Chell, Kylah and even Kay began provocative dancing while Ava and Finn leaned on the wall, sang and clapped their hands. Finn laughed delightedly.

'Voulez-vous coucher avec moi, ce soir
Voulez-vous coucher avec moi, ce soir.'

Chell kicked her heels away, leaped onto Kay's bed, showing off, pushed the dress hem further on her thigh, using her hand and splayed fingers to caress, in imitation of the music video. She jumped to turn round and, one suspects, bend over, but her head spectacularly impacted the ceiling and she came to a quick bouncing halt in the middle of the bed, her dark hair cradled in the spread, electric-blue talons of acrylic fingernails.

A taunting burst came out from Kay, and Kylah: 'Holiday insurance. Holiday insurance.'

'We *told* her to take out holiday insurance,' screamed Kay in laughter and the others joined in.

'Oh baby. Are you okay?' Kylah reached up to her.

'I've banged my nut. A headache and I ain't had a drink yet.' Chell looked through tears of laughing. They all crowded round just as there was a knocking at the door.

'It's Lady Marmalade herself,' whispered Finn wonderingly, and this set them all off again.

'Come on, come on.'

Chell began pumping her clenched fist up and down.

'Pub, pub, pub, pub, pub.' She jumped off the bed and stepped back into her shoes. The chant was joined, 'Pub, pub, pub, pub, pub,' and they formed a line-up in the bedroom corridor and out the door, where Manda stood in changed clothes and too short a skirt, but she unquestioningly joined the chant and followed on down the corridor of numbered hotel-room doors, in unison, 'Pub, pub, pub, pub, pub.'

The chant fizzled out on the stairway beyond the twin fire doors. Conversations began to static betwixt them as the girls moved across the hotel lobby.

'Hello,' Manda called out and she waved across the lobby

at the receptionist who returned a distressed expression. Though Manda could not comprehend such a possibility, the receptionist now no longer recognised her in the white, short denim skirt and white tassled boots and her grey top with a low, gaudily hanging neck. On the top, in shimmering gilt lettering, tautened over her bosom, was the motto:

Some Won't
Some Might
I Will

Manda owned three such identical tops, in electric red and indigo as well as this grey one – which she had brought with her on the holiday, anticipating them as a sure means of opening the doors to all male society.

Some of the girls, especially Manda, were disillusioned that, as they entered the Flight Deck Hotel bar, more heads did not turn to them.

Finn and Ava were now accustomed to the general anonymity and nonchalance of great cities – the curtailed glance on entering an establishment had replaced the shameless but acceptable scrutiny of their home places. In their village and small town, Ava and Finn were scrutinised for hopeful signs of incipient dissolution and decay; in the great city of London they were only scanned for their possessions; assessed for any edge. Once upon a time, people looked and evaluated the face of a stranger, nowadays they first noted clothes, handbag and your wristwatch when you got to the top of the queue in McDonald's on a Saturday night; perhaps your shoes as you walked away.

The hotel pub was now occupied by surprising eclectics; men who looked like airport workers haunted the end of the bar with its area of gambling machines and an electronic dartboard which they pranced before as if it were some tender oracle.

Numbers of women, occasionally quite young but harassed-looking, slumped in bad postures in quieter seating areas. You soon noticed they all had name tags still hung upon one blouse breast – they probably worked in the terminal franchises and shops or as waitresses in the fast-food joints, lived locally and met here for some after-shift relief before pitching themselves into various modes of transport, homeward to modest Sussex bolt-holes. The whole place was oddly lacking of actual air passengers in transit.

'Finn, we don't know what you drink any more,' Manda claimed.

'I drink what I always drank, Manda. But I don't really want to get on the plane tomorrow hung-over.'

'Oh, come on, Finn. We were all out on the lash night before last, celebrating coming here. We were at Rascals. You should of seen us. It was brilliant. You really missed yourself.'

'Mmmm.'

The bar obviously served food as there were packets of condiments in small ceramic dishes placed upon all the large, rectory-sized tables on which years of spilled alcohol had excoriated away long sections of varnish into blackened strips of bare wood. The tables were enclosed as booths by elevated frameworks of varnished, lathe-turned wooden ballisters. Kylah pointed towards the largest table and the squad began to squeeze in, giggling and crouching down around it in a swift deployment to avoid being she who must go up to buy the first round.

The single ashtray was soon being slid up and down the large table like a curling stone until someone grabbed one from the next table. Since Ava, Finn and Kay were too polite to shove in, they were inevitably the last left on their feet – by default the outer seats, facing away from the bar, were theirs. At least Finn laughed, affectionately, admitting defeat. 'My round then.'

Kay sat down while Finn and Ava took the orders and got in the drinks.

> Manda: Pint of Guinness Extra Cold and a
>   packet of pork scratchings.
> Kylah: Vodka and Coke.
> Chell: White-wine spritzer.
> Kay: Glass of red wine (large).
> Finn: Dark rum and Diet Coke.
> Ava: Dark rum and Diet Coke.

'Ah. Drinking identical drinks, is it now, girls?'

'Here's your pork scratchings.' Finn tossed the packet across the table in an openly hostile way.

'Jeez, Manda, how can you eat them things? They're like scabs from the willy of a skanky boy.'

'The voice of experience, Chell?' Manda held a singular curled pork scratching to her bottom lip and licked.

'Uh. Don't scum me out.'

'Ah brilliant, "Don't scum me out." Haven't heard that in ages.' Finn smiled at her.

Chell winked proudly and aimed at Finn, her hand a shooting pistol; her thumb came down.

The tenderness of Finn's nostalgia had thawed out already and she spoke to Manda with a gruff, tolerant familiarity. 'Where's these photos of wee Sean then?'

Manda took out her purse and began delving.

Chell, looking across at the photos, caught Finn's eye then looked away, her smirk wiped invisible as she lifted the glass to her lips.

'Here's my wee darling,' Manda professed, handing a sieve of small colour photos over to Finn across the table. There was an open-eyed honesty in Manda's adoration that Finn couldn't ignore, until she looked down on the photographs. The infant already appeared to have a ginger-headed, receding, iron-filing hairline. The nit-discouraging skinhead. And sure enough, the regimental ear stud was in place; blue eyes, a look of startled helplessness and certain perplexity at being in existence. Also, most unfortunately, Sean's baby face bore little trace of Manda but was a familiar, warped plaster cast – like a crisp packet shrunk in an oven – of Manda's ghastly impregnator.

'Oh, he's just lovely.' Finn obediently passed the pictures to Ava who cagily shuffled the images while smiling.

'Are these recent?' Ava enquired neutrally.

'About a month back.'

'Oh. Lovely,' which could not help sounding as if it was more lovely that the photos were taken a month back rather than that the subject was lovely.

'What's all the gossip from home then?' Finn changed the topic as Ava passed the photos back. Manda shrugged as if Finn should already be fully aware of all the latest gossip, carefully sliding the photos back into her purse, but she leaned in forward and said, 'Here, but listen to this. Isn't this brilliant? It's a classic: mind bitch Rita Robson from school; won the beauty pageant in fifth year?'

'Aye.'

'She become a screw.'

'But . . . she was always dead gorgeous,' said Finn and looked up and down the table, confused.

'Naw. A screw. A prison officer. In Glasgow. That's what they call them. Screws. Like *Prisoner Cell Block H*.'

'What did she do that for?' asked Finn, genuinely bewildered.

Kylah deadpanned, 'Probably cos all her exes are in the fucking jail?'

Chell chipped in, 'Nah. She really wanted to. A girl looking like that. She had a great body and arse, now she's dressed in that awful uniform every day.'

'It's a disgrace,' Kylah added.

Finn tried to move things quickly along. 'What else's doing in the town?'

'Don't you phone your mum?'

'Aye, but I'd like to think you know stuff my mum doesn't get to hear about, Manda; unless you're leading a really dull life.'

Manda narrowed her eyes challengingly. 'Tell her about the old Madonna.'

'Madonna?'

'No, *the* Madonna on top of Our Lady's.'

'Oh aye. Classic.'

Even though she'd initiated the tale, Manda now interrupted everyone, holding up a hand to stop any comment until she had demanded, 'Here, listen to this. Isn't this brilliant? Listen to this. Explain it to her,' she snapped aside at Chell while stabbing a finger towards Ava.

Chell explained, 'Ava. To light her up at night they've gone and fitted a floodlight in front of the statue of Our Lady of

Perpetual Succour who's always stood way up high on the roof of our school in town. But the way her cloak thing and one of her legs sort of goes sweeping backwards and the actual shape of the floodlight on the roof, down at her feet, you can see the shape of the floodlight – so's from wherever you're stood in the town now, it looks as if the Virgin Mary is about to kick a football.'

'Take a penalty no less.'

Ava and Finn laughed.

'Aye. A penalty shoot-out to see if you get to go up above or down below,' shouted Chell, roaring.

Finn said, 'C'mon then, Chell, tell us the latest about tourist info.'

'Oh, this is classic, brilliant, aye, listen to this. Classic.'

Chell went – as if it was a familiar speech – 'Dealing with tourists, girls, it's more like a form of social work. I don't even know how I got the job in the first place. I think it was more that all the other ladies there and the boss aren't actually from our town.' She lowered her voice. 'Some are no even Scottish. Can you believe that?' She scanned incredulously across all the eyes round that table though she sped past Ava's. 'So that was pretty bizarre. Like they learned where everywhere was in the town from maps. They used to memorise the town map when they were chewing their piece at lunch rather than having a gossip with me. Like someone would come in and ask where St John's Square is, and I'm ignored as if I don't live there, while all the staff round me have to dive for a map. And you know, they're all full-time employees and one's married to a Fed who was transferred to town at the same time and pretty fishy to me how she got the job at the same minute he got one, but anyways, they soon all had mortgages for houses within just months of coming to the town and I'm from the town and can't afford one. I can barely pay the rent with Kyles. Anyways. They're nice folk and all that and I think the thing is, some of them – like Ava here – speak dead good French and German and all that stuff. But there's no much call for using all them foreign languages. All we have is geriatric Americans and geriatric

37

bus parties. A good-looking young guy has never once crossed that threshold. Anyways, tourist info had to be seen to employ someone local. When I went for the interview it was with an Englishman and he goes like, "Are you interested in the history of 'our' area, my dear?" . . . I says, Eh nut. "Do you know what times the three trains a day go to Glasgow?" . . . Eh, the morn, the afternoon and the night? "Do you know the times the boats go out to the isles?" . . . Eh nut. "Do you know what islands they go to?" . . . Eh nut. "Do you ever go to visit any local castles or places of interest?" . . . Eh nut. "Will you work for five thousand a year and be part-time in the winter?" Eh, if I can come out on your Christmas office party as well. Aye. "You have the job then, Miss McDougall."

They all laughed.

She lit a Marlboro Light and frowned in concentration. 'You find out some interesting stuff though. Like did you know, to get to this place called Malin Peninsula in Southern Ireland you go to Northern Ireland and head north from there?'

They all looked at her.

'It's true. But try telling an American with white runners that. "No, it's in Southern Ireland not Northern Ireland; but Malin Peninsula, though it's in Southern Ireland, is north of Northern Ireland." Aye. I mean, I can see why they were confused. And some of the folks. Americans. I mean this time a guy comes in . . . his tam-o'-shanter bunnet and all that, white runners, going on about his ancestors. Fair enough. But like it's "Hey, young Miss" this and "Hey, young Miss" that, and then he starts asking what ferries he needs to go to this place called Ten NA that I'd never heard of.'

'Ten NA?' Finn furrowed her brow.

'Aye, Ten NA. I say to him, "Ten NA. That's not in Scotland. I never ever heard of it." He goes, "Yeah, young Miss. Ten NA. Sure sounds like a military base to me, but it's meant to be a real beautiful spot there, Miss," and all that. He goes that he knows roughly where it is. So's I step over to the trusty ancient map – you know the big old one where the centre of town has been poked out by all the fingers jabbing onto it – and I ask him to show me where this place is and he went and goes, "Yeah, look right out here, young Miss, that's it right there. Ten NA," and I look. He's pointed at Iona.'

All the girls from the port burst out into the hysterics – especially Finn – but Ava didn't quite get it.

Finn saw Ava's hesitation and said, 'Iona. It's a wee island off the coast. They used to bury the ancient Scottish kings there. Spelled I-O-N-A.'

'Ten NA, eh? Yanks.'

'That's fucking brilliant. That's a classic. St Columba made a monastery there,' Manda nodded with authority. She ventured further, with sudden conciliation. 'Don't worry. Like where you're from, Ava. I bet we wouldn't know stuff there, eh? Where *are* you from?'

'It's just a tiny village. It's in the Vale of the White Horse, near Didcot, or Oxford.'

Kay piped up, 'Oh, I've heard of that; there's the actual horse shape in chalk or something cut out a hillside?

'Oh yeah. Seen that on telly. We know of that. Up in Scotland,' claimed Kylah, nodding.

Manda remained gloomily silent.

'Is it nice there then; is it out in the sticks; is there dances to go to and that?'

'Oh it's deadly dull. I mean, it's adorable-looking, very . . .' she gave the slyest look to Manda . . . 'English. But the only dances are young farmers' dances and hunt balls and all of this sort of thing. Quite brutal.'

'That's like up our way though, out at Silvermines and down the Pass and that, isn't it? No that there's much left of the farming.'

'Is it like *The Vicar of Dibley*?' asked Manda, cautiously.

'Well . . . I suppose it is a bit; it looks like that.'

Finn shifted her body a little and went, 'And so how are *you* doing, Manda? How's working at the salon and all that?'

'Well, I'm Practice Manageress now of course.'

'What?'

'Practice Manageress.'

'Does that mean you're practising at being Manageress?' Finn slyly suggested.

'No! Most certainly not. I *am* the manageress of the practice. Two days a week. You call a salon a practice now, like the doctors and dentists do. After all, it is that important to the community.'

Finn laughed a little too loudly. 'Practice Manageress of the Best Little Hair House in Town.' Finn turned to Ava with a glance of condescending appeal.

'You *know* fine it's not called that. Any more,' Manda said, coldly, firmly and hurt.

'What's it called then? Gentrification of the Bog Lands?' Finn turned again and made a smart smirk at Ava.

'Eh? What's that meant to mean then, Finn?'

Finn suddenly looked serious and stated, 'Hair Today, Hair Tomorrow, is quite a weird name for a hairdresser's.'

'Isn't.'

'Is too.'

Manda put on a formal, businesslike tone, actually changing her accent. 'Well, we did want to call it Hair Today, Gone Tomorrow, but the bank wouldn't give my big sister the loan if it was called that. They says it was self-defeatist when we was asking to borrow money; they made it very clear they wouldn't back a business that might fail, called Hair Today, Gone Tomorrow, cos they'd be a laughing stock if it went bust. So the bank made us change it to Hair Today, Hair Tomorrow. We didn't think of it at the time but I see their point of view now.'

'Hair Today, *Here* Tomorrow?' Ava asked.

'No. Hair Today, *Hair* Tomorrow.'

'Oh, okay,' nodded Ava unsmiling, as if a contention of logic had been challenged.

Outright, Finn just asked, 'If it's not a sore point, have you seen anything of wee Sean's dad?'

Her accent changed back. 'I've no seen nothing of that prick for months.'

'Have you got any money offof him?'

'Nut, love. Not a penny recent. Gave us a hundred quid two months back.'

'You want to get the Child Support Agency onto him.'

'Aye, but there's downsides to getting those loonies involved in your life; cause more hassle than they solve. I mean, people jump to clusions, but it's great having a wee boy; it's just great. I'm happy with it. He'll be all growed up away to school one day and I'll still have good years ahead of me, kind of thing.'

'Aye, Manda. We all love wee Sean, but it cramps your style a bit now. Not being able to go out nights and not working full time and that,' Chell reminded her.

'Aye, but there's all the practical benefits.'

'Like what?' shrugged Chell.

'Well, for one, it's much easier wearing six-inch heels pushing a pram cos you can kind of lean in on it for balance.'

They all burst out laughing at this.

'Your ex still had money for new wheel hub things on his bloody boy racer car though, didn't he?'

'Aye. And know what he went and did? He tried to get wheel hubs on the pram that would match his car. Honest, I'm no joking. Och, what the hell. It's no like I was going to marry just cos I had a kid. I mean, even if I was living with wee Sean's daddy, do yous think I'd be marrying him? The only aisle we'd both be walking down together would be in the supermarket. I'm far too young to marry; especially the likes of a waster that he is. Marriage the now? No thanks. I watch yous parents. Getting old in marriage means having sex less and less and farting more and more in each other's company, until your life is just one big, long fart.'

They all laughed but Chell pointed out, 'Your life already *is* one long fart.'

'Aye, but I don't have a husband to compete farting with as well.'

More laughter.

'Any more gossip from the town?'

'Nah. Not really.'

'What about school? Your wee sister's in third year now, eh?'

Kylah went, 'Aye. She is. Jesus. I know we's were once no angels ourselves – we were holy terrors – and my wee sister and her mates might no be able to get in any pubs yet, but those

41

wee besoms rule the streets. They've all got mobiles, some of them better than mine, drinking ciders down the piers and Jeez, girls, the stuff they're into would make us blush: smoking joints in micro-skirts and going down the street bushing, y'know, commando with even Brazilians and worse in the dark down that pier; snowballing and all sorts . . .' Kylah seemed to run out of steam, shrug and inhale from her cigarette.

'How's Woolies, Kylah?'

Manda interrupted, 'I go into Woolies with wee Sean to see her. Don't I, Kyles? Sit on the floor on my black overcoat and let wee Sean play with the toys for an hour. He pulls everything down, doesn't he, Kyles?'

'Aye he does. No crack really. Young lassies aren't working there these days. It's all part-time older women and that. Pauline MacKinnon that we was at school with's bloody mum works there now. With me. It's like having fifteen mums, telling me I was out too late on Saturday night and all that. Tell the truth, I'm a bit browned off with it.'

'But with your talent you should be a singer, Kyles, you should have been in Hear'Say if you'd listened to me. You can compete.'

'It's no that music I want to compete with. That's all a bad dream for me, Manda. Marianne Faithfull was in the charts when she was still in school and hanging out with the Rolling Stones. How can you compete with that? Candy Givens, Betty Davis, Maggie Bell, Sandy Denny, Grace Slick when she come onstage at Woodstock. How can I compete with lassies like that? I hate that *Popstars* shite.' Kylah hoisted her cigarette and glared at it. 'I've got to give up the fags.'

The others looked around blankly.

Manda enquired, 'Are you saying you like Mick Jagger? He's ancient.

'Mick Jagger was sexy back then.'

'Don't scum us out, Kylah. I seen him on VH1 singing his songs with those lips moving. He looks like a tapeworm being electrocuted. Is that his father in the band with him?'

'The hell with Woolies. Studio engineer. That's what I'm going to become. Then a record producer.'

'Listen, girls. Sorry to be a bore.'

'You can't help it,' Manda smiled sweetly.

'I feel we should really think tonight about where we're going, because we've left this late enough now and we need to book it. Can we all say our bit again about who wants to go where?' Kay looked round the table.

'Well, we all *had* seemed to be agreed where we's are not going.' Manda turned a challenging glare at Ava and Finn.

Kylah immediately backed Manda up on this matter. 'Aye. No bloody Ibiza overpriced rave.'

'Ibiza is plug.'

Kay said, 'I don't want to go either, but you've never been.'

Chell shrugged. 'Don't need to. *Ibiza Uncovered* and all that; thirty quid to get in one of these nae-charts-superclubs and felt up by some skinhead who thinks he has a right to scream in my ear and touch my tits. What tits I have.' She looked down.

Voice heavy with perturbation, Manda said, 'I admit I'd like to be featured on *Ibiza Uncovered* though. I'd be so brilliant. They'd get me on *Big Brother*. Do you get paid? Do you think you get paid to be on *Ibiza Uncovered*, girls? I'd be brilliant on it.'

'I hate DJs that think they can force their crappy record collection on three thousand people at the same time. Back to your bedroom, boys; get a band of actual musicians.' Kylah nodded and lifted her drink.

'That's Ibiza out then,' Finn muttered from the side of her mouth to Ava.

'Why? Do *you two* want to go there?' Manda showed her teeth.

'No. I says I'd like to go to Paris for a few days. Don't think we could go, cos I think it's too pricey.'

'Paris. Paris? How will we know where the good bars and the good dance floors are and the boys might no speak English?' Manda was wide-eyed with distress.

'So you want to go back to Magaluf. Just cos you know it?'

'What's wrong with that? Magaluf is magic. It's the opposite of Ibiza. All the uncool people are on Minorca not Ibiza, and uncool people are fun. Or at least I'm more likely to get a ride off one.'

'Majorca. Magaluf's on Majorca. Not Minorca.'

'Aye, aye, whatever, Finn. Jesus. I never knew we was back in geography class with Mr Eldon. Thought it was phil-o-suphy you were studied. Listen, girls, Magaluf is just fantastic; you go down a street where there's brilliant bar after bar, every one with a dance floor and a proper DJ that plays actual chart stuff, not rave crap. Cheap shots of drink and loads of guys gagging for it — if you can fight your way through the English slappers. And know what there is? Actual karaoke in loads of bars. "Final Countdown" by Europe or songs by Roxette. You can do all that. I did that. I was brilliant. That's my karaoke song. "Final Countdown".' Manda directed this straight at Ava who smiled, tightly and cautious, only a little afraid.

'We know. Sounds idyllic.'

Kay interrupted, holding up a hand, 'Chell, can we hear from you? Can we hear other people's opinions about where to go as well?'

Manda went, 'Humph. Tut.'

Chell looked both ways as if momentarily confused. 'Ah. Well. I'm easy.'

'All the boys know that,' Manda leered and looked around. She was ignored.

'I don't have a fixed place or that. I guess I'd like to go to a beachy warm place a wee bit more than a big, like, foreign city. I mean. I did take nine bikinis.'

'NINE!'

'Nine?'

'So? I took seven,' Manda was swift to announce, lest she be outdone.

'What on earth do yous need nine bikinis for?' Finn asked.

'Well . . . I thought yous all would of took about the same, I mean, you know? You have a beach party bikini with sequins and embroidery and then just a swimming bikini. They're . . . different.' Chell shrugged in a self-explanatory manner. 'And you don't want to be on the beach or by the pool with the exact same bikini *every* single day.'

'That's what I would take if I was getting marooned on a desert island forever,' said Kay.

'Wish you were,' the voice of Manda murmured among the general hubbub.

Chell said, 'Bikinis is nothing. Do yous want to know how many bras I brought with me?'

'Oh God. Don't tell us.'

'Okay, right, Chell's leaning to a beach holiday. Kylah. What about you?'

'Of course I'd like to go to San Francisco. Cos of all the music stuff. Or somewhere in America, but I know we might only manage a couple days there with the prices.'

Finn was shaking her head; doubtful, 'I'd like to go to America too but I just think, it's going be a good couple of hundred quid flightswise and more for the cheapest accommodation, even for three nights or that.'

Manda shook her head solemnly. 'Why would yous even want to go there? We'll be raped and murdered.'

Ava broke ranks and spoke up. 'Wherever we go, we'll need somewhere with a swimming pool for Chell.'

Manda managed a thin grin and everyone else laughed, even Chell.

'Right, Manda, you want to go to Magaluf, Finn is all for Paris.'

'Aye, but I mean, in the end I'm easy, whatever the majority want.'

'Ava?'

'I'm of the same mind, whatever most of you wish is fine with me.' Her darker, more mature and restful voice declared, 'Well what about you, Kay?'

Finn nodded towards Kay, 'Where do you actually want to go to, since you've gone to the trouble of bringing your computer and you're letting us use you credit card tonight?' Finn looked around authoritatively.

'Well. The computer I need for a little uni work and email, so it's not any bother. Of course I'd like to go to New York or Paris or Rome too, I'd really like but –'

'Rome; that would be brilliant,' Finn said.

'Tut . . . trust you to bring homework.' Manda raised her eyes. 'And Rome. What is Rome? Eh? Rome is just . . . old buildings and that.'

Kay ignored her. '. . . But look. The whole idea . . . I mean, when we all first talked about this back home, the plan was, come here and book something, anything, at the very last minute to get it the cheapest poss, but since then everyone's started to get a little bit carried away with their own ideas about where we're going, but don't forget the original idea: just to go wherever was cheapest. I would be led by the cheapest price to anywhere. Rather than anything else I'd be led by that. So that's almost definitely going to be a resort rather than a city. I mean, I looked yesterday for flights going tonight, just out of curiosity, and there's great low prices and if the flight is cheap enough we can even worry about accommodation at the other end, once we get there.'

'Aye, but where are all these cheap flights going to? I'm no going back to Turkey. Turkey and Ibiza: off-limits.' Kylah put her drink down for emphasis.

'A lot are long haul but there's European destinations as well.'

'What's long hauls?'

'That's far away. Thailand–Australia–all–that.'

Manda kicked off, 'I'm no going to Thailand. You need jags and stuff; I can't be bringing weirdy diseases back to wee Sean.'

'Other than malignant VD, from Magaluf.'

'Fuck off, Fionnula. Just cos lesbos get off scot-free.'

Ava quickly asked, 'What happened to you in Turkey, Kylah?'

'What didn't happen.'

Manda guffawed, 'Aww, listen to this. It's a classic.'

'It was me on my own and all bloody hen parties. There was only one organised night out to this theme park, called Medieval World, where they could hire a male stripper or pay extra and get one dressed up as a knight in plastic armour – you're paying extra for all the armour he has to take off. He was all hairy. Rubbish. And the local guys there would follow a girl round all night from bar to bar and try and get you down on the beach with them. Man, they'd know what hotel you were in and be waited outside the hotel complex when you went out at nights. They'd follow you from bar to bar and there were only four or five bars open that time of year. Standing in the distance, talking to you when you went up to the bar, trying to buy you a drink in each place. Jesus, girls. Every night you ended up walking home to the hotel backwards, telling them to go away. If you'd had a letter box, you'd have needed to say night-night through it. Persistent. They didn't just want to jump your bones – worse – they all wanted to marry me. Like this one says, "Kylah. Marry me. You are so beautiful, your eyes are like our sea, your hair is like silk and your teeth. Are they *really* all your own?"'

'What?'

'Aye. What a wee tiddler of a boy. Never mind silicones, this guy was only used to women with false teeth.'

'Jesus.'

'Yeuch.'

'Oh, don't scum us out again.'

'And I'll tell you another thing too. I was nice to him.'

A familiar smile appeared on Manda's face; she turned, stared greedily at Kylah just as she had stared at her and others for years – whenever a teacher had shouted at Kylah, Manda had been watching her, as if awaiting some ultimate breakdown or catastrophe, even if it only ever manifested itself upon the face. Manda drawled, 'What she means is she shagged him.'

'Aye, so? It was so nice to see his dark skin against mine. But he wasn't a Duracell: didn't exactly keep going all night.'

Ava found this very funny and laughed until she was quite flushed. Kylah looked at her and chuckled back.

The round was finished.

Manda barked, 'Right, who's for more?' Then she frowned. 'Are you not smoking?' Manda nodded, accusingly.

'I'm cutting down,' said Finn.

'Oh. Right. And do you ever smoke, Ava?'

'Sometimes. No thanks.'

'Hmmm. Well, aren't yous the party animals.'

47

'Let's all have an early night so as we can go mental tomorrow,' Kylah wisely counselled. Chairs screeched and jamp back and cigarettes were cradled in the mouths and handbags and shoulder bags were grabbed or hoisted.

'Bloody hell, girls, what's happening with yous? I thought we's were out for a laugh?'

'Come on, Manda. We don't even know where we're going tomorrow.'

Manda casually threatened, 'Och well. There's always the minibar. Eh, Kay?'

3

Kay and Chell's hotel room was poached balmy with electric central heat. There was a scatter of discarded high-heeled shoes in the corner. Finn and Ava had delivered their backpacks to their own room then quickly returned. Manda wasn't there. She'd remained alone, huffily in the room next door – her absence heavily palpable; Kylah smoked on the bed with Chell, offering lighters to each other.

Kylah said, 'I know fine what Manda the Demander's up to. She's drinking out this minibar contraption.'

Kay sighed, 'I told her it costs a fortune.'

'She was crabbit cos we left the bar early.'

'She's turning into a right old alchy. The amounts she guzzles. I tell you.'

'That's right enough, Finn, I meant to say that. After we moved in to our wee flat together, Manda came round for a house-warming, didn't bring any booze and guzzled all of ours, and of course she never left either. She crashed out drunk on my bed, takes up all the room and hogs the downie and I wasn't sleeping beside her, farting all night, so's I had to sleep with Chell. When we got up in the morning, Manda had already made herself a giant breakfast, a whole packet of bacon and four eggs from the fridge and she'd wolfed the lot. Tried to hide the empty packets deep down in the scullery bin.'

'And she had a bowl of my variety-size Coco Pops,' Chell added.

'Aye. And a bowl of her Coco Pops.'

'That's near all I eat some days.'

'Hey, Finn. Last guy she shagged, she met at fucking Weight Watchers.'

Finn laughed.

'Imagine it. The big Bridget Jones granny knickers on, that the tummy bit goes *way* up.'

'Oh Jesus,' went Kylah.

'Aye. The control underwear.'

'It's support underwear. She's wore it on every night out since the baby.'

Angrily, Kylah said, 'Yous should see Manda's medicine cabinet that she's took with her. She has these water retention tablets and she was going on about taking them for the beach. Water retention. It's pizza and Big Mac retention she suffers from.'

'Och, don't be so mean. Her ears'll be ringing next door.'

'She has high standards of preparedness, that girl – the sheer number of flunky packs I saw her stuffing away in her suitcase. She'll be able to open a contraceptive stall, selling them on the beach the amounts she's took. Wee Sean's no getting a brother or sister.'

Kylah confessed, 'I'm not sure I'm in the mood for days on a beach with Amanda Tassy. One blink of sun and she's topless with them swinging about all day, yet they're all white cos she's aye wore her bikini in the tanning machine at the salon.'

Finn groaned. 'She's always getting her kit off in front of us.'

'Not in the tanning salon at her sister's place she doesn't.'

'Chell's nine bikinis and Manda's nine bellies. She'd go mad, walking around in . . . Rome or that for a few days.'

Finn mimicked with a bitter tone, '"What's Rome? Just a load of old buildings."'

'Mind that time we all went to Glasgow, Finn? At the railway station?'

'Aye.'

Ava asked, 'What was this?'

Kylah said quietly, 'It's quite sad really. Manda's a small-town girl through and through. She'll never, ever leave our town. She'll always be there cos she feels insecure anywhere else. I'm not slagging her for that. If you like your place and if it makes you truly happy, grand. That's what a home should do. But it can be sad. A good few years back, we all went down on the train to Glasgow for just the day, window-shopping and that, but Manda on her own, went back to the railway station two hours before the train was due to leave and she just sat there on a bench, waiting, with all them city weirdies about. We got there fifteen minutes before the train went and Manda was just sat there. Four or five hours in Glasgow and she just couldn't cope, it was amazing.'

'Aye, she'd been in Glasgow an hour and she was saying stuff like, "I wonder who's walking up and down the esplanade back home right now."'

Finn said, quietly, 'I mean, London still amazes me, I'm still from a wee Scottish town and I miss my folks and that, but really . . .'

'It's cos she's so bloody nosy. Manda's terminally nosy – the perfect nosy hairdresser – and she has her specialised subject: our town and people's goings-on – and she's simply dying if she doesn't know the latest.'

'Aye, that's true.'

Ava nodded acceptingly.

'There's a thing.'

'What?

The girls were very still within the room.

'Notice anything?'

There was a thick silent night over the place, a silence that now seemed powerful and special, like the restful expectancy of a Christmas Eve.

'All the aeroplanes have gone away.'

'It's too late for them to fly. They have restrictions,' Ava quietly explained.

They were all quiet.

'Oh. So the people in England can get a bit of sleep?' said Chell.

'Sort of,' Ava muttered quietly.

Again they listened, a stillness in the room and then the awareness of a huge tomorrow was suddenly upon them.

Saturday

1

In the so called Business Hub of the hotel, which looked like a provincial polling booth in some UN-sanctioned general election, they had made their last-minute booking that morning on Kay's computer, and ever since, Manda had been shouting at people: alarmed and complete strangers, even at the bus driver who wasn't the same guy as the night before, when they boarded the Hotel Hoppa for the terminal: 'Aye. That's us all booked up, mister. Self-catering in Benidorm. Seven nights. It's going to be brilliant, mister.' Manda had not showered and her eye make-up hadn't been renewed since the previous night. While it wasn't badly smeared it had achieved a sort of insubstantial presence which added to the vagueness of her gaze, though those eyes did show, blue and sprightly and ready.

Kylah, Chell and Manda were allowed to occupy the back seat without question.

Manda announced, 'Aye. I says to the gay gadgie at the going-in place – reception – whatever it's called. I says, Look, mister. It really would be easier for me to list what I *didn't* drink out that minibar thing rather than list what I did drink. I told him, I told him that I drank near everything; only didn't not drink two things. I told him, I'm no good at adding up, especially in this state. All I didn't not drink was that cognac-brandy stuff and peanuts. I don't like cognac-brandy stuff and don't eat minging monkey nuts. Don't worry, Kay. I'll write you a cheque for it all.'

Kay nodded glumly, unconvinced. 'Eighty pound, Manda.' Kay raised her eyebrows with expectation.

Manda noticed they weren't very well plucked.

Kylah went, 'A cheque? You don't even own a chequebook.'

'I do too.'

'It's your sister's, from the salon account.'

'I can write a cheque on it. I do it all the time for stock.'

'Your big sister's going to love that on the accounts, isn't she? Eighty Quid, Minibar Expenses, Gatwick Airport,' Finn sneered.

'I'm famished. Can we get some food somewhere?' Chell asked.

Manda lifted her chin off the vibrating seat back, 'Pizza Hut. Do they have that here? Bet they do. That's brilliant. They've got it in Glasgow. I go every time I'm down there with my big sister. Cheese Feast with extra cheese. Brilliant. Bungs me up a bit, mind you.'

'Spare us the details, Manda.'

Chell carefully said, 'I'm glad we's plumbed for self-catering, eh, girls?'

Kylah took over, explaining, 'Aye. Cheaper. No point paying – there's Mackers and there's Burger King and KFC in Benidorm. Everything. From the photos it just means you get a wee scullery in each twin room with an electric cooker hob and a kitchen sink, but we'll just eat out, girls. We're no going to they buffet meals and all that. It's all families and kids at those crappy buffets – we'll be off, getting leathered, too hung-over for breakfast queues. We had those buffets in Turkey. Like school dinners. Telling you, the meat was goat or something.'

'What are you wearing out tonight in Spain then, Finn?' Chell asked.

'Depends on weather, doesn't it?'

'It's going to be mild though, isn't it? For little tops.'

'Little tops, aye,' said Finn, then she yawned.

'It's going to be heatwave, isn't it?' Chell asked.

'I doubt it,' Kay said quietly.

Kylah said, 'Anywhere else is heatwave when you come from Scotland.'

The Hotel Hoppa minibus moved away from that small area in front of the Flight Deck Hotel, the neat organisation of the ground, like an English miniature village – the dainty driveways similar to a go-kart track. The bus hesitated then it edged out into the traffic on the road and they headed off, making a bamboozling configuration of odd manoeuvres over and beneath bridges, through the airport hinterlands.

When the presence of the terminal, or indeed the actual moulded grey of its bulk, its curved edges and its almost window-less facings, revealed itself ahead, the Hotel Hoppa would then perplexingly move away, onto a dual carriageway, gaining speed, often in the opposite direction to the terminal, seemingly sounding out, for some far place. Just as oddly it would use the next slip lane exit to slow down, move round in a direction and come to the car park of another revealed hotel – each of which appeared more salubrious than the Flight Deck Hotel.

Throughout this journeying, an anomie of provincial, cautious silence was observed by the young women as they brusquely observed all around them; they judged their new surroundings now revealed in the filtered daylight: the moving, tattered flags outside one hotel, the obedient boarding of a few more older passengers, adjacent traffic, then the recommencement of the journey once more. All this provoked no comment as the heads and shoulders of the young women compliantly cooperated, lazily moving back and then forward as the bus accelerated or slowed.

Close up, the exterior architecture of the southern terminal resembled one vast air-conditioning unit. The building nurtured more air conditioning among its honeycomb interiors, haplessly revealed along tunnels and corridors, where roof inspection tiles were removed, exposing the baking-foil-wrapped ducts, the rectangular, unpainted aluminium of small cooling and heating machinery.

The six young women and other passengers de-bussed below the open-sided storeys of a car park, its perma-dusk illuminated by strips of fluorescent lighting; the shy, polished wings of occa-sional parked saloon cars showed on the lower floor and the tannoy of what seemed to be a railway station could be heard, garbled among the bus fumes in the distance.

Finn and Ava stepped in under the minibus, grabbed and hoisted their backpacks. Finn skilfully hoiked her backpack onto her shoulder, put her face down, so her black locks of hair fell forward, past her cheeks, as she secured a strap around her waist. Ava's backpack seemed so light she was able to casually hang it upon one rounded shoulder, with a strap dangling loose. Manda observed this with disappointment, Chell with a kind of horror.

'You've no took much clothes with you, eh? Ava?'

'Mmmm.'

Ava, with her slung backpack, and Kay, pulling her single smaller case, moved ahead through the sliding doors, then came Manda, Chell and Kylah, each pushing a heavy trolley and two cases apiece, with helpless expressions. Finn morosely ambled in at the rear, her hands hung on the straps of her backpack.

Immediately, they had entered the new world of the terminal; disembodied voices on the public address, which would never cease, began to speak. Even in toilets there would now be no escape.

'*For security reasons please do not leave baggage unattended. Unattended baggage will be removed and may be destroyed,*' the voice blankly threatened from a round, sieve-like speaker up on a ceiling tile above.

'Jesus. Hear that? Need to keep a close eye on our cases. Imagine all my shoes being blown up.'

Finn walked easily backwards and gave the trolley shovers a cold eye. 'They'd need some amount of explosives to blow up all your luggage, girls.'

Now a series of yellow-and-black signs on light boxes, illuminated from within and suspended at roof level from vertical, chrome bars, gave orientation; the young women obediently lifted their chins, to obey the information upon these signs, as – apart from Ava – they had once lifted their faces together to the bright stained glass of their school chapel where a turquoise-and-rose light would fall upon their foreheads.

Caution. You are approaching a moving walkway.

They stepped or shoved their trolleys onto the moving surface. The walkway was bordered by walls of long thematic narrative advertising strips which passed by at their sides. Manda and Chell paid more attention to the regular Emergency Stop plungers which they passed, with their mass of instructions and admonitions on red adhesive stickers.

Suddenly, on the adjacent walkway, coming towards them were three teenage girls, in their blondeness, holding out mobile phones like totems, turning their faces from one to the other in an animation of their own self-importance. One wore a very short, golden lamé dress.

Manda put her devoted gaze onto these girls as quick as a bored cat would turn to a daddy-long-legs halfway up the wall. As the moving walkways carried the parties opposite each other at a combined velocity to a point of convergence – and then away – Manda's head swiftly swivelled and followed her prey; her lip also curled as she examined the low-hanging cut at the back of the girl's lamé dress. Manda turned to Chell loudly, 'Jeez-o. You can near get a view right up the wee hoor's downtown bonanza.'

The auto door flipped for Finn and, following her, under the burden of their trolleys, the party of young women slowly entered the great hall of South Terminal.

Above them was the cathedral height of roof cables and the realisation that most of the volume was just circulating air space – its own atmosphere – above the unseen, dust-filthy roofs of airline counters and shops.

Highest above were the bending silver pipes, large horizontal fans and mysterious boxes clinging onto the ceiling. This grand hall was made from components rather than structures, everything was readied to be renewed or changed in an instant – the sensibility of impermanence and lack of faith was in every plastic wall and bulkhead. Once, architecture spoke of permanence and a future; here it was always ready to do a runner, like those huge moulded warehouses which now lay across this part of the kingdom – parcel hubs, super-hypermarkets, furniture vasthouses, or sinister human detainment areas.

'Bloody hell. Look at the size of this joint.'

Massed banks of TV-sized monitors showed the serried flight arrivals and departures in figures and letters of buttercup yellow, the same colour as the credits on American TV shows. To their right were the flashing bingo screens of a bureau de change and the open area of the arrival plaza, producing a steady inflow of trolley pushers. A lethargic paparazzi of chauffeur drivers held up handwritten names of arriving passengers.

Placed against the one wall of windows was a confusing array of placticised booths; although they were hotel booking agencies and obscure airline contact desks, with their child-friendly moulded corners and infantile colours, they could all have been legitimate Lego sales franchises.

A scarlet Royal Mail box stood there, its plastic slit fiercely muzzled against parcel bombs, its collection hours an archive of stuck-on and pulled-off amendments and half-hearted paper commitments, resecured with Sellotape.

Kay spoke and they all listened attentively. 'We might be able to check in right now.' They all collectively tipped their heads back and looked up again – as they also used to do together at the screen in their small town's cinema. 'Says we can. Area C.'

To the left of the young women lay the vast, alphabetically demarcated check-in areas A, B, C, D, E, F, laid out in formations beneath two minstrels' galleries. Large yellow cubes hung from the heights, their four sides displaying A or B or C on each side, above the rectangular arrangements of check-in counters and the luggage conveyors behind the seated staff, which sunk down hellishly into the floor.

'So we don't have to lug these bloody suitcases about all day then?'

'Nut. We'll be able to get shot of them at last.'

The concourses of the check-in areas were thronged with those intent on embarkation. The young women all saw a family pushing a loaded trolley, each lending a push or a symbolically placed hand upon the huge suitcases bound with string and laid flat; the man was small, a tweed jacket, a pullover underneath; his wife and perhaps her sister in burgundy saris and two teenage daughters or grandchildren, in blue saris with bright golden nose piercings – each young girl as beautiful as if it were their wedding day.

Manda stared with a blatant intensity which even Chell had never witnessed before and she tried to give Manda a cautionary look, to prevent her delivering some inappropriate utterance, but

Manda soon found something else and she remained speechless, inwardly quivering. She was observing two skinny girls: pink tracksuit tops, their roots-neglected hair scraped back, gold hoop earrings, white sweatpants revealing their coloured G-strings through the fabric, and their trite, small-of-the-back tattoos, flagged there lustily to encourage alternatives to the missionary position.

'Lots of foreigners here, uh?' Manda said, suspiciously, as if some vast hoax was being carried out upon her alone.

'It's an airport.'

'I suppose.'

'Besides. We're foreign.'

'Lots of *weirdos* here then.'

Kylah tutted and raised her eyes.

With Kay and her small suitcase leading them, they were moving on ahead. Kay was looking around with purpose, the armada formation of three trolleys trailing her. They came to the appropriate desks under Area C.

'You'll all need your passports.' Kay turned and went back to Finn and Ava who began walking on ahead, joining the short queue.

'See, we're forming gangs already,' Manda darkly claimed, turning to Kylah as they all began to rapidly fumble for their passports, as if a policeman at a border control had demanded them.

Kylah held her passport between her sparklingly white front teeth as she clipped down the top of her vanity case; she also had the disposable camera out again. 'I'm going take a photo of us checking in, girls.'

'Here. Wait.'

Chell turned and looked at Manda who had her purse in her hand but a blank expression.

'Hell's bells.'

'What?'

'Hold your horses.'

'What is it?'

'My passport is no here.'

'Look proper, Manda.'

'Honest engines. I'm no jesting, Chell. It's not in here.'

Chell stepped over. 'Where was it?'

'Here. Right here in my big purse. That's where I keep it.'

'C'mon, it'll be in your bag. It's a right Mary Poppins job. Look in it.'

Manda lifted her shoulder bag up onto the basket of the trolley and stood over it, both her forearms plunged within, up to her elbows. 'It's not here, it's not here,' she hissed, both aggression and panic in her voice at the same time.

'What is it?' Kylah drawled in a bored voice.

Without looking at Kylah, Manda rummaged roughly. 'Can't find my passport.'

Kylah said nothing for a moment, dropping her eyes to Manda's kneading, scuffling arms in the noisy congeries of her deep bag. Quietly Kylah said, 'Maybe you put it in your boot with your money?'

Manda looked around and then she surreptitiously put weight on one of her legs. 'Naw, I can feel my notes in there but there's no ways I'd've put my passport in too. It was right here in my purse. I'm positive.' She had fear in her face now and she was looking from Kylah to Chell. 'Oh no. Now I'll need to go all back to that bloody hotel–thing–stay–place.'

Kylah said, 'What about in your suitcase; I mean, you're hungover? Mightn't you have put it in there when you packed your clothes?'

'Och I'm daft but there's no ways I'd put my passport in there cos I know I need it to get on a plane.'

'Look again. Look again.'

'I'm telling yous it's not there.'

'Here.' Kylah stepped in and took the shoulder bag from Manda and began rummaging.

'Have you tried all your pockets?' Chell reached out and patted the side and the breast pockets of Manda's white Levi's jacket.

'I've looked.' Manda brushed Chell's hands away testily, but then rechecked the pockets herself, patting at them. Now the tearfulness so familiar to Chell and to Kylah began to appear on Manda's face.

Kay was beside them. Manda hadn't noticed her approach so wasn't prepared.

'What is it?'

Manda looked up and Kay also immediately recognised the symptoms of a pre-bawling, hysterical fit.

'She's lost her passport.'

'She can't *find* her passport,' Chell snappily amended.

'When did you last have it?'

'Umm. I dunno. It could be anywhere. I mean, I had it in my purse and that's all I can remember.'

Ava and Finn had been glancing over at them from the check-in queue. They crossed back in a lackadaisical, studenty manner, each now with their backpacks slung on shoulders, halting where the trolleys were.

'What's up?' Finn asked.

'Manda can't find her passport.'

'You had it down in the bar last night when you showed me the photos of wee Sean. I saw it.'

'Yes. I saw it too. You had it in your purse,' Ava nodded.

'I know. I know. I've got my purse here, safe. That's where I always keep it. But my passport isn't inside it. But. Oh, I'm sorry.'

'Don't get upset, Manda. We'll find it.'

'She definitely had it last night,' Finn stated.

'What about your cases?'

'That's what I said.'

'I wouldn't put it in my case. My money's in my boot. That's where I keep my cash. It can get a bit pongy.' She stamped her foot hard.

'Her passport's not in her boot. I asked.'

'I could feel it if it was there. It's just my bit of cash.'

Finn said, 'Look. We'll go to a cafe or something and we can all sit down and Manda can go through her stuff there.'

'Maybe we could go to Mackers. I'm famished.'

'Let's go to a pub?' Manda brightened immediately as she said this.

'Wait though.' Chell looked down at herself.

Everybody now turned and looked at Chell.

'Eh. If we're no going to be flying I wish I hadn't wore these runners and trackies.' Chell indicated down at her cotton track-suit bottom and her running shoes. 'Maybe I should change?'

Kylah sparked up. 'Aye. Right enough. If we're not going, I should change back into decent clothes. If she won't be able to come, I need to get ma Topshop skirt out my case if –'

Manda burst out crying as if it were a sneeze.

2

The four girls stood by the three trolleys and they watched Chell with her arm over Manda's shoulder and Manda's scuffing, bandy gait as they melded into the milling throng of others – heading off for the toilets.

'That's done it now,' Finn shook her head.

'Do you really think she's gone and lost it?' Kay turned to the others and she opened her mouth wide at the ramifications of this.

Kylah said, 'You bet your ass she has. She was steaming last night. Bouncing off the walls.'

Ava said, 'Oh shame. I feel quite sorry for her actually. She's upset and I think she's really quite sweet.'

'Mmmm. You'll never hear the last of this. If she's gone and lost it, there'll be hell to pay. And if she finds it she'll never quit gabbing either.' Finn looked around.

Kay went, 'Gee. What if she really has lost it?'

'That's that then, isn't it?'

There was silence. Everyone looked at Finn.

'She'll have to go home then, won't she?'

'Oh, don't say that.'

'No ways she'll go back home all on her own. Look. She can't even go to the bog without an escort.' Finn's face hardened. 'No, but sorry – it's her problem. I saved like a bastard for this holiday and I'm not cancelling cos of Manda. We'll have a better crack without her. She's worse than a bad wedgie tight up your ass all day.'

Kay said, 'We can cancel but we won't get a refund on a last-minute booking this late. We'll lose one hundred per cent. One thousand four hundred quid, on Dad's card.'

Finn looked at Kay. She clenched her fists at her sides and she lifted her head up to the ceiling, slowly shaking her head.

Ava took control. 'Look. Everyone. Listen. There's a real good chance she has simply put it in these suitcases or somewhere a bit silly.' Ava slapped the top of Manda's distinctive pink cases. 'We all need to go, sit somewhere and help her search through everything and I'm sure we'll find it. And if it is lost it could turn up at the hotel or on the bus and get handed in over the next few hours and we have the rest of the day.'

Everyone took stock and nodded sensibly.

'Bet you anything her passport's back at that hotel.'

'Aye.'

'I'll go back,' said Kay. 'It's a free bus; only takes a jiffy. If Manda goes, God knows what she'll get up to.'

'I'll come with you,' Finn suddenly announced.

Ava observed how Kylah gave Finn and Kay a briefest, help-lessly pejorative stare. Kylah asked, 'Got your phone with you?'

Kay ruffled into her shoulder bag – the beautiful, large calfskin one she'd got from her parents that last Christmas, only noticeably more worn now – and she lifted her mobile phone out between two fingers and shook it daintily at Kylah.

'C'mon.'

Finn looked at Ava and said, directly, 'We'll phone in half an hour.'

Ava and Kylah watched as Finn and Kay moved off into the crowds.

Ava looked at Kylah, smiled and shrugged her shoulders. Kylah looked back a little uncomfortable to be suddenly isolated with this beautiful new stranger. With relief Kylah said, 'Look, here they are back.'

Chell and Manda moved towards them through the people. Manda moved as if she carried urgent letters for the King. Shouldering in front of someone's trolley, her lip instantly reacted into the beginning of a huge tut. She jerked aggressively aside, holding a twisted face upon the perpetrator – a look designed to judge their mentality in a crushing and final way. Chell's little head bobbed obediently just behind Manda's shoulder.

Manda was flushed from crying and you could see she had splashed her face with water but this had only served to mash up her already undefined eyeliner even more; she opened her mouth to speak before she noticed, then changed her question, demanding, 'Where's Kay and Finn?'

'They popped back to the hotel to see if they could find your passport,' Kylah said flatly, with a condescending inflection. 'C'mon and we'll go somewhere and take a deech through your gear.'

'I hope all your knickers is clean in there,' Chell added.

Angrily Manda snapped, 'But I'm telling yous it's not in the cases. I'd never have put it in there.'

Manda was leading them now and she had been turning around anxiously to shout back at the others but then, before traversing much of the area at all, she let the brake handle snap up on her trolley as if she'd noticed her passport itself, lying on the ground, and she shouted, 'Kay's case is on my trolley!'

Kylah had to stop abruptly behind her.

'What is it, Manda?'

'Kay's case is on *my* trolley.'

'Well, she couldn't very well take it with her.'

'Aye.' Manda thought about this, then stated, 'I suppose it is my passport she's away looking for.' She nodded to anoint the situation and pushed on.

Chell, Kylah and Ava too, could only conceal a certain admiration. For up the escalators, Manda was seated, somehow dominating the small smoking section of the Gatwick Village Inn pub with a full pint of Guinness before her; its white disc of surface had descended down enough to show considerable inroads had already been made upon its quantity. Manda indicated the drink by revolving the grubby thumb of her smoking hand towards the Guinness and called loudly, 'Hair of the dog that fucking bit me,' then she jammed her cigarette back in her lips. Ava was sat next to her and you could tell that Manda was badly hung-over because she did not even bother to turn and mercilessly scrutinise this pale and fascinating addition to their group. 'Oh, girls.

If they find my passport it's going to be brilliant. You'll really see how to party with us, Ava.'

'Mmmm,' Ava purred, doubtfully.

Just reaching that upstairs pub hadn't been easy for Ava. She had politely followed behind them as they had toured the South Terminal shopping village.

'Boots,' Manda had formally noted aloud to Kylah and Chell, who both nodded in confirmation.

'Hey. Body Shop. Oh, and a La Senza, girls. Wow. Sunglass Hut. It just sells sunglasses; mental.'

They were in a large lobby, intersecting with two main promenades. On the far side of the escalators, some coin-operated public phones remained, and although they were gradually being phased out to provide more retail space, there were also short rows of electric-blue-coloured seating. There were no armrests on the seating – so people could stretch out to sleep upon them in time of delay-crisis.

'Look at this joint. It's humungous.'

'It really is a village.'

'Let's nose round.'

Ava followed as they peered challengingly into the open doors of the Body Shop where the assistants – seemingly the same age as themselves – looked back blankly. Edible coconut and heavy cream-like smells came to their nostrils.

'What were they stared at? Stupid bitches,' Manda said indignantly.

'Body Shop. Pricey, but their peppermint foot lotion, that's just brilliant,' said Chell.

'I don't see the point of it. Just makes your socks greasy and your feet smell like Polo mints,' Kylah said.

'It's good sexual lubricant. It kind of all tingles,' Chell smiled, knowingly.

Manda remained uncharacteristically silent.

They all passed Ultimate Gift, glumly unimpressed, but now

they came to the intersection with the long promenade which led away to their right and to their left.

'Bags Etc. We'll need to take a damn good look at that.' Chell pointed with a certain aggression.

'Look, look here, it's a balcony thing and you can see all down onto folks' heads, wow.'

Manda left her trolley and dashed forward with excitement to the very edge, to find herself elevated high above the Arrivals plaza and check-in forecourts. You could stand at the railing and look down upon the steady inflow of arrival passengers and also, over to the left, towards the security area before Departures, where people moved to go airside.

'You could gob down on their fucking heads. Dare you, Chell.'

'Nut, fuck off.'

'Where's Finn and Kay? Oh. Be brilliant if they could see us up here.'

'Aye.'

Manda took off again, like a child in a fairground, excitedly running from ride to ride but too worked up to decide on one. Her missing passport seemed forgotten.

Ahead, the view down to check-in was blocked by a temporary-seeming structure called Caffè Nero, serving sophisticated varieties of coffee and packaged sandwiches; people sat on tall stools in some skewed, jet-lag dream of what Milan might be. Businessmen held mobile phones to their ears but mysteriously said nothing – emoting the concentrated intensity of people judging albums through music-shop headsets.

Then Manda spotted it ahead, she actually ran with her hen-toed gait, stumbling in her smudged white boots – she gaped and glared into the wall-less open entrance. 'Look at this place,' she called. In a downtrodden voice she admitted, 'It's even bigger than Rascals.'

The Village Inn was a themed English pub. The pseudo-rustic beer pumps curving their pipes in retro-obedience, the shire horse mural, the grand old varnished bar bending to a central point like a plough abandoned on the edge of some Hampshire meadow. There was a burgundy-and-purple imitation Turkish carpet which had drunk deeply of spilled beers, sticky colas, sauces, gravies and even presented the occasional flat pale disc of directly spat-out chewing gum. Above all this, a smog of beer ozone manoeuvred at nose level, although an overpowering pink-grapefruit-scented disinfectant pummelled for dominance outside the swinging toilets door.

Manda had stared, entranced. In the smokers' section nearest the open entrance, steady creameries of fag smoke curled around the visors of various baseball caps and arose towards brilliant illumination from brass disc fittings on small down spotlights in the ceiling.

Hanging like chimps from trees, in the crannies and against the cosmetic roof beams, were a gang of flat-screen televisions. Soundless, every television was tuned to Sky News, its scroll narrative ticker-tapering out along the bottom of the screen with a steady inflow of updates on the latest child molestations and inner-city assaults, supported by lingering and repeated mugshots of the accused. A non-verbal form of justice was being meted out already up there, dramatised by the constant, incongruous accompaniment of the upbeat CD jukebox. Then sport came on and males shifted their positions.

'Oh. This is just a brilliant place,' Manda sanctioned.

'Aye,' Kylah said.

A moody pocket of lads were stepping out from beneath the screens and glancing up at the sport (or perhaps they had been deftly noting the mugshots of the accused) and they had already spotted Chell, Kylah and Manda with Ava standing behind, at the mouth of the Village Inn, gawking.

There was a gaggle of Irish golfing bachelors in jumpers, an excess of disposable income blatant among a mass of black shiny Guinness arrayed along the wet bar top.

Other mature males blocked the bar, leaning casually, pretending to give all attention to the flat screens but also appraising the seated tables of females off on hen holidays. The glum horse-racing contingent was also represented. These men still pondered the form in their folded-out tabloids. Meditative lagers at their elbows, they glanced up at the screen for any racing news, bets sown and dangerously committed before departure.

Those two separate tables of girls didn't present much of a challenge to Manda who had evaluated them thoroughly. For a start they were mostly all wearing black dress trousers – nothing like that wee hoor back there in the gold lamé dress. Perhaps they were just off-duty office workers, not a glamorous traveller, like Manda?

A trolley park of luggage at their side was taking up the space of a small car and the four of them sat in the Village Inn, waiting for Finn and Kay to text. Manda casually fished out a twenty-pound note, dropped her purse on the tabletop, then with killing *coup de grâce* elevated the note before Ava's face. 'Ava. Away up to the bar and get us all another round in, would you, beautiful?'

Chell stiffened, but quicker off the mark than Manda had anticipated, Ava stood and said, 'Sure. What would you like?'

'Guinness Extra Cold for little old me and whatever you and the wee monkeys are having?'

'Just a white wine and lemonade.'

'Can I have a bottle of cider with ice please?'

'Right.'

All three young women at the table watched Ava move towards the bar. Let's be frank: Ava was wearing boot-cut jeans that afternoon and all three scrutinised and evaluated her arse as she went. Manda was looking for some avenue of criticism; but it was pretty clear there was absolutely none.

'I think she's really *gorge*ous-looking,' Chell uttered in a low, matter-of-fact voice.

'Me too,' Kylah quickly seconded.

'Lady Di here?' Manda shrugged, mock indifferent. 'Huh. No a bad figure I suppose but . . .' She paused . . . 'You can tell, even though her clothes is crap, she's very high maintenance and I don't buy the butter-won't-melt-in-her-mouth thing. Mark my

71

words though, girls. She's a dark horse this one. There's something afoot about her. Just haven't fathomed out what it is yet.'

'She seems quite down to earth to me, for a posh English bird; we'll see in Benidorm.'

Manda suddenly lowered her voice. 'Do you think she's munching Finn's carpet in London then?'

'Manda. She'll hear you.'

'So? C'mon, 'fess up, we're all wondering it. You know what Finn's like, when she spews up, it's fur balls she spits.'

'Manda. Finn had a London boyfriend last year. She's not like that, you know; get over it.' Kylah shook her head in disapproval.

'I don't care. It's disgusting whatever. And though everybody's too feart to mention, we's all know fine well what Finn McConnel's been up to in the past. It turns your stomach.'

'Manda. Why don't you chill out? I thought we'd all timed this bloody holiday so's we wouldn't be on our period.'

'Fancy her too, Kyles?' Suddenly Manda loudly sniffed at the fingers of her non-cigarette-holding hand.

Chell jumped at the sudden attack but Kylah just stood and tightly said, 'You've a filthy mouth on you for a wee boy's mother.'

Chell winced and stiffened her legs in her seated position. Wearily she said, 'Girls, let's not fight. In front of Ava. On the very first day.'

'I'm away for a wander. I'll text. Meet Finn and Kay.'

'Sit down, Kyles,' Chell hissed.

Kylah looked at Chell. 'Chell. Hear what she just says. Don't put up with it.'

Kylah turned back to Manda, but before she could speak, Manda squeaked, 'Bye then.'

Kylah replied in a slow, deliberate manner which scored its target all the more, 'Pick up your phone and talk to your poor wee son, for fuck sake, girl,' and she turned and walked towards the arch.

Manda's raised voice turned bitter now with a familiar edge of tears to it. 'I'll phone. I'll phone when I'm good and ready to phone,' and then at Kylah's receding back came a full shout, Manda's voice cracking slightly, 'Hear me?' Her face beetrooted up with anger and she gave a wet-laced glare of feigned wrongness to Chell.

People observed from close at hand and turned round over at the bar; there was a sudden drop in conversational volume across the interior. Ava herself turned from the beer pumps where she stood, to look.

Then Ava was approaching with a bottle of cider and a half-pint glass in one hand, her own dark chinkly rum and Coke in the other. 'Is that too much ice for Kylah, do you think?' she calmly asked, diplomatically putting the glasses down. She departed to a taut silence.

As Ava walked away again, Manda looked in Chell's face. 'I'll drink Kylah's cider,' she snapped. It was hard to decipher if this was a practical move, to deal with the abandoned beverage, or a specific act of revenge. She gathered her thoughts a moment and darkly stated, 'I forgot to phone last night. You know, I was excited. I don't get away much like all these . . . students.' She nodded angrily at retreating Ava. 'Away from home and wee Sean. I 'fess up, I was buzzing a bit, and after a few drinks from that minibar contraption I sort of forgot, and it got too late to phone home. The cheek of Kylah, bloody telling me how to be a proper mum.' As if to counter her own argument, she hoisted the remaining pint of Guinness and nuzzled away at it then smacked her lips.

Chell sighed. 'I know, honey. Don't fret. You can call in an hour.'

'Aye.' Manda nodded decisively.

Ava returned and placed another full pint in front of Manda and the white wine and lemonade before Chell; perceptively she said nothing and circled the table to reseat herself by Manda's side with her own rum and Coke.

'Ta,' Chell said quietly.

All was not plain sailing though as Chell noted Ava suddenly hoist the twenty-pound note insolently before Manda's face. 'Do you know what?' Ava said. 'That barperson questioned your twenty-pound note. It's a Scottish one, so I paid with an English note.'

73

Chell widened her eyes and experienced a swift burst of admiration for Ava; subtle, but she knew fine how to hold her own.

'Eh?' snapped Manda, rising straight to the bait.

'I mean, he was willing to take it, but I said no problem and paid with an English twenty. Imagine. In an international airport as well.'

Manda didn't even have the gumption to look at Ava; she squeaked her arse round on the seat and glowered towards the beer pumps. 'That's fucking ridiculous. That's . . . completely favour-atist to English money,' she declared.

'Never mind. Let's just call it my round and you take this back. I'm sure you'll be able to spend it perfectly well, somewhere else,' Ava stated in the plummy accent but with an inflection of doubt, and she put the rejected Scottish twenty down on the wet table, close to Manda. 'Can I mooch a cigarette please, Manda?'

Delighted, Manda was impressed now. 'Aye, sure.' She went so far as to lift the pack invitingly and Ava plucked a Marlboro Light from within.

Chell saw Manda's expression: the mind collating then suddenly detouring back to where she wanted to be, and with a fresh tone Manda commenced, 'So, Ava.'

Chell bit her lip.

'Philosophies and that. You and Finn are working at, in the London University.'

'Yes?'

'What's that all about then? I mean, I've read *Harry Potter and the Philosophies' Stone*. Most of it. It's a bit long, is it no for a book? But what's that going to do for you? You know? When you come out of uni and that and you've read. Books. It is all in books, is it? Philosophies?'

'Well . . . that's . . .'

'What I'm digging at is this. Is it like. The meanings to life and stuff?'

Ava lit her cigarette as a slight barrier, buying her some thinking time, and cautiously reminded her, 'I'm reading French as well.'

Manda nodded sagely. 'You read French. I can see that'll be useful, aye. The French language. We did that at school. A bit.'

Ava just smiled. 'Philosophy sounds very clever-clever, I know, and irrelevant, but all you really do is look at what people have thought and believed through history, not just about how to live your life. What different thinkers have thought. That's all it is really. And also . . .'

Manda raised her eyebrows in expectation.

'. . . philosophy is about *how* people think.'

'How d'ye mean?'

'Ancient philosophers thought differently from how we think today, in an ideology of science and specialisation. Ancients thought clouds in the sky were spirits and things. And even how people thought fifty years ago has changed.'

'Is that right enough?'

Chell was surprised; she was expecting a cutting aside but Manda seemed – however momentarily – cautiously curious.

Manda enquired, 'Why do it then? I mean, you could have chose to study . . . like a health and beauty therapy course that I'm going to do one day. Or a hotel and catering course. That'll get you a job. Look at yon Internet of Kay. There must be hundreds of hotels across the world. In all the places. There's so many *places*. If you do hotel and catering you're quids in for a decent job. Or for you . . . I would bet hotel management would be a good bet.'

'Listen to you, Manda Tassy. You sound like old Leary Neary, the pervy careers guidance gadge at school,' Chell chuckled.

Manda turned sharply to Chell. 'Well, that's what it is, I'm saying; what job will she get, with philosophy when you leave the uni? Know what I'm saying, Ava? You might know the meaning to life and that by then but . . . well, it's like my old Nana says: if you want to grow your roses, you better follow the milkman's carthorse.'

Chell went, 'What?'

Ava said, 'Well, there you are. Your Nana is obviously a philosopher too. And you're right. I won't get a job out of it. There isn't a big factory somewhere full of philosophers, sitting at desks, thinking. It would be nice if there was. It's just a very interesting thing to do before I have to get a dull, proper job.'

'You must have to be dead clever, all the same though,' Manda queried.

'Oh no. I'm very slow.'

'Nah. You must be dead brainy. To read all those philosophies and understand what it all meants.'

'Well, some of them are just impossible to understand.'

'Can even you no understand some of them?'

'I'm not very brainy, Manda. Finn is the whizz-kid at it.'

'Aye? She was always a brains-trust,' Manda nodded, frankly excited and turned in appeal towards Chell. 'Finn was aye good at covering it up. That she was brainy. Like she was one of the girls. You know, out on a Saturday night downing the drinks, sometimes chasing lads?' She paused and coughed theatrically. 'But she could also swot up and pass the exams.'

'Could she?' Ava quipped.

'She got *tons* of Highers.'

'We have Highers in Scotland but yous have A levels down here don't yous?' Chell nodded seriously.

'Yes. It's Finn you're best talking to about philosophy. She understands everything. Even Baruch Spinoza who's a complete old bore, but Finn can talk about him with the top professors.'

Manda barked suddenly. 'Hear that, Chell?'

Chell was astonished; Manda seemed genuinely impressed.

Manda opened her bruised eyes wide. 'One of our gang, talking to *the professors*,' she chuckled to herself amusedly. Private images of grandeur were buffering up in her mind. 'Well I never.' Now Manda looked down, rueful and a touch vulnerable. 'Well. I was brought up Catholic, like all us were. Are you Catholic?'

'No.'

'If you don't mind me asking.'

'Not at all.'

'What are you?'

'Lapsed Jewish.'

'Oh right.' Manda began toying with the new pint. 'Is that where the reindeers are from?'

'Pardon?'

'Lapsed.'

Quietly Ava said, 'That's Lapland you're thinking of. Lapsed means when you once did, but no longer believe in an ideology. Any more. Like a religion.'

'Oh. I'm like that too. That's just like me then. Lapsed. When I was a wee girl I believed in all the stuff. All of it. I believed in little baby Jesus, and the Virgin Mary, and the words on the Sacred Heart that hung in our house. I used to stand on a chair to reach down that picture frame from the wall and to read through the words. No understanding them though, but kind of scared of them?' She explained, 'That meant Jesus was living in our actual house. And underneath was writ my dad's signature and me and my big sister's names were writ there too and the priest had signed it, just to confirm Jesus was in the house. Though as my dad says, when the poll tax form came each year, thankfully Jesus was exempt.'

The three of them laughed out loud at that.

Manda smiled. 'And I believed in all that too; doing good and not doing wrong things. But as I got older I started to think a lot of it was fibs. Fibbing to make us do what the school and the nuns and church wanted us to do and not what I wanted to do, or even maybe Jesus too, and what I'm saying is, is that philosophy? Cos that's mine. You should do what you want to do in life.'

'It certainly is. It's called scepticism with a touch of the Epicurean. That's my philosophy as well,' Ava quietly said.

'Oh aye. Septicaemia. I've heard of that right enough.'

'Scepticism it's called.'

'Is it? You're the same as me then, philosophy-wise?'

'Sure.'

'Oh, Chell. Hear that? Philosophy is brilliant!' Manda called out.

3

KYLAH	Big Mac	large fries	large Coke	apple pie
MANDA	Big Mac plus a cheese-burger, a dozen Chicken McNuggets in two packs of 6	2 large fries	strawberry shake, strawberry sundae	
CHELL	Cheeseburger	small fries	chocolate shake, Fanta	
AVA			Grande latte in paper cup from Caffè Nero	
FINN	Nothing			
KAY	Nothing			

Finn and Kay had returned from the hotel without locating the passport and Manda was in some curious state of semi-denial. Once again, Manda gave a scowl over towards the young girl behind the counter and spoke none too quietly. 'Dippit cow. I says to her: twelve McNuggets, right? She goes, we don't serve twelve. Well, yous sell boxes of six, don't you? So give us two of them then. You thick, skanky townie hoor. Must of got Higher maths, that one. Or is it A level? End up working in a bank she will.' Manda shook her head. Irritably masticating with her mouth full, she added, 'I so wish there was a McDonald's in our bloody town. My sister drove us up to that Mackers in the Fort. A hundred mile for a Quarter Pounder. If there was a Mackers in

78

the town then I could leave wee Sean in the play area while I got myself a Big Mac and a good blether with all us mums. Mackers is a sort of brilliant crèche. I've heard they have *News of the World* there on Sundays. Are yous really no having a single bloody thing to eat, Ava?'

'No. I'm okay for just now, thank you.'

'And are *you no* having anything, Kay? After your big adventure.'

'I don't really like McDonald's.'

'Yous would scare Kate Moss. You won't have a shadow soon. Puts you off your food, yous not eating any. This is brilliant.' Manda shook the Big Mac like a trophy in both her fists towards Ava; a moist rip of ketchup-weighted lettuce fell heavily to the table. There were the sounds of eating and the suction of straws.

'Yous'll have a brilliant time in Spain without *me*, girls. Just think. You'll be there tonight. Spain is brilliant. Well, Magaluf is brilliant at any rate. But there is one thing I should point out to you about Spain.'

Chell frowned. 'And what's that?'

'The bright light from the sun there. It really bloody shows up your complexions. Deep pores, every plook. You know? And all they restaurants and a lot of the terraces of the bars, they have light like this light. What's this shitey light called?' she nodded upward.

'Fluorescent?'

'Right. Did you learn that in philosophy university, Ava? Well, this light, it makes you go all green. And not yous two but if you're blonde, like me and Kyles is, the swimming-pool water turns your hair green as well. It's a constant battle against going green. And you're green in the morning with a hangover too. And yous're in swimming pools all the time it's so scorching hot there. You sweat between your tits. If you have any.' She nodded directly across the plastic table at Finn.

'It might not be so hot now. You were aye there in Augusts.'

'And the light shows up everything. I hope you all brought plenty of concealer.'

'I always do.'

'Aye. It was so boiling hot when we were last time in Magaluf, my sister snogged one of the Birmingham boys most of the night lying in a fountain, to keep cool. I told yous everything about it.'

'You did. Aye.'

'Aye, we went there, me and Catriona, with that bitch Shelly. What a bitch that bitch Shelly is.'

'Shelly McCrindle? Did she go with yous?' Finn pursed her lips in surprise.

'Aye. You really missed yourself.'

'But you're not a blonde,' Finn suddenly pointed out.

Manda looked at Finn but then she addressed her response directly to Ava. 'Aye but my big sister did a good job with my hair, eh?'

Ava nodded politely.

'And the boys would never have been able to tell – if I was going with yous – cos my collar matches my cuffs. My sister did that too.'

Finn turned away again.

'Another thing about Spain, girls. Watch out for yon food they're aye funnelling down your gullet. Pie-elle-yah it's called. It's minging. It's bright yellow rice, like yon you get with a carry-out from Light of India, but it's got all sea monsters and stuff in and you try to lift a spoonful and it's got the broke-off creeper pincer things of those sort of sea cockroaches mixed up into it. When all you want's a good burger, eh? Got one of the pincer feelers in my mouth once and they've got the wee black eyes all stuck out. Uh!'

'Sea cockroaches?'

'Aye. Like, what are they called, those pink things?'

'Prawns. She means prawns.'

'Anyways, in Magaluf. Oh girls, the times we had there. You really missed yourselves.'

'You told us.'

Manda turned sharply, 'Ava. At Water Lands there's this slide, the Kamzey-kazee or something it's called, and all this crowd of boys is stood at the bottom with their cameras going and you wonder why, but it's cos when you come down the slide and splash into the pool at the bottom in your bikini, you're going so fast it takes off all girls' bikini tops, unless you know to hold it on.'

Wryly Ava said, 'So Chell with her nine bikinis is prepared for several shots on that.'

All the others laughed at this and you could see Manda was furious that attention had been diverted. She went on though: 'And also, Ava –'

'Oh don't scum us out.'

'– you hit the water with such a bang that when you climb out the pool, all this water is running down your leg and know what that is? Do you know? Ah, they dinna teach you that in philosophies. It's cos the water's been forced right up your fanny and it just comes gushing back out. It happened to me. There again, I have given birth to a lovely wee boy, so maybe more would come out me than say . . . one of yous.'

'Gee, Manda. I can't believe you'd boast about a talent like that. Why don't you quit yapping and have a good look through your suitcases; see if you can't find that passport?' Finn said, which was enough to drive Manda into a broody, and doubt-less brief, pause.

Chell looked at Manda out the sides of her eyes. 'Were you sick in the night, Manda?'

'Nut.'

Kylah went, 'You were too. I heard you fine. I wasn't sleeping. I couldn't with the bloody racket you were making, blundering about.'

'I was not. Anyways. Tell them about last time you were sick, lassie. It's a classic.'

Chell said, 'Oh, Selwyn? That Saturday before I moved in with Kylah? I drank so much that when I got home and tried to sleep, I threw up beside my bed. Couldn't be bothered to clean it right then, and I crashed out but was woken up by this sound. It was old Selwyn, our dog, eating up my sick. He must have been forgot to get fed that day cos when I did get up next afternoon there was hardly any left to clean away.'

Everyone else went, 'Awwww.'

'Sorry. Some of yous is eating. Do you have dogs, Ava?'

'Dogs and cats. Well, at home, not in London; they're my parents'.'

Chell leaned over the table. 'How many?'

'Two dogs. There's Wilbur and McLean and two cats called Hector and Buggers.'

'Buggers!'

'What kind of dogs?'

'Bulldogs,' Manda interrupted.

'My two Weimars.'

'Oh, the blue dogs. They're adorable dogs,' Chell pined.

'Blue dogs?' Manda muttered. Then she wiped her hands on a napkin from the huge wad she'd brought from the dispenser.

Suddenly Ava said, 'Can't you travel within Europe using any kind of photo identification? That's their condition of carriage.'

Manda looked at her puzzled. 'Are carriages no pulled by just trains?'

'Can you?' Finn sounded hopeful.

'I'm convinced you can. We'll ask at the information desk,' Ava said.

Finn looked around the table and addressed everyone, 'Aye. They told Kay and me if any passports was found and turned up at the hotel or on the buses it would be sent to the information desk downstairs.'

Manda didn't look up or show any interest.

'Cos it might still turn up. Manda. Manda!'

'Eh? Aye. I was thinking. Anything I've got with photos is in the drawer in the front room back in Scotland with wee Sean's birth certificate.'

'Don't you have a driving licence or something?' Ava asked.

'Can't drive.'

'You must have something?'

Manda shrugged.

Finn impatiently challenged. 'Look, Manda. Why not just go through your suitcase, once, for us?'

'See yonder suitcase?' Manda pointed to one of her cases on

the trolley. 'That case has no been opened since back in the town in my bedroom. I know fine, cos me and Dad had to sit on it to get it shut. There is no ways on earth I could have opened that last night while I was stocious. Open it now and we're no getting it shut again. I'm warning yous. The other one I *did* have open last night, to get changed to go down to that grotty bar, and I did close it up this morn.'

'Help us get this down then.' Finn flicked her head at Ava. The two of them surrounded the trolley.

'What one's the one you've never opened then?'

'That one with your hand on.'

The others watched as Finn and Ava lifted the other suitcase – with difficulty – down together and slowly placed it on its side.

Manda announced, 'You'll need the combination for that lock.'

'What is it then?'

In an incredulous voice she said, 'I'm no telling you. Here.'

Finn straightened up and she raised her eyes to the ceiling.

Angrily Manda stomped to the case and she kneeled down with her big bare knees placed together onto the actual floor. She used her hand to shade the combination as she entered numbers on the small dials and unlocked it.

Manda stood up, put her hands on the seat of her skirt and looked around them all. 'I'm not a fool, you know. I didn't lose my passport. Someone here has took it off me as a tease and someone knows it fine. One of yous, or more, knows better than any.'

'Oh God.' Finn looked to the others in appeal. 'Manda, give it up. Don't be so ridiculous.'

But once the idea had been aired, Chell and Kylah suddenly looked as if they were completely excited by the whole concept. They chortled richly. Kylah leaned forward with her arms crossed, frowning. 'Why would any of us bother to nick your passport?'

'Why do you think? Cos yous can't stand me any more. You don't want me coming with yous.'

'Manda!' Chell actually cried it out. 'Nobody would do that to you.'

Manda glared round them all.

Finn said, 'We're just trying to help you out. Me and Kay went all the way over to that hotel to try find your passport. So thanks very much.'

'Knowing you two, yous booked a room and had a right old brutal gang bang.'

A percolating silence.

Kylah said, 'You're hardly away from Sean and you're drinking and snapping away at all of us and going on about stuff and getting on our nerves. I'm sorry, but you've just got pished and gone and lost your passport. That's all there is to it.'

'Sean, Sean, Sean. Yous are aye throwing Sean in my face as if I cannie go pee on my own.'

'Well, you did have to take Chell with you to go to the bog.'

They saw Manda's temper froth up even more. She might have self-induced a haemorrhoid her face went so red.

Finn leaned into Manda. 'You're going to feel really daft if your passport is in there,' she said flatly while she pointed at the suitcase.

'Well, it isn't. Cos I had it in my purse last night and it should still be there.'

'Go look then.' It was an order.

Manda kneeled again and lifted the large suitcase lid open. Several belts with sparkling buckles fell down from the lid netting, twisting and snaking awkwardly and she angrily swiped them aside as she dug in with both arms, tugging out layers and reaching deep, as if she were digging a hole in beach sand. 'There. See. Nothing. Hope you're happy.' Manda leaned down on the top and relocked the case lid then turned and looked Kylah directly in the eye. 'Now I have to go and phone my wee boy and talk to my dad about what to do.' She brandished her mobile phone the same way she'd been waving the burger about before, then lumbered up and away. She rounded the corner of the rear entrance to the McDonald's.

Slowly Finn bent forward, let her hair fall from behind her head, and she lay her nose on the table. They could see her pale scalp where the long hair parted a bit.

'I know, Finn. I feel like that too,' mumbled Kylah, chewing.

'Jesus,' hissed Finn. 'Are you thinking what I'm thinking?'

'What?

'See the suitcase she's not letting us into?'

'Aye.'

'Do you think she maybe has it hid in there?'

'What? Why?' said Ava.

'She'll do anything to be centre of attention. I wouldn't put it past her, after we've been nice as pie to her all day, an hour before the flight is due, she'll mysteriously find her passport. She'll have been centre of attention and got us massaging her arse all day then she'll be satisfied and whoops! That's it. The passport strangely materialises.'

'Naw. Never. She wouldn't,' says Chell.

'Girls,' went Kay. They all turned to her.

'What?'

'What is it?'

'None of yous are like, teasing her, are you?'

'What?'

'None of yous have her passport, do you?'

'Are you joking? Come off it.'

'Seriously. Are we all being straight up here? Because at first it did cross my mind one of you may have nicked it, to wind her up and warn her.'

'Come on. She's a pain in the arse but I wouldn't go that far.'

'Yes. I feel sorry for her.' Ava shrugged.

'What are we gonna do if she really has lost it?'

They all looked at Finn.

'Don't look at me.'

'We can't leave her, Finn.'

Kay said, quietly, 'Listen, girls. We went back to the ticket place. There's no refund on these tickets or the hotel bookings. It's twenty-four hours' notice at the best of time and there are no refunds of last-minute discount bookings. If we don't go today, and we cancel, we've lost all the money.'

There was a long silence.

Chell looked at her burger ruins before her. 'I don't think I can leave her. If she's not going, I think I'll have to stay with her. I'll pay you back, Kay.'

'Chell!' Exasperated, Finn looked at her. 'You've got to get your own life.'

'That's easy for you to say, all down in London and that. You know fine what she's like. If I go with yous, Manda'll be at me about it for ten fucking years. You don't have to see her near every day. I do.'

Kylah said sardonically, 'It's true. Manda'll have it put on her bloody gravestone. "Here lies Manda Tassy. Died of VD. Was abandoned by her rotten friends once at Gatwick Airport."'

They all looked towards the rear exit then sat in silence, reprimanded by guilt.

Kay said, 'Maybe we should cancel.'

'I can't believe this,' Finn huffed out.

'No, listen. We cancel. Make the gesture. Make sure she's safe home on a train out of London and we'll all rebook tomorrow and be away.'

Finn said huffily, 'All that money wasted and gone for her. I worked in that fucking flower shop for this and I get hay fever. There's no need to cancel. There's time for one of us to take her up to King's Cross now, pack her on a train and make it back here for the plane. We'll go. Me and Ava will go and see her safe onto the train, cos I wouldn't trust her on her own in London.'

'You've got it all worked out,' Chell said quietly.

'What do you mean by that?'

'Jesus, everyone.' Kylah shook her hair. 'See? The minute she mentioned that we'd nicked her bloody passport, she had us all thinking. Didn't she? She's a genius. She's sneaky as hell.'

'I'll need to go back with her, girls,' Chell said flatly.

Finn tutted. 'Well, I don't trust either of you to get to King's Cross. And you've to change stations in Glasgow with those monster suitcases.'

'Finn, I know how to change stations in Glasgow,' Chell snapped. 'Just cos you live in London.'

They all sat gloomily. Finn pointed. 'Till we find her bloody passport, why don't you get all those bloody cases off our hands? Take them down the stairs to left luggage. And check them in there. I'll help you. Sod's Law being what it is, her passport will turn up the moment you check your cases in to left luggage.' Finn groaned, 'I must say, girls. I thought Manda would ruin these holidays, but I've got to hand it to her. I didn't think she'd manage it in twelve hours straight, before we'd even got anywhere.'

Ava said, 'Look. If we want to rebook tomorrow we can put it all on my father's credit card, but I somehow don't feel we should tell Manda that.'

'No, Ava.'

'That's kind, Ava, but none of us could agree to that.'

Kay chipped in, 'You can put half on my card too. Don't tell Manda for God's sake, but I've seen my dad put thousands and thousands on this card when the builders were in. Sounds snide, but he'd hardly notice and if you *want*, you could each pay it off later in the year to me and I'd pay Dad back. But it doesn't matter. I mean. I'm kind of saying I'll pay it for the moment.'

'That's awful kind, Kay, but . . . if the passport doesn't turn up it doesn't turn up. Today, tomorrow or the next.'

'Tomorrow. Jesus. Kylah, yous can't *all* come up and crash out at Ava and I's place up in London. It's totey-wee. And we'd need to leave all your cases here in left luggage overnight and that'll be pricey and the Gatwick Express costs a fortune.'

'Then we'll need to stay another night here in bed and break-fast or that. Her passport might get found later today?' Kay said. 'Before we make any big dramatic decisions maybe we should chill a while.'

'Pub.'

Manda: Pint of Guinness Extra Cold placed on table
    awaiting her. The spumous honeytop thinning.
Finn: Double gin and tonic with bottled tonic.
Ava: Double gin and tonic with bottled tonic.
Kylah: Bottle of Strongbow cider with ice in a
    half-pint glass.
Chell: White wine with lemonade.
Kay: Glass of medium-dry white wine.

'Whesh–it. Here she comes at last.'

Self-importantly, Manda moved between the tables.

'Where have *you* been then? We took all the cases down to left luggage.'

'Just scoping round. I got your text. Yous should see. It's amazing, on round there. You really missed yourselfs.'

'What's there then?'

'Oh all sorts.'

'We got you a Guinness.'

'Oh. Wow. Cheers. That was nice of yous.' She whipped out a hand. Her rings chinked on the pint glass as she clutched and lifted it all to her mouth without sitting down, so she could dominate over the group.

'Know what I saw?' Manda said after smacking her lips.

'What?'

'This bunch of girls. They haven't come in here yet. Probably don't drink. Six of them.' She looked around aggressively. 'You'll never guess what?'

'What?'

'They had a football with them. Carrying it. A football. What's happening to girls that six of them would go on holiday with a football? For fuck's sake. Silly cows. You should of seen them marching around with their ball. I mean, fucking posers.'

'It's this ladettes thing that you read about.'

'It's probably to play volleyball?' Kay suggested.

Manda protested, 'Why can't they buy a ball when they get there?'

'You don't know where they're going,' Finn put in.

'Aye, it might be Turkey. Could be a major operation to buy a bloody football in Turkey.'

Manda sneered, 'They probably pass it round and snog it at night, pretending it's David Beckham's head. Fucking silly sporty bitches. Losers.'

'How's wee Sean?'

'Fine,' she snapped. 'Yous should see round the back. There's everything. A CD shop. A Starbucks.' She'd plonked down now and lit a fag. 'Then there's a restaurant – really humungous, called . . . I've forgot. Gargoyles, Carbuncles?'

Ava smiled. 'Garfunkel's?'

'Aye, that's it. Then there's another place, that Pizza Express.'

'Is there Pizza Express?' Kay raised her eyebrows.

Ava said, 'Oh, I *love* Pizza Express. And they do great salads.'

'Mmm, it's good. The spicy pizza they do is . . . yummm,' Finn nodded quickly.

'I hate spicy stuff,' Chell stated.

'Great salads, yes,' said Kay.

'And the dough balls. Have you had those dough balls?'

'Oh yes.'

The other three girls went gloomily quiet. 'I've never been in a Pizza Express,' Chell admitted.

Manda glared suspiciously. 'I looked in the window and they didn't have a salad bar. You don't go up to help yourself to salad like you do in Pizza Hut. I love a Cheese Feast with extra cheese. Bungs me up a bit though. And a salad with kidney beans and mayonnaise. Pizza Express was like a real restaurant with waiters and that. It looked posh. Pizza for snobbers.' She cut off at this point; criticism had been accomplished.

'I don't like mayonnaise,' Chell stated, almost inaudibly.

Kylah frowned objectionably at the music coming from the Village Inn jukebox and Chell said, 'To me rap music sounds like a whole load of televisions all turned on at the same time.'

Manda hurriedly pulled her pint away from her mouth and licked her lips. To exclude Finn and Ava, she said, 'Kylah. Chell. I'll tell you a classic. When me and ma big sister and Shelly McCrindle –'

'You told us that.'

'Aye. I know what one you're going tell us. You've already told us, Manda.'

'Oh.' Crestfallen, bereft of audience, Manda resigned herself to the hard facts. Then she sparked up. 'Aye. But I haven't told *them.*' To tell her story she turned towards Kay, Ava and Finn and carried on regardless.

'When me and ma big sister and Shelly McCrindle went to Magaluf. right? We was coming back at Magaluf Airport. And there was this guy there. A bonk. A right spunker. Gorgeous suntan. Tattoos. In the cafe-bar-thing-place, where we was having a drink. So fucking Shelly tried it on with him – like he'd be interested in her – but he was Spanish. Or that. From the Magaluf island. Majorca it's called. So Shelly starts sliming up to the guy and he speaks really good English. They all speak English there. And so they should, the money they make from like, British, English and that. So McCrindle goes, "Oh, and what is it you *do*?" As if he'd be interested in her, typing letters and doing the hoovering in that dodgy solicitors' office that makes her think she's in fucking *Ally McBeal.* So's he says, "I'm a rapper," and McCrindle is straight off, gabbing away like a right spacker about rap this and rap that and you know, M&M's-Ice-Vanilla-Cube-T and all of that shit, and the guy just sort of looks at her and he's away, down the stair. And I tell yous,' (now she swivelled and looked Kay in the eye) 'he'd fancied my Catriona cos he was giving her the eye. My big sister Cat is just totally gorgeous-looking. Isn't she, girls? She's a hairdresser like me, Ava. As you probably know. So off the guy goes. Away. So a bit after, me and Cat and Shelly go down the stair to the toilets and what do we see?' Here Manda paused and let out a long and private, theatrical laugh. 'We see that same guy in the middle of the airport floor with his brilliant suntan but stood beside this machine and I can't explain the name of it but it's a machine that you put your suitcase into and the machine all wraps it up in plastic cling film stuff, so's you can see if your suitcase has been robbed, when they take it away on the plane. So me and Catriona just start pissing ourself at Shelly. Oh, it was hysterical, cos he's a wrapper of wrapped-up suitcases. That stupid cow Shelly McCrindle, eh?'

Surprisingly, both Finn and even Ava chuckled openly at this. Manda looked encouraged by their mirth.

Finn said, 'I was surprised Shelly went on holiday with yous lot, cos I didn't think she actually got on with you and your sister.'

'Well, she doesn't. No now anyway. We just had our holidays same time as her and stupidly, we were generous enough to let her tag along with us. She's popular, but Shelly McCrindle's a dumb slag. All that ever went into Shelly McCrindle's mouth during that whole holiday was McDonald's burgers and guys' cocks – and once – when she met a guy from Inverness – both a McDonald's burger and a McDonald's cock went into her mouth on the very same night.'

Even Finn laughed out loud.

'I'll tell yous another that'll prove how gormlessly stupid Shelly McCrindle is. When we was there in Magaluf we was meant to meet at this place and – you know – I was that wee bit late getting ready so didn't Shelly get bored waiting. So she goes into some bar for a drink. When I arrive outside the shopping centre, where we was meant to meet up, where I'd *told* her to stay put – she's nowhere to be seen. So I call her mobby and says, Where are you? and she says, In a bar, and I says, What's the name of the bar? She says she doesn't know what the bar's called, so I says to her, Away outside and read the name of the bar then and I'll soon find it. First off, know what she goes and does? She puts her mobile down on the table and walks out and leaves it there. Can you imagine that? I hear the bump as she puts it down and I says, Shelly? Shelly? She's no there, so's I shout, You slag. Then I can hear her coming back – those plod-ding feet – and she picks up and I says, Why didn't ya take the mobile outside with you? You're just burning credit, you doofus. I just says to never mind, just tell us what the bloody bar's called that you're in, and do you know what she's sayed?'

'What?'

'She says, It's called Guinness. I go, Eh? She says that it's called Guinness, and the street number is one thousand seven hundred and fifty-nine. I says, Shelly McCrindle, you stupid fucking hoor. That's just a *sign* outside the pub advertising that it sells Guinness, and one seven five nine is no the number of the street, it's the year in all olden times and that, when Guinness was first ever invented or something like that, cos if you look over there on the beer pumps now, yous'll see that number written. Anyone knows that. Seventeen fifty-nine. Dumb hoor.'

Finn said, 'Guinness,' and she laughed and shook her head in commiseration.

'That *is* pretty thick,' Kylah admitted.

'Very sheltered,' Ava ventured.

Manda was quick to confirm. 'Aye, that's the word, Ava. Sheltered. And thick as shite.'

Suddenly Finn seemed to relax. 'You know, I was thinking what you were saying there, Manda, about being in an airport bar. I was thinking about this bar here.' Finn looked around. 'I'm not so sure a bar like this is a very cruisey place. It's not much of a pickup bar for guys.'

Manda looked deeply serious. 'How do you mean?'

'Well, think about it. Here we are in this place. We're going on holiday. Maybe. So are other folk. But the chances we're all going to the same place is really rare. So what's the point in blokes and girls chatting each other up? They're no going to see each other again. And if there are guys here who've arrived back, there's no point anyone chatting girls up either, cos they're leaving to go away. I was wondering that this might be the one bar where a girl can just sit and not get chatted up by guys. This is a pickup-free bar. I think that's quite nice.'

'Aye. I like it here and it's true. No guys hit on you.'

Manda's face had darkened. And she nodded slowly, absorbing all this. 'Jeez, Finn. You might have a point here.'

'Ha, ha, ha. Look at Manda. She's fucking broken-hearted,' Chell laughed.

Finn ruminated. 'Airport bars might be sort of . . . free zones. We can drink and talk together but the way things normally are in a bar between lads and lassies don't apply here. It's quite nice.'

Ava nodded seriously. 'Yes. Everyone is just passing through. In transit,' but she did a smile Finn alone recognised as a private one.

Chell said, 'I think that's *perfect* for chatting guys up. No commitment,' and she chuckled dumbly.

'What?' Finn asked, looking at Ava.

'Nothing.' Ava shook her head.

But Chell changed the tone and pace by interrupting. 'Here. Girls. Talking of Inverness. This guy comes into the tourist info in July there and he's like dead posh and he goes to me, "I *need* to purchase theatre tickets. I have heard upon the wireless that there must be new plays on in Inverness in a new theatre and I'm very interested to visit," and he starts going on about Shakespeare and *Macbeth*, that Sister Condom tortured us with in Higher English, and how it happened in Inverness or something and the new theatre there he'd heard a snippet about on Radio Scotland news. But none of us knew anything he was talking about. So this Victor Mildrew guy made a right old fuss that we don't know about the new theatre and off he goes in the huff. Couple of days later I'm looking through the newspaper at lunch break and Inverness hospital has opened a new operating theatre.'

Finn, Ava and Kay suddenly burst out laughing.

'Stupid old dickhead. Thought he was so smart and all that. I hope he went up there.'

Finn was laughing; she shouted, 'Aye. Can I buy tickets for this evening's performance? Sure. Two vasectomies and a hip replacement.'

Everyone else moved their bodies laughing, but Manda just smiled and she tried to snub these jokes by turning aside dreamily and putting a lighter flame to a cigarette end.

Ava said, 'I had sex in an airport bar once.'

This produced a startling and paralysing effect not encountered by the group thus far. Manda turned back to the table in a tracasserie of moving legs. Each gaze settled upon Ava. The flabbergastation was enhanced by the fact the others clearly witnessed Finn turn her head to look at Ava, unable to hide a certain surprise.

Finn coolly countered any personal fluster by banter. 'Hey. Are you challenging my airport bar theory?'

'No. Because the chatting up happened on the plane, not in the bar. So your thesis holds. Paul. Very sincere. My first American. My only American. Sitting next to me, London to Seattle. Had to change planes at Chicago. Started snogging. We wanted bad to do it on the plane.'

'Mile-high club,' Manda shouted.

'Couldn't. Not as easy as it looks in films. Two of you sneaking into a tiny plane toilet together, with all those ratty, frustrated stewardesses hallucinating from five hundred people's farts and looking for a fight. By the time we landed, we were fairly randy. Kept trying to open airport broom cupboards. You see that in movies but everything in an airport is locked.' Ava nodded towards the toilet doors. 'So we resorted to a bar's toilets. The big toilets were just too busy.'

'Classy, love. You'll be just fine in Bemidorm.' Manda nodded smartly.

'Be*n*idorm.'

'So your theory hasn't been refuted but I never let myself get picked up in an airport bar. Yet.'

Manda narrowed her eyes. 'When was this?'

'Why would that matter?'

'Oh, sorry, I didn't think it was an issue.'

'It's not.' Ava shrugged. 'When I was at Oxford. And we didn't have sort of *full* sex. You know.'

Kay jumped, sensing a greater priority. 'Oxford? Oxford University?'

'I was at the university for a year but I dropped out and re-applied to London.'

Finn said nothing.

'Gosh. You got into Oxford?' Kay couldn't help wondering out loud.

Manda twisted her lip straight at Kay's face. 'That's dead posh, isn't it?' Manda insinuated universal disapproval, with a sly, appalled edge. She looked at Finn and sneered. She knew fine Finn had kept that little fact from them.

'Yes,' Ava curtly came back with. 'Of course it is.'

'Is that why you dropped out?' Chell asked.

'No. I just did not do any work. At all. And it was so close to home it was easy to skip days. I had my little Mini Cooper. Vintage. Which is too much bother to park in London, so I stupidly sold it. I miss it. I drove Mum's car down last month, didn't I, Finn?' She laughed, carefree.

Finn said, 'Aye. She did. *And* she all scratched up the side of the car. She can't reverse for peanuts. So's when we went back up to Oxfordshire for the weekend, she went and parked her mum's car with the bashed side away from the house and right up against a giant hydrangea. That was what, four week ago, and her mum hasn't even noticed it yet. They've three cars,' added Finn crisply, with a tone of defensive warning attached to it.

Ava laughed again and furrowed her brow. 'I mean, I had digs in Oxford but I liked going home too much. Walking the dogs.' She shrugged.

At the mention of the dogs, Finn had helplessly remembered the river beside Ava's parents' sickeningly beautiful house. The river's English essence so complacent – compared to the tossing, bucking, rocky burns and amber falls from home. That English river had soft clay lips on its shallow banks, amounts of delicate willows actually surviving along them. Among the rich, emerald weed of the shallows, the water was truly mild as they had both lowered their torsos into it and breaststroked out, close to the deep river middle, the current utterly benign. Ava had turned, treading water, and shouted to the dogs to follow – a bit breathless – but water never even splashed on her lips from the gentle surface. Wilbur and McLean dodged and swerved frantically, barking, getting in each other's way upon the banks, frustrated – not following.

Finn recalled how, as Ava had quickly undressed, in case anglers wandered up the pathway, she had lifted her dress over her head with a swift, familiar but thoughtless coordination, the same way she had instinctually touched aside and politely held the weeping-willow curtain at the bottom of their gardens. Later, she had given her hand to help Finn climb out the river and up the bank, then Ava, underwear transparent, had tilted her head to one side, her arms angled over her shoulder, sharp elbows, squeezing the water out her ponytail with both hands, as you do in the shower, while the dogs fussed gratefully around her long toes.

'Are you a few years older than us then, Ava?' Manda snapped.

'I'm nearing the age of reason. Twenty-three.'

As if she had solved a crucial pub quiz question, Manda went, 'Ah. Knew you were that wee bit older-looking.'

'Thank you, Manda,' Ava said cleanly.

'No. I mean –' she looked at Chell and Kylah as if for assistance '– I think you look nearly like a supermodel, lassie. I just meant you were that bit more mature than us.'

'Huh,' went Finn. 'She isn't, girls.'

Ava suddenly put a finger up to her eye and played with the perfect skin underneath it. 'Worry, worry, worry, made me a fool forever.'

Nobody knew what it meant, not even Finn, but they laughed. Ava was quirky and now, clearly, a dark horse. Apart from Manda, the others staunchly approved of this.

5

There were spotlights above the three of them – Ava, Kay and Finn – in that Pizza Express, and Kay continually noted how a reflection of Ava's silver watch on her thin wrist was stupidly circling on the ceiling above their table, like a lost moth.

'She's a psychological study,' said Ava.

'A psychiatric study,' said Kay.

A Niçoise salad was in the middle of the table and each of the young women had a pizza placed before them. There was also a bottle of white wine and a bottle of water because of the spiced pizza.

'But with Chell, why is she so acquiescent? Does Manda have something over her?'

'Nah. It's not like that. Is it, Kay? Chell is just a good wee soul. Always been like that. She'd do anything for you and so she sticks by Manda.'

Kay said, 'But Manda's so bloody needy, we all have everything over her. We know she got knocked up by an idiot on the first night, we know she's no good at hairdressing but gets kept on cos her sister owns the joint. She has zero financial interest in the business but pretends she does; we know she can't look after her own child and her dad and Nana do most of the work.' Kay took in a big breath and added, 'Ava, I'd be interested to find out how much longer it takes Manda to tell you. How many more *hours*, that is. If she hasn't told you already. But I might as well say now, that when I was seventeen, I had an abortion.' Kay deliberately leapfrogged into the next sentence of her statement, but she was aware of her own curiosity as always, and as she spoke she looked directly at Ava, watching for a reaction. 'There's no way I'll pretend to be cool and lie that it was easy, for me or my parents, but it happened and of course

97

everyone knew about it. And we're Catholic. My parents had to decide what was more important and so did I. Middle-class mores or our religion.'

Ava stopped eating, but more out of politeness and concern rather than shock; she frowned and nodded compassionately.

'I don't mind the whisper-whisper stuff. I lived in a small town then and that's the way of the world. And I don't even mind that Manda was, of course, chief among the town whisperers; she always is. What I resent about Manda since she had little Sean — and let me say now, that girl has issues about deeply resenting having had Sean —'

Quickly, casually, as if she were supporting the early stages of a point in a line of argument, Finn nodded sharply and said, 'Yes, that is true.'

'— when she mentions Sean in front of me, every time, every single time, Sean is brought up in front of me, Manda turns and gives me a look in the eye and we all know what that look means.'

'Mmmmm.' Ava and Finn were both nodding, frowning, gazing straight at Kay with their knives and forks held tensely still in the air. Kay faced Finn and because she'd had a good few drinks said, 'Say it, Finn.' She turned aside to brief Ava for a moment. 'Finn and I have talked before about this. Say what Manda's look says.'

Finn glanced around the restaurant and then she lowered her chin so it almost touched her pizza on the plate and she said, quietly, 'Manda's look says: "Kay Clarke, you murdered a wee unborn, whereas I've had an angelic little ugly brat, therefore you are a wicked, wicked person and I am blessed earth mother incarnate."' Finn raised her voice and her head. 'Something along those old lines?'

Kay smiled. 'Exactly. She's a wicked bitch for trying to lay a guilt trip on me.'

But now Finn quickly turned and, in a boyish way, clicked her head and winked at Ava. 'And that's a look you know all about as well, dear.'

Kay raised her brow.

Ava said, 'Well, Manda gives me a fine eye every time she uses the word "English".'

'Ha. Aye. I'd noticed that too.' Finn nodded enthusiastically with her mouth full.

Turning to look at Kay, Ava forked at her plate and said, 'I terminated a pregnancy too.'

'Oh. Wow.' It came out terribly. It sounded like Kay was commenting on a photograph of a Voysey or Frank Lloyd Wright house, turning the pages of some architectural coffee-table book. 'I mean, what I mean is. What age were you? Can I ask?' She sounded daft.

'Nineteen; up at the Oxford adventure.'

'Oh. That's why you had to quit there.'

Ava sounded tetchy and Kay clenched her teeth.

'No. No. I didn't "quit" Oxford. That's too dramatic. I just wandered away. Quit implies one makes an effort first. I didn't expend enough energy to quit. Though the pregnancy thing was an added complication.'

'Was it a long-term boyfriend?'

'Hardly. Good bloke, but he had his university degree too and he was more freaked out than I was. Thought he'd have to come to the clinic and hold my hand. He was convinced he'd faint. I mean, I caught it real early so it wasn't so bad.'

Kay said, 'Amazing thought, thinking it. I mean, you and I could have a four-year-old or something right now. Like Manda. Or worse. Be married.'

Ava said, 'Leibman wants to marry Finn,' and she giggled, surprisingly childish for once.

'Get lost. It's you he's mad about; I bet he has all your essays pinned to the ceiling above his bed every night. Falls asleep reading them.'

'Who is this?'

'Dr Leibman. Doc Leibman's our philosophy lecturer and our personal tutor; he's kind of sexy; single, with his flicky-back hair and his floppy suits and he smokes *a lot* and he's had books published. Tough impenetrable ones, not silly student guides.'

'Tony Leibman; he's quite famous. As far as famous can be in

British philosophy. And he's completely in love with Ava. It's rocked the foundations of his life's theory he's so fucking in love with you.' Finn yelped a laugh.

'He is in love with you.' Ava flicked her fork.

'He's in love with you and you're both Jewish so you can be wed immediately.'

'He's in love with you cos he finds Catholicism romantic and exciting and doomed.'

'It would be doomed. He's a logical positivist. Imagine having sex with a logical positivist. They're so unromantic.'

Kay had to try not to curl her lip – at the very least – because of the use of a Christian name towards a lecturer. Ava, at last, turned to gaze at Kay. All previous exchanges had been unintentionally private, an intimate two-hander betwixt Ava and Finn, but now she deferred to Kay. 'To drive Anthony mad, Finn and I tell him we're going to retire to the lodge in my parents' garden and just read and write philosophy for the rest of our lives and be happy spinsters.'

Now Finn turned aside, looked at Ava and once again, their world closed in, excluding Kay. 'But we'll live off Pizza Express, like this, and when the pizza boy comes we'll pull him in and ravish him every night.'

'They don't deliver, do they?'

'Don't spoil the fantasy, Kay.'

'Till we're too fat to drag him in through the door.' They looked at each other, laughingly, their faces all lit up, delighted at themselves.

Ava smiled at Finn. 'Since yesterday your accent has changed too now you're back among your . . . old pals. Your accent's gone all Scottish since yesterday. It's ever so cute.'

'Don't be condescending, you devil. The linguists will tell you that's just normal. When you come back from the mill on the bloody floss, your accent's changed too. You English, combine-hitching, cider-swilling, yokel hay tumbler.'

'On the second count, I never drink cider. And you're usually with me at the mill on the bloody floss these days, you freeloader.'

Finn was playfully reaching out and slapping Ava's arm softly.

Suddenly Ava said, 'Right. I'm quite full and I'm going for a wander, get a *Guardian* and check Information for a certain somebody's passport.' Ava looked up amiably and she smiled.

'She hardly eats. It's really annoying,' Finn said, neutrally.

Ava announced, 'I'm blessed with Manda's mobile number so I might even risk giving her a call to find out what pub they're all in on their wanders.'

'Bloody hell,' said Finn.

Back in the town, it cannot be emphasised too much, how Manda viewed possession of her personal (non-work) mobile phone number as a massive social kudos for any other young woman to possess. For men less so. Manda had given her number to scores of men but they never called back. Impressed by Ava's looks and curious exoticism, Manda had demanded Ava lodge her number in her mobile phone address book that very morning.

Ava said, 'Manda. What hubris.'

Kay noted how Ava slightly aspirated the H.

'Yes.'

Ava thumbed at the keys of her phone which made minute noises of resistance. Kay noted how elegant her hands were but the nails utterly unadorned and the fingers free, apart from a single attractive, slightly hippyish or Celtic amber ring.

Kay sat and fished up another pizza slice. Ava made her feel fat, she thought, but she chewed away with a slightly aggressive relish, staring at Ava.

Ava just then swiftly turned aside and she opened a long floppy pocket on the rear of her backpack. Kay had seen her make use of this pocket before. Ava carried no hand or shoulder bag, except a small leather reticule on a leather cord, so she dipped in and out of this backpack zip pocket frequently for money and various items. As Ava idly dropped her mobile phone in there, Kay innocently let her gaze follow the beautiful hands. Ava pushed the phone in deeply so the backpack shifted its form a little. Then Kay saw it and immediately looked away across the table at nothing, gnawing at the ration of pizza.

Ava zipped up the pocket and put a twenty-pound note on the table.

'That's too much,' said Finn, deadly.

'I'll get the change later,' and she was up on her feet.

'See you.'

'See you soon.'

'See you.'

With her backpack hooked on her shoulder, Ava took herself between tables and away, without her even looking back.

Kay stared down at the table. She looked at Finn.

Finn asked, 'Are you okay? You've gone pale as a sheet.'

'Ah. Yes. I'm fine. Didn't offend her or something, did I?'

'Oh. No. She does things like that on the spur of the moment. She's dead impulsive. What is it? It's something bugging you.' Finn looked straight at Kay.

Kay said, 'Nothing.'

To Kay's delight, Finn suddenly went bright red. The smile that was on Finn's face now evaporated. Slowly the flush was cooling to paleness. She moved her face a fraction forward, as if trying to will Kay not to say something embarrassingly profound and affecting for them both.

'What?'

'I don't know if I should say it.'

Finn just froze. Unable to speak, she looked down loathingly at the glasses of wine, already blaming them.

Kay put her out of her misery and said, 'It wasn't anything. It was something I saw. In Ava's backpack.'

Finn physically relaxed, her shoulders dropped and her voice changed tone. 'Her backpack?'

'In that pocket in her backpack when she put her phone away. I just looked down.'

'What?'

Kay dropped her voice so it was almost inaudible, though it was a huge distance to the nearest occupied table and they had heard that the rising and falling conversations of its two occupants were in some vowel-heavy Nordic tongue. 'She had two passports in there.'

'What?'

'Clear as day, I saw her put her phone in beside her passport, then some bits of paper and stuff and a paperback sort of fell aside, and lo and behold, tucked in at the back there, was another passport. A second one.'

'Oh. But she has a French passport. She has dual nationality. She has a French one that she uses in France; if we'd gone there.'

'No. No. It was red. It was a red British passport. French is blue or something. I remember from the exchange student that stayed with us. The British is red and this one was definitely red.'

'No?'

'Yes. Yes. I saw it, I swear to you. I saw two red British passports in there.'

'You're jesting?'

'No. I saw two passports.'

'Bloody hell. Manda was right enough.'

6

Through the huge tinted windows they could see the grey concrete curve of the monorail track to the North Terminal. With a selfless, servile abandon, the flanks of road vehicles hurtled along from left to right, over on the A23. Sometimes a windscreen caught a flitting sun, muted by the tint. There were the blue gaps of a southern-skied English afternoon.

Chell and Kylah each resolutely clung on to their metallic vanity cases; out of a traveller's curiosity they also both held up and continually checked and rechecked the reception quality on their mobile phones, as if they had been dropped by chopper somewhere in behind enemy lines.

Manda nodded affirmatively and she became animated as the automated public address voice at last began the countdown for the arrival of the three-carriage monorail. Through the glass, Manda was able to watch the vehicle's low, lithe approach, slithering over the elevated concrete track until it vanished behind the perfectly aligned metallic entry doors. She was already leaning against the door, palms impatiently flat against its coolness. The transit offloaded passengers from the far side for a few moments before the auto doors opened, to permit boarding. The doors slid aside just in time to witness the last passengers stepping out on the other side of the carriage, onto the exit platform; Manda scowled at their backs, at tugged suitcases and at the lifted, scuffed heels of shoes. She whisked her head round then rushed directly aboard – passing through a forest of enamelled, vertical handrails – to the very front of the forward-facing windscreens with views of the rail-less tramway before them. Chell and Kylah slowly followed.

'No driver, eh? If only buses were like this. Nobody'll believe us back in the old town.'

The Gatwick Transit moved, suspended sixty feet above the earth, then the capsule took a long curve, so the occupants leaned over and, quickly, original vistas became visible. To their left, on the oil-streaked apron, a huge, impeccable jet aircraft appeared very close, wildly cosmopolitan and intimidating, white paint along the crown of its fuselage, a streamlined engine nacelle somehow precariously supported, way up in its thin tailplane. Manda frowned disapprovingly but now the coach was twisting even more. Beneath the elevated monorail track they all passed over a busy road but a wider vehicle tunnel actually descended, passing beneath this road, so the monorail formed the third level of these crossing ways.

'Hey,' went Chell. Their position now gave a broad view backwards towards the South Terminal building, where they had just been. Everything in these airport lands was seen through tinted or affected glass, which seemed to magnify, distance or distort the whole world. They glimpsed the Sussex skyline, fat with some dark trees. Looking out across the tops of more parked aircraft, the protective jet blast screens created the optical illusion of the louvres vibrating with the monorail's westerly motion.

Just then, an outgoing, wide-body Airbus shockingly lifted up off the runway, its nose skyward, lumbering east, seizing the complete attention of the three young women.

'Oh, for God's sake,' Chell admitted.

But already the transit was slowing and approaching the huge white cube of the Meridian Hotel with its geometric black windows, which rose above them. Suddenly the barn-like nest of the transit terminal enclosed them within. The monorail rapidly decelerated, halting at more perfectly aligned doorways. The doors flew open and Manda barged out and ahead.

'C'mon, girls, let's go,' she ordered and strode on.

Following at a distance behind, Chell and Kylah glumly followed. Another branch of Boots appeared on the left and a bureau de change on the right. They were now entering the central area of the North Terminal's middle level, its operating floor spaces striated with ascending and descending Thyssen escalators – upwards escalators to Check-In and Departures and downwards to UK Arrivals on the lower floor. The flanks of these escalators were sealed in clear perspex, displaying the absorbed, intently busy interior mechanisms of the stairways, winding, like the mantelpiece coach clocks of the stockbroker belt.

Ahead was the Avenue shopping mall, beyond the seating areas. Manda stopped and pointed the accusatory finger. 'Look. Another Tie Rack.' Sure enough, beyond the huge WH Smith was a Tie Rack.

'Another. Och, that's no use. There's one back in the other place,' Chell nodded.

They walked in a large circle, passing Caffe Uno Presto, (where there was a queue), the Bridge Bar, which didn't impress them by its size, a Garfunkel's, Impulse, Sunglass Hut and Watch Station, yet another over-fragrant Body Shop, Costa Coffee. Another Monsoon and another Accessorize brought more derision that the terminals were merely duplicating their shopping facilities. Glorious Britain was passed in contemptuous silence, but after the cash machines, Nine West raised some excitement; the shoes were studied intently in the window but the young women didn't enter the premises. They understood, frustratingly, that their suitcases were already full enough. They discussed the possibilities, the multitudinous permutations of buying shoes and clothes on their way back home while pointing over hopefully at the Rolling Luggage suitcase shop. Then the apparent available space in Ava, Finn and Kay's backpacks and suitcase was contemplated in hushed tones.

They moved onward, skirting a McDonald's but peering within; they conceded it was even bigger than the one back in the Village of South Terminal. Then came Serendipity Games which was one of those coyly titled 'amusement centres'. There was a debate over the pronunciation. Within, Sega arcade games were slyly blinking and bleeping their furtive lights – like the bridge of a spaceship in a bad sci-fi movie. They briefly entered the games arcade. There were Ezzy Dancers beyond the bank of logjam coin machines forlornly sawing back and forth. The girls excitedly consulted one another on the desirability of a quick dance but concluded against it just for the moment.

'This place isn't near so good as Gatwick Village. I thought there'd be millions and millions of shops.'

'Aye, me too, but it's just all the same old thing again.'

'C'mon then. Let's head back.'

They took only two steps before Manda spotted the hanging yellow sign.

Short Term Car Park
&
Meridian Hotel

Ava moved through Gatwick Village, leaving WH Smith with a *Guardian* held awkwardly under her arm and then she dumped everything down on one of the blue chairs over by the escalator. She leaned, removed her mobile from the zipped pocket in the backpack and frowned at the front of the phone while turning and sitting down. She sighed and looked away into the distance then dialled up a number. She spoke softly. 'Well, well. I am in London. Sort of in London. And now you have my new number. Bloody Gatwick. Nowhere. That's the problem. I'm with some daft bint who's lost her passport so we're stuck here for just now. No. Pals of my pal, from Scotland. Okay. Victoria then. I'll come up. Your choice. Phone me. Of course I have. Phone me. Kisses.' She ended the call. Within seconds it rang again and she smiled, sitting, hunched over, her thin knees pushed way out in front of her, both hands holding the phone up to her smiling face so it was close to her eyes. She took pleasure in pushing the off button, holding it in until the trilling phone died like a small bird.

'Oh. My. God.' Kylah then Manda and Chell entered the giant eight-storey interior atrium of the Meridian Hotel, looking up. Its vast capuchin of glass and white aluminium was capturing echoes of the flowing water feature which was producing a slight and constant tinnitus. The high, white inner walls of the hotel with their square bedroom windows loomed down over the diamond-shaped expanse of the atrium, lit by glass canopies; two elevators rose in glass tubes on either side, the occupants precariously exposed and gazing downward.

To the right was a long reception and concierge desk with an orderly queue; suitcases were bunched alone in outposts and seats were lit by cold blue neon floor strips – a design feature inspired by the emergency lighting on aircraft aisles. Checking in or out of the hotel and stepping crisply forward was a fresh gaggle of super-efficient-looking aircrew. The pilots in dark suits with honeyed cuffs of rank, leading five or six stewardesses and a single steward. Manda scowled in disapproval at the stewardesses' gear: burgundy pillbox hats, mustard tunics, matching burgundy skirts; the handsome younger pilot, pulling his wheeled flight bag and manuals behind him like an obedient dog.

Kylah handed over a lighter. 'There's a big No Smoking sign over there.'

'The whole of England's a fucking No Smoking sign,' Manda muttered.

On the left mezzanine lay an expensive-looking cocktail bar with square leather armchairs, and above it, on the first floor, accessed by a twisting, angular staircase was the Sports Bar. A Thai restaurant and a bistro restaurant entrance stood on either side of the mezzanine bar.

'Look at this joint. It's like out of Las Vegas or something.'

Manda whispered, 'Rascals doesn't have a look-in.'

'Jesus. It must cost a fortune.'

'We could share one drink or that.'

The water feature was beside them, an infinity pool perfectly filled to a suspended mirror of surface encapsulated within an inch rim of black marble. Water trickled somewhere invisibly. Manda used two fingers to draw back her hand like a dart thrower and she precisely tossed her ciggy butt onto the surface then walked ahead.

The near bar had its glazed, sleary surfaces animated by

reflections of the frantic and synchronised movements on three very large television screens.

Manda took her place by the beer pumps, two impatient fore-arms laid flat on the bar surface as a means of summons. 'Hey. How much does your Guinness cost, mister?'

'Sorry?'

'I said. How. Much. Is. Your. Guinness?'

Kylah and Chell visibly winced.

'Two pound ninety.' He stated it coldly.

'Two pound ninety!'

'But Mands. We can't share Guinness. We hate Guinness. It's like river mud.'

'Och. They've no got Extra Cold anyway. It's that warm stuff.'

'Well, how about three wee shots? We could do three wee shots?'

'Much are your vodka shorts then?'

'Two eighty.'

This was met with an astonishingly long silence. As if they were awaiting a better offer. When nothing came, Chell's quiet little voice peeped, 'Do you have vanilla vodka?'

'Stolichnaya.'

'What's that?'

The barman turned round and looked at the backlit bottles, 'But we don't have shot glasses here. I'd need to serve that in a whisky glass.'

'You don't have shot glasses?'

'No. It's the same measure but I'd need to give you standard glasses.'

'Do you no have egg cups? In Magaluf they serve shots in egg cups.'

He was unmoved.

'Shots is a sad idea. It'll look like eye drops in the bottom of a big glass.'

'Let's just have bottles of Smirnoff Ice.' Kylah pointed down to the fridges with their glass fronts lit up in behind the bar, gladly recognising one drink beverage.

'Aye, okay then.'

'Suppose.'

To defuse Manda's mood, Kylah announced, 'My treat.' Kylah put her vanity case up on the bar top with a clatter and began opening and rummaging in it for her purse.

'Three Ice,' the barman said indifferently and placed three glasses upon the bar top.

'We don't need glasses,' Manda snapped, aghast.

'Bar policy. I need to give you a glass.'

Manda scoffed. The girls looked at each other and tittered.

'Whatever.' Manda shook her head mournfully.

The three of them diligently watched the barman's every movement.

'No wonder this joint is empty,' Manda quietly mentioned. The barman ignored her. When he topped the first bottle and put it on the bar, Manda immediately snatched it and rudely walked away, plugging her mouth with the neck end and swigging as she suavely sauntered back to the bar edge smoking area and the leather armchairs.

'Another gay guy. It's like the Village People down here.'

This was said with no accounting for acoustics. Chell and Kylah followed with the regulation drinking glasses and sat on the armchairs with their backs to the bar, unable to risk looking round.

Quietly, Kylah leaned forward and informed, 'You mean the YMCA,' and she did a shy, censored version of the arm positions from the dance as she mouthed the letters.

Manda's ringtone jittered. As if her life depended on it, she beached her latest ciggy in the ashtray gap and removed the phone, frowning suspiciously at the incoming number. Her face lost all wrinkles of displeasure. 'Hello, Ava!' Manda looked at Kylah and Chell with a beaming smile on her face. 'Oh. And how are you? Oh, just having a wee drink at the Meridian Hotel in the other terminal-thing-place. You take the transit contraption. It doesn't have a driver. I'm with the girls.' As if this were private business, Manda swivelled and she gave her full back to Chell and Kylah. She was putting on quite a pompous voice – 'Sure. Of course. You're welcome. You're really missing yourself, we're having an amazing time. Where are you then? Oh. Where's Finn and Kay? Oh, of course.' Manda tutted scoldingly. 'Just you phone me now if you get lost and I'll come and get you. See you soon, Ava.' She slowly took the phone away. Now she moved round to face Chell and Kylah. Manda cleared her throat. 'You might have heard. That was Ava. Calling me. She's coming over to join me for a drink and –' she changed her tone suddenly '– Fucking amazing, eh? She must be fed up to the back teeth, being with Finn and Kay, fawning over each other.'

Chell and Kylah just nodded obediently.

'She'll be checking if there's any luck with the passport as well at the information desk.'

'Oh, that's nice of her,' said Kylah with an edge of implied criticism. Manda gave her the eye but seemed to plump for ignoring it. 'I mean, I bet if wipe-my-arse-with-cotton-wool-Kay Clarke had gone and lost her passport, those three'd all be run around like headless chickens, calling, eh, lawyers and diplomatics and that. And she's the type would get an escort to the plane and be allowed on, cos her surgical dad works in the Health Trust. Eh? If Kay shags a single boy on your holiday, she'll probably get a wheelchair to the plane on the way back. But don't tell her I says that.'

'Mmmm, I don't think it would quite work like that,' Kylah shrugged.

Manda admonished her with a broody silence and took another long draw on her bottle, generating soapy-looking bubbles and frothings within, she had it tipped back so far. She smacked her lips. The bottle was almost finished. 'Well, Miss Moneybags might stretch to a few rounds for us – where all the crack is.'

By the time Ava's tall figure appeared across the atrium, over by the just-audible water feature, a single spare leather seat had been jealously pulled up next to Manda who guarded it diligently. All three of them began waving their arms excitedly in the air, as if they were marooned on a desert island and Ava was a passing ship.

'Here she is, here she is,' Manda stuttered.

Ava hopped up onto the mezzanine smiling, the backpack hooked on a shoulder. 'Howdy.'

'Hiya.'

'I saved a seat for you. I saved a seat for you.'

The girls went silent as they watched Ava put down her back-pack against the glass partition and sit. There was a slight pause.

'What would you like to drink? It's amazing. That barman guy actually comes and asks you what you want and brings it you. It's pricey as hell though.'

'Are we still all drinking?'

'Of course. We're on bloody holiday.'

Ava turned to address Manda. 'Look. I popped in at that information desk and nothing. Yet. It's a terrible worry.'

'Oh.' Manda nodded, uncomfortable. It was clear she didn't want to talk about the matter of the passport. 'So you left Kay and Finn alone then, did you?'

'Well, I didn't leave them as such. We just had some pizza and I felt like a little stroll and I wanted to buy a newspaper.'

'Oh. You read them newspapers then, do you?'

'Yes. Don't you?'

'Nah. Never. I mean, I take a look at *News of the Screws* when it's in the salon on a Monday, or the *Sun* and *Mail* and that, but I'm no into, like . . . news. All politics and that. Gordon Blair and them.'

'Mmm.' Ava nodded with a serious look.

'I'm into the magazines. You know, *Heat* and that. Stuff with celebrities in them. I like to hear about the celebrities. Kylah's probably going to be one before me, though I will be one. Wait till you hear her voice doing karaoke in Spain, Ava. She's amazing. Kyles has the voice of a fucking angel. I'm no joking you.' Manda said this with an aggressive, protective conviction, a commitment rare to hear from her.

Ava nodded curtly. 'I'm sure you do.'

'We told her; oh, we said it all right, especially me, we told her to go for *Popstars*; she could be in any band with that voice.'

Kylah raised her eyes to the high atrium.

Manda continued, 'I'm glad you've come over to us. It's just the way it is that you split into gangs. It's like in *Big Brother*.

If you watch *Big Brother*, and I always do. If you follow it, you see the group always splits into gangs. It's amazing to watch and –'

Quietly but formally enough to make it sound like a reprimand, Ava interrupted, 'Manda, it's not gangs. I don't want us to be in gangs, I just thought I'd come for a walk and see you all, I don't want us to split into gangs.'

'Oh no. Gosh. Neither do I. But I was just . . . observing that's what sort of happens sometimes in *Big Brother*.' She carried on though. 'Now Ava. Tell us a bit about Finn's London boyfriend she had. They have split up now?'

Cautiously Ava said, 'Yessss.'

Manda guffed, 'Haw haw. What was he called?'

Ava played along for a bit, looked round the table conspiratorially. 'Oh, girls, it's bad.'

'What, what, what?' Manda lurched forward greedily.

'He was called "Gilbert".'

The other three girls screeched in laughter.

'Gilbert. You must be jesting?'

'Gilbert Grape?'

'Haw haw haw.'

'He was astonishingly good-looking,' Ava said, loudly.

The laughter switched off.

Manda narrowed her eyes. 'Good-looking, like who?'

'Well, just that look. I don't know what kind of blokes you like, but he was quite slight, tall; he had those features.'

'What features?'

'Those features.'

Chell nodded, trying to be polite. 'Oh those.'

'You know, like cheekbones and a jaw that goes down like this, and tousled brown hair. One of those guys that goes to bed good-looking, and steps out of bed good-looking in the morning, or afternoon, since they were in bed for weeks.'

'Oh wow,' went Chell, enthusiastically.

Manda tutted loudly in disapproval. 'Why'd they split up then? Who chucked who and why?'

'Can I steal a cigarette?'

'Aye, aye, go on, go on,' Manda snapped impatiently and shoved the pack over towards Ava.

'To be honest, he was a bit . . .'

'Aye, aye . . .'

'He was a bit over-obsessed with Finn.'

Manda's face hit the floor.

'He wanted to spend all his time round at our place so he was forever there and it's small. I'd want the shower or even Finn would, and he was in it, for hours. He hated the guys he was sharing with so he just sort of moved in. He was cooking there and never washing up and he was sort of hanging on Finn every minute. Sometimes she'd be reading and he'd just stand there behind her, looking over her shoulder, twisting her hair. I've seen that go on for an hour.'

'Oh, that's so sweet,' Chell voiced.

'No, it's no,' Manda insisted angrily, glaring at Chell.

'So Finn asked him to, you know, cool it a bit and he got quite nasty about things.'

Manda looked about; you could see her formulating something then out it came. 'So he was, kind of getting in you and Finn's way. Maybe stopping yous swotting so much. Sort of . . . he was coming between you and Finn.'

Ava was ready for this. 'No. Because, after all, it was in the summer when they split up and I wasn't around. When Finn was working in that flower shop.'

'Oh,' groaned Manda, beached for a moment.

'Och, what a shame,' went Chell.

Kylah kept out of it. Smoking and looking away disinterestedly.

Manda leaned back, cautious about risking any more, so she went back to the source. 'So is old Gilbert Grape off the scene now?'

Ava leaned forward. 'Actually, I think they meet up now and again.'

Manda realised the opportunity was there and swiftly said, 'Are you single yourself, Ava?'

Ava held up both hands as if she were carrying an invisible

tray in each. 'Looks like it,' she laughed and dropped her hands. 'I did *have* a boyfriend, up in Oxford, a really nice bloke, but we split.' She looked hard into Manda's face, willing her to ask more. Manda must have sensed danger and she backed off expertly, stating – using a pompous vocabulary acquired from many years of DHSS and solicitors' letters – 'I have terrible relations with the father of my son.'

'Oh dear.'

'He's a waster and an arsehole,' Kylah contributed.

Ava said, 'I'm sorry about that.'

'Aye, I've been through a lot.'

'I'm sure. Manda? May I ask you something?' Ava deferred in her voice and immediately saw that Manda responded to that.

'What?'

'What's childbirth actually like?'

'Oh. My. God. Ava. You would not believe the agony. I mean, look, I was okay, wasn't I, girls?'

'Mmmph.'

'I was trying to stick to a healthy diet. Well, a healthier one. I didn't lapse with the fags and the booze. Hardly at all.'

'Except when your manky ex was about.'

'Aye. He did lead me astray with the odd fag packet and bottle of voddy or that – when I paid for it – but I'll tell you something, Ava. And remember it. You don't really believe in your pregnancy till your gut starts poking out. You don't really believe in it till you get bigger and you start to feel the wee blighter, and then I got serious, didn't I, girls? I mean, you really can feel it when he has hiccups inside you. And Nana said that meant he was going have a good head of hair on him and that was true. Though I like him with a skinhead. When I went up the hospital the first time I was, "I don't want drugs, I want natural child-birth," and then that was false alarms. When I goes up next time, when my waters broke, and ruined my fucking electric-blue pencil-line skirt – I could never wear it again after that for some reason – it was fucking ten hours' labour and I was like, "Fuck sake, you mean old bitches, give us more of all the drugs you can lay your hands on, for the love of Christ." And the gas made me giggle then my blood pressure goes way up so's they don't like that and it was Caesarean section and they whips out my wee fat darling. "An heir at last," I yelled.'

Ava laughed at that.

'He had an ear stud on when he come out,' Kylah drawled,

Manda snarled aside, 'Shut it, Kyles. I'm talking to Ava here. And that was me. Don't know what drugs they's give us. The names of them and that, but wow . . . I was out of it and it's true, I did say, "Oh look at his wee ear stud," and they was all laughing at me, cos I'd wanted it to have an ear stud so badly I was − what's it? − hallcey-inating it, cos of the drugs.'

Kylah snapped back, 'Aye, and baby Sean had a Rangers Football Club tattoo right across his arse that its daddy wanted too.'

'Will you shut it, Kylah?'

'He's a right blue nose the father. He'd dye his lawn blue,' Kylah said.

'If he had one. He's a right idle perisher,' Chell added.

'Will yous two shut your gums?' Manda turned back to Ava and rattled out, 'So-that's-what-childbirth-is-all-about-do-you-want-to-have-babies-yourself-Ava-I-expect-so-eh?'

'Eh? Oh. Hi. Thanks.'

Manda whirled round furiously, perhaps expecting Kay and Finn but it was just the little waiter, tentatively holding out a wine list towards Ava. Ava took it and opened it out. The other girls fell obediently silent.

Without hesitation, Ava ordered three bottles of Chablis.

'Thanks very much indeed, Ava. You know your wines and all that then?'

'Like we say back in the town, Ava. If you're going to be a bear −'

And Chell and Kylah took up the chorus of three − 'Be a grizzly bear.'

Chell, Kylah and Manda all laughed, delighted at themselves.

Suddenly Manda lumbered upwards onto her feet, slightly unsteady. 'I'll show you my section scar, Ava.'

'Oh, no. Please. It's quite all right.'

'Quite, quite, quite; lassie, away with you. It's just here. I don't need to get my bits out or anything.'

'Jesus. Put on your sunglasses, Kyles,' Chell moaned.

Other customers now helplessly glanced over to see Manda standing, pushing down the front of her skirt – with difficulty – her pale belly, ring-marked red by the waistband, was revealed, and the top of her knickers, which were quickly peeled over and pushed down cautiously.

'Don't be feart, everyone, you'll no see my pubes, I got such a stoater of a bikini wax offof my big sister.'

Just where the visible dots began was the purple and black little envelope of scar.

Ava just nodded cautiously.

Kylah said, 'Manda's third eye.'

'The emergency exit,' Chell quipped.

Manda snapped back the knicker elastic and tugged the skirt up then plonked herself down.

Ava could feel the tense, middle-class patience running out among the few tables surrounding them – but she just smiled, caring surprisingly little for such values.

'It's brilliant, cos they cut your section now – if they can – so's it's hid down under your bikini – for when you goes on holidays. Really considerate, isn't it?' She nodded seriously.

'Right.'

Manda leaned forward. 'Did you get a bikini wax yourself for this holiday, Ava?'

Ava looked at Manda then she looked left and right at Kylah and Chell. She presumed they might put up some sort of resistance to this line of frank questioning but to her amazement, they were looking at her quite expectantly as well.

Ava chuckled. 'Are you really interested?'

'Of course.'

'Well, I did, but only because Finn advised me to. She actually said, "Now you better go have a bikini wax in case we end up at a beach, and you're in for a good old interrogation about that area of your body the minute you get to the airport."'

A darker look came upon Manda's face. 'She did now, did she?'

However, Kylah and Chell smiled and looked at each other. 'Ach, good old Finn.'

'The Mighty Finn.'

'She can read us like a book.'

Manda snapped, 'No she can not. She can't. Well, Ava, you must understand. I am Practice Manageress and a professional beautician, so you know, I do take an interest. A bikini wax is interesting cos everyone's skin reacts different. Like you being brunette – I'm blonde just now myself, you probably couldn't tell, Ava, but as Finn went and blabbed, I'm mousy-haired.'

'You're brown with hints of ginger, ya minge-er.'

'Amn't. Amn't. I'm mousy brown. Well. You're classic brunette, Ava, with pale skin, so I suppose you know what we mean.'

'Mmm,' Ava hummed. She was clearly bored with the girly talk, but Manda wouldn't let up.

'So I suppose your skin reacts to waxing, Ava? I mean, as well as a bikini wax, did you wax your legs for this trip?' Even though Ava was wearing jeans, Manda stared hard and aggressively at Ava's thigh.

'Actually, I'm not too bad. A razor does the job for me. Even a man's razor. I don't get bumps or ingrown hairs or anything. Hardly.'

Sceptically, Manda drawled, 'Really? So you didn't get a leg wax then?'

'No. I thought I'd live dangerously.'

Kylah said, 'I saw when those bloody wee fifth years – the daughter of Pauline from work and her mates – when they all went to Ibiza together this summer – aged bloody seventeen, they all got bikini waxes. The works. At aged seventeen, off to Ibiza. Imagine we could have, when we were that age?'

Manda dropped her voice to a whisper, 'Well, if you have any unsightly razor bumps or ingrown hairs, Ava, at our salon we recommend a bottle of In Grow Go.' Manda suddenly veered round on Kylah. Some other niggling matter had achieved mental domination. 'Well, we don't like Ibiza. Do we?

But I hope none of they wee bitches end up on *Ibiza Uncovered* when I haven't been on it. That would be one reason to go to Ibiza. Think you get paid to go on *Ibiza Uncovered*, eh? That would be brilliant.'

'Nah. Never. You don't get paid.'

'Mmmm.' Manda looked deep in thought. There was a delicate tinkling behind Manda and she whipped her head round again. The waiter had arrived with an ice bucket on a stand. He was accompanied by a waitress who could have been his sister. She placed the four glasses on the table.

'Oh. Posh.'

'Are you hotel resident?' asked the girl.

'No we're not. Here's my card.' Ava handed over her credit card. Manda deftly noted the colour of it but was disappointed it was not gold like Kay's. It was some silvery colour.

The waiter placed the ice bucket beside Manda. Chell and Kylah didn't talk. The three young women carefully watched the waiter's every move. Cradling the bottle in a white cloth, he showed it to Ava who nodded and smiled and he then started uncorking.

'I went to Ibiza,' Ava ventured to break the intense silence which she was sure was making the waiter nervous.

The other young women turned to her accusingly.

'You know? Doing exciting things in exciting places; that's what we're told life's all about these days. I didn't go super-clubbing though. It was a total chill-out thing, somewhere else on the island. A bunch of us hired a villa with a big pool. We filled the pool with fresh melons but they ended up tasting of chlorine. I can't remember the name of the area. It was nice. There were wheat fields. I was very surprised at that.'

Predictably, the agriculture of Ibiza didn't elicit much excitement nor any response.

The young waitress appeared and Ava signed off the chit and said, 'Thank you.' The waitress silently retreated.

Meanwhile, Ava said to the waiter patiently holding the bottle, 'I'm sure it's fine. Please,' politely indicating all the glasses. The waiter's arm went in front of Manda to pour and Manda looked around his white-shirted arm and said, 'Do any of yous think there's a *Bemi-Benidorm Uncovered*?'

'Nah.'

'There might be?'

'The only thing getting uncovered in Benidorm will be your tits, Manda.'

She laughed. 'We sunbathe topless on the beach. Don't we's, girls? Trouble is, ya cannie really snog boys topless on the beach. It just doesn't feel right. Anyway, snogging boys on the beach just interferes with getting your tan. Do you sunbathe topless, Ava? In Ibiza. Among the wheat fields.'

'I sunbathe topless in Oxfordshire. And there's a dude who flies around in a helicopter, taking pictures of the big houses, then he turns up at the door trying to sell photos to the owners. Needless to say, we have a big house and didn't he turn up and show a photo to my father. There I am in the picture on the balcony of the outhouse, where I live. I'm lying naked, sunbathing. And the bloody date the photo was taken was on it. It was a Wednesday and I was meant to be up in Oxford, at uni. Not only embarrassing that my father sees me totally starkers but I got a terrible row off him for dodging university. Then the heli-copter bastard phoned up and tried to ask me out on a date. For a helicopter ride. I hung up on him. He'd got me in enough shit already. I told Daddy he'd asked me out on a date, and the one framed photograph he had bought – which was taken from the river angle, to the south, so that I was out of shot, akimbo on the balcony – was quietly taken down and hidden away in a cupboard.'

The others all laughed at this, deeply impressed by the wealth of information contained in the short revelation.

Presciently, Manda pointed out, 'See. Always pays to have a good bikini wax.' Then she added, 'Huh. So you lot really do call your old men "Daddy".'

Chell gritted her teeth but opened her eyes wide. 'Wow. You mean you have a whole bit of house yours?'

'Yup. A converted mill house.'

'And your place's so gigantic you could dog it off from a uni or a school and nobody would notice?' Kylah asked.

'Well, not from school. I went to boarding school. I'm spoiled. Or at least I spoil myself.' She giggled.

'I don't think you seem spoiled at all,' Chell insisted.

Manda now looked at Ava appealingly. 'I suppose you must be well known and dead popular in your wee village, Ava?'

Ava frowned, actually curious where this one was leading.

'You see, Ava. I'm knowed and popular wherever I go. Like when I walk into Rascals on Saturday nights, everybody knows me. I think I'd be great on *Big Brother* and that. That's what I'd like to do in the future, like Kylah has her singing and Kay has her house-building whatever it is: arkatercka, and you and Finn have your philosophies and I'd like sort of fame in the public eye, and loads of money from it.'

'Uh-huh,' Ava responded.

'Bottoms up; probably mine, you bores,' Manda blurted, in an imitation posh English voice.

'God bless us and all who'll sleep with us,' said Kylah, lifting her glass.

'Cheers,' Chell lifted hers.

Sloshing the wine as she carelessly gestured with the glass, Manda leaned across and frowned at Ava's upper lip. 'So, Ava, do you get electrolysis?'

7

Back in Pizza Express they'd finished the wine. Finn was saying to Kay, 'But the reality is you saw the passport. That's your burden.'

'Christ. You're a philosophical version of Manda.'

'No I'm not. Go on.'

Kay frowned and she said. 'I feel like a cigarette.'

'I never knew you indulged.'

'Sometimes. When I've an essay to write and that. I see you've cut down.'

'I can't afford it. The price of them these days.'

'Straight off – if I do it – you're still landed in it, cos how did I get hold of her mobile number?'

'Say I give it you?'

'She's far from stupid. She'll know fine you're sat right there.'

'I'll go away then. Okay, I won't. She might not say anything. She's awful. Polite.'

Kay sighed.

Finn actually made eyes at her. 'I'll owe you big time?'

'Tell us all the dirt about your boyfriend.'

'Oh my God. Who's being Manda now? His name was Gilbert.'

They laughed.

'Have you had many boyfriends?'

'Have you?'

'I've sort of still got that one now I told you about.'

Finn shrugged and said, 'I haven't been a slut. But I haven't been an angel either.'

'Me too.'

'I'm only doing this cos I don't want to be stuck in this place and if Ava's planning to pretend to find the passport before we go, then she's fast running out of time.'

Kay looked at her watch.

'Yeah, I know, she's cutting it fine but it's not funny any more. It's sort of creepy.'

'Your friend's mad, Finn. I should have guessed.'

Finn dragged her chair round to beside Kay. They sat next to each other as Finn peeled the cigarette packet.

Finn divested the tight packet of two cigarettes then held the flame to the incongruous cigarette held in Kay's lips.

'Ta.'

And then lit her own.

Kay blew out too much smoke. While she dialled Ava's number, Kay looked into Finn's face, slightly loathingly. It was answered mercilessly quick. A babble of excited voices were suddenly encircling Ava's presence, most noticeably the unmistakable loud bray of Manda. Kay's spirits immediately slumped. She could even have sworn she made out the well-worn and dreaded phrase, 'practice manageress'.

'Ava. It's Kay.'

'Yes. Helloo.'

The voice of Manda clearly crowed, 'Who is it?'

'Where are you?' Kay asked.

'I'm over in some hotel with the girls.'

'A hotel?'

Finn sat more upright, frowning.

'Ah. With Manda? Cos that's a bit awkward considering.'

'Yeah. Hold on.'

'Who is it?' Kay heard Manda's voice demand once again.

There were sounds, presumably of flight, away from the others and Kay heard Ava say casually, but with sufficient authority to quell them, 'I can't really hear. Just a moment please.'

Kay carried on talking. 'I wanted to talk to you about something.'

'Yes? How are you two? Are you coming over?' She sounded drunk.

'Well. The thing is.' Kay groaned at herself. There was a slight echo on the line and she was sure she could hear her own voice: soft, unmistakably Scottish, cowering before Ava's clipped tones, so it seemed. 'The thing is, Ava. I have to just say to you. Inadvertently when you were back at Pizza Express with us, putting away your phone, I saw . . . in your bag. I know I sound like Miss Marple but I'm not trying to be her. But I could have sworn on my life I saw two passports in your bag. I hate to sound horrible but I can't help what I saw. Sorry. To babble.'

Finn nodded encouragingly but infuriatingly, still smiling. Kay angrily turned away from her.

Ava said, 'Yes?'

Kay didn't want any silences. 'Being a nasty sort, you know, I just . . . couldn't help wondering.'

Ava let out a bright quip of sound. 'Ah. I understand. Sorry. You saw in my pouch on the backpack. Both the passports I've there. You saw both passports? I see. And you think . . .'

Helpless with the silence. 'I'm afraid so.'

Ava was laughing down the mobile phone with its hot, physical presence at Kay's ear. 'Did you tell Finn?'

'Finn? No. I didn't mention it to her.'

'So she's there then? Put her on.'

'Eh?'

In an epileptic fashion, Finn shook her head.

Kay asked, 'Is it Manda's passport?'

Ava laughed again. She was enjoying it too much, Kay realised. Ava said, 'I wanted to renew my passport two years ago. Hated my old photo. Last time I went to France, Christmas past, I got in the car outside the house and checked my tickets. I had picked up my old passport instead of the new one and almost hadn't noticed. When I was packing yesterday I was late, so I just grabbed both, to make sure I didn't take the wrong one. I should just chuck it, but I want to keep it for the awful photo. That period of my life. I have a French passport as well, since I'm dual nationality. I took it here too, in case we ended up in France. I usually keep all three in a small plastic folder together but it snapped. The old British one has the corner clipped off it. I'll show you later. Oh, that's so funny, Kay.' She dropped her voice to a whisper. 'You thought *I* had stolen Manda's passport.'

Kay was mortified. 'Sorry.'

'Are you coming over here?'

Kay couldn't believe how casual and friendly she still seemed. 'I'm so sorry, Ava.'

'It doesn't matter; I think it's very funny. You must think I'm very naughty.' She laughed a surprisingly hearty and dirty chuckle down the phone.

They had all agreed to meet up back in the Gatwick Village Inn so Manda, Chell, Kylah and Ava were off, leaving the empty wine bottles upside down in the melted ice bucket and a crowded ashtray on the table.

The Gatwick Transit moved back along the elevated path, above the roads on one side and the runways, taxiways and aprons on the other, consecutive airliners evenly spaced at distant gates.

'What's the name of our airline? Suppose any of those planes is ours?' Chell quietly said.

Manda pointed a finger, like a pistol, at the others. In her alarm she seemed to have sobered up; her voice suddenly sounded clear and purposeful. 'My round in the pub, girls, cos that's it. Might be the last time I see yous for this holidays.'

'Oh, don't say that.'

'Face facts, Chell. Passport's gone.'

'It might turn up yet.'

A turbulent silence descended on the four girls as the South Terminal drew back in towards them. The sky was battleship grey but the light was fading; the terminal seemed cut out of the skyline as a much bolder, dark bulk. Corners and angles now seemed to be submerged in darkness, sheltered from any illumination.

'*You are now approaching the South Terminal. Exit on the left.*'

Manda wanted to say something cutting and nasty but a sickly emotion was lifting in her, a pain evolved from the days of crying alone in the primary playground, the point of her blouse collar chewed in her teeth. For the first time Manda experienced the realisation she might not be going on holiday with the others and it became concrete to her. She contorted her face in concentration trying to fathom where her passport had got to.

8

They arrived back in the Village Inn and met Kay and Finn at their table, noting Kay was smoking. Manda got a round of drinks in when her mobile phone rang again. She fiercely scrutinised the incoming number. 'Oh shit. The big sister. Knew I shouldn't have took her suitcases.'

'Does Catriona no know you took her cases?'

'Nut.'

Kylah and Chell looked into each other's eyes with hearty anticipation.

'Hiyaaaaaa. Nut. We're still in this airport; haven't gone any bloody place yet. It's a classic. You're really missing yourself. Oh. I didn't know you were going to Aviemore. Why didn't you . . . keep me informed? What are you going to Aviemore for? I'm sorry. I'm sorry, Catriona. I didn't think you'd mind. Eh? You said I could take them any time. I thought I did ask you.' Manda's voice climbed to indignation. 'Well, I don't know why you're fussing so much. I'll be toddlin back home soon enough anyways, 'less my passport turns up. Yes. My passport. Why are you going to Aviemore? You're going with a guy, aren't you? Aren't you, Cat? Dirty hoor. I know it's no my business.'

Chell and Kylah stared at Manda's features, shamelessly spectatorial, but the others looked away, pretending to find sudden interest in aspects around them, and they moved or shuffled uncomfortably. Especially Kay who took repeated little sips of dark wine from her glass.

'You can use my case. It's under the bed. I cleaned that sickness off.' The voice on the other end of the phone grizzled audibly like a fly against a window. Manda lowered her head. 'Mmmm. Uh-huh. Mmm. Do you want to say hi to the girls? *Kay's* here . . . Hello?' Manda looked away from the mobile phone that she twiddled in two fingers, loosely, like a piece of waste paper. She made a formal statement: 'She's hung up. I got a right bollocking. So I did. Silly cow.' Manda sighed and looked off to the side. All the others, even Ava, could now judge her mood – it was all surfacing. Manda had tears budding in each eye.

Trying to be gentle, Chell said the wrong thing as usual. 'Ach, don't fash about her, Manda. Like you say, she might be getting them back soon enough anyway.'

'Aye,' said Manda curtly, leaning on the table and looking off to one side to avoid eye contact.

Finn said to her, with true sincerity, 'You're not really having a very good day, are you, pet?'

Manda's eyes bubbled up. 'No. Everyone's against me. It's pure victorisation,' and she rubbed her eye with the back of her hand. Then she looked at Finn and said, 'Finn, I think you and me need to have a talk together about things.'

When Manda cried – which she did a lot – her face sort of pulled back, giving her an odd mask; it made her look even younger and her mouth seemed to widen in the process as she gulped air. Her head jerked and she managed a few more sobs.

'C'mon then,' Finn nodded. They both stood quickly and moved off out of the Village Inn with a sort of electric urgency, as if this moment were long overdue. Ava watched with amazement. The others at the table just silently looked on – they also saw Manda's head go forward and her shoulders jerk from sobs, her coiled fist flying to her own mouth; Chell and Kylah recognised the familiar biting at the knuckles.

At a distance, Finn, and Manda halted to confer. In their history of ill feeling, these two young women were used to a youth of street confrontations and confabulations, so even in Gatwick Airport they didn't bother sitting quietly together anywhere, this open, public *strasse* was perfectly exposed for purpose.

Manda faced Finn. 'Finn, do you have a problem with me being here?' She sniffed and touched her nose in imitation of wiping snot, but truly, none was there.

'No, Manda, I have no problem, you being here. It's your

holidays too. I just don't like some of the stuff you come out with, stuff that you just say to people without thinking.'

'No I don't.'

'Yes. You do. The fact you don't think you're doing it doesn't mean you're fibbing; you just genuinely don't know when you're doing it. You should have asked Cat if you could take her cases as well. You were in the wrong there.'

Manda nodded. A sudden, effective tear slalomed down her cheek and tucked in somewhere under the chin. 'I know I'm doing wrong. I know. It's just, I just come out with it. You know that story you told me last year, about the scorpion thing crossing the river on the back of the frog and he went and stung it, cos it's his nature? You were beeling at me about something I can't remember and you says that story to me? You can't change the way you are, and I was that way? This way. I think of that story all the time.'

Finn laughed. 'Ach, Manda, it's just . . . I said that to you, right? All this year, you know . . . this philosophy crap I do. All year I was writing an essay, saying – arguing – there is no such thing as a fixed nature and folk can end up being what they please. Maybe.'

'Oh. Is that no true any more then about the scorpion and the frog? Have yous disproved it at the university?'

Finn let out a big sincere laugh. She leaned forward and softly placed both their foreheads together, laughing. 'Oh, Manda baby.'

'What? What is it?' Manda, though tearful, let slip a giggle, in her own oddly unselfish way, always delighted to produce mirth in others. 'I don't want to go back home. I want to stay with all yous and go away somewhere dead brilliant together and have the memories of it and be able talk about it with everybody. In Rascals.'

Finn smiled. It felt the same, Finn thought, as that anxiety between lovers, when one word can change everything and a twisted pity riles in your gullet, capable of elevating the food up from your stomach.

Manda was still shivering with racks of sobbing but they were dry sobs. 'I really admire you, Finn. I think you're brilliant. You have opinions. I'm so proud of you, that you're talking in philosophy, with the professors.'

Finn frowned cautiously.

'I mean, we've been through a lot together, you and me, with Orla dying and wee Sean getting borned.'

'Aye,' said Finn bluntly.

Finn had heard this speech before, about how much the two of them had been through together, which really amounted to how many times Manda had slagged Finn off behind her back, been confronted, burst into tears, then lectured Finn once again on how much they had been through together. Finn was powerless to change anything, racked up on her personal history in a way she wasn't with Ava or her London acquaintances. Finn knew all she had to do for a quiet life was say it. She held those words in and savoured the pain in her chest for a moment longer. The two of them leaned together there, like blown boxers. Finn said, 'Aye, okay, Manda. If you behave and be nice to everyone, then I won't go away on holiday without you, whatever happens.'

Manda's chin came up immediately. 'You mean that?'

'If you are nice to me and all the girls and other people too, then if the others go, I'll stay with you. *If* you behave yourself. I can't make the others do what I want, but I'll stay with you and I think Chell'll stay too.'

Rapidly Manda added, 'That means Ava'll stay too, cos she's your pal.'

Finn shrugged. 'Ava's her own woman. That's up to her.'

Manda scoffed conspiratorially. 'She's no going to go off alone with Kylah. Mind you, Kay might talk her into a posh holiday thing in a Rome sort of place, just looking at old buildings and that.'

Manda ignored Finn now, turned and walked back towards the table in the Village Inn. Finn followed. Then she stopped abruptly a few steps behind Manda, and remembered, in Oxfordshire, she and Ava had suddenly halted, their bare feet in long dry grass, just to listen to that bird calling.

To the whole table, and indeed beyond, so people at other tables turned round to look curiously, Manda announced, 'Aye.

Just wanted to say. See, if we don't find my passport tonight or ever, that's Finn staying here in England or Britain with me and Chell or maybe going another place and that. I just thought I'd tell all the rest of yous that.'

The occupants around the table looked at each other.

Ava suddenly said, 'If your passport doesn't get found why don't we all go to Brighton? We could hire a car.'

All eyes turned to Ava.

'Brighton?'

'We won't all fit in one car.'

'We'd have to hire a bloody minibus for us lot.' Manda said. 'That's a good idea. What's Brighton?'

'Let's vote on what we should do then,' said Kay. 'Perhaps we should just cancel, stay here for the night, just in case the passport turns up tomorrow? It could be at the Flight Deck Hotel in the morning. Take a vote,' Kay said.

'Vote, vote, another bloody vote.'

'All those who vote on staying another night –'

'And losing all that money,' Finn reminded them.

Kay raised her hand.

Chell raised her hand.

Kylah looked around the table and felt Manda glaring at her. She raised her hand.

Ava raised her hand without looking at anybody.

'That's it then,' said Manda, in a matter-of-fact voice. 'It's circumpherential.'

Finn rumpled up her nose in curiosity.

Ava said, 'There's a Hilton here somewhere.'

'What? That's deadly posh.'

'My father stayed at it once I remember. When he was going to the Far East.'

'Where's that then?'

'What? The Far East?'

'No. The hotel.'

'It's somewhere here. Unless it's gone.' Ava looked around as if it could have been behind her. She said, 'Look. Since we've just all blown a thousand quid, what we could do, is take shifts.

We did that on holiday once in Nice. Just get two twin rooms with four beds and four people get some sleep then two stay up, then after a while the others give up their beds; or some of us could sleep on the floor. We used to do that when I was small too. My parents wouldn't pay for an extra room and I used to sleep on the bedroom floor, or my father would, and I would sleep with Mummy. Daddy can be very mean with money. And he's a terrible bloody snorer.'

'Great,' Kylah chewed her words off, 'I'll write that on my postcard home: "On holidays and sleeping on the floor." Better than Turkey, I suppose.'

Manda said, 'I think that'd be a right laugh, sleeping in shifts. Oh, girls, it's going to be brilliant.'

Ava shrugged. 'Really, it doesn't matter. We could get doubles too . . . in a Hilton they'll be nice big beds so maybe at a pinch, three of us could crash out in one?'

Matter-of-factly, Manda nodded in a quick sequence, which obviously included Finn and Kay. 'That'll suit you two.'

Finn slammed her drink down so hard on the table it was a serious matter for a physicist that the glass did not crack.

Chell jumped up in her seat.

A huge gollop of drink had shot up out of Finn's glass and gathered on the table, round the base, and the drink bushed up within. A mad fizz, almost comical in its animation.

Manda stared down at the fizzing drink. She was a little scared – but not enough. Her degree of triumph was so huge, Manda turned her whole body in a leisurely manner away from Finn and mimed at casually looking out over the bar. She expertly allowed her body to tremble with feigned waves of suppressed laughter, just enough for Finn to be aware of the shimmering surface of Manda's clothes.

Finn had to respond. 'Aye, laugh away, Manda. Two minutes and that's you being wicked after us jacking in our holidays for you. You're helpless. You really are.' She lifted her drink free of the spilled puddle, took a swallow from the glass and put it back down in a dry place.

Manda kept wise counsel.

'Well,' Ava uttered in a crisp way.

A few other drinkers at tables close by had looked over at them. Trying to change the subject, Kay said, 'Perhaps I should go tell the airline we won't be boarding then?'

Ava chirped, 'Oh, leave them be. The passport might turn up yet. They make no bones about cancelling flights on you. We definitely have lost the money for the self-catering in Spain as well. Yes?'

'For sure.'

Manda turned, risked a quick mocking peek at Finn, then retrieved up her Guinness pint and swung around away from them all again, taking the glass with her, tipping the pint into her invisible face so they saw the base held out almost horizontal, as she suckled on it deeply.

'Well, we should all go to this Hilton and sort out, eh, rooms then.' Kay raised her eyebrows.

Ava snappily said, 'Twin rooms.'

Chell giggled then stopped.

'Well, yes,' Kay said and coughed.

Ava brightly trilled, 'No *ménage à trois* tonight,' and rolled her eyes.

Manda immediately swung round, back to the table, and let off a throaty laugh. Her Guinness was almost drained. 'I don't know French but I know what that means.'

Ava said aloud, 'Threesomes are just awful. I hate threesomes.'

The table's very low spirits immediately revived into electric interest. Apart from Finn's, all the heads again moved to Ava.

'Is that right now?' Manda demanded, the voice a combination of police inspector and saucy comedian, turning her body all the way back round to the table, to become part of the group again.

'Tell us about them then?'

'I'm too embarrassed to say it.'

'You and two girls,' Manda sighed, with a feigned inflection of boredom, and she shook her head.

'No. Me, a guy and a girl.'

Finn humped her shoulders a few times and smiled. 'I have

heard this before,' she confirmed, to fend off the stares in her direction.

Manda snapped, 'I had a threesome.'

'No you did not,' Kylah roared. 'We both fell asleep at Big Tosh's party and skinny Barry McLean lay in between us on the coats' bed. And I have a horrid feeling, while he was laying there between us, the wee mink . . . you know . . . boxed the Jesuit while we was in the land of nod.'

All the other girls called out in lamentation.

'Cos I woke up and caught him shoving someone else's hanky into someone else's coat and then he creeped off somewhere. And I wasn't putting my hand in the pocket to find out – ah tell yous. I went and pulled the coats off and curled up on the armchair and that was our threesome, Manda.'

'That is a threesome,' Manda insisted. 'We both snogged him,' she snapped.

'Two hours apart, Manda. I mean, whatever floats your boat. I'm not criticising you, Ava, but I'm no into all that, yeach, two boys going at me, or worse, two girls. In bed with one guy is trouble enough. The kingdom of the sneaky hand, aye wandering down to my bumhole. A threesome would be like being trapped in a room with two pickpockets going at you.'

Ava laughed.

'Aye. Two boys or that. It would scum me out,' Chell told them.

'Huh.' Manda scoffed at Chell. 'Dinna knock it till you've tried it, love.' Then she turned and greedily asked, 'Going to tell us, Ava?'

'This was really unspeakable.'

'Oh. Brilliant.'

'No. I mean unspeakable in a bad way. They were this nice couple at the art college in Oxford, both terribly good-looking, I thought. They'd been going out together since they were fifteen or something. Like a dream couple that looked so cute together, always holding hands in the street and whispering and smiling. I knew the girl from my school but she'd left in third form and then we met up again at Oxford. Both of them, really awfully nice. Really gentle people. They were actually living together. So some nights I'd be out drinking with them and smoking a little bit of dope back at their big flat where they painted their pictures. One day I'm in the student union bar with the guy and he told me, "Do you know that Joanne and I have never made love?" Never. Never. And on another occasion I was with her – Joanne – in the Oxford Arms and she told me, "Do you know, Ava, that Ben and I have never really snogged." I was intrigued and I asked why, and she replied, "We don't really enjoy the sensation."

'But that's. Incredible. A classic,' Manda said in an awed voice.

Ava continued, 'And then I asked Jo – knowing fine – about their sex life. She told me, "Well. We just sleep together and cuddle but we don't ever do anything. Ever." So I was at theirs again one night and I was completely blotto and they were too, but they're very mellow so it's hard to tell, and I was just so very curious – so intrigued by them – so because I was drunk I said, "May I kiss Ben?" and Jo said, "Yes, of course," and so I did.

'And?'

'He didn't move. Tongues, nothing, and then I said, "Well, may I kiss you?" and . . .'

'Wooooo . . .'

'. . . And I do. I kiss the girl. Gosh. But look, I went to an all-girls' boarding school. That really wouldn't get very far as an interesting item of gossip in the school dorm.'

Manda gave a sour look.

'But with her, it felt like kissing a dead girl. She was so un-responsive. You could feel she wanted to, and he too, but they were. Sort of troubled. I was afraid they thought I had a terrible venereal disease or something. Then I start taking all their clothes off and I take off my clothes and I lie on the bed with them.'

'Ya hoor.'

'They're just, lying there, and I try to get them to, you know, kiss each other. Nope. So then I try something with him. After quite a while he says, in a very cold voice, "Don't do that please," and she's . . . very pretty . . . so I try something . . . a thing . . . with her and she says, "No way." So. We all three just lie on the bed like that, one on one side of me, one on the other, in the complete dark. I remember they wanted it dark. No lights. All of us starkers with no clothes on and his voice says out of the blackness, "My father molested me," and then the next minute on the other side of me, her voice says, "My uncle did things to me." And so we just lie there. I felt like crying. I was shivering on the bed because it was cold by then. But we still didn't move. I was too scared to cough or to cuddle them and they were too. And the three of us just lay like that. For what felt like hours. Silent, never mind speaking. Then we must have simply fallen asleep again because it was morning and do you know what Ben said to us?'

'What?'

'"Would you like some dandelion tea, girls?"'

There was a long pause.

All of them started laughing; cautiously at first but then with more enthusiasm at the horror of it.

Kylah asked. 'So like, was that it? What happened then?'

'We put our clothes on. I remember, *all* of our clothes, because it was a cold winter – jackets as well – and we sat in the kitchen and drank dandelion tea as if nothing had happened. We're all still pals but we never mention it. Fucking hell,' she cursed in her genteel accent.

'Oh that's so sad.'

Ava frowned. 'Yes. It is sad, isn't it? Very. It's funny, in a perverse way, but it's so serious. I was being so frivolous, literally, and just walked in on something I couldn't handle. It just all twisted round horribly and backfired on me.'

Chell went, 'Oh, Ava. You're just so wild. That's mental. It's brilliant.'

Manda's mouth was hanging open. Then Manda pointed at Kay and said, 'She had one okay and they went all the way.'

The others stiffened. But an odd thing happened. They realised Manda was not criticising. She was showing off.

Kay's face was still concerned at Ava's story but she smiled, said, quite calmly, 'Back at school. With Manda's big sister and a boy.'

And Manda, instead of taking offence, now nodded enthusiastically. She wanted to impress Ava. What for so long had been an unspoken weapon in Manda's hands, suddenly felt defused and passive. Manda had said it proudly, actually fondly, smiling at Kay as if she was giving her permission. 'Aye, she did. My bloody big sister – who's gorgeous – and Kay and that blinkin Iain Dickinson. Dirty bastards. How about that then? Eh?' boasted Manda, clapping her hands together with full civic pride, nodding thirstily, desperate to score points by association. 'Kay's a right old shagger, eh? You're a legend, Kay,' Manda claimed, to the astonishment of the others.

Kay bowed her head. 'Thank you.'

Ava wagged a finger. 'Beware of threesomes.'

'Ach. Never say never again, Ava.' Manda let out a big, throaty and vulgar laugh.

'Ava's mental, Finn; she's completely brilliant,' said Kylah with glee, as if Ava were absent.

They all sat among the potshots of reflection, reaching out for the dregs in a glass, a cough, the lighting of a ciggy.

Soon Kylah and Finn marshalled more beverages along the bar top then made the crossings back over to the table, holding the drinks. There was a curious hush from the table. Kay, Chell and Ava were sitting silently with a knowing smirk on each of their faces.

'Oh my God!'

'She's putting it on.'

'She isn't.'

'Oh wow.'

Manda was sitting, slouched backwards in her chair, with her arms folded but her head had fallen forward. She was asleep.

'Jesus. She's falled asleep.'

'Christ. She hasn't died, has she? That'll be the next thing on this bloody holiday. *Weekend at Bernie's*.'

'After all Ava's threesome excitement, it's wore her out,' Chell insisted drily.

Kay and Finn laughed.

'Manda.'

'Nae, shush.'

'Just shush. Quiet.'

'Is she just pretending?'

'Shaddup.'

'She really is asleep.'

'If she is, she'll fart any second now.'

Finn breathed out. 'God. The peace is unbelievable.'

'Look at the size of her double chin.'

'She really is asleep. If she was pretended she'd have woke and slapped you one.'

'Shame,' Ava said.

'It's not a shame. Put cigarette ash on her forehead.'

'She was covered in enough mascara all day.'

'Write "Knob Gobbler" on her forehead with lipstick.'

'Nah, don't. We have to get her into this Hilton Hotel now or whatever.'

'She'll never drink that Guinness now.'

'Oh aye she will so. Minute she wakes up.'

'How many's she had? Maybe she's about to go that comatose way she does?'

'Aye. That's what I'm afraid of. How much has she guzzled?'

'About five or something but it's the wine that must of made her sleep. She was drinking wine with us.'

Finn said, 'I'll need to buy her more wine then.'

Ava laughed.

'She never drinks wine. It's right enough.'

'She'd have been drinking it to show off to you.'

The waking table began to nibble at their drinks.

'Well, Manda. Scratch that holiday and all my money. Thanks a lot, you stupid bitch.' Kylah addressed this to Manda's still face.

'Aye. She's definitely fast asleep.'

'Will we really get two rooms at this hotel then?'

'Depends on what it costs, but aye. Look at this one now. By the time she's quaffed another, she'll be ready for her bed. And I'll tell you right now what'll happen. Put her in a twin bed and you're not getting her out of it, if we do a shifts thing. She'll be in it all night long and the other person'll have to sleep on the floor.'

'Maybe we should go on ahead and see what three rooms in the hotel costs?'

'Oh, hold on the now. I'm no getting dumped with old Steptoe here.'

'Wake her up to drink her beer.'

'No, don't. Let sleeping dogs lie.'

'Finn!'

'Seriously. It's peaceful.'

'It is restful, I admit.'

'Be great if she had an Off switch.'

'I'd take the batteries out.'

'I bet her passport's in her case and the daft cow has forgot, locking the case back up last night.'

'Look.' Chell pointed.

Manda was stirring, moving one arm.

'The kraken awakes,' Kay said, through her teeth.

Manda nodded upwards, awake, eyes opening.

Finn loudly said, 'Good morning, Vietnam.'

'Eh? The crack? What is the crack; what were you saying? Oh hell. Did I go and nod off there for a wee minute?' Then the arm went out like a shot and grabbed the Guinness.

Everyone laughed.

'What? What?'

The three trolleys moved along the tunnels. Dead slow. Manda with Kylah's sunglasses on and her head down, pushing her trolley with difficulty, hardly watching the way before her, lifting her gaze reluctantly. She was followed up by both Chell and then Kylah, pushing their own trolleys. Kay, Finn and Ava walked side by side far up ahead, transporting their own light luggages. 'Slow down. Why don't you?' Manda groaned. Other passengers stared at her, seemingly talking to herself.

They had paid up at left luggage and checked one last time at the information desk. The usual ladies had changed shift, gone home, but the new shift – a woman and guy this time – told them no found passport was to be had. They even phoned through to the Flight Deck Hotel where nothing had been handed in and Ava had asked for directions to the Hilton.

They moved onward under the high, air-conditioned ceilings in the great hall of South Terminal with its constant audible hum which the present mind – like the sounds of aircraft on take-off – adapted to, and did not hear.

They passed the magazine roundels of the newsagent on the corner and through the ridiculous, ceaseless, swift batting of the swinging auto doors. They moved on down the draughty corridor and then onto the moving walkways, repassing the long narrative strip of advertising hoardings for luxury goods. They glumly reversed their hopeful journey of earlier in that day when they had decamped from the Hotel Hoppa.

Kay, Finn and Ava were approaching the end of the moving walkway when Ava slightly swung her backpack towards her at an angle to unzip and grab out of the pocket two British passports. 'Now we're out of earshot of Manda, do you ladies at passport control wish to inspect these?'

Making no effort to keep up the pretence that she was not involved, Finn confessed, 'No. But I do want to see your old photo,' then she reached across Kay and took the passports from Ava's hand.

Kay felt herself reddening. 'I'm sorry about that, Ava. I just saw them both in there and jumped to the wrong conclusion.'

'No, it makes sense. I'm actually quite excited you thought me capable. You must think I'm very naughty.' She looked at Kay and raised her eyebrows cheekily.

Finn let out a laugh, Ava's old passport opened in front of her; sure enough with the top corner clipped off its front cover. 'No wonder you were keeping this under wraps, you goth hussy.'

'That was a very special era.'

'Too right,' Finn said. 'Look.' She raised the passport, a single finger jamming open the photo page before Kay's eyes. The way an American cop on telly arrogantly flaunts his badge. Kay smiled. Ava's photo-booth image looked alluring; perhaps she was a touch thinner but Ava actually looked younger now. The goth effect wasn't make-up, it was the Pre-Raphaelite waifdom of huge dark bags under her eyes. Her hair was unkempt too.

Finn said, 'I wish you'd really nicked Manda's passport. Jesus, see if I saw it now on the ground, I'd grab it and chuck it in the nearest bin.'

Kay looked at her watch and said, 'No way. If we started running for check-in now, we could still make the plane. Just.'

Finn said, 'I'm serious. I've really been thinking about it. What a great holiday it would be, just the five of us without her. I'm getting older. I'm getting too old to put up with her bloody carry-on.' She turned round and gave a false smile back at Manda, shoving her trolley far, far behind.

They followed a corridor with glass walls sharply around to the right. It gave a view down, through grim girders spiked with anti-pigeon pins, onto the stained tops of trucks and buses passing quickly and silently below. The three lead women now turned left into a wide corridor. As usual, the only opening out of the airport building was to give access to vehicles. The storey of a fluorescently lit car park was off through swing doors, rows of cars glistening in an artificial, showroom light.

At the top of the incline, the automatic doors opened and the space widened into the hall of the Hilton Hotel. A small bar was to the right with a restaurant behind it and to the left were ordered queues for the reception.

When Manda wheeled her trolley in she just continued onward among the armchairs of the bar so the stacked cases actually contacted with an unoccupied chair and pushed it a small distance, the legs squeaking on the floor. She slowly took off the sunglasses and looked around.

Ava, Finn and Kay had just taken control and already stepped in to the queue at reception. Manda had not the energy to intervene.

Kylah and Chell pulled up behind Manda and eyed things. 'This is not as amazing as yon Meridian joint.'

Manda looked glumly at the bar. It was more like a portable

counter set up at a wedding. 'I don't know if I can drink any more,' she announced.

'Come on. It's Saturday night.'

Chell sat down on a seat, one hand out protectively on her trolley.

Eventually Kay, Finn and Ava crossed back over to the weary group.

Ava said, 'We got three twin rooms next to each other.'

'How much was that?'

Finn said, 'A-fucking-lot.'

Kylah shook her head. 'Oh, I don't want to know right now. I think I'm wiped out money-wise already.'

Kay explained, 'These hotels always cost a fortune cos they're actually in the airport. You only get cheap deals by going out to the ones that need the bus and we're jiggered now with all this luggage.'

Manda frowned. 'You've got to have your stuff, Kay. You cannie be yourself without your stuff. It's no our fault you've come along on a bloody holiday with just three pairs of knickers or whatever's in there. Some of us have got cool clothes. At least you'll have room for a wee bit of shopping to bring home?'

Kay gave a warning look.

'We're living the high life, girls. They says normal they'd be fully booked, but there was a conference thing here that cancelled.' Finn nodded around the lobby.

'What's a conference?'

'Manda. No touching the minibars here. Right?'

She held her arms up in surrender. 'Aye. Honestly, people, I'm jiggered. No sure I can drink any more.'

'That would be a first for you on any Saturday, before two in the morning.'

'Aye. I suppose we could do a wee sit-down here and watch folk but I actually feel like crashing. Look! Look,' Manda yelled. She was pointing back at the doorway area. All heads whipped.

'A hairdresser's. Will yous watch my stuff?'

Sure enough, a hairdressing salon was over there within the

hotel confines. With urgent authority, Manda actually trotted towards the establishment.

'She's off.'

'We'll get an hour's lecture on the faults of this place now,' Kylah warned.

'Fuck sake,' went Chell. 'I thought she was on about something exciting. There's always the chance Johnny Depp is around in a posh airport joint like this.'

'Aye, and with luck he's left Vanessa Paradis home with the wee girl,' Kylah suggested.

'Johnny and Vanessa are a lovely couple. He's well taken.'

'He hasn't seen me yet, with my new La Senza bra and knickers on,' growled Kylah.

'We might as well enjoy ourselves and have a drink then,' Finn shrugged.

'Maybe Manda will piss off to bed and we won't have to hear any more of her . . . pish,' Kay openly voiced, suddenly bright and hopeful.

'More like pish the bed.'

'Right. Aye. Who's sharing with her? No me. I did last night.'

Chell said, 'If I promise not to kick, can I sleep in your bed, Kyles, rather than share with Manda?'

Finn went, 'Och, that's a waste of money after paying full whack for a twin room.'

'Be our guest then, Finn.'

Chell nodded. 'Look. She's away inside. British Hairways. Hah.'

'What she doing now?'

'She'll be making an appointment.'

'She'll be asking them questions and that. I can hear her.' Kylah spoke in a cynical voice: '"Hi, I'm Practice Manageress in the most amazing hairdresser's and I'm here to give you advice you don't need, cos you are actual professionals, but I'll make spiteful comments about your prices.'

Finn nodded sagely.

'I'll share with her.'

They all turned to look at Ava.

'You're joking?'

'Okay then, Ava. Cheers.'

'No, I will. I'll take it on.'

'You *are* crazy, Ava.'

Manda: Pint of regular Guinness.
Finn: Red Bull and double vodka.
Kay: Red Bull and double vodka.
Ava: Red Bull and double vodka.
Chell: Red Bull and double vodka.
Kylah: Red Bull and double vodka.

They had bought Manda a drink in anticipation of her return and the five of them sat at two small tables pulled together. They had established a small compound by pulling the trolleys up close around them.

Manda emerged from British Hairways with a smile on her face. Only halfway across the lobby she shouted out, 'Ava. They do leg wax; you could still get one done!'

Most people in the lobby turned round to stare.

Finn put her face down, and through the gritted teeth, cursed. 'I'm okay thank you.'

'Got you a Guinness, Manda,' Kay obediently nodded.

'Oh, oh, what's this? Red Bulls and voddy? Mmm.' She sat down with a thump on her seat, sighed and reached out for the Guinness without thanking Kay. 'All drinking the same thing again, girls, eh? That's an amazing place there. You really missed yourselves. I was talking to the manageress in there, telling her I'm a Practice Mana— Hey, Kay. This is regular Guinness. It's all warm and that.'

'They didn't have Extra Cold.'

Manda's eyes went back around the Red Bulls. 'I wish yous had got me one of those.'

Each girl bit her lip and pretended to look around, to try and not laugh.

'What? What? Maybe I could change this?'

'You just took a big glug out it, Manda.'

'Well, I want a Red Bull and voddy now.'

Kay sighed and stood up. 'Very well then.'

'Oh, cheers, Kay, that's brilliant of you. Might as well finish this. Aye, what a place. No as good as our salon of course.'

'That's a brilliant name it has, British Hairways.'

'Eh?'

'British Hairways.'

'Hairways. Like British Airways.'

'Oh. Right. I get it. The airline thing, eh? Oh, I didn't get that. At first. Aye.'

Ava said, 'When I was in Ibiza, I saw this bar called Al-Cojones; I thought that was dead smart. Al. Cojones.'

'What do you mean? Al Capone, like the gangster?' asked Manda.

'Well, in Spanish, *cojones* means balls. Bollocks. You know, Al-Cojones? Alcohol.'

'I don't get that.' This was bluntly and accusingly put.

'Do you speak Spanish as well?'

'No. No. But. I mean, I know *cojones* means balls.'

There was an unappreciative, judgemental silence from Manda.

To try and back Ava up, Finn said, 'There's an Indian restaurant in Fort William called Poppadom Preach. Like the Madonna song. I thought that was brilliant.'

'Aye.' To snub Ava, Manda overenthused. 'Now that is funny. That's just hilarious. Classic. Poppadoms. Aye. I've ate they from Light of India. By the way, girls, watch out. Pie-ell-yah . . .'

'Aye, Mands. You've told us; you've told us before a hundred times about the Spanish food. Don't forget we're not going to fucking Spain any more. The flight's just gone.'

'Oh, have I? Aye, anyway. That salon. Pricey as hell, but everything in England is. They have good products and a beauty salon in at the back.' She paused to drink from the Guinness. The others couldn't help watching as the muddy liquid stirred within the imperial pint glass but also diminished hugely, in consistent and sluggish jerks. Manda lowered the glass which only had about a quarter left and smacked her lips in full relish. 'Aye. I says I had a friend who might be wanting a leg wax cos we were, unavoidably, delayed.'

'Not unavoidably.'

'Has our plane definitely gone away yet?' Chell asked.

Finn looked at her watch. 'It's too late to check in. It might not of actually took off yet.'

'It'll probably crash and we escaped, cos of brilliant me,' Manda said blankly.

Everyone was a bit discomfited by this and said nothing.

'Oh.' Manda looked at her watch and squinted. 'Is that? What time is it? My watch has stopped at quarter past three.'

'It's quarter to.'

'But the second hand's going round.'

'Manda. Fuck sake. You've got your watch on upside down, you spacker,' Kylah yelled.

'Jings. So I have. Never even noticed,' she stated proudly, adding, 'And I've had it on two days.' She yelped a laugh but made no move to correct this. Manda's attitude was that others handled organisational matters on her behalf.

Kay appeared back with a Red Bull and vodka. The others noted it looked suspiciously like a single measure. Theirs were now safely disguised by the mixing.

'Oh cheers, Kay, for that. I'll get you back. Sometime.' Manda put the almost-drained Guinness aside and immediately splashed the Red Bull from the narrow can into the tube glass, among the ice cubes. Before it had even settled, Manda lifted the drink quickly to her mouth and began lapping at it.

There was a bit of a silence.

'Ava's sharing with you tonight, Mands.'

'Is that right now?' she said, wiping her lower arm, in that familiar motion, along her mouth – using the full length of the lower arm. 'That's great, Ava. We'll have a great time sharing. You can show me your make-up and I'll show you mine.'

'Great.'

'It's the best. I get it through the salon.' Manda added, 'I do use Lancôme on a regular basis but not . . . frequent. I didn't take none this trip.' There was silence as she lit a cigarette which she had placed in her mouth. 'Now my big sister. My big sister. My big sister.' Manda leaned forward and vomited a sudden brown liquid gush into the remainder of her Guinness pint. The cigarette was helplessly propelled in there also, its filter and white flank briefly visible as it spun in the sewerage-like swish.

Immediately the other young women yelped out sounds of exclamation: a strange meeting of revulsion and delight, simultaneously swinging their legs away from the table to save their bared thighs or trousers from the coming torrents. But it just as quickly stopped coming out of Manda's mouth. It had not filled the pint completely.

Finn looked at Manda's instantly ashen face; Manda's mouth had stopped the vomiting but now gulped air, desperately sculpting itself into a bizarrely aquatic O shape. Finn's mind fervently speculated that if she now drove a huge cork stopper into that pursed mouth with a good heavy mallet, it might silence Manda forever.

Ava sprang into an emergency action mode, crouching down beside Manda, taking her arm and lifting her, cooing, 'Come to the toilet, quickly now.'

All other eyes rested with a horrid fascination on the pint glass, trying to discern if they could identify Chicken McNugget fragments therein. You could define that the Guinness was already carbonated from just that single, unfortunate gulp of returned Red Bull and vodka.

Ava was leading Manda away, across the lobby. Other hotel guests were staring, rightly suspicious, turning heads and slowly following the route of the two young women. Ava had detected the toilets sign which pointed down the corridor at the far end of the reception counter and it was towards this target they now unsteadily moved.

'I'm . . . again . . .' Manda held her head back.

'Hold it in. Just a little further.'

The door to the Ladies was there, ahead.

They reached it.

The toilet interior was softer lit than Ava had expected and thankfully no one was in there. It contained that hushed Ladies toilet ambience, awaiting a drip somewhere. In urgency, Ava led Manda to a sink, not a cubicle. Manda stood there, her palms spread on the edges of the sink, her head hung over the designer porcelain. Nothing happened. She swayed back a little and went, 'Oh, I'm so sorry, Ava. Oh.'

'It's okay. It doesn't matter. If no more is coming now, perhaps you should visit a cubicle?'

'Aye, maybe just.' Manda entered a cubicle and Ava leaned over and lifted the toilet seat for her, but Manda just placed her back and her full weight against the partition. It creaked mutely in protest.

'Okay?'

'Aye. Aye. I'm okay. Like I wasn't sick really. It was just my drink came back up on me a little. It was just the drink. That's Kay pushing that fucking Red Bull shit on me.'

'Yes. Maybe I'll just leave you here a moment.'

'No, no. Stay with me please. Maybe I should just have a wee lie-down. Maybe you and me should just go to *our* room. I'll put my head down a wee minute and tell you more.' She burped but nothing came. 'Tell you more about my hairdressing salon.'

'Okay. But Kay or Finn have the room keys. You stay there, I'll go back and get one. Okay?'

'Aye. Did I get any boak on my top?'

'Don't think so. Can't see any. I'll be right back.'

'Aye. Okay.'

'Wizard,' Ava smiled.

After Ava had exited the Ladies, a lone, echoing voice, weak but still aggressive, growled, 'Wizard. Fuck sake. Who says that any more?'

Ava crossed back to the delighted gathering and their trolleys of suitcases.

Finn just raised her arms in the air, a look of satisfaction and incredulity on her face. 'It was a classic,' she mimicked.

'Do you have the room keys? She wants to lie down.'

'Thank God.'

'How are we gonna get that off the table?' Kylah pointed at the pint glass.

'Don't tell the barman, just hide it underneath.'

Kay quickly dealt out the room key cards and gave one to Ava.

'Is she okay?'

'Yes. She's in a toilet cubicle.'

'Her natural environment. Either with her skirt up and a guy behind her or her head down the lavvy pan,' Kylah sneered.

Finn said, 'She's probably managed both at once on occasion.'

Ava recrossed the lobby.

Manda was still in the cubicle, huffing, puffing, breathing dramatically. But she had shut and locked the cubicle door.

'I've got the room key, Manda,' Ava called from outside.

'Aye, aye; just a wee minute.'

'Have you been sick again?'

'No. Is my stuff safe?'

'Your suitcases? Of course. They're fine, don't worry about that. I'll get them once you're in the room.'

'How far to my room?'

'Oh, I'm not sure. Perhaps I should go and check?'

'Right you are then.'

Ava smiled and left the Ladies. She strolled calmly down the corridor, looking at the room number signs which were displayed on the wall with directional arrows. The numbers were all in the thousands.

Their bedroom was in the old 1970s wing of the Hilton, down a long corridor with fire doors. Ava passed conference-room double doors then some housemaids' dens and lonely alcoves with attentive vending machines standing in them, humming steadily.

Ava wisely checked the electronic key worked. The door opened first try, releasing a scent of neutral, hygienic blandness. The windows faced into the enclosed courtyard. She slammed it back shut and returned slowly to the Ladies out by the lobby. When she re-entered the toilets, Manda was now at a sink, leaning over it.

'Look at the state of me,' she lamented.

'You're okay.'

'Feel bit better now.'

'Good. Do you want to head for the room? It's quite close by.'

'Aye. I'll have a wee nap in the room then come back and join yous all. It'll be brilliant.'

Manda seemed restored, alert, her nosy head turning to observe everything around them as Ava led her back down those reconnoitred hotel corridors. The only uncharacteristic trait was her almost meditative silence.

'Okay?'

'Aye. Just overdid it a wee bitty there. You know how it goes?'

'Very much so. You have been drinking since this morning, my dear.'

'Aye. That's me. I always just go for it. Always having a good time, me.'

'Just down here and to the right.'

They passed through some fire doors.

'I'm going to be sick,' Manda suddenly announced in a morose and fateful tone.

'Oh God.' Ava looked both ways. It seemed too far, both from the Ladies toilet and to the bedroom: the right turn away ahead, and that long distance after the turn.

Manda began to run forwards; her hand went to her mouth. Ava took off after her. Manda ran surprisingly fast.

'Not on the walls!' Ava yelled, sinisterly, for those perhaps cowering within their rooms.

Manda had come to one of the vending machine alcoves, she stumbled to the right and then into it. By the time Ava rounded the corner, Manda was upon her knees, her face desperately against a vending machine. But it was not a vending machine. It was a six-foot-tall ice dispenser and Manda was vomiting more of the brownness into the dispenser grille where the ice fell down when requested. For support, Manda's arm went up above her, against the burnished, specious metal of the machine, but her palm hit the Dispense button. Vast amounts of the brown liquid were now emerging from Manda's innards in long bouts – too much for the shallow, melt-ice grille to cope with – then the gouts from Manda's lips were joined by a generous, clattering downfall of ice hitting the back of her head. Forced out by the gathering ice pile, hot vomit began to spill down the front of the machine and gather on the carpet along with thudding, resting ice cubes. Ice cubes lodged in Manda's hair at the back of her neck. 'Ohhhhh,' she exclaimed.

Ava had to throw her arm around Manda to get her to their bedroom. Then support her against the door as she got the key card in. Manda fell over in the short room corridor. Ava wasn't strong enough to lift her, so she sat, her thigh beside Manda's drained face, and she stroked Manda's forehead which was popped with sweat beads. 'Manda, just a few more feet and you're on the bed.'

Manda slowly got on all fours. She crawled.

'That's it,' Ava called, then used all her strength to wrap both arms in, under the mighty breasts, and haul.

'No. Oh no! A nail. I've gone broke one of my acrylic nails,' Manda keened and she held the hand up: one breached nail was tipped over. She rolled on her back upon the bed nearest the net-curtained window, which layered in a grey pashmina of half-hearted light from the courtyard.

'My nail,' she mumbled and she fell asleep immediately.

When Ava grabbed the boot, unzipped it down the back of the calf and hauled it off from Manda's heavy, pale, bare leg, a modest wad of elastic-banded money – and a passport – shot out and slid across the hotel room's purple carpet.

Sunday

1

The four-door Toyota Corolla motored through sunny English lanes and leaf-shuttered glades, north of Dormansland, moving out towards March Green. The sunroof, front and rear windows were open about an inch, so a metronomic buffeting of acoustic was monotonously marking the passing tree trunks which came up so close to the pavementless verge. The sound laid out into a steady, whispery threat, as a farm wall was beside them, then half-mile bursts of uneven hedgerow made transparent by their velocity. Occasional, momentary vacuums of silence as metal access gates in the hedges gave view across harvested fields to a horizon. Always a horizon of more fields or more distant, large dwellings clustered among mature oaks and elms. The acoustic variation included the approach and retreat of close or faraway Sunday steeple bells. Then came another new-build villa: paved driveways, mass-production nymphs, second and third new cars, the occasional azure lip of an outdoor swimming pool.

Ava was driving – relaxed – one hand annoyingly holding the steering wheel at the bottom with just three fingers and thumb. To Manda's earlier fury, Kay – the only other holder of a driving licence – was navigating in the passenger seat, the *Big Road Atlas Britain*, bought from WH Smith in South Terminal, spread out upon her thighs. Kay kept touching away hair from her forehead, displaced by the window draught and she sometimes glanced down at the hem of Ava's floral, summer tea dress, high on her thighs. Kay did not approve of the reckless and casual manner in which Ava held the steering wheel, she told herself.

On the rear seat, Manda had her mouth up to the inch of window gap as if she were trapped underwater, sucking on an air pocket. Her thigh occasionally compressed tackily against

Chell's – everyone having daringly plumped for sandals, skirts and halter-neck dresses after studying the weather forecast in the hotel rooms. Then came Kylah, and on the right, Finn was gloomily pressed against the centrally locked rear door.

Manda took her mouth away from the window for a moment. 'This is brilliant. I'm going to learn to drive soon. Aye. Ma big sister's gonna teach me. What a place you've got down here, Ava. England and that. Tennis courts, swimming pools, horse-race stuff,' (they had passed through Lingfield), 'traffic jams with just BMWs in them. Yous are all loaded.'

She did crudely reflect what Chell and Kylah were observing with a sort of horrified, glazed absorption. As they had watched Sussex and then Kent go by, they had an open-mouthed, sinking feeling; as if they'd caught their best friend stashing away goodies for years, without them ever noticing.

'Manda. You've been sent to Coventry. Save your breath. Today is for your benefit. Rest and recuperation.'

'Eh? Where's that?'

A series of trees popped by, their out-drooping branches were leaf-thick; fast-moving bands of shadow striated through the sunroof between crashes of light, until they came out aside hedgerow for a while.

'Read what was on the list again.'

'Not again, Manda. We've made the decision. We took a vote.'

'I know, I know. Vote, vote, vote. It's like . . . a government or something this bloody holidays. All votes. It's like all Finn's politics and stuff; Tory Blair or Gordon Blair or whatever he's called. What was on the list again? Please.'

Kay sighed and peeled over a sheet of paper, sealed in the atlas pages.

'For the last time.' Kay read, 'Leith Hill Tower.'

'That was a tower.'

'Yes.'

'So what? We've a tower back in the town.'

'Yes.'

'What else?'

'Lowfield Heath Windmill.'

'That's a windmill.'

'Yup.'

'Gatwick Zoo.'

In a childish voice, Chell pined, 'I wanted to go to the zoo to see Cocky the cockatoo.'

'I don't like zoos.'

'Christ. Your hotel rooms looked like one this morning,' grumbled Finn.

'It's no a big zoo. It's a tottey wee one. There's no polar bears or that.'

'But you can touch the animals.'

'Lingfield Racecourse.'

Manda had a way of converting a statement of intent into an ongoing, mumbled, interior monologue of her thought. 'We went past that; could of popped in there for a drink, couldn't we of not of? Isn't horse racing and that all big posh birds in silly hats like Lady Di had? And they wouldn't want my kind there. In my miniskirt.'

'Don't mention Lady Di when we're drived fast in a car with no enough seat belts in the back for all us,' Chell frowned.

'Leonardslee.'

'What was that?'

Kay said, 'Can't remember. Yet another garden or a stately home.'

'Our flat is a stately home,' Kylah claimed. 'It's always in a state.' Kylah and Chell laughed together, next to each other.

'It's in a state cos yous two never do the hoovering.'

'Well, when you next come round you can do the hoovering for us, Manda.'

'Next!'

'Nymans, owned by the National Trust, it says here.'

'What's that?'

'Big house.'

Ava said, 'Actually, that's run by the National Trust, I think, but it's owned by the Scientologists.'

'The what?'

'It's a religion. Big in America.'

Chell spoke up. 'Aye, it's true. John Travolta and the Cruiser and them Hollywood people are into that stuff. Do you think we'll see them if we go to America? Imagine.'

'*Grease*'s still brilliant, though John's got fat.'

'What's it?' Manda looked around.

Finn said, 'It's a belief system. Dianetics. Freud and the occult.'

'Philosophy?' said Manda, darkly suspicious.

'Well, sort of. Not proper.'

Manda slowly pronounced all this to get it clear. 'A weird religion that John Travolta's into. Called: The National Trust?'

Ava, Kay and Finn laughed.

'No, Manda. Not the National Trust. Scientology.'

'Wakehurst Place.'

'A big house?'

'Sheffield Park.'

'A big . . . gardens?'

'The Bluebell Railway.'

Manda went, 'A railways. I mean a railways. Girls. Are yous trying to kill me here? Why would we's all want go to a railway?'

'It was on the map. I simply underlined everything of interest to visit on the map, then looked them up on the Internet. It's old steam trains. Might have been quite nice.' Kay humped her bare shoulders.

'A railways. Fuck sake.'

Thoughtfully, Ava muttered, 'I think they filmed *The Railway Children* on that railway.'

'What's that?'

'*The Railway Children*.'

'What is that?'

'Have you never seen it?'

'Is it a black and white?' Manda asked, with really savage contempt.

'It's in colour. It's on every Christmas. The kids get sent to live by the railway side.'

Ava quietly said, 'I read the book when I was a little girl.'

Manda made it perfectly clear. 'I hate Christmas telly.'

'I love it,' Kylah snapped.

'And Jenny Agutter gets her knickers off to wave them at the train,' Kay announced. 'She was so beautiful, young Jenny Agutter. She looked a bit like you, Ava.'

Manda perked up. 'Wait a minute. This film sounds quite good. My kind of thing.'

They all laughed.

Ava corrected, 'Her bloomers please, Kay. Her bloomers. Not her knickers. It's made for children.'

Kay laughed. 'When I was little, I was really shocked when she got her . . . bloomers off. And my dad quietly went over to the telly and changed the station.'

'Never?' went Ava.

'Honest.'

Ava said, matter-of-factly, 'That's a strict upbringing, when *The Railway Children* gets censored.'

Manda sneered, 'Aye. And look how Kay turned out.'

Another silence.

Kay continued, in a severe tone, 'Saint Hill Manor.'

As if it was the Tuesday-night pub quiz in the Mantrap, where she had notoriously never contributed a single correct answer, and was thus used as the tester in guesses, Manda yelped, 'That's a manor house.'

'Yes.'

Manda let out a half-genuine, half-exaggerated yawn. 'Anything else on the list, Kay?'

'Just Hever Castle,' said Kay.

To annoy Manda, a chant began within the car, revived from earlier; even Ava joined in with pantomime gusto: 'Heave Up Castle. Heave Up Castle. Heave Up Castle.'

'You'll be feeling like a Red Bull and Guinness, Mands?'

'Shaddup. It had better be a good castle.' But she smiled proudly at her fame. Manda held up her broken acrylic nail. 'You don't reckon they'll have a nail clinic at this castle, do you?'

'Got the Guinness monster's passport safe up front there?'

'Oh, I have it right here, safe and sound,' said Kay, with mock authority.

'Make sure it doesn't go back near her.'

'I have officially seized your passport, Manda.'

Manda said nothing but donated a smile of playing along.

Ava said, 'It's meant to be one of the most beautiful castles in England.'

Manda declared, 'Och. We've got gallons of castles up our way. You'd have castles coming out your ears if we were in Scotland. Oh, Ava. It's going to be brilliant when you come to visit us. You will come visit us, won't you? She says in her bed this morn she would.'

'I will, yes.'

'Do you promise?'

'I promise I'll come and visit sometime. Don't know when. I've never been to Scotland.'

Manda said, 'I'll show you everything. Finn doesn't know it up home now.'

'Yes I do, Manda. I go back all the time.'

'It's near a year since you been back. You don't even know Rascals.'

Finn just tutted. 'I had to work in London all the summer. To afford this banjaxed holiday, Manda.'

Manda ignored this. 'And I'll be taking you to Rascals on a Saturday night, Ava. It'll be brilliant. Everybody'll go: "Who's that beautiful girl?" and I'll say, "This is Ava, my pal from England," and they'll all be amazed to see you.' Manda went silent for a split second then said, with intense contemplation, 'Wonder what happened in Rascals last night? I might need to text Shelly McCrindle to find out. Eh?'

'Mmmm.'

'Oh, look at this village. It's quite cute.'

'It's very. English,' said Kylah.

So loud that Kylah shoved against Chell and squashed Finn against the door, Manda yelled, 'A pub! A pub, look the . . . stop stop . . . stop . . . a pub. The Wheat . . . Shelf Inn.'

'Wheat Sheaf,' Kay said.

The car made no motion of slowing.

'I need to pee,' Manda lied.

'We're almost at Hever Castle.'

'But that was a great wee pub,' Manda groaned, turning to look back, forlorn. 'And we really need to discuss where the hell we're goed on holiday. Tomorrow. Not vote. Natter about it over a pint and that. Like adults. Wine.'

'We've got wine for the picnic.'

They had halted earlier at a huge BP service station – and as if it were a place of historic interest or outstanding natural beauty, every girl except Kay had insisted upon leaving the car to look around. From a shop there they had purchased three half-chilled bottles of Mâcon-Villages out the fridges and eight pre-packed sandwiches. There had been debate and argument over the variety of fillings. Manda bought four packets of crisps which vanished into her bag. These purchases formed the back-bone of the picnic project.

'Las Vegas. We've only got a few days. We should go to Las Vegas. We should have flown out the night. Not tomorrow. I feel grand now.'

'Course you do. You were in your bed by ten. That must be a first on a Saturday night for you, Manda, since you were twelve year old and we's used to hang out down the bus shelter. *We* were in the bar till midnight. Weren't we's, girls? After we'd taken your pint of spew to the toilets and left it there.'

'Aye. We had to leave it till it cooled down so it didn't scum us out too much, carrying it.'

'Oh, don't talk about it in the car. It's making me ill,' groaned Kay.

Manda said, from the back of her throat, 'I heard Ava come back to our room. I was that wee bit dozy. You know, you might be right enough about that, Chell. It's donkey's years since I was in my bed at that time on a Saturday. Even when I was expecting Sean. I'll have to take a very close look in my Nights Out Diary. It goes right back to . . . the beginning.'

Ava said, brightly, from up the front, 'Did you and Manda grow up living near one another?'

Chell answered immediately, 'Above and below on the Complex at number twenty-two. They were first floor and we were third. Know how we become good pals, Ava? Well. When we was twelve or thirteen and that, you're trying to smoke cigarettes to be grown up, aren't you? And that summer me and Manda were smoking for the first time. And I used to steal two or four cigarettes from my Uncle Buzz's packets, cos he'd never notice, then late at night, when me and Manda should of been sleeping, I'd lower a cigarette on the end of a long piece of string down to her, down from my bedroom window to Manda's bedroom window under, and we'd both lean out smoking and waving down or up to each other before we went to sleep. Isn't that right? That summer, eh?'

Manda laughed at the memory. 'Aye. It was brilliant, eh, Chell? We used to send each other wee notes and letters and everything up and down on that string.'

Chell said, 'Me and Manda were in touch all the time with the string. Swapping letters and cigarettes and *Buntys* on it. Our folks couldn't keep us apart.'

Manda went, 'It was sort of like the first time in history of texting, that string.'

Chell laughed. 'I've still got those letters, Manda.'

'Me too. Me too.'

They both fell silent, a little tender at the memories.

After a period of respectful quiet, Kay said, 'I tell you, the American flights tomorrow were all much cheaper compared to tonight. I don't know why.'

Ava said, 'Because this is the weekend.' She changed down gears for the junction ahead and looked both ways.

Kay said, 'Left,' and imitated Ava, turning her head left and right to view the traffic as they did the turn. Ava continued talking as they geared up. 'If you book later tonight, much more will have come online. You could save hundreds by booking early tomorrow morning too.'

Kay looked down at the map. 'The paper makes me queasy if I look too long. We go up to Edenbridge, turn right, have to go just under a railway and we should be there. Okay, we need to do a right here, up one of these little lanes.'

'This one?' Ava questioned.

'Yes.'

'There's no signpost or anything whatsoever.'

'According to this, that should get us there. We go under a railway.'

Manda contributed, 'Is it the knicker-waving railway?'

The soporific clicking sound of the indicator began, the car slowed and came to a halt in the middle of the road awaiting oncoming traffic. Ava's hair – she had pinned it up today, making her even taller – tipped slightly backwards, she was steadily watching in the rear-view mirror, not making any contact with the eyes in the back.

Softly, Kay said, 'Here's the railway.'

They descended. In perma-shade lay the dried mud puddles of the cupped dip beneath the girdered bridge, bearing the zigzag prints of verge-hugging tractors and a perfect set of ascending horse turds, maintained intact between the average tyre width.

'Look. Hever Castle sign.'

'We're here. We're here. Well done, Kay.'

Manda said, 'Can we please now put on the bloody radio and get some music, since Kay has finished with her navigate stuff?'

Ava stabbed out a finger and the radio came to life through low, spread-out speakers in the front and the rear. The pleading, steady churning of a Romantic symphony was in progress.

'What's this? What's this music? Now, this is crap music,' Manda shouted.

Kylah plugged her ears again.

'Turn it off. Just turn it off. It's like a bloody funeral. We'll have to get a decent station that plays the charts on the way back.'

The music cut off.

They were driving through an outbreak of sudden mock-Tudor buildings on either side of the road and ahead was a sharp left-hand bend. They all peered out the car windows, Chell and Kylah lowering their heads to do so. Looming on that very corner was the wisteria-clad, weathered red brick of the Henry VIII public house.

Up front, Ava and Kay gave each other an anxious eye, hoping Manda would miss it.

'A pub. An amazing English pub of England. Stop. We've got to go in.'

'We can go on the way out, Manda.'

'Och. Why?'

'Manda, we can't have you throwing up in the moat,' Kylah warned.

'We're off to meet the gentility, Manda. You don't want to show us up in front of our betters,' Finn pointed out.

Sombre, devotionally, Manda asked, 'Are the posh owners actually inside of this castle? Do I have to meet with them?'

'They're on their holidays. Away to Magaluf.'

'You're jesting me.'

Near the gated entrance to Hever Castle, a stood-down police car was parked that day.

'Fuck sake, it's the Feds. Duck down, Kylah. Duck down. We're no meant to have four in the back of the hire car, like the gadge at the airport was greeting about. You know it fine.' Manda physically began to push Kylah's head down into the gap between the front seats.

'Hoi. Get offof me. You near banged my nut on this.'

'Shush.'

Kylah actually remained ducked down.

'Now they'll think we're trying to sneak someone in free,' said Chell nervously.

With her hand holding Kylah's head down, ringed fingers on Kylah's bare neck, Manda swiftly informed her, 'Oh, it's brilliant up here. You're really missing yourself, Kylah.'

Finn laughed out loud and shook her head.

'There is no actual Feds anywhere, Manda.'

'Can I come up now then, please?'

'It *looks* safe,' Manda considered.

Kylah rose up gingerly and began fixing her hair.

Manda popped a snigger. 'Hey, your fizzog's gone all beetroot. Do you go like that every time after a blow job, love?'

The car drove slowly onwards, obeying the fifteen miles an hour speed limit and following the small, hand-painted car-park signs plugged into the manicured verges on pointed strips of wood. In a mock-Tudor gatehouse there was a small booth with an electric traffic barrier. They paid the entrance fee, all of them fumbling and bustling for their contribution, to an attendant through a small window. 'On the right please, follow the marshall's directions.'

As they drove ahead, Manda spied the traffic marshall in his yellow reflective vest; he smiled at their party and waved Ava on through, flicking his hand this way and that, indicating Ava could choose whatever parking she wanted in this area. Ava just lifted one finger, now placed atop the steering wheel, in acknowledgement. Loudly, though the window was wound right down, Manda yelled, 'That bossy nerd looks like fucking Moby.'

The car park was an ordered, huge open field, neatly ranked with cars and sports utility vehicles. Free parking spaces of grass were pressed dry and flat with some bleached, yellowed car outlines when there must have been long-term events.

They were rolling and bumping on down the broad field then suddenly came a heat-hazed skyline and the view to the blocky castle, framed by the perfectly cut verging of its square moat — a vast mass of complexes, annexes and interconnecting outbuildings were visible behind the castle. Formal gardens were over to the right.

'Oh wow. What a pad. I wish I'd of had ma twenty-first in that then, girls, eh?' Manda shouted.

Grandiloquently, with an air of glamour and high jinx, Kylah said in hushed tones. 'God. Manda's twenty-first.'

'This is brilliant. I'd love to live here. If I was a Spice Girl or won the lotto or a *Big Brother* and this was all mine, I wouldn't let anyone near the place.'

'Course you wouldn't, Manda,' Finn shrugged.

'But I'd let you and Ava in, to have one of those totty wee cottages over yonder to do your philoso-pissing in.'

'Thank you, My Lady Heave Up,' Finn bowed.

'Not at all, Fionnula McConnel.' Manda waved her hand regally.

'Manda'll win the lottery for sure. It's aye someone like Manda wins it.'

'Why shouldn't I win? I deserve it. I've worked hard for it, figuring out my bloody numbers every week and trekking to the newsagent in the pishing rain. I've only won a bloody tenner so far. Unless I win *Big Brother* as well. Which I would, when they let me on. It's the only way I'm ever going to get money.'

Ava said, glancing in the mirror, 'Have you auditioned for it, Manda?'

'Nut, love. But I will. One day. When the salon can cope without me for a few months while I'm inside the house. Cos I'll be in till final night for sure. I'll get on it easy-peasy.'

'Let's park here,' Ava said to herself and suddenly swung the car round dramatically and they came to a halt.

Finn muttered, 'So you don't have to reverse out, Ava. Health and safety.'

The left back door sprung and Manda was away, sheltering her eyes against the sun with her hand, yelling something, running off down the slope, waving her hands in the air, shoulder bag jumping out at her side, the miniskirt fabric stiff, but flapping up distressingly high.

'She's off going mental already.'

'Just leave her to fall in the moat. Might as well get it over with.'

The others got out of the car slowly, softly and respectfully, closing the car doors as if they might damage them. Ava had popped the boot using a switch by the steering wheel and they all ambled around to the back, while studying the form of other parked vehicles. Two rows of cars back they saw four large tour buses drawn up tightly together.

'Ooo, so lovely here. And the weather's just gorgeous,' said Kay.

Ava lifted the boot lid. The vast bulk of overweight suitcases were back once again in the South Terminal left luggage. The pristine boot interior contained Kylah and Chell's vanity cases which they anxiously lifted out, intending to haul them about all day for cosmetic updates. Kay's smaller suitcase and Finn and Ava's hollowish backpacks were layered over to one side. Manda's horrid leather jacket was bundled like a rats' nest in a corner against the wheel hub shape. Ava grumbled around in her backpack. The top of it was carelessly loose, and hung open. Ava dragged out a straw sun hat then balanced it on her pinned-up hair.

Finn shook her head briefly, said, 'That'll mess up your hair when you take it off.' Then, 'But I guess you want to keep your complexion milky, to woo the squire from the next county. Deep down, you're genetically hard-wired to Jane Austen.'

Ava turned to look at Finn through her Wayfarer Ray-Bans and smiled, breathy admiration in the voice. 'Oh, Finn. That is so brilliant.' She leaned over and kissed Finn on the cheek. Finn accepted the kiss, nodded and smiled back with full affection while Chell, Kylah and Kay redundantly looked on.

Ava and Finn then lifted out the two plastic carrier bags of sandwiches, and the doubled-up bags hammocking the three bottles of wine. Chell took the first sandwich bag, Finn the other and Ava took jurisdiction of the wine bottles, which clunked familiarly.

'We should take all the passports; we can't go through *that* again.' Finn nodded conclusively in the direction of the castle, towards Manda's unseen presence there.

'Has everyone got their passports safe with them? I've got Manda's. Where is she anyway?' called Kay, like a teacher on a school outing.

Manda had run down a great deal of the polite reverse slope beyond the parked cars, then in open grass she had stubbornly halted and she stood, staring down at Hever Castle, its grounds and environs, absorbing what possibly might be of use to her and what might divert her. Kent bubbled in that heat-hazy distance, bulbous trees washed dark by their downward shadow were like smoke rising from artillery hits as they popped up on the horizons. It was all almost silent. She slowly watched wandering bands of figures in short-sleeved shirts and children running quick bursts, moving freely in the many distances. Small people circled among the patterned order of far gardens. Other stick forms seemed to let themselves down into a mysterious sunken area of pleasing, controlled landscaping. There was the puddle-like spread of a huge grey-green lake, something fake about its domesticated and perfect banks.

Manda scrutinised the castle itself, its improbably small windows and its propped-up, perfect magnificence centred in the square moat. When her mind moved to wider speculations, she wondered if the lavvy pans emptied into the moat.

But then her eye settled on a dark privet of topiary to the right of the castle walls. She sucked in a breath slowly between her teeth as she squinted and comprehended what the form actually meant. She had seen such a thing only in the picture books of her youth and on television. She felt she deserved it and she called out loudly, some buried, wordless exclamation perfected on the visiting fairgrounds of youth, swelled by the fact she had been the first to discover it.

Manda turned and slowly ambled back over the ridge to the reverse slope and its ranked vehicles. She was breathing heavily, pulling out her mobile phone. But then squinting to precisely identify the target car. To her shock there was reception coverage on her phone even though everything around was bloody country fields. England was amazing. Her multi-ringed fingers began, with a swift, expert dexterity, texting Shelly McCrindle.

> *wht hppned rascals lst nite who snog thatz*
> *fowl who slow dnced ur really missing urslf u slag*
> *cant tell u how gr8 its here wht a storey classic tell*
> *im NOT in magaluf its secret*

Manda sent the text with a commanding thumb push as she closed in on the hired car, feigning casualness and slowing her pace. She noticed everyone now had sunglasses on as well as Kylah, so she quickly fumbled among the metallic, frazzling protest of the crisp packets in her own bag for her shades, while she called, 'I *know* something amazing yous all *don't*.'

Chell nodded to Manda's phone, now clutched in two hands. 'What went and happened in Rascals last night then?'

'No, not that, girls. It's something to do with this place.'

'What?'

'Not telling. Just remember it was me found it out first. Yous'll see; yous'll see. Come on then. Let's get going.'

Kay said, 'I think I'll take my computer with me.'

'I'm sure it'd be safe in the car.'

'Aye,' said Finn. 'Check it out. It's the Glastonbury set on a day off, swigging their French wines out the back of Range Rovers. These are your people out there, Ava. I'm surprised you don't have your pink wellies and your over-the-knee stripy socks with you, like at Glastonbury.' She playfully grabbed Ava by one arm.

Ava was adjusting her straw hat. 'More Royal Ascot. No?'

Manda said thoughtfully, 'But if the computer got nicked, we'd be jiggered for booking America the night.'

'But there's computers at all the hotels though?'

'Oh aye. That's okay then. Let's just leave it here then. After all, I'm gonna leave my leather jacket, it's so sweltering. And that's worth a fortune.'

'Thank you very much for your consideration. But I have all my emails in this computer; it'd be a little inconvenient for me as well if this was swiped.'

'Oh. Right. I suppose so. Aye.'

'Everything out the car then, everybody?'

They nodded.

Ava pointed the remote-control central-locking keyring at the car and it beeped deep somewhere within. Even in the bright sunlight, the orange indicator lamps bloomed up dramatically and they heard the locks, almost simultaneously, clunk into place.

They began to assemble at the front of the car, but as Chell moved there, she halted. She pointed severely to the front wheel, the tyre fixed snug in the grass but turned at an extreme angle due to the way Ava had quickly swung in to the parking place. Chell said, 'But Ava, look. Your wheel thing is at a very thought-less angle for any dogs who want to pee against it.'

It was a very Chell thing to say. Everybody laughed.

'Well, at least it won't roll all away down the hill and into the moat. Just the kind of thing that would happen on this holiday,' Kylah pointed out.

Everyone uneasily surveyed the vehicle a last time. Prissily, Kay checklisted: 'Handbrake on and in gear?'

Ava nodded her hat brim once and so they headed off down-hill. Chell and Kylah's burnished aluminium vanity cases flashed hugely in the sunlight. The handles creaked annoyingly as the boxes swung from side to side. Kay looked a little overburdened and technologically out of place with her summer dress and the huge black lozenge of the computer flat against her hip bone.

The hill was steep enough so their forward feet came down heavily on the grass.

'Looks shite but we's was right to wear flat shoes, eh, girls?' said Chell.

'Mine have a wee bit heel,' Finn pointed.

'They're nice. You get them in London?'

'Aye.'

'Sandals, even flip-flops, look grand if you've had a very good pedicure. Say from our salon,' Manda told everyone, ignoring – or probably insinuating – that Finn and Kay were wearing handsome sandals with unadorned toenails. Ava was wearing battered trainers that she needed to drive in, but with her height, they suited her short dress with its shoulder straps.

Ava suddenly pointed to the left. 'Oh,' she said. 'The pavil-ions are up there. We need to go to the pavilions. There'll be cafes and we could get plastic cups. That silly petrol station didn't have any. We might be able to get strawberries and cream.'

'Ice cream would be nice.'

'Aye. A good fat strawberry Mivvi.'

Ava took off up the hill and the others followed.

After a short climb – everybody looking around or staring down in concentration – Manda went, 'So. Do yous see it yet?'

'What?'

'Can't yous see?' She held out both hands, exasperatedly, towards the castle as if she were presenting them all with some vast gift.

'What?'

'Look over yonder, beside the big castle.'

Finn saw it first. 'Oh. A maze.'

'Oh aye. A maze made of bushes and things. Oh, what a scream. That'll be brilliant.'

'What brilliant crack that'll be. We must go after the picnic.'

'Oh, come on. Some of us is bound to get lost in it forever. We'll never find our way out,' Chell frowned.

'Aye. Manda'll be stuck in it for days.'

'Maybe sexy firemen would come to rescue me out?'

'Brilliant.'

'They'll find her by the smoke signals going up.'

Sure enough, despite the ascent, Manda had a gasper alit and shoved in the corner of the mouth.

They walked on. Upward. Manda said, 'Christ. This is a bit of a pech in the bloody heat. It's fucking roasting.'

'You should get more into sport, Manda,' said Kylah.

'Eh? You're no into sport.'

'Aye, I am.'

'What sports are you into?'

'Watching *Gladiators*.'

Nobody talked. They all concentrated on the steady ascent until they stood on the metalled surface of the road, before the pavilions.

There was some kind of self-service restaurant within. Others were snacking under Coca-Cola umbrellas on the terrace.

'We could of bought the whole picnic here,' Manda complained.

'It'll be dear as anything.'

Ava ordered them, 'Stay here.' She carried the bag of wine bottles on ahead and pulled off her sunglasses before she entered the pavilions, disappearing within.

'Why'd she take our wine?' Manda lifted her sunglasses and glared.

'Better get off the road,' said Kay. She flapped hands towards the others as if they were a trail of ducklings being herded from danger. They all stared down at the tarmac under their feet then looked left and right and stepped back up onto the verges of grass. Chell and Kylah began lighting cigarettes.

This road was beyond the car park turn-off though, and only seemed to give vehicle access to some buildings downhill, to do with maintenance and gardening. They could see an old-style, dark green Land Rover with a trailer attached, parked down in the shade of fine mature trees by some administration buildings. They idly turned their heads, looking around.

'God, we're miles from home, eh?' Manda speculated. 'Who would have thought we'd end up somewhere like here?'

Finn grimaced. 'Aye. Who *would* have thought.'

Kylah said, 'My Old Dear offered to send me money somehow. I was trying to explain to her what was going on this morning but she was right bamboozled. Thought I was asking for money. Mind, I was using up bloody phone credit. That's the thing about Old Men and Old Dears, eh? You can't text them or that, cos they can't work it, eh?'

'Mmm. My Old Man doesn't even have a mobile. What a fucking loser.'

'Is the castle built . . . good, Kay?' Chell asked.

Kay turned round to survey it. 'Well, it's all restored. The only original part is in the gatehouse. I'll look later.' She pointed. 'The Astors completely restored it. A lot of what you're looking at was built in the thirties.'

'What do you mean "original"? Like a good idea?'

'No. Well, what part is actually from Tudor times. Or even later. It's not really an old castle. It's a jazzed-up modern one. Nothing much, you see, would have been here in the time of Henry the Eighth. The gardens too.'

'He chopped off his wives' heads, eh?'

'Yes. Anne Boleyn lived here for a short time, it said on the Internet.'

'What happened to her?' Manda frowned.

Kay drew her finger across her throat.

'Dozy cow. Must have been asking for it. If she had this place, what more did she want?'

'I can't believe you even have a bad opinion of Anne Boleyn.' Finn shook her head disappointedly.

'It must have a ghost, the castle, eh, Kay?' Chell said.

'I would suppose. We could ask.'

Chell went quiet at this. A certain inchoate gloom gathered over her, despite the bright weather. 'I don't really want to go in the castle,' Chell quietly said. 'Ghosts go for me. I'm telling yous.'

Kylah and Manda laughed.

Finn said, 'Any ghost in there'll soon be quaking in fear when it hears Manda coming.'

They all laughed, even Manda. 'Aye,' she agreed. 'Aye, that's right enough. I'd say to it. "Hoi. What've I got to fear from you, ya headless cow? You can't even give my boyfriends a blow job.'

Laughter.

Now she furiously demanded, 'Who is Astors?'

Kay said, 'They were very wealthy Americans. Who owned Hever Castle. It was a huge family. Teams of them. They owned Cliveden House as well, I think.'

'Any bonkable sons about?' Kylah glanced around, as if hoping for a stray male heir, stumbling through the verdure.

'Oh. Like the horse race Ava says? Royal Astors?'

'No. That's Royal Ascot.'

'Och Jeez. I can't keep up with it all. There's so many rich posh goings-on and folks. I only thought there was one or two of them but there's bloody millions and millions of the idle perishers round this way.'

Chell said, 'Ava's very . . . confident. In a good way. You can see she's very confident. She's at ease.'

Finn nodded. 'Aye. They get taught that at the boarding schools. They're all like that. It's like, their lives are there, intact, never under threat, anything is a possibility so everything – even what they believe – is sort of tagged on. Their beliefs are like, options. We believe things that grow out of our lives. Their beliefs are a series of choices, like off a menu in a posh restaurant.'

'I don't know if this philosophy course is good for you, Finn,' Kylah said.

Finn just laughed at herself but looked at Kylah. 'You might be right.'

'Nah. You're still the Mighty Finn.'

In pompous mode, Manda began, 'I must say, despite her threesomes and sort of tartiness, cos miniskirts, wellie boots and over-the-knees socks is pretty tarty – if that's what she was weared at Glastonbury – but what I *do* like about Ava is her generousnesses. She's generousness itself with money. Like she doesn't give a toss. It's going to take us a year to pay back all those hotels' bills stuff, but she's laid-back as you like about it, with that America Express card. Though you've one too, I know.' She jutted at Kay. 'That's big of her,' Manda nodded, and seemingly utterly without guile.

Finn nodded, slowly. 'That's true. She is generous. I could tell yous crackers of how funny she is too, but there's time as the holiday goes by. She used to be madder but she's calmed down.'

'Aye?' Manda suddenly cheered. 'Hey, girls, look. Here we are. It's going to be a classic. It'll be brilliant. We might be going to America. Everyone else is really missing themselves. Look, I'm sorry about that wee passport thing yesterday. I don't remember even taking my boot off to put it in.'

The four of them now looked at Finn. Finn stared at the grass by her feet then she shook her head, but a smile came up on her face and she glanced at Manda. 'Fuck sake, Manda. You're something else, I'll say that.'

They all smiled at this public forgiveness.

'I think Ava's lovely,' said Chell. 'I think you have a good friend there, Finn.'

'Hey.' Manda turned to Finn and nudged her with an elbow, so Finn tottered ever so slightly. 'Shame Ava didn't have a gorgeous bonk of a brother, just that wee bit younger than her. Our age?'

Surprisingly Finn nodded in agreement. 'Aye. I've thought that. Yous should see her parents' fucking house.'

Manda nutted her head at Kay as if she were not present, 'Bigger than her folks' place?'

'Oh aye. It's got a long driveway and that, going past trees for ages, like here, but not as big as this and it's not a castle or anything, but I'm telling yous, it's more beautiful. It's dead, dead beautiful with roses and creepers stuff growing up the walls. You think you're in a film when you first go there. And a river goes past the bottom of the garden, a tributary. To the Thames; all clean, and they own a section of the riverbank and hire it out to like, fishermen, and you can swim in the river in summers. It's lovely. Just bloody lovely. Hey. Mind when we used to go out on the bus, try and swim at Tralee Bay, kicking our way through the jellyfish and our legs turned blue with the freezingness? Seeing who could just stand longest in the water without your legs going dead?'

They all laughed out loud at this.

'Bloody murder,' Manda nodded decisively, exhaling smoke.

'We were just daft wee lassies, girls,' said Chell.

Kylah went, 'Aye. We thought we were so cool though. We were all topless, going –' she put on a baritone voice – '"Why is everyone staring? Don't they know it's cool to be topless?"' She changed back to her own voice. 'Folk weren't perving us, they was looked at us going, "They must be freezing. Wrap them up in baking foil, someone."'

They all chuckled.

'As if we were going to get a tan. The skies was grey.'

'Grey? It was fucking raining proper.'

They all laughed, apart from Kay who just smiled. She had not been allowed in their gang back then.

'We were cool okay, we were having like, what is it . . . hypothermia.'

They all laughed again at the clear memory.

Kay said, 'I didn't want to ask, but do you know if Ava's house is listed, Finn?'

'What's listed?' Manda snapped, feeling they were drifting off-topic without permission.

'Listed means it's of historical or architectural importance. Grade Two or even Grade One, if it's really old. It means you can't alter the original features.'

Finn said, 'Oh aye. Her French Old Man says something about that.'

'Know what yous two is like? Know what this is like? Know what yous are reminding me of? That boring bloody thing on the telly. *Antique Roadshows*.'

Kay and Finn profoundly ignored her and just looked across her butting face.

Finn nodded, oddly melancholic. 'Can I mooch a fag for later?'

Manda jammed out the packet at her in a businesslike way. Finn stuck the cigarette in, behind her ear, hid underneath her hair.

'Here she comes. Shoosh now,' Chell went.

Ava herself was crossing back towards them from the pavilions. They all watched her very tall, long-stepping progress with pride. A row of white plastic cups now in one of her hands, all slotted together into a tube. The slightly sweated wine bottles lying flat in the other bag. Bananas and perhaps three green apples were also visible in a depressingly transparent white plastic bag which also hung from her right hand, and piled on top of the fruit within, they could see the pressing, rounded corners of two punnets. 'Strawberries,' Ava pleasantly called to them. 'Probably rock hard; nasty apples, bananas. I got them to open the wine bottles as well. I jammed the corks in quite tight. I hope we can get them back out.'

Manda's face took on a dark, cheated air since she hadn't thought of this.

'Oh Jesus. Smart thinking, Ava. I never thought of that. We's had no corkscrew. Let me carry that,' and Kylah hurriedly took the fruit bag off Ava.

This gave them all some kind of skipping, increased momentum and they began to excitedly descend the slight brae towards the castle but then veered over to their right. As their vantage widened across the slope, they espied nest after nest of settled picnickers on open grassland, close to a lush and generous copse of trees. So they shifted course in this direction. The dark claret of a huge copper beech rattled in a burst of breeze beside them. A percussive prattle shivering up the tree, lifting the heavy reclination of the branches before they slowly dropped into stillness once again. Ahead, some green leaves reflected back the white sun from among all that generous abundance of sluggish chlorophyll. They could also now distinguish some purpose-built picnic tables and carved logs – but all seemed occupied.

Kay moseyed over beside Ava's strides. She had to hold a hand down on her computer to stop it banging against her bony hip.

'Ava, I don't want to appear to be a nosy parker and all that but can I ask? Finn was saying how beautiful it is and I was wondering, is your parents' house a listed building at all? I'm very interested in dull architecture stuff.'

Suddenly, Ava deliberately stopped, allowing the four others to haplessly draw ahead. Manda kept going onward across the pleasant hill flank for a short spell. Then Manda stopped aggressively and looked back, but equally resigned to the exciting advance of the three others, her nature wanted to pioneer onward, so she continued, yet repeatedly and frequently snapped her head back around to view Ava and Kay.

When the others had covered some ground in advance of them, Ava and Kay ceased standing in silence and Ava nodded in a Napoleonic, 'walk-with-me' gesture.

'Yeah, I was going to tell you about this, Kay. I thought you'd be interested. Doing architecture. And I didn't want you to think I was blowing my own trumpet or my parents or whatever.' Ava nodded on ahead at the young women. Manda was now screaming. Then dancing, and she started swatting out at some invisible insect. 'And I didn't want to bore the girls. It's Grade One listed.'

'Oh. Grade One?'

'Yes, but that's automatic because of the Tudor and Elizabethan parts and there's additions from the seventeenth century. You can see the numbers, fifteen twenty-two, carved inside the main door on the old lintel. But also, it was partly built by Elvetson. Adam Elvetson.'

'Oh. Oh, he's so famous. God, I know his stuff. It's really likely I've seen your house in one of my books in the uni library. I mean, I'm no scholar, I'm getting trained as the usual bog-standard office builder. But I waste hours with the monographs and photo books in the library. A Basil Spence library no less. I love domestic English architecture, Elvetson, so much. He's amazing. He was an associate of Lutyens.'

'Yes. But perhaps it's not in the Elvetson coffee-table books and such. We've two or three in the house and Daddy groans when they arrive from the book club, because our place is never in them.'

'No?' Kay smarted slightly.

'There was huge reroofing and enlargement renovation carried out in the thirties before it was protected. A young architect from Oxford built the new wing and the music-room extension on the other side and he put in extra floors, and gable and dormer windows in complete *imitation* of Elvetson using the same materials he found still in storage. He was a slavish admirer and then someone told Elvetson himself that there was a filthy plagiarism of one of his houses up near Cholsey, where we are, and the story goes, between the wars, the great man himself came up from London in the car for the day and he viewed the house and said, if his memory wasn't sharp he'd think he'd really designed and built the house himself. However. He didn't like some parts of the roof and interior, so free of charge, with the owners paying only for materials and labour, Elvetson drew up plans for big changes to the gable windows and the interior, in the water garden parlour and to the main hall staircase. But the plans are all lost now. It's mentioned in his correspondence but the specific plans are gone. So if you look in the Berkshire and Oxfordshire architectural guides and almanac today, there's argument and debate about what parts of the house are Elvetson's updates and what parts were the original pastiche. When I was small, on three or four occasions I can remember young men appearing outside my bedroom and it was some young architecture student from London or Oxford excitedly taking photos of our roof beams and gables and arguing the point as to what were Elvetson's improvements and what was fake. I thought it was all very impressive. Daddy always forgot to warn me he'd invited these students down. I fell in love with one for a month when I was thirteen. He had sideburns.'

'That's just amazing,' said Kay. 'You're really lucky to live there.'

'Yes. I know.'

'I'll look it up when I'm back in Edinburgh.'

'Well, it's bastardised Elvetson basically. It's not major work, like Kitchenly Mill Chase, do you know that one?'

'I think I've seen that.'

'That's his most famous house. Not so very far from here.'

'With a moat?'

'Yup. Stunning. Come up to our house sometime. Stay the night; there's tons of room. It is sublime. Under the Lambourn Downs and the Ridgeway. Don't know what we'll do when Daddy retires. I whine at him already. Not to sell. There's a railway station at Cholsey. Or I can pick you up in Oxford. I don't know what the trains do from Scotland.'

'Ooo. I'd so love to. That would be lovely.'

The conversation petered out and they just walked on.

Up ahead, Kay and Ava could observe the deeply controversial debate had begun as to where they should settle for their picnic. Arms pointed and gestured. Kylah and Manda favoured a pitch suspiciously close to a picnic in progress – not even upon tartan rugs but upon large, laid-out, hopefully imitation Persian carpets which must have been hauled down from a large vehicle. The party included, what appeared to be, late-teenage sons with a mother or aunt.

Finn was having none of it, waving instead to a completely free area closer to the trees.

Ava yelled in a strident, but shameless, posh call (which obscurely, somehow embarrassed Kay), 'Go closer to the shade. Closer to the shade. Some of us can sit in it and some out of this dashed sun.'

Manda stared blankly through her sunglasses towards them then she continued to scan around, frustrated at the family nature of every visible picnic group and the utter lack of young, exclusively male groupings. This just wasn't the beach in Magaluf.

Ava turned her lenses to Kay and in a unburdening voice sighed, 'I hate the sun really. Hate it. I've been dreading a beach holiday.'

'So. Have. I.' Kay elongated each word.

The other young women were settling just on the fringes of the shade.

As Kay and Ava approached, Manda, sitting crossed-legged, yelled out and pointed, 'See they? See they gadgies yonder. Carpets with them, man. Now that's posh. I'll say when I'm back home, England's so posh the parks have carpets.' She burst out a scoff of spittle and air and cigarette smoke. 'We don't have nothing to sit on,' she added bitterly.

Kylah had collapsed flat, arms out. 'Ooo, the grass is nice and cool and tickly.' Then Kylah sat up suddenly to watch everything.

Ava stepped into the shade and lay down the carrier bag with the others, and the tube of cups. 'We can swap about the plastic bags if our bottoms get wet but I don't think it's rained for days. The ground should be dry.'

Finn had sat down and waved a hand. 'It's fine. No problem. It's dry.'

Manda leaned and she began hauling everything out of the plastic bags and dropping the sandwiches and fruit to the grass like a four-year-old child. Her fist closed on the greasy, slidey flanks of a wine bottle and she began squeaking the semi-plunged cork back and forth as if she were wrestling with a cat. Then Manda stood up, holding the bottle in one hand. 'I'm gonna sit with Ava. And Kay. In the shade. It's fucking roasting. What a scorcher.'

Chell, Finn and Kylah remained, sitting just out in the sun; Kay, Ava and Manda sat along its frayed edging within the lolling shade from the branches shifting the border minutely, eddying it back and forth in the breeze. Kay looked at Ava's crossed legs, and from her calfskin bag, Kay took out a full-sized bottle of Evian.

With a low plug sound the bottle cork came off in Manda's fingers. Surprisingly, in good etiquette, Manda now lumbered up once more and began dispensing the wine into the held-up plastic cups. Kylah and Chell got their slosh then Finn. 'Ta,' went Finn.

'Kay?' said Manda, standing before her, the bare knees close to Kay's face, and Kay held up her cup. 'Thank you, waiter.'

'Ava, you don't have a cup.'

'No thank you, my love. I'm driving. I'll just have water.'

Manda looked astonished. 'You're no drinking?'

'I'm driving. I can't.'

'Och, you can have one or two wee doochts?'

'Nope. Once I start I'll want to go on. I'll be having Kay's water.'

Manda looked slighted. 'Ava, come away. You were drinking last night. Have a wee doocht.'

'Leave her when she's driving,' Finn growled quickly from out of the sunshine.

'Okay then.' Manda made a huge, pushed-out-lips shape. She went about pouring her own share into the plastic cup, holding both at the same height, the bottle almost horizontal, its lip on the rim of the fragile plastic cup, as if she were decanting from one test tube to another, back in the old chemistry lab, committing some hazardous atrocity. Manda was clearly helping herself to Ava's forfeited share. 'Jesus, that's the first bottle tanked already. We's're mental.' She tossed the empty bottle recklessly over by the sandwiches so it bumped heavily, just missing Chell's kneecap. Gingerly squeezing her plastic cup, Manda slurped the surface off.

'Careful, Manda.'

'What is it your parents do for a living?' Kay almost whispered.

'Father negotiates merger deals or something for French companies in England and the Far East. Mummy was a college teacher in the early eighties but she stopped when I first went to primary school. Your father's a surgeon, isn't he?' Ava asked. 'That's amazing.'

'Well, he doesn't really practice much any more, which is crazy. Just now and again for major operations, to test out new equipment and procedures. He has a big overpaid job in Glasgow to do with the Health Trusts so he's away from Mum a lot. He pops through to Edinburgh to take me to dinner. I think I see more of him than Mum now.'

'What. Are you two talking about?'

Ava and Kay turned. Manda was looking directly at them, sunglasses off. 'Do I hear bloody political politics going on about again? Come on, lassies. Lighten up. Have a crack. Drink your wine up now, Kay. Less of yon Evian.'

'We're fine thanks, Manda.'

'What'll we talk about better then? I know what we'll talk about.'

Finn shouted over. She was keeping a close, supervisory eye on things. 'What will we talk about then? Manda?'

Manda clapped her hands. 'The topic today, girls, is . . .' She looked around the group.

Chell predicted Manda's train of thought immediately and shouted, 'No. Not truth or dare. I can't be bothered. I've no truths left for you, nosy besom.'

'*Or* spin the bloody bottle, Manda.' Kylah shook her head.

'It won't spin on grass.'

'Aye, it will so.' Manda showed her teeth but she was only toying and she continued: 'The topic today, girls . . . is . . .' Her gaze stopped at Ava.

'Ava. Ava . . . sorry, what's your second name again, Ava?' She dropped her voice politely.

'Hurmalainen.'

'Who am I laying on? That's brilliant. Who am I laying on!'

Finn lowered her head down and called across to Ava, 'She's impersonating one of our teachers at school.'

'Quiet!' Again, Manda's head had stopped at Ava. Her eyes hard to judge as she'd put sunglasses back on to intimidate. She suddenly pointed. 'Ava Who Am I Laying On?'

'Yes?'

'What tampons do you use?'

Someone let a burst of air out their lips.

'Manda,' Kylah yelled. 'You just can't ask someone that.'

'No. No. I don't mind. I've been asked worse.' Ava held up her hands in submission.

'Ha ha. See? She's all right is Ava.'

'Lil-lets. And I'll tell you, Lil-lets are a British institution.

Bloody hard to buy abroad. I use non-applicator. So I get a thrill at least once a month.'

Everyone laughed.

'Why Lil-lets?'

'Don't leak. Tampax expand that way and Lil-lets that way.' She illustrated with her long hands. 'I can get stuff trapped here. They're much, much better. And I use towels.'

'Manda's concept of intimacy *is* the venereal, Ava,' Finn called squinting from out of the sun.

'Don't try tell me that's philosophy. I've had a kiddy and I know fine what gynaecological is too.' She snapped round on Kylah. 'Is that right enough, that Lil-lets expand that way, Kylah?'

'Aye.'

'I'm going try them then.' Manda turned round, smiled and explained proud-as-punch to Ava. 'I know what all they use. Even Kay told me. It's interesting.'

'I've a better one to talk about than periods,' said Kylah.

'What?'

'Why are the sizes in Topshop and Gap so totally different?'

'Oh tell me about it. My sunglasses is Topshop. Sunglasses from Topshop is all that fits me. Nothing fits me. Like I'm size twelve.'

'Manda. You're not twelve.'

'I am so. In Gap I am too.'

'Just cos you can crawl yourself into one thing out of Gap that's twelve, don't mean you're twelve. You're fourteen to sixteen,' said Chell, knowing fine Manda was sixteen to eighteen.

'Fuck off, midget. I am twelve.'

'No in Topshop.'

'Nut, love. I admit. Not in Topshop.' She chuckled then shouted out, 'Even you're no twelve in Topshop.'

'Gap is American. You'll see if we go to the States, it's so reasonably priced.'

'And Mango is Spain.'

Quickly Manda added, 'And Zara's. Both's in Magaluf. But no in the resorts. It's a pain. It's well out of Magaluf and you need to take this bloody weird bus with local people only speaking

Spanish language to this main big town that's called Palma. And wait till you hear this, right? Catriona tried to pay on the bus with her credit card. It's no America Express or that, it's fucking Visa. Famouser! And the bus driver asked to see her passport. On a bus. Like she was getting on a plane or something. So's we paid cash.'

'Catriona tried to pay on a bus with a credit card?'

'Aye. What's wrong with that?'

'Just as well they didn't ask for *your* passport, Manda.'

This was ignored. 'But we didn't have them. In Spain they do that thing. They take your passport when you get to the hotel. So's you canna do a runner it's for.'

'And now we've got your passport, Manda.'

This was ignored. 'And I'm telling yous, it's sickening. How cheap it is; Zara and Mango over there compared to Scotland.'

'That's like Kookai in France,' Ava said.

'What?'

'Kookai in France. It's French, so it's so very cheap over there. I can never buy anything from Kookai in England now. It's so expensive here and so cheap over there. This is from Kookai in France.'

'It's really nice, Ava.'

'Like it? Thank you.'

'I wouldn't have thought you'd worry about that, Ava.'

'Well, of course I do. Why should I pay twice the price for the same garment? It doesn't cost that much to take it across the Channel. You're being ripped off in dear old rip-off Britain.'

Manda pursed her lips in concern and disapproval, then turned to Kylah. 'I am so a twelve.'

'Well, show's the size on that skirt.'

Finn said quick, 'Don't, don't, or she'll take it off.'

Just then the double timbre of Manda's mobile phone went, then silenced, signalling the arrival of a text. Manda leaped for the phone as if there were a race; only her nine remaining acrylic nails steadied the aggression she buried into her bag with.

'Saved by the bell, Mands.'

Manda had the phone out, devouring the information on its

face. 'Aye. Aye. Thought so.' She nodded. 'It's from Shelly McCrindle.'

'Herself. Out the blue?'

'Nah. Nah. Actually decided I would text her. She's no my pal or that. Though she's popular. Just to ask what happened in Rascals last night. Here it's.' Silence fell as Manda read the text, lips moving minutely as she spelled out the words to herself.

The others began to talk about sundry matters, Kay again to Ava; Finn, Kylah and Chell taking up conference about clothing sizes, but Manda held up an insolent arm, to silence them. 'Hoi. Hoi. No. Shut up. Listen to this. Shelly claims she snogged Angus Robb. Bull*shit*. More like he stood next to her for two minutes at the bar. I'll be getting to the bottom of that when I'm home. And wee Michelle McLaughlin's meant to have got off with fucking Poggle and gone back to his place. His place!' Manda yelled out loud, still staring down at the face of her phone in fury at such ignorance. 'Poggle lives with his folks, Shelly. Ya daft cow liar. And also Shelly says she was all night in the VIP area. That'll be fucking right, unless she fell in there, unconscious-out-of-her-mind.'

Finn suddenly took notice. 'The what?'

'Shelly's claiming she actually was in the VIP area all last night. No ways she was.'

Finn's jaw opened wide. 'Are you really telling me there's a VIP area in the new club in town? You're joking me?'

Manda looked straight at Finn. 'Aye. What's wrong with that? All clubs have them now. It's dead nice in Rascals. All glass and that. Great seats.'

Finn let out a long mocking laugh.

'What?'

'Well, for starters, I mean, who exactly are the VIPs in our town, I'd like to know?'

Manda physically recoiled in deep offence. Was it not obvious she herself was one?

Kylah shook her head. 'Ach, it's just called the VIP area. Anyone can get in if you buy a bottle of bubbly above a certain price. So's old pervs'll buy a bottle of thirty-quid shite like, just so's they can go up the dance floor and say to some daft wee fourth year, "Come to the VIP area with me, darling," and wee lassies fall for it. They don't snog but they sit in the VIP, looking down their glasses of bubbly at you. Bunch of wee hoors showing their knickers.'

'If they have any on.'

'Aye. I swear, some nights, that Timmons girl, I swear she had nothing on. Eh? I could of gobbed at her and scored a direct hit.'

Chell nodded in complicity at Kylah. Kylah and Chell were using an identical technique to support their soft-sided, plastic cups of wine. The grass was too unstable a surface to put them down upon, so they were kneeling on their lower legs and using the space between their bare knees to semi-clench and support the cups between. They needed to smoke and light cigarettes with the free hands.

Manda was lost in thought then proclaimed defensively, 'Catriona and I are in the VIP area all the time.'

In exact synchronicity, Kylah and Chell barked out, 'Twice!'

Finn laughed out loud. 'VIP areas. Christ. We used to go to clubs to meet people, now we seem to go to avoid them.'

Chell elaborated, counting using her thumb and forefinger, for emphasis. 'Manda, you was in it on your twenty-first with us and you was in it with Catriona the Saturday yous reopened the salon and yous didn't invite me and Kylah in.'

Manda sneered, 'Still beeling about that then, are yous, girls? Tut. That was a business event for regular customers and business associates.'

'We are regular customers.'

'What you have to understand, girls, like I already explained after to yous, is, like, we have regular-regular customers, spending tons in the beauticians and the salon every week. Obviously we have to reward our biggest and best clients. So that's why I couldn't permit yous two to come into the VIP area that night. I'm afraid.'

There was a silence.

Finn laughed again and shook her head at the profusion of new words that had been forced into the daily lexicon, 'clients',

'VIPs', all with segregation and social division as their basis. The Social Exclusion Boogie. And here was Manda, of all people, using them unquestioningly.

'And the DJ's always in the VIP area. Especially that old baldy twat plays shite,' Kylah said, her face turned to Finn.

Finn nodded, expressing predictability with a shrugging gesture.

Chell turned a look upon Kylah. 'You rubbed his baldy head with your hand once, when he was stood at the bar.'

'Right enough. So I did. To take the piss. It was smooth as my leg the first time I ever shaved it.'

Ava said, 'I went into a club in Dublin.'

All heads turned to her.

'We were pretty wrecked, me and my bloke of the time. There were plenty of empty seats where we sat down and really excellent waiter service, except for up at one end of the club. This one end of the club was absolutely packed and heaving yet our end was completely empty. There was nobody else in our end. Up that other end people were pushing together so they couldn't move and everyone was screaming at each other and it was actually quite ghastly. Hellish-looking. I asked, "Why is everyone squashed in that place over there?" and the waiter bloke said, "Oh, that's our VIP area." Everyone in the club was in the VIP area and they wouldn't come out.'

Manda looked stunned, her well-developed sense of exclusivity shattered further by a concept that one day there might be more people in the VIP area than in the ordinary area of a club, and how she would possibly solve such a huge conundrum. In a low, shocked voice, she said to Ava, 'Is that right enough, Ava?'

'Yeah. Sure.'

Almost whispering, crushed by the implications, Manda asked, 'Didn't you want to be in the VIP area?'

Ava shrugged. 'I don't give a shit. I'll drink French champagne anywhere with anyone. I might be posh but I'm not a snob. Those are two different things.'

'You're right, Ava. I never thought of it like that.' Chell nodded.

Manda looked confused and fell into rare silence. To occupy herself she crossed and began de-corking operations on the next bottle.

Half-heartedly, Kylah reached out and began picking up the sandwiches, studying the fillings and dropping the sealed packs back onto the grass hopelessly, from her disinterested, loosened fingers. Manda circulated, topping up plastic cups.

'This is nice. This is chilled out,' stated Kay.

Ava stood and crossed to the strawberries, lifted a punnet and wearily returned to Kay's side. She seemed a little bored, Finn noticed. Ava poked at the fruits, smelled them and began tearing off the plastic. 'They're not fresh; irradiated or refrigerated for ages. They need to be eaten fresh. We have them in our kitchen gardens. I ate so much in August, it was actually disgusting.'

'I'm not even really hungry yet, after Manda dragging me to Mackers for McMuffins this morn.' Chell reached out for a banana. 'I'll have a nana.' She stubbed her cigarette and began, ever so delicately, peeling the banana.

Finn fished the cigarette from in behind her ear then leaned right over so you could see her tits – bare, braless – hanging down, to grab Chell's lighter. She used it and tossed it back.

Manda fished out a packet of crisps. She gave a sly look at the others, thought better of it, then put the packet back in her bag and she crossed over to the sandwiches.

Kay and Ava fell silent. Eating strawberries together. It looked like the strawberries were quite good and they weren't letting on.

'Ach, come on. Let's play spin the bottle.'

'Manda, I'm no doing dares. What are your dares gonna be? The usual same old stuff. "Go over to those picnickers and show them your tits; go over to those picnickers, ask them for a snog." Those is always your same dares. And I'm no doing snogging with just girls either. Again. I'm no doing any of that today. I'm not even pished yet.' Kylah looked away.

'Fuck sake, Kylah. What a bore. What's wrong with yous?'

Finn said, 'I'll play if it's original truth or dares. Not childish ones.'

Manda leaped right up. 'Form a bit better circle but not too close together.' She arranged one of the empty plastic bags flat on the grass but suddenly a breeze seized and shifted it.

'Ooops.'

'Got it.' Manda kneeled over the empty bottle and placed it on the plastic bag. 'Come a bit closer, Ava and Kay,' she insisted.

Ava got up. Kay raised her eyes to the branches and followed her.

When everyone was in position, Manda leaned, her hand on the bottle, craning her arm. 'Everyone ready now?' Manda spun the bottle. She did it quite well, so on the static, plastic surface, the bottle revolved around efficiently then quickly slowed.

'Kay!' Manda screamed. The name rang out across the still, restful, afternoon parklands.

'Fame at last,' Kay murmured.

Ava chuckled.

'It was almost you, Manda,' Kylah shouted.

'No ways. Look. That's pointed to Kay for sure. Truth or dare, Kay?'

Kay held a strawberry idly before her lips.

'Kay?' Manda yelled again.

'Truth.'

Manda sat back, raised her hand to her mouth and went into great thought.

Kylah warned, 'Manda. Not sex. I'll buy you a drink, Manda, if you don't ask her something about sex.'

'Okay.'

'Nor gynaecological speculations.'

'Huh. I'm thinking, I'm thinking.'

'C'mon then.'

'Right, Kay. Ever been in love?'

'Wow.'

'Good question. For once, Mands.'

'No,' Kay said, then smiled. 'I'm a user and abuser of men.'

'Oh, sure.'

'Och, that's no a good answer. You have to . . . what is it, Finn?'

'Elaborate,' Finn drawled.

'Elaborate.'

Ava was looking at Kay, quietly smiling.

'I don't think I've been in love. I've been obsessed. I've had TWCs.'

'What's they? Like a VD?'

'Two Week Crushes. But I don't think I've ever been in love. Maybe?' She shrugged her shoulders once, in an offhand but mysterious way.

'You've been obsessed though?' Chell quickly asked.

'Yessss. Who hasn't been obsessed with guys?'

'I think she's answered it,' Chell stated. 'I don't think I've been in love. Apart from with Johnny Depp.'

'Who was the guy, Kay?'

Kylah rattled off, 'Stephen Hawking.'

'Depends what love is.'

'When something hurting another person would hurt you as much; when you can't stomach the thought of something bad happening to someone else. That's love,' Kylah nodded.

'Nice. That's how I feel about my wee Sean. Who's Stephen Hawking? From the town?'

'Course you do. But that's not very sexy. That's a bit like how you love family.'

'But I feel like that about Johnny Depp. Imagine something happened to him. I'd be devastated.'

'Give it over to the philosophers.'

'Och, they'll be there hours, yabbering about it. So you haven't been in love, Kay?'

'Maybe.'

'Now she's changing her tune.'

'It's not with Johnny Depp, is it? He's mine.'

Kay laughed. 'I'm not sure. You can feel love for your friends. I feel love for all of you.'

'You must love Manda most, otherwise you wouldn't put up with her.'

Kay said, 'I think sexual love . . .'

Manda mocked it, sucking in her lips toothlessly to repeat and sneer, 'Sexual love . . .'

'. . . starts mixed up with desire. You admire the other person and maybe part of you admires them because you want physical things from them, so by admiring them you're giving yourself permission . . . to let them bonk you. They might not be admirable at all. I think women do that.'

'Interesting.' Ava nodded.

'Then as you become closer to a lover over time, it turns into a familial love, like our parents.'

Manda drawled, 'Kay wants to change universities to philosophy.'

Chell said, 'I agree with Kay. That's all right enough but more cleverly said than I could.'

Manda announced, 'And we must all of loved Orla for how we cried at her funeral.'

'That's right.'

'I thought I'd die when she died,' claimed Manda.

Finn said bluntly, 'I didn't.'

The others looked at her.

'I'm not being cold. Think about it; the minging thing was we were alive and she wasn't. I didn't think I was going to die. I just knew that she had died. And we couldn't be with her ever again. Each breath I took felt more real. I haven't forgotten that. We were all young and that was death coming right up to us.'

'That's true,' Chell nodded. 'I was so sad but part of me was scared for myself. I admit it, cos I'm a scaredy-cat.'

'That's what death does.'

Ava said softly, looking around as if for help, 'It was a cancer that . . . took her, wasn't it? Finn said that to me.'

'Aye,' Chell nodded sombrely. 'What's it? Hodkin's, Hodgkinson's lymphonia or something? Kay? Your dad's a doc?'

Kay smiled. 'You always get it wrong. It's not Hodgkinson or melanoma. My dad told me it was classical Hodgkin's lymphoma. But it was a rare subtype and it was late diagnosed.'

'Oh. Mind the time when Manda says nymphomania!'

'Oh, we shouldn't laugh.'

Chell turned to Ava. 'One of the teachers, no in our school, up at the mixed high school that Catholic girls don't go to, he met Manda in the street on a Saturday and asked her what Orla died of and Manda says, Hodgkin's nymphomania.'

They all laughed, softer, more cautiously than usual, under the green trees.

'I did,' Manda confessed. 'I didn't know what a nymphomania was then but I do now.'

'Aye. You are one. That's your disease.'

Manda said, 'But Orla would have laughed at that.'

All, except Ava, concurred with smart nods. 'Och aye. Sure. She's up there laughing the now.'

Kylah said, 'She'd've cracked her shite laughing.'

Manda commented, 'Know how in Magaluf and that you put your scarf up on your head over your hair? Well, every time I do that myself or see a lassie doing it somewhere, it brings a tear to my eye, cause I think of wee Orr and her scarves after the chemos.'

'That a sweet thing for you to feel, Manda,' Kay actually said.

Manda shrugged. 'Well, of course I do.' She looked vulnerably towards her and said, 'I do have feelings, Kay.'

Kay frowned. 'I know you do.'

Manda said to Kay, 'So. Are you. In love. With Finn a wee bit, Kay?'

Kay pretended to look aghast.

Manda laughed, transitioning between a look of severe inter-rogation then looking oddly content at the response. 'See, she hasn't gone beetroot with a big brasser, but she hasn't answered the question either.'

'Are you then?' Ava asked it.

A silence tightened out among them and Kay held her legs very still, and put out her palms in offering. 'Who couldn't be in love with the Mighty Finn?'

'Thank you, Kay,' Finn barked out, businesslike, and nodded.

Manda said, 'But —'

'Spin the bottle, Kay.' Ava said it and, surprisingly, Manda shut up.

'Spin the bottle.' They all cheered. Kay leaned forward and spun the bottle. It went a little to the side and rolled and its spin brought it back . . . to Kay.

A huge roar went up, so loud a pigeon at the next tree burst and careened through the leaves, its whipping wings thrashing and away. They glanced up.

Kylah cynically mimicked, in a semi-*South Park* voice, 'Kay. Are you in love with Finn?'

'What happens now?

'She gets to go again.'

'No,' said Ava. 'She gets to ask herself a question.'

'Aye. Gets to ask herself a question. That's right.'

'Or set herself a dare?'

'Pee in the moat, Kay,' Manda yelled.

'Kay gets to go again; that's the rules this time.'

'Okay then. Come on, Kay.'

'Okay. I dare myself and Ava to eat all the rest of these strawbs.'

'Ach. Boring.'

Kay leaned forward and spun the bottle again, better this time, but it juddered to a halt on Kylah.

'Hurrah. Kyles with no piles.'

Kay said, 'Okay, Kylah. Truth or dare?'

'Trooooth,' she said in an exasperated tone.

Kay went, 'Okay. Living together with Chell. What really, really drives you potty about her?'

They all murmured again. 'Good one.'

'Great question.' Even Manda was enthused, perceiving the possibility of conflict.

'Well. Where do I start?'

'Get lost. I'm no that bad.'

'Mmmm. Chell. Bras! Bras. Leaves her bras on the couch. Home from work, off comes the bra, her watching telly. Next day the same. Once there were four bras on the couch and down the cushions. You can't take a boy home without worrying about bras everywhere.'

'We haven't taken any boys home. Yet.'

'Aye, that's why no. You'd be trying to snog on the sofa and he'd have one your bras between his teeth. And she can't fill the dishwasher proper.'

Finn said, 'Hey. Yous have a dishwasher?'

'Oh aye.'

'Jesus.' Finn looked at Ava. 'Lap of luxury. Eh, Ava?'

'We're no students, Finn, we're working professionals. All bloody mod cons we have. The town's leaped ahead since you left. And Chell, she puts like three mugs and three teaspoons in the dishwasher and sets it going. That drives me . . . potty for the electric bill.'

'Okay. Very good. Spin the bottle.'

Kylah leaned and spun. It went round the most times yet, and an incremental 'Woooooooo' went up.

'Chell! Oh boy. They're equal now.'

'Truth or dare?'

'Dare. Do a dare, Chell.'

'Nut. Truth.'

Kylah leaned forward and turned to look at Chell.

Chell puffed out her cheeks in anticipation.

Ava said, 'Ask the same question.'

'Aye. Same thing. Let's stir it up in their household a good bit,' Finn shouted, laughing.

'No, no. Eh? Chell. Have you ever let a guy go up your bumhole on the first date?'

Manda screamed, delirious with joy.

'Only joking. Only joking.'

Chell slapped Kylah's bare arm in a reprimand; it cracked stingingly.

'Owwww.'

'I know the answer,' Manda bawled.

'Fuck off. At least not on every date, Manda.'

'Okay, Chell. Same question. Seriously. Same question. What do I do that drives you nuts in the flat?'

'You have that music going in the front room and your bedroom as well, at the same times. Like different musics but the same time. Loud.'

'That's cos I'm tidying up, from room to room. Clearing your bras away.'

'Spin the bottle.'

Chell leaned forward and spun it while Manda warned, 'This is boring.'

The bottle only made half a revolution and pointed immediately at Manda. Another huzzah of commotions went up.

'Dare. I'll do dare and I'll tell you what to dare me. Right? Dare me go over there and pee behind a tree. I'll need to soon enough anyways.'

'Nut. Cos that's no a dare for you. That's normal to you.'

'But it's a challenge cos I don't even need to pee yet.'

The noise and laughs calmed down and Manda leaned forward anxiously on her folded legs.

'A dare? Aye?

'Aye. A gidge yin. A gidge yin.'

Chell said, 'I . . . dare you . . . Manda . . . to . . .'

'Come on?'

'Go back up that hill. To that restaurant pavilions thing that Ava went in. Drink two Guinness and come back.'

Everyone stiffened, their eyes trained on Manda for her reaction.

'Och, Chell . . .'

But Chell turned her wrist to look at her watch. 'And do it all . . . in . . . Mmmmmm. Do it all in ten minutes flat.'

Kylah raised a hand of objection. 'What if there's no Guinness?'

'Beers then. But it must be full-pint beers, like Manda drinks. Men pints.'

'How'll we know she done it?' They went into quick conference.

'Give her Kylah's disposable camera. And she'll have to take a photo.'

They had been waiting for an adverse reaction but this was the bait. By allowing Manda to draw attention to herself up at the pavilions, the challenge became irresistible to her.

Manda leaped to her feet in new animation, her bare legs ringwormed with grass compressions. 'Oh brilliant. Oh brilliant.

Aye. It'll be brilliant. I'll say to them up there, quick, quick, you gadgies. I'm on truth or dare here. Hurry it up. All my mad mates have dared me. The girls have dared me, so's quick. Two pints Guinness quick. It's a *dare*.' She emphasised the word with feverish glee. She horked up a big chortle but went on, 'I'm on a truth or dare, give me beer quick. And I'll ask the barman. Take a photo of me. Bet he's a right bonk. Oh, yous'll really miss yourselves. Right, I'll do it.' She clapped hands.

'Give her the camera, give her the camera.'

'Right, get ready and we'll do it from the second hand at the top. Ten minutes, eh?'

Manda frowned. 'Yous won't run away and hide on me while I'm gone, will yous?'

Kylah says, 'Don't you worry, we'll be here and counting. It'll be amazing if you make it.'

'Aye,' said Manda, taking sporty breaths.

'Here's my disposable. Don't lose it running. It's only got so many photos, so only use two. Don't go wasting them, cos I'm saving them for if we ever get anywhere. I've just used one of us checking in at that first hotel thing and one of your pint of spew last night.'

'Aye, that'll be brilliant but I want a copy.'

'I want a copy too.'

Kylah turned a dark, angry face on the entire party. 'I can't believe I'm the only one took a camera. Bloody hell.'

Chell had been museful. 'How'll we know if it's no two photos of just the same pint of Guinness?' she wisely aired.

'I won't cheat. And I'm thirsty.'

'That's a good point. Right, you have to have one pint lager and one Guinness.'

Manda shrugged casually. 'That's easier to down; a lager. Do I have to pay for it?' she tentatively added.

'Chell and me'll pay; get a fiver, give her a fiver, Chell. I owe you anyway for no asking just your usual truth-and-dare sex-with-boys questions.'

Chell dived for her purse.

'Righty-ho.'

'Ready?'

'I'm ready.'

'No, wait. I missed last time. Wait till my second hand gets exact to the top. It's seven minutes to now, so you've till three minutes past. Exact. To get back to this tree and touch it. Okay?'

'Okay?'

Manda seemed anxious now. 'What if someone'll no understand me or that?' Then she stiffened her resolve. 'Ach, I can take a photo of myself.'

'Aye.'

'No cheating.'

'Ten, nine, eight . . .'

'Seven, six, five, four, three, two, one. GO!'

Manda took off suddenly at a speed which surprised all of them; with utter conviction, her feet stamping down heavily onto the rubbery turf.

'Go, Mands!'

'You mental case.'

'See your knickers.'

'You're brilliant, Mands.'

They shouted encouragements and taunts then their voices died out and they began laughing at Manda's odd figure, her head held down, moving out against a green flank of sloped English meadow, her deceptively powerful legs forcing her upwards. After a few more moments, Finn started to slumber into chronic laughter that became so afflicting, she let her legs lower and she crumbled to the ground, but lifting her head twice, to watch the now distant figure receding.

Smiling, the others glanced at Finn's collapse as well as the distant figure.

'Chell. You are so brilliant.'

'That was the best ever, Chell. What a stroke of fucking gumption that was.'

Kay yelled, 'We're free. We're free.'

'For ten minutes at least. Five quid to get rid of her for ten minutes.'

'Fifty pence a minute. Money well spent at last,' said Finn.

'If she gets a taste for the Guinness she'll be gone an hour.'

'She'll be an hour even if she doesn't. There's no ways she can make it up that hill.

They all took breaths and began sitting back down.

Finn threw herself from sitting-up position, backwards on the grass, so her hair slapped out, a sudden black slick upon the green, and as she lay there, she said, 'Oh. The peace that surpasseth all knowledge. She's gone.'

Kay smiled down at Finn's figure, adoringly; a complex frame of twig shadows shifted on Finn's pale, bared legs.

'Thing is, Chell, I think she'll bloody well do it,' Kay warned, and turned away from looking at Finn.

'She'll have a heart attack.'

'She'll give someone else a heart attack with those tits going up and down. Did yous see the other folk staring at her?'

'Aye. She'll have gravity on her side on the way home, girls.'

2

A rare lethargy had overcome them, the country minutes elongating out as perfect boredom, and none of the young women moved in the dowless afternoon.

Finn sat with Ava and nodded over to the prone figures, smiling once.

'That wine's made me sleepy, but I can't nap during the day with contact lenses in,' Kylah quietly informed them, lying back under the great tree, shadows shuffling over her figure among milk saucers of fallen sunlight.

Distant human voices called for straying children and the children themselves called meaninglessly into the huge airs around them.

A light aircraft moved over, changed direction above the castle itself and sped away. A huge, vengeful ennui fell over the landscape and another vast cloud's shadow raced up the fairway. The leaves lifted once more above them then settled.

'I'm bloody knackered, I could have a right wee nap,' Chell groaned.

'It's the nervous energy of being around Manda,' Kylah said.

Kay turned her head on her shoulder, looking up at the distant brae slope.

All heads turned. Chell looked at her watch. 'Wow. Three minutes-ish more.'

'She's sunk. Should have set a forfeit if she lost. Suicide.'

'Hush, Finn,' Ava said.

When they stood, they were all checking their clothes for marks, casually reaching out at one another to brush dried grass spindles off.

Up on the fringe of the bank where it met the horizon, layers of cumulonimbus were banking up in accumulative ledges over the Kent meadows and against them an indistinct figure materialised.

'I don't actually believe it.'

They all turned.

Chell flicked her wrist and nodded at her watch. 'A minute left still.'

Manda was racing downhill in a flat-footed motion, coming closer. There was something odd about her stance and only then did they make out what the stance signified. Thrust out before her, almost at full arm-straightened length, a black dot bobbed: Amanda Tassy was carrying a pint of Guinness in her downhill flight.

'That cheating besom's carrying her pint.'

Kay snapped defensively, 'There was nothing in the rules said she couldn't.'

'In fairness, that's right enough.'

'She must be sloshing gallons out, which is not drinking it all.'

Finn blew out air. 'Manda? I doubt she's spilled a drop.'

As the figure moved onto the mown grass of the fairway, her pace slackened only slightly and the pint went towards the face in a very familiar manner. She was taking gulps while in swift motion. Then the arm went out at full length in front and she was close enough to distinguish her shorter blonde hair, bouncing.

'That's a remarkable sight,' Ava nodded, her shoulders starting to vibrate. 'She is just . . . amazing.'

'We've got to hand it to her. How's the time?' Finn asked.

'Forty-five seconds,' Chell shouted.

'Come on, you dafty!'

'Come on, Manda!' screamed Kay.

They were all on their feet, prancing up and down, waving her in with urgent hands.

Manda detoured towards the carpeted picnickers. She altered course slightly to avoid them, and as she passed, one of the teenage boys of the party, seated with his back to her, actually flinched in alarmed recoil when Manda battered across the very edge of their carpeting and she yelled, 'Out the way!'

Manda's new course took her directly towards the target tree. She was unseeing of her enthusiastic audience, only the tree was within her attention. They could hear her feet now, hissing across mown grass, could see roughly a quarter quantity in the plastic pint container, so beloved of student unions and concert venues.

'Twenty-five seconds.'

Manda's face was wild with panic and determination, the downhill momentum gave it a crazier edge than was normal. As the others still urged her on, Manda entered the border of shade, and the midst of their noise, put her other hand out and stopped dead as her palm impacted the tree. She'd hit it a little fast and she turned round on the impact, stumbled, rocked unsteadily stepping backwards. Not spilling a drop she straightened, lifted the pint to her lips and began gulping.

'Ten, nine, eight . . .' Chell called out for everyone's benefit.

But Manda sloughed the beer draught in one sliding tip, holding the plastic pint near vertical for a few seconds longer to drain off the possibly controversial dregs of Guinness into nothingness; only some Rorschach mosaics of dried foam adhered to the inner sides. Manda tossed the plastic pint container aside into the grass.

'Seven, six, five —'

'Finished.'

Manda allowed herself to fall helplessly backwards on the grass — arms splayed out. As a group, all five girls now threw themselves forward. The girls fell upon Manda, placing their chins upon her torso, their hands upon her, as if she were a shamanic being. Finn kneeled at the crown of Manda's head and she grabbed her hair and the back of her head in both hands, cradling it and lifting her head slightly, and though upside down, Finn bent right over and anointed Manda's forehead with a kiss. Chell had shoved her head in under Manda's vibrating chin and threw her other arm across the bosom, embracing her. Without self-consciousness, Kay had lain two palms on a thigh in congratulation. She noticed Manda's mottled skin was slick with perspiration.

'Manda, you looked so brilliant coming down the hill like that!'

'You got my camera?'

Manda smacked her upper thigh where, sure enough, the camera was a snugged, tight lump in the skirt pocket.

Ava kneeled on the other side, using both her hands as an inadequate fan to disturb air upon her.

'Get offof me. Lezzers,' Manda breathed and just stared directly upwards, at the leaves of the tree above, her chest hurtling up and down, the cleavage in her low-cut top varnished in sweat, the corners of her eyes smiling, but the mouth sucked air, until it wheezed, 'Fuck me. I'm dying for a cigarette,' and this set up another symphony of exclamations. Cooried at her neck, Chell produced a cigarette pack, her head still rested on the shoulder as she lit a Marlboro Light in her own mouth and tenderly directed it towards Manda's lips. Instinctively, Manda raised her arm and two ringed, stubby fingers took the filter and placed it gently in the corner of her mouth. Her whole face had broken out in active sweat now. 'Did I do it? Did I do it?'

'Course you did.'

'You're a hero, Mands.'

'I'm telling yous. Everyone was watching me. I was a classic. Must have been a thousand people or something watching me.'

'Aye.'

'What's been going on here then?' Manda moved her head from side to side. With a deathbed croak she still managed, 'You fucking lesbos. Oh God. I'm dying.'

'You did it though.'

'Aye. Right enough. Spin the fucking bottle again then, it's someone else's turn.'

Everyone laughed.

'Am I a VIP?'

'Course you are!'

202

'It's bloody clouding over a bit,' Finn said.

'Good.'

They silently watched the picnickers roll up their carpets. The two teenage boys carried the large one drooped betwixt them. The mature woman carried a small carpet rolled under one arm, the traditional picnic hamper of woven wicker in her other hand. The figures moved slowly off up the hill. Manda gave them an insolent and deeply unacknowledged high wave.

'We'd actually better get a move on or things might close.'

The shade line had disappeared and the sky was more cloudy now. It was cooler. Side by side, in a line, the six young women walked further down the hill towards the castle. There was another large crescent of mature trees to pass through then the castle was straight ahead of them, very close.

The castle was surrounded by a wide gravel way and a bridge over the moat which gave access through the gatehouse and portcullis. At the rear a caponier connected to the mass of out-houses and the fake Tudor village. As they drew onto the crunching gravel, the others slowed but Manda kept moving ahead.

'Look,' Chell tittered, 'there's actual lifebelts for folk like Manda who fall in the bloody moat.'

Oddly, Manda didn't bestow her constant, contemptuous once-over, up-and-down scrutiny on other afternoon strollers and tourists with cameras who passed very close to her. One couple even had to halt their progress to give way to her imper-ious passage. Almost at the moat edge, Manda stopped. Slightly behind, the others caught up.

'What is it?' asked Kylah.

Manda was looking up, at the side of Hever Castle, at the small windows, at the edging of the restored and perfectly main-tained twentieth-century roofing, its serious, pure-leaded guttering to stop staining on the stonework: fine limestone and the gentle colouring of the flint inlay. Manda looked at the flower beds and topiaries on the far edging of the moat, even at the base of the castle walls – areas that could only be accessed by gardeners in boats. Some of the small diamond-framed open windows were canted out daintily and the shoulders of circulating tourist figures could be briefly glimpsed moving within the building. Something in the moat gurgled pleasingly in the cinnamon waters which were slicked with long-legged flies and water-lily roundels.

Manda suddenly turned on Kay accusingly. 'One family lived in all this Disneyland to themselves?'

'Yes. Well, it said so on the Internet. One guy lived in it. I think he owned *The Times* newspaper and his father gave him this place. Before him they didn't live in it all the year round.'

'What do you mean? No all the time?'

'It was a holiday home for them, I think. You'll need to buy a guidebook.' She laughed.

'A holiday home. Like a cottage up our way? This wasn't their all-time house? Jesus. And theys're gone now?'

Kay said, 'The Astors were very wealthy. Maybe the richest in the world once. I think one of them went down on the *Titanic*.'

'He did. John Jacob Astor,' Ava nodded. 'But he might have been part of another family branch. There were a lot of them.'

Kylah piped up, 'Hey! That's right enough now. Isn't he one of the guys when Leo goes to the posh dinner? He was quite nice to Leo though. Friendly. Not like crazy Billy Zane.'

Manda had been nodding – strangely quiet. She said, 'When I look at this, I'm scared cos you see it real, how rich they was. And in your mind you can imagine being stood outside, like now. Their house, and them shut up in it and you out here cos you're just ordinary. It's pushing down on me how rich they really was compared to me and my dad. And how rich, rich is, is scary. I can't believe folk could have all this and no one else allowed, cos it'd been all private with them gamekeepers and the old butlers and that and I guess, you know? They would be doing the big parties like my twenty-first but bigger – ones that last all night long – and think of the servants they had. I've never seen richness like this and when you just see it. Fuck. I thought I admired, you know, rich and that. Spice Girls and David Beckham. If you earned your money and worked hard. But I'd never really thought of what rich is. They only thing I feel sorry for them is they might have had their own maze but they didn't have good mobile phones. Imagine how awful that'd be.'

Finn nodded. 'I know what you mean.'

'About the mobbies?'

'Naw. About the rich. You look at that and you know they had real power. Like the kings of old but the power is money.'

'Aye. That's it. That's what it is. It's the power they must have had. That's what's scary. Like if they were against you, God help you. If they had all this.'

'You're right, Manda. I agree with you.'

'It's so much. There's rich and that. But. It's so much all this. I mean. Well, I hope they appreciated it.'

Chell said, 'Sure they did. They're no stupid. They would probably be running round and round this moat, screaming for joy every night.'

Finn added, 'But it's all relative, isn't it? Before I go condemning them? If you grow up with this you're like a fish in water.'

'How d'you mean relative? All in rich families?'

'Naw. Well, look us last night. Thanks to Kay and Ava's credit cards. I was snugged up in a posh hotel at the airport and there are homeless people on the streets of London who I see every day – a wee ginger Scottish guy at Holborn who calls me "doll" that I talk to, and bought coffee for once, before Christmas when it was freezing. I wasn't over-thinking about him myself last night, was I? With my mitt on the remote control? Compared to him I'm in unimaginable riches. Maybe if I was whacked up in this castle, dressed in silk, a good-looking gamekeeper sneaking up to my room, I'd be the same. Selfish and complacent.'

'What's complay what . . . ?'

'Not giving a fuck about anyone else cos you're okay.'

Manda turned to Ava. 'You're rich, Ava, but no this rich. Are you?' She jerked her head at the castle and twisted her lip.

'Well, no. Not this rich.' She chuckled. 'I mean, we have a lovely home and a holiday place in France and investments but my father still works. I was at school with girls whose parents didn't even work. Anyway. Very few can afford these big castles any more. Even the hereditary ones. The upkeep, you know, heating it and everything.'

'The Spice Girls could.'

'Not this.'

'Could even Spice Girls not afford this?'

Ava grinned wryly. 'No.'

'Richard Branson could afford it easy. He has a whole island some place.'

'Telling yous this as well,' said Manda, with a scathing look at Kylah. 'No ways could any of Hear'Say afford this.' She shook her head dismissively.

'I never said they could,' Kylah snapped back.

'Do you have servants, Ava?'

She laughed. 'Noooo. Mummy does everything, and in the garden. She looks a right hippy, out in her dungarees with her hair.'

The girls all looked at Ava, not without slight disappointment at the failure of her family to employ the necessary help for their acres.

'C'mon. Let's nose around.'

They began to stroll towards the ornamental gardens.

'Would you like a cigarette, Ava?' Chell offered.

'Yes please.'

Chell lifted the lighter graciously for her and Ava mumbled thanks then she smoked, looking down at the cigarette as if it was a new conundrum.

'All right?'

'I used to smoke tons but I sort of quit but I used to smoke the reds. The long hundreds. But these are pleasant.'

Finn, Kylah, Kay and Manda – who was still laying off, sweeping her arm around in a revolutionary condemnation of the topiary – had drawn on ahead, but down to Chell and Ava's right were stairs and a large sunken garden area.

'It looks nice down here,' Chell said.

'Shall both of us go?'

'Hoi! Yous,' Chell shouted.

The four girls up the path stopped and turned their heads.

'We's are going down here for a dander.'

'Okay, we'll catch up.'

'No lezzing,' Manda barked.

Chell and Ava moved off towards the sunken porticos of the ornamental garden. The lake lay beyond.

Chell and Ava walked side by side for a few moments without talking as they descended the stairway. There were few people about and they strolled ahead across grass, beside the ordered verges of the flower beds.

'Manda's a cheeky cow,' Chell whispered, then in a louder voice, 'Aye. Marlboro Reds. Wow. They're strong, Ava. We all smoke the Lights. Also, I know fine we all smoke the same cigarette so's we can nick one another's when we're short.'

Ava smiled. 'Practical.' They walked onward.

'Manda went through a phase of Lambert & Butler.'

Ava said, 'Lambert & Butler Yeats.'

Chell looked at her with a blank smile and then added, 'We noticed one pack was doing her on two nights out, cos she was offering them round and no one was taking and then she was no smoking a single one herself but taking ours when we offered round. Lambert & Butler. Yeuch. She's a fly besom at times. Minute we pulled her up on it she was back on the old Marlboro Lights.'

'Manda's okay. It's like dealing with a cat.'

Chell nodded. 'That's true, aye. She is like a cat.'

'That was nice story you told in the car. About –' and she held up her own burning cigarette '– lowering cigarettes and notes on the string.'

'Aye,' Chell chuckled.

'Being an only child, you know. I missed out on that kind of thing. Which is to do with how I've turned out. I'm a bit of a loner. I'm spoiled.'

'I don't think you seem spoiled at all.'

'Oh but I am. I love my own space.'

'Is it good sharing with Finn in London? She's nice Finn, eh? She's laid-back.'

'Finn's great to share with. She is laid-back and independent and trustworthy.'

'Aye. She's aye been like that since she was little. Like, she's a strong independent woman type. That'll be why yous two'll get on. You're sort of strong loner types. If you don't mind me saying?'

'No. Not at all. I think you're correct.'

'Like, I mind her in primary playground; Finn playing wee games all by herself, nattering away to herself, and it makes sense she's doing your philosophy stuff. You know: thinking great notions. She was always looking up in the sky, thinking away to herself all her life. Like Kylah was aye singing, and Manda was getting on people's nerves sort of thing. And I was just fretting about stuff.'

'I was quite nervous coming on this holiday. I've never been on a girls-in-a-gang holiday. Boarding school put me off gaggles of girls. Actually I've been on holiday with more gangs of blokes than girls.' Idly, Ava said, 'Kylah's nice. You share together, don't you?'

'Aye. She's amazing. Wait till you hear her sing. She's not show-offy. She's shy; writing songs on her wee piano keyboardy thing. She's got all the music gadgets and she sits there with the headphone on. Ava.'

Ava jumped.

'She's actually writing songs and you wouldn't believe it. I was coming in the house one day and there was music on the radio and it was just brilliant and then I realised it wasn't the radio. It was a song Kylah'd made and sung, playing on the stereo, and I swear it sounded like a real Top Forty song. She's amazing . . . I says to her, get out of this town and to music school, but she willna listen to me nor nobody. She's stubborn as a pony.'

'You'd miss her if she left?'

'Oh aye.'

'And Manda?'

'Manda's stuck in the town, but her sister's ambitious and got the business and Manda is happy to be in the town. Me and Kyles is more unsettled. Insecure.'

Ava stated, 'I believe you find the things you want in life when you're not looking for them.'

'Do you?'

'Yes. You have to not try too hard and then you'll find them or they'll find you. It's like trying to remember a word that's on the tip of your tongue. Sometimes you just can't, then if you stop thinking about it, it pops into your head an hour later.'

'Do you think it's like that for finding guys too?'

'Yes I do.'

Chell looked across at her. 'Have you had a few boyfriends, Ava?'

'A few, yes. An older guy once. I love it when you make a connection with a bloke. You can talk all night and you want him to say, "I love this and this about you and I think this and this and I hate this and this about you." But that's a struggle. Blokes won't talk about feelings. Sometimes you want him to define you. You want your relationship to tell you things about yourself and then you find you're only learning things about him, not yourself. Then you see the whole relationship's about him. Men are tough-minded and selfish these days. And sometimes the nice ones . . . you don't fancy them. So they become friends but with awful crushes on you and this spoils it. And with good-looking guys, they all think they're God's gift. You must fight them down and tame them and I'm just not sure I've the energy for all that any more. I like men to come ready-assembled. No work necessary. But I'm not in a position to demand it as I'm something of a mess myself.'

'You're no a mess.'

'Oh, I am really. So I go for the flawed blokes and two wrongs never make a right. So far.'

Chell and Ava had come down to the old lakeside boating area. It was oddly deserted, not a soul there, on the elegant curve of stone jetty, inset with pink pebbles polished smooth. There was a splendid stillness, heavy with absence. Behind them was the colonnaded shelter, the still, grey-green obscurity of the lake laying out flat before them. Possessing its own sluggish permanence. The lake was so large its distant edges were vague, the overall shape of the water mass only hazily defined by buff discs of young and middle-aged trees on far banks.

Drawn to the long sightlines and that sublime space, suspended hugely over the water, Ava and Chell placed their feet on the very edge of the steps' curvature. The first step was two inches above the water, bending round on either side of them with a perfect, flush conformity, the surface like a glaze affixed along its edging. As they looked down, the first four inches of water were clear enough to see the porridge of silt lying undisturbed on the submerged step – the step below was absolutely invisible.

These long curving steps had been clearly designed for boarding into and alighting from small fleets of pleasurable rowboats while wearing elegant clothes.

Ava said, 'Just imagine it.'

'What?

'Maybe I've read too many Henry James's, but I bet you that after partying all night at the castle and in the Tudor village, house guests, young ladies in their dresses and their beaus, came down here. Not at night, but always at dawn, as the sun was coming up. They'd all be tired.' Ava moved her arm across the vista of the false lake. 'The water and the sky would be white. Mist in the trees. A bird or two calling. I bet you there wasn't just three or four boats. I bet you Old Man Astor had a fleet of ten or twenty boats on call, with rowers for the older people, but for younger house guests, the men would row themselves with a girl sat snug in the seat. All her skirts piled up at her shoes. Skirts of silk. All handmade up in London. And they'd row out onto this, calling to each other. But the calls would become less and less, and eventually all the boats would just be floating apart out there, the oars lifted. The odd champagne cork popping but maybe the sound not reaching the other boats.'

'Oh God. How beautiful. I can just see it the way you're saying it, all so nice.'

'The posh English are mad for a rowboat. Like when I was at Oxford, punting.'

'Punting. What's that?'

'It's sort of a third-rate Venice in Oxford, and the student guys are mad for getting girls in these small boats and they push them along the river with a big pole. Punting it's called and it's silly. All these Hooray Henrys, and you're forever there, pretending you're having a gay and jolly time, flat out in a smelly canoe, ducking your hat for bridges and waiting in terror for the hand sliding up your leg. It seems to drive men mad, getting a girl trapped in a boat and then lunging at her. Groped or drowned. They're your choices. They know we love our clothes too much to dive for freedom. Have you never been in a boat with some guy?'

Chell nodded definitely. 'I once gave a guy a handjob out on the deck of the ferry to Lochboisdale.'

'Oh.'

'Sorry. I've mucked up the atmosphere now, haven't I? I'm sorry.'

Ava was silent.

Chell added, 'It was night-time. The wind was howling like fuck, I was terrified, the boat was going up and down, felt seasick, so I tried to do it double-quick, looking out over the white horses that was getting their tops tore off soaking us and I got a cramp and finally got some on my jeans. And ma hair was ruined. Och. I'll shut up now. Just you do the nice talking.'

But Ava laughed loudly and the laughter echoed out, back from the portico behind them, but it immediately fell dead just feet out, across the still water. The falling death of that laughter startled them both and they became silent and looked at each other.

Ava coughed and said quietly, 'Well, that is just the same as punting in Oxford, Chell, just more . . . Scottish.'

They both chuckled.

Chell frowned again. 'Hey, Ava? Do you think any boats couped over out there in the water . . . and the lassies drowned, arms held up in their big dresses?'

'I don't know.'

Chell said, 'I've seen ghosts – I think – and read the tarot and that but I've never screwed with the Ouija board. You don't mess with that. It's just. My stepdad was drowned off a fishing boat and they never found his body.'

Ava stiffened up. 'Oh, I'm sorry.'

'No. No. It doesn't bother me so much.'

'I'm an insensitive idiot, because Finn actually told me some of this when we were in first year and I must have forgotten. I'm sorry. Pardon me.'

'It doesn't matter, Ava. Really. It's not like a no-go thing for me to talk about. Far from it. I'm more, sort of haunted.'

'Haunted. Yes you are, a little.'

'I was at primary school when that happened but I still mind it well, so poor Mum lost a father to me then she lost the man she loved so she's kind of a nervous wreck too.'

'That's so, so awful. So awful,' Ava repeated.

'I sense spirits though and I can tell things about people.'

'Yes. I felt that about you. I just sensed it off you.'

'It's probably . . . it's probably just rubbish.'

'I don't think so.'

'I didn't think you'd be into all that stuff. You being sort of scientific-thinking. But when I was young after Daddy Patrick was lost I used to have horrid nightmares. Pale faces in the sea. I don't like boats at sea and that. Not really here. It's just a big pond.' She chuckled and threw out a hand. 'But I don't like the sea and big boats.' She looked at her feet. 'I always think I'll see the shape. The black shape of Daddy coming on a wave. If I look at the water long enough, I can make myself see something, but it's usual like, the sun, sliding along the top of the water. But I do see him there. They say death walks behind you but it floats too. And you can't escape the sea. Take me anywhere. Benidorms, America or the Caribbean places or that. If there's sea, I'll be smoking my fags squinting out waiting for. Oh . . .' She shivered.

Ava put a sudden arm round Chell's shoulders. 'Want to sit down where the posh girls sat? And have a cigarette together?'

'Aye. Where the posh girls sat.'

They crossed in under the curved and covered portico, Chell put down her vanity case which scraped on the pebbled ground and they aimed for the stone bench there, but just as they turned to lower their rears upon the cool stone, Chell flashed out an arm and said, quietly, almost a whisper under the echo of roof tiles, 'And they had all cushions along this.'

Ava nodded and whispered, 'Yes.'

'They'd had all lacy bright cushions all along this.'

It was a long bench, forty yards of moulded curved stone slabs, and both girls looked along it cautiously in both directions.

Chell went, 'And not just cushions, there was a made cushion here, so it wasn't hard against your back, a long . . . blue cushion was here that stretched all the way along, tied with ribbon, and it hadn't been out all night so it wasn't damp from the dew at dawn. It was put out by the servants just before they all came down boating here.'

'Yes.'

Chell produced the Marlboro pack with the lighter inside. There was a silence; both of them quickly fumbled for the cigarettes. Chell lit hers then cupped her hand to Ava who leaned forward and caught the flame on the tip. They both blew out smoke. 'And a girl was here who had . . . something big going on. Maybe in love with a husband of another lady.'

'And did they go out on a boat?'

'Sure they did.'

'And what happened?'

'She put something overboard in the lake, a ring or a locket or something, I don't know what. She did it for a reason. To mean something. Something started or something finished.'

There was a pause. Chell was looking out at the dead water.

Ava said, 'All those people will be most likely dead now. This must have been before the war and they would have been in their twenties at least.'

Chell nodded authoritatively. 'No. She might have been younger, twenty even but married to another. Or even pregnant.'

'So they went out in the boat and she put something in the water?'

'Aye. She dropped something in the water without telling the man, something that moved quick to the bottom, and it's out

213

there. Out there right now, still in the mud, and you could spend your life looking for it but it wouldn't be found. Oh.'

'What is it?' Ava asked, excited.

'This is starting to sound like *Titanic*.'

Ava laughed loudly.

'The girls try to get me to watch it every year, the insensitive besoms. I grin and bear it once or twice but give us a break!'

They both laughed.

Chell said, 'Sometimes I really don't know if I'm making it all up. If it's imagination or a real thing.'

Ava said, quietly and shy-seeming, 'Do you know, do you know if they touched on the boat? Were they doomed lovers? Doomed is sexy.'

'Touched?'

'Where they shouldn't have?'

'Men in boats.'

'So that's a yes. Maybe they did everything in those boats?' Ava suggested.

'Oh no. Those huge noisy dresses. The water's so smooth, the ripples would show.'

They both laughed and Ava said, 'That does make sense.'

Chell said, 'But they're laughing and joking here. These people had everything going for them but were just like everyone else, they knew fine you have to grab at life. But sometimes, life won't let itself get grabbed or you do a lot of damage because you're scared of having regrets. You're more scared of not doing something and missing out than you are of doing it.'

'That's true.'

'People thought they had everything, but down here at dawn with girls in the white dresses, they realised there's things you can't have. Men want everything and these were men who had loads but maybe on a quiet water like this, out floating there, they felt they were just like everyone else for a minute; they couldn't have everything. A hollow boat sinks the same for everyone.'

Ava nodded.

Suddenly an odd thing happened. Chell leaned over towards

Ava's ear, her lips almost touching the flesh of the lobe, and quite harshly she said, 'Ava. You're confident but look after yourself.'

And now Ava nodded, maybe a little paler, and looked at the stone ground.

They both lit cigarettes again after a long silence. Chell said, in a softer voice, 'And all the men smoked but not the lassies, so we'll make up for that.'

Ava laughed, that understanding laugh again, and it came back down from the roof.

'I did talk about it with a lady doctor. Once. When I was depressed, cos I was like . . . creepy.'

'What?'

'I was hanging around, when I was fifteen and that, hanging around all the shores on my own, looking out at sea. You know, going a bit potty. We all do at that age. I'd lie to people I was going places but really I'd be down by the wee lighthouse or on the black shingle, watching.'

'Oh. That's giving me the goose bumps. Look.' Ava held out her arm. It was shadowed with many erect pores. Chell put her fag in her mouth and with two hands took and rubbed the arm with both hands until the skin was abrased.

'Och, I'm sorry. I'm scumming you out,' she mumbled. 'Like there's no widows' walk in the town, though there's a pub called that. I won't go in it though. Drives Manda mad.'

'Sorry? What's a widows' walk?'

'That's where in the olden times before they had radio on boats, the wives of the fishermen would stand up on a platform on the roof of a high building that gave the best view of the fishing boats returning back in and if a boat was late, the wives would stand up there on it waiting and waiting and sometimes a boat would come in a day late, or two in the olden days, and it would be bad weather but the women would be up there, waiting till the boat came back. Or didn't.'

'Was the whole boat lost with your stepdad? Others too?'

'No. Thankfully. He went over in a big wave off the deck and that was that. But it's like. My mum's been out on the widows' walk every day of her life, since. The sea off Scotland isn't the same as in other places of the world. Like if you go to Benidorm or the Greek islands, it's another sea on maps, isn't it?'

'Yes.'

'But that won't stop me. Like here. Okay. It's just a big duck pond.'

'Oh Chell, don't say that. Old Astor will be hurt. It cost him so much to make it.'

'Aye.' Chell looked up. 'Sorry, Mister Astor. Sir.'

Ava laughed.

They sat in silence a while.

Ava said, 'The Greeks or the Romans used to think all the seas were connected by subterranean tunnels. That someone could fall in a fountain in Rome and come out in another place.'

'Never?'

'They did. I read it.'

'Wow. Cos I think this. That Patrick could be anywhere. Or his bones and bits. Or his spirit.' She gave a ridiculous but nervous look out across the water.

Ava suddenly dropped her cigarette and stubbed it under a trainer. 'Give me your hands.'

Chell dropped her cigarette and gave Ava her hands. Ava took them and held them, looked at Chell and said, 'But not here. There's no subterranean tunnel into this place. Men dug it, not the gods. So on this water, your stepdad is at peace. His spirit isn't in this place.'

Chell nodded and smiled enthusiastically.

'But is someone else?' Ava suddenly asked.

Chell frowned and still massaging her hands into Ava's she looked out at the lake. 'I can't see through the water. People drowning in these lakes is something that happens on telly programmes. On just films.'

'Maybe.'

'I think this is a good place.'

'Do you?'

Chell said, 'There were bottles chinking and people laughing.

The worst that happened here . . . is that some randy wee bitch got her stockings wet getting out the boat.'

They both laughed loudly.

Manda, Kay, Finn and Kylah had descended the steps into the huge sunken arena of the patio and approached the porticos of the boat jetty. It was Manda who turned to Finn and sneered, 'We've come upon a tender moment, Finn. Chell's closing in on your bird.'

They were looking hard to their right and they saw Chell and Ava, sitting alone on the long curved bench. Very clearly, Chell had her hands locked up in her lap with Ava's in hers.

Finn returned a look at Manda, head slightly tilted, in a weary rebuff.

However, Ava spotted the group just then and Chell's head turned too and smiled, the comradely hands didn't even shift, laying in the lap.

As they came up to them, Finn laughed, plonked herself down next to Chell.

Ava said, 'Chell was telling me all about her poor stepfather.'

Finn nodded acceptingly.

The hands remained entwined. Then slowly separated as everyone started offering cigarettes round.

Finn seemed perfectly cheery. 'Nice here, eh? Perfect spot for a party at night.'

'We were just imagining it in the old days. Boating parties and stuff.'

'Aye. I bet there was plenty of those.'

Kylah tipped her jingly bangles to look at her watch. 'Let's let wagons roll.'

Ava lit a cigarette and she quickly stood up and stepped out from beneath the roof. She squinted up into the sky where the cloud was bright. She realised how shaded it was in the portico so she unhooked her sunglasses that were hanging on the neckline of her pretty dress, and put them on.

Manda's brow furrowed as she formed the snide put-down in her head. 'See you're smoking, Ava. There had best be plenty cigarettes in yon duty-free shops when we get going tomorrow to – wherever brilliant place we get going to.'

Finn, sitting on the stone bench, stooped far forward smoking and looking out to the lake.

'Can you swim in this muck?' asked Kylah, squidging up her nose.

'There's a big No Swim sign there, Kyles.'

'No ways should you swim in that,' Chell claimed.

'Maybe we should get a sprint on,' said Finn.

Ava was smoking noticeably deep, sucking the smoke in and blowing it out, her slightly flat, perfectly featured face held up as if she didn't want to get smoke on her dress. 'Your accent has gone all Scots again,' she observed.

'Well, that's cos I'm Scottish,' Finn said testily. They began moving away out from the portico and back across the vast sunken lawn.

'You look like bloody medics with your vanity cases, girls,' called Finn.

Kay walked out ahead of the group then sometimes stood patiently, smiling, allowing them to catch up. The computer bag still hung at her side. Her calfskin bag on the other.

'Poor Kay hoiking that round with her all day.'

'Ach, she's used to it.' Manda nodded.

They marched on slowly all the way to the maze entrance. A man was standing there. 'Ladies.' He bowed, courteous but somehow familiarly authoritarian. He looked at the sky and then dropped his gaze straight to his watch.

Chell's small voice came, 'Is it easy to get lost forever in there, mister?'

The man replied, amiable, with a countrified local accent, 'Oh no, no. Don't you worry. It only takes minutes to get out. Three minutes or so from the middle is the record.' He chuckled. 'You must go to the stone marker in the centre. Find that first and then start back from there. We had a party of blind chaps in there once, and they made it out. Quick. Clever fellows. Judged it by listening to the voices from outside as to how close they were to the perimeter bushes. Seeing folk would have no advantage now, would they? Hear a pin drop those fellows. All with one hand on the shoulder of the other, like those soldiers in the trenches who'd been gassed.'

Ava nodded.

'Eh?' went Manda.

'Don't worry.' Kylah held up her metallic vanity case. 'I've got a good pair of nail scissors in here. We'll cut our way out.'

They made an excited lunge for the opening in the hedgerow, but the man held up his hand and halted them once again.

'Have you visited the castle or have you just come to the grounds for today?'

'Do we have to visit the castle?'

'No, dear. Just to say. You're the last to go in the maze. I don't think anyone else is inside and the castle closes at five prompt, the gardens themselves close at six so you won't have time to visit the castle.'

'Okay then.' They bundled in under the grown lintel as if it were an emergency exit and they entered into the yew-hedge maze. They immediately bunched up against each other in the first corridor, the foliage close on each side of them. It was oddly gloomy in there and suddenly damp-feeling. Manda had blocked the way, and began rostering them. 'Right. Right, listen. I go first. Kay, you follow me? Then Kylah, then –'

'Manda. Hoi, Manda. This is just the way in. It doesn't matter. It's when you're in the middle and the way back out what counts. Finding your way back out is what a maze is for.'

Manda gave Finn a look. 'I know what a maze is for, Finn. They dinna just teach that in philosophy.'

Chell said, 'It's thick tree stuff, isn't it? You can't see through it to the other side, even from here.'

Manda continued, 'Right. It's me. Then it's Kay, then Kylah then Chell then Ava then Finn. Follow me.' Manda moved on down the corridor in an odd, small-stepping walk. Kay moved trudgingly behind, holding the computer flush to her side,

Kylah followed. Resigned to her doom behind, came Chell, then Ava and Finn.

'Wow. Ava,' Chell yelped hopefully, 'you can near see over the hedge tops. You should of brought those espadrilles you wore last night. They make you so tall you could see all the way over.'

'What espadrilles?' Manda barked back from the head of the line.

'I put them on after you were sick last night.'

'Oh aye? Dressing up after you got shot of me, were you?'

There was a beat of polite pause. 'Actually, they were just handy at the top of my backpack,' Ava said as they walked on, turning a right-angled corner.

'Oh. Were they?'

'Yes,' Ava called back in an insistent voice that was haughtier than usual. In fact it was a tone she hadn't used among them before. Manda probably didn't heed it, but the others did. 'If you must know, I got your sickness on the shoes I was wearing, so I walked back to the bar in bare feet and put on the espadrilles in the bar. Thank you very much.'

Manda fell into brief silence, sensing something.

At the bottom of the corridor was a hard left which turned into a long, long curve of hedging, circumscribing a semicircle.

Chell tried to help out and called, 'Hi, Kylah. You took enough. Leave a trail of condoms behind us so we'll find our way back out.'

'Like a Hansel and Gretel, for the promiscuous age,' Kay murmured.

But Manda snorted from the front. 'Nay chance, girls; all the dirty hoors behind us is bound to pick them up, and your trail will be lost.'

They now had advanced up a small corridor – their line had drawn out longer with gaps between each of them. Ava saw Manda's shoulder turn another corner. Immediately Ava shot out one hand to grab – quite hard – at Chell's arm and stop her. Ava put a finger to her lips and jerked her head backwards. In last place, Finn was forced to halt. Kylah disappeared round the corner ahead. Ava whispered, 'Come on. Let's scarper for a scream.' Finn nodded immediately, turned tail and led off, Ava and Chell right behind her, retreating back the way they had come in a soft-stepping, theatrical manner, indicative of not making heavy footfalls.

As they sneakily withdrew, Chell was making a repressed but excited keening. They rounded the next corner. Ava whispered breathlessly, 'Turn right. Left, right then left again. I was counting.'

Somewhere over to their far right, through the foliage, Finn, Ava and Chell heard a shout of alarm from Manda.

'Keep going, keep going,' whispered Ava and she broke out in a wild fit of girlish giggles at the unexpected adrenalin rush.

'I thought it was back to the right?'

'So did I. All looks the same.'

'Eh. It's a maze, Finn.'

'Shit.'

The three of them stopped stock-still and began whispering.

'We're lost.' There was panic in Chell's voice.

'Don't start, Chell. It's only that way or eh, that way.'

Ava hissed, 'Oh gosh. I suddenly just could not stand Manda's presence any more. I'm sorry, but really. Did you hear what she said?'

'Och, I don't think that was directed at you.'

'Well, I don't care any more, to be quite honest. Look what she says about everyone. Not just me. I think it's because Chell and I got a bit of a break from her and then suddenly. Boom. She was back up in my face again. She's so . . . heavy. I must have got inured to her before?'

Deep within the metallic skin of her vanity case, Chell's mobile phone burbled urgently. All three young women turned their faces to each other with horror.

'It's Manda! Bloody phoning it so she can hear us.' Chell looked around.

'Switch it off. Switch it off!'

Chell put down the vanity case with a crunch in the path at her feet and there she kneeled.

'If you open it, the ring will get louder and she'll hear better.'

'But she won't be able to find us.'

Finn looked at Ava and in a hushed manner said, 'Our phones will ring next.'

Wind oddly shook the yew-tree hedge at their shoulders, as if someone had grabbed the other side in two fists and tugged it just once, violently; they were buffeted by a cool wind from outside the parameters of the maze.

All three of them turned to frown at the hedge. Chell stiffened especially. A cold wind sucked down the corridor of leaves they stood in. They frowned oddly.

'Jesus Christ.' Chell's bared shoulders jumped and she looked directly up. There had been a peal of thunder, so loud it seemed immediately above them. Their days at the airport had made them more aware of the attendant airs above, the presence of aircraft, slithering invisibly and hazardously, and now new, angrier gods seemed low and manifest. A huge electric ambience had bustled into their blinkered sphere. The mobile phone ring went silent as the gloomy lane was lit up for an unearthly fraction by the vicious spit and kick of bone-white lightning across their heads. The frizzle suddenly obvious around their nostrils was of seared ozone.

Both of the girls looked concernedly at Chell who was wide-eyed and asked them, 'Oh no, God. Where did this come from?' already openly petrified.

There was thunder, so loud it moved the ground beneath them like back at the airport.

Chell looked straight to Ava. 'It's her. Them from the boats. Maybe there were the dead ones, laid out along the bottom of the lake?'

Finn said, 'What?'

Ava took Chell's hand. 'Nothing. Come along.'

But it was too late. Above them they could see purplish unstable dimensions of cloud, vapid at the edging. A single black bird crossed the sky, panicked. The sound of batting came from the very top of the hedges and fat, singular, cold raindrops with generous air spaces between hit at their faces.

'We've got to get out of here.'

They took another turn but it ended in dead hedge so they

doubled back. The raindrops stopped but then they came again with huge hysteria; a strange pea-shooting sound came from Chell's metal vanity case. Skittering along the lid were tiny white pellets as a cloud of hailstones began firing at them from side to side, hitting off the leaves.

They heard a distant scream, but mingled with excited delirium, somewhere off to their right: Manda.

The hailstones came in again, huge amounts of them multiplied and funnelled in by the narrow walls of the maze – and then just rain. So heavy, sudden and so violent, Finn considered trying to bury into the hedge.

'Oh, for fuck sake.' Ava looked romantically tropical; water drops were dawdling and spasmodically rushing down her cheeks and jawline, pulling long stands of black hair with them.

'Jesus. It's actually freezing.' Finn grasped the bared roundels of her own glistening wet, narrow shoulders. 'Oh. What a bloody disaster, this holiday.'

'Try this way.' Puddles had already gathered, so deep, Chell felt their cold depth seep in over the soles of her flat sandals. They were splashing along, the leaves pouring rain off their points, like ten thousand tilted soup spoons. Another crack of lightning made daylight of the ground by their footwear. Then they heard a male baritone call to their right and they stopped moving.

'Hands up?' The male voice seemed to come from the sky itself and was lost in several reports of thunder moving in succession eastward, leaping inhuman distances with no effort.

Chell appeared terror-struck and looked above, her right hand reaching for her childhood crucifix which she no longer wore on her neck.

'What? Hello!'

'Can someone put their hand up?' It was the matter-of-fact male voice of the man at the entrance but he seemed to be slightly above them as if he'd climbed a tree. Ava shot up her hand, wiggling her fingers for additional prominence, letting the rain pelt her skull.

'Yes. I can see you.' The voice came from their right. Chell

223

was bent over now, the water pouring down her back. She was shivering.

The male voice called, 'Sorry, everyone. I was just fetching my raincoat. The weather was looking ominous but you were off in there like a shot.'

There was another, more distant shout.

'Oh,' the man's voice added, humorously, 'this'll be a challenge; there's another group as well.'

'No, no,' Ava called, turning, trying to define the man's location. 'No. Those are our friends. We've been separated into two groups.'

'Well, you are the lucky ones. They're off up in the top corner. Very tricky. Okay. Keep your hand in the air. Go straight ahead and turn right then stop.'

'C'mon.'

Their light summer wear added to the grudging exhilaration of water flowing over them – each hitting drop was felt through wetted fabric on the skin and so unexpectedly out of character for the balmy afternoon. Their legs and arms goose-bumped helplessly. Their clothes weren't just wet through, they could feel the outline of any underwear, stolid and defined there against the clinging cotton.

'Okay. Turn immediately right and follow this curve you are in all the way to the top of it and then you must turn left. Do you hear me?'

Finn ran ahead, as if it would aid the escape. Ava pulled Chell by the hand after her. Their feet splashed, a pebble became jammed solid under Chell's heel, but she could feel how it was lubricated in its movements by fresh, slick mud. The hedge curve was the longest yet, drawing them far away from the man. At the top Finn waited until she was joined by Ava and Chell then they moved to the left. There was only one route so they followed it back down.

'Hello?'

'Helloo,' Ava called but the voice did not reply.

'Okay then.' They jumped as his voice was almost next to them and above. Their upheld eyes were closed against the rain.

'I'm here at the exit. You must go back along to your right, turn left at the top and follow the route all the way back and you're out.'

They set off. The man now began shouting louder and it was apparent he was calling to Manda's group, but the sound of the rain was so loud on the ground, nothing could be heard of them.

'We've gone wrong.'

'No. To the end.' At the end sure enough there was a bowered arch. Finn stepped through it and there was the exit on her right. She hurried out.

On top of stepladders, like those used by a tennis umpire, glistening against the sky, stood the man, in a slicked oilskin, hood pulled up. He didn't look down at them, just shoved out an affirmative, jolly thumbs-up. He shrugged and the oilskin slithered. 'They can't hear me and I've to watch for damned lightning up here; let me tell you.'

Now Ava, Finn and Chell were actually out, it was difficult for them to divine much advantage. It seemed less sheltered and the rain gave an impression of increased vigour.

The parkland and low country had been utterly swept free of humankind. The long slope away from the moat and castle, up to the car park, was ill-defined by the very thicknesses of the rain, moving in a smoke of slow-shifting curtains. The drops were hitting the grass so hard at a spot near the summit, a small white wavering ribbon on the ground could be discerned, heading across the flooded grass flanks as the heavy drops kicked up a thin advance band of froth.

The man shouted after them, 'Don't shelter under trees please. It's very dangerous.' He turned briefly and jerked his arm to the right. 'Try the gatehouse but I think it's closed.'

'Should we wait for Manda?'

'Fuck her, let's try and get wee Chell in the castle. Thanks,' Finn called back and they ducked their heads and ran.

Halfway there they stopped running. The grass was too slick underfoot and they were utterly inundated by now anyway, the hems of their skirts slapping their bare legs or sticking, plastered inside out to the thigh. It was obvious as they approached the gatehouse the castle was closed. The portcullis was down for the commoners. Literally.

'Might as well head up for the pavilions place.'

Ava said, 'The car's closer and I've the keys.' Ava had the tiny leather reticule on the long leather string that she'd been carrying with her all day. The leather had turned black but she slapped it tackily.

'Surely the girls will have the gumption to head there?'

'I'll flash the headlights till they see them.'

But the ascent of the hill was no easy matter. The rain came on down in thick, hysterically intense pillars. The horizons had vanished in brighter areas of vapour and they seemed enclosed in water.

Finn laughed first then Chell and Ava followed.

In her plummy accent, Ava declared, 'Don't fall on your bum whatever you do. Better to be wet than a huge muddy bottom, and it's a hire car.'

They looked back down to the maze, but in the distance it was obscure through the differing muslins and buntings of rain intensities, just its dark, regimented shape and the corners of its glistening wet hedging were clear. The whole earth steamed around them.

'They're still stuck inside.'

'Fuck. I hope Kay's computer is okay in this?'

Ava spat water away from her lips and shook her head. Drops came shooting off the very tips of the dark strandels of matted hair.

'Come on. We'll dry out and warm up in the car.'

The gardens were shortly to close but the car park still contained many vehicles, though it had noticeably emptied since their arrival. The rain was not easing but still pinkled, hit and played upon the polished metallic finishes of the cars, or clung in adhesive medallions upon waxed bonnets; these little puddles vibrated and shifted irritably under the deluge.

The parked cars had changed in the vicinity of their Toyota Corolla during the absence, with some sports utility vehicles drawn across the few spaces which had been created next to them. Ava thumbed at her small bag. The leather tie was difficult to undo in its sodden state. She could physically feel Chell shivering next to her now, her vibration somehow communicated through the wet turf.

When Ava pointed the remote at the car and pressed it to unlock the doors, there was absolutely no response. She tried again. 'Oh no. Oh no. The rain has fucked up the remote now.' Ava pressed it again and again but their car was unresponsive. 'I don't fucking believe this. Let me try from the other side.' She crossed and pressed again but there was no response.

'What now?'

'Can't you just open it with thingmy car keys?'

'No. All these things are remote locking only.'

'What about the boot? Manda's got that jacket in the boot and I'm bloody perishing cold.'

Ava walked round to look at it. 'Oh, it's just a button anyway. You can't even open the boot till the central locking is disabled.'

'Hey. Where is these bloody folk from all these cars? Can't they help us?' Chell stooped in her wet dress.

'They must be sheltering in the pavilions. The pavilions are still open.'

'Let's go and see the car-park attendant guy. He might be up in yon pay-booth thingmyjig.' Chell flapped her wet fringe.

'No sign of them lot yet.' Finn was looking down into the valley. 'Not to worry though. If lightning hit Manda, it would retreat.'

They turned and trudged up the tyre-mark track, past bonnets and boots of other cars. The car-park barrier and pay booth had eaves and an awning over the electric barrier, forming an area of shelter, and though it was far too late, the three young women couldn't help rushing the last few yards for the novelty of its rain-free feel, even if this was purely psychological by then.

Through the open pay-booth window was the car-park attendant they had seen earlier in the day. He was wearing a waterproof jacket and sitting by a computer screen which seemed unnaturally bright, such was the exterior gloom.

'Excuse us?'

'Ah. You'll get shelter in the pavilions. Still open.'

'We were trapped in the maze in the middle of all this.'

'An umbrella is a marvellous thing,' he heartlessly droned.

'It's not actually that, though we're drowned as rats.' Ava held up the keys to the car with the keyring attached. 'The rain seems to have sparked out the remote lock on the keys for the car and the thing won't open for us. We can't get in it. And leave.'

'Oh dear.' He had begun to take a greater interest in the three forms outside, rising and crossing to the women. Initially, Ava assumed their vulnerable aspect, their body-hugging, sodden vestments – underwear-revealing in Chell's case, non-underwear-revealing on Finn's breasts – or their impassioned, wild hair, might have been what roused the man. But he took the car keys with great keenness and glared through the lenses of his thick glasses at them. This was the nirvana he sought: a mechanical problem to assist with.

'Ahhhh. What kind of car?'

'Toyota Corolla.'

'Really? Usually very reliable. These are pretty waterproofed with a small rubber sealant, so I don't see the rain as a problem. You probably just need a new battery. A new battery will do the trick and Brian's just coming over in the Land Rover now, so he'll see to it.' He made no motion nor showed any intention of inviting them inside the office.

The girls stood close together, outside the pay-booth window, heads bowed, their own arms embracing themselves. The rain did seem to ease a bit though it still tumbled off the sheltering eaves in distorting plates and huge warped lenses.

'I'm freezing.' Chell shivered. She put down her vanity case, kneeled and lit up, rising with a cigarette which showed a transparent grey water splotch halfway along its length.

'Do you want me to ask for a loan of him-in-there's jacket?' Finn asked, in a lowered voice.

Chell made a funny face and dropped her voice to a whisper. 'Nah. It'd scum me out; he's a bit weird. It's probably got earwigs crawling around in it.'

Surprisingly quick, its cross-eyed headlights very close together and switched on, a Land Rover suddenly came round
the corner and approached the pay booth. They stepped back.
Its noisy engine edged in under the awning and the vehicle
halted; the engine chuckled to a stop. A younger, fast-moving
man, quite handsome in a long-faced way, swung open the
driver's door and stepped out, flat-footed in rough gumboots
with the tops folded down. He didn't keep eyes on the young
women for a moment but looked around at the car-park scene
while they watched him. He approached.

Ava said, 'We're locked out of our car. The remote lock won't
work in the rain.'

Without introduction he said, 'Let's see your keys.' Ava darted
them out at him a little quickly.

He dropped his gaze on the keys immediately. 'Ah. These
don't have a light on them, so you can't tell if the battery's dead
or not.'

He didn't say anything else but turned his back on them. 'I'll
change the battery. Timmy. Hoi, Timmy. Got a screwdriver in
there? Oh, it's okay, I'll use my penknife.' He turned to them.
'I'll just go inside for the light.'

'Okay. Thanks.'

As he disappeared round the Land Rover and inside the
building, Chell looked at Finn. She whispered, 'He's quite dishy.'

Ava looked at Finn.

Finn shrugged. 'In a it's-late-in-the-day-kind-of-way, yeah, I
suppose he is.'

Ava shivered and leaned down; she lifted her dress a touch,
took a hunk of hem and wrung it out with both her hands. A
good deal of water spattered down on her sodden training shoes.
'Oh, this is just ridiculous.'

'You've got such great legs, Ava.' Chell looked.

Brian appeared back, moving in his quick way. 'Okay. Where's
your car?'

'Ah, down that line there.'

'Hop in.'

'In this?'

'Yeah. You can't walk in that rain any more.' He opened the driver's door and reached in to clip the seat forward. Chell pulled her dress out, away from her underwear which had become visible through the wet fabric, and used her hand to urge Finn in first. Brian suddenly said, 'Oh sorry. There's something on the back seat there,' and he dashed off round the other side and jerked the door open to lean in and get a circle of electric cable off the rear left seat. Chell used this opportunity to duck ahead of Finn, clamber in the back and shuffle over to the other side.

Brian carried the cable to the office door and left it there while Finn got in the back seat beside Chell. Ava banged the metallic passenger door closed behind her. Brian dashed round again and climbed in, starting the engine, leaning in eagerly over the steering wheel and slamming his door shut behind him, all in one interconnecting moment.

'There's no seat belts in here,' Chell said, doom-laden in the back.

'Don't need them. You're on private property.' He drove off. He was pleasingly threatening in some way, Ava thought. He drove craned forward as if he had bad eyesight.

'Going to become a quagmire this, when they come out the pavilions,' he told them. 'They're all sheltering in the pavilions. It's these Chelsea tractors. Weigh a ton. Literally. Carve up the park when it rains now, they do. And you look at the garage names on the plates. All London. Huh! They all come down to the country and they have off-road vehicles. Crazy. What's that accent?' he said and put his eye to the mirror.

'Scottish.'

'You're not Scottish though.'

'I'm from near Didcot and Cholsey.'

'Oh yes. I'm cockney. Left years ago. It's not my manor any more. All my mates . . . What's your car?'

'Blue Toyota Corolla.'

'All my mates from school. Not one of us lives inside the M25 now.'

Ava turned to glance at him.

'Here it's,' said Chell from the back. The man braked abruptly, hauled on the handbrake and he was out, holding up the car keys across the bonnet, compressing the button before Ava had her door fully open.

'Stay in, stay in, don't get wet. Isn't bloody working.'

'Oh, I don't believe this,' said Ava. She was half out the car, showing a good bit of wet leg, she admitted, and then stepping over beside him. She suddenly thought how pathetic she must appear. Chell and Finn followed her out of the Land Rover.

He pointed to the Europcar sticker in the back window. 'Hire, is she? Where you coming from?'

'Gatwick.'

Out of curiosity he tried pushing the remote again and then walked around the Toyota, continually pressing in a frustrated wrist movement.

'Nope. You're gonna have to phone your hire company and tell them you can't get in it. Their problem. They'll send a taxi for you. Maybe. You flying somewhere tonight?'

'Tomorrow.'

'Well, that's not too much of a downer then. What a day for it.' For the first time, it seemed, he gave a tight grimace and actually looked at Ava, but she was staring off down the hill.

'Oh God,' she said.

It was falling gloomy now and slightly below the hill ridge, up the wetted slopes, came the stooped but unmistakable figures of Manda, Kylah with her now dulled vanity case, and Kay. Kay was noticeably hugging the computer to her chest.

'They're with us.'

'Oh. You can get a lift back with them then, can you?'

'Naw. We're all in the same car.'

'Six of you? What a squash.'

Chell watched the others, their bodies leaned in, ascending the slope. They climbed slightly further to the right and they were glaring with fascination at the actions up above them: at the Land Rover with headlights on, at the rugged male stranger, all outlined against the comprehensively purple sky above, in its dying light.

Then Chell suddenly pointed. 'The wheel's gone wonky too.'

'Pardon?' said Ava.

'The wheel. You had the front wheel twisted round. Remember? When I said about the dogs not being able to pee on it and now it's straight.'

Ava stepped quickly into place. 'My God. So it has.'

'What's that now?' said Brian.

'Eh. It must be the power steering has gone too or something. That wheel was bent when we left.'

'Bent? The power steering?' Brain gave a gruesomely critical look at them.

A sodden Kay, hair pressed absolutely shapeless and flat, was approaching. Alone.

'What are you all doing?' called Kay.

'We can't get in the car. Something's wrong with the lock and the power steering's failed.'

'But. Isn't our car over there, where Manda is?' Kay pointed. 'What?'

They stepped forward and looked across. An awful realisation came upon Ava. 'Oh God, no.'

Thirty yards away, beyond two of those large, off-road vehicles, previously hidden from view, stood an identical blue Toyota Corolla, its nose pointed forward in the same position. Kylah and Manda were standing impatiently before its bonnet.

Ava called out, 'It's identical. They're bloody identical! But this has a Europcar sticker too . . .' She leaned over and peered in the window. 'But the road map's not there. This isn't our bloody car. It's someone else's. Oh my God. How completely embarrassing.'

'It's exactly the same.' Finn scowled.

'You are joking me? Oh holy roller, that's a first.' Laughing, Brian marched forward towards the second car, his arm held out straight before him, echoing Manda's stance when she had run down the embankment with her beer, earlier in the day.

In seconds they heard the familiar bolts shift out of lock. Ava, Finn, Kay and Chell helplessly followed behind Brian.

Manda looked at the stranger. 'Who are you? What's going on? Where were yous? We're totally soaked.'

Brian turned to Ava. He placed the keys in her helpless palm. 'Women drivers. Seen it all now, my love. Keep the battery. Memento of Hever Castle.' Laughing up at the metallic sky, Brian flat-footedly marched off into the gloaming towards his Land Rover. In seconds the engine shuddered and the vehicle whined away in reverse.

'It's so embarrassing. We thought that other car was this one. It's like, exactly the same. Same make, same colours, it's even a Europcar hire one with a sticker in the back window; like you just couldn't tell, girls.' Chell shrugged.

Manda eyed them all but her contemptuous look soon rested on Finn and Ava. 'Fucking hell. University education and yous two can't even tell your own car from another. I don't know. What the fuck was all that disappearing act in the maze? We's got soaked to the skin. Look at the state of us. Kay here thinks her computer might be jiggered with water.'

'Oh, it'll be okay. Don't exaggerate,' Kay reassured.

Manda ignored her. 'So that's the holiday up in smoke, botched by you fucking idiots; and yous were blaming me for screwing up the holiday. Was that meant to be funny or something? Running away and leaving us stuck in there?'

'Manda, we got soaked too. What possible difference did us not being there make to you? You'd have got soaked anyway.' Finn shrugged.

'Can we sit in the car and not stand in the rain arguing, since we've got in it at last?' Chell asked, reasonably.

'Friends-so-called should no run out on other friends in a crisis.'

'Crisis! Manda. We were in a maze together in the rain. Chell was scared.'

'It's this I'm-all-right-jack-looking-after-number-one now, these days; isn't it, Finn? Want to go off talking philosophy and groping each other in the rain?'

'Was that directed at me?' Ava said. It was in a completely new voice nobody had heard before, and Finn only on a few memorable occasions. This new voice shut everyone up.

Ava snapped at Manda, 'I'm sick of all this sapphic innuendo as well.'

'What's Suffolk?' Chell frowned and turned to Kylah.

Kylah replied, 'Suffolk? That's another bloody place, isn't it?' and she shrugged.

Manda looked at Ava. There was a considerable distance between them but Ava began walking towards Manda.

'Ava,' Finn said blankly.

Ava kept moving.

'I'm no talking to you. Fancy-pants-whatever-your-name-is. This is all between old pals and you're no included.'

Ava said, 'Oh really? Everyone's sick of you, Manda. Me included. You are driving me . . . batty and I'm not the only one. Everything for two days has revolved around you and your selfishness.'

'You don't know anything.'

Ava was getting closer.

'Don't you come closer to me. Posh psycho. Look at you. I knew you weren't right in the head.'

Only a body length separated them.

'Ava!' Finn shouted, this time very loudly. 'Don't touch her.'

'Aye. Don't. Or I'll . . . get my big sister on you.'

Ava put her nose down to Manda's face; Manda visibly leaned back, intimidated. 'Warning you. Don't touch me.'

'Or what? Or what? Don't you ever disrespect me,' Ava said quietly in her face.

Manda blinked.

Ava canted in her right leg behind Manda's calves, then using both arms, shoved with force from her shoulders. Manda went stumbling backwards but she threw an arm out wildly, trying to balance on the wet slope.

Chell let go a cry of fear.

Manda wasn't down. She moved her strong legs round to try and get footing and was actually running forwards, downhill, back-pedalling to fight the momentum of the push, but the grass was completely slick. A foot shot out from under and her buttocks hit with a tremendous bump, bouncing once on the grassy slope. Manda began sliding, spectacularly, back down the wet hill on her arse. With her acceleration, her upper body immediately flattened, her face up to the metal sky, arms swept back behind, fingers extended in shock as she gathered speed like a toboggan sledge, feet in the air. Her weight flattened the grass which her buttocks skated over, but then, gradually, her progress gouged up a mud smear behind her arse before she completed a slow, full revolution, miniskirt forced under and back, like a tailcoat of pure muck, white control knickers utterly revealed before they darkened with shiny mud. She rolled over once and came to a complete halt, lying belly down, pushed up on her elbows.

Kylah, straining to enunciate the words through laughter, declared, 'That. Is the funniest thing I saw. In my entire life,' and she ran alongside Chell to the boot of the car where they both bent over as if vomiting – trying to conceal their hilarity from Manda.

Calmly, oddly reasonable, Ava shouted down the hill, 'Hey, Manda, I'll put the headlights on so you can see your way back up,' and she walked towards the unlocked car.

3

The traffic police car flashed and stopped them just past the roundabout where the B2028 joins the A264 at Copthorne.

The patrol car had been on the slip road of the roundabout and had jumped forward, following them immediately.

From the back, in deadpan voice, Manda uttered, 'I told you to duck down, Finn.'

Ava drove onto a sensible lay-by on the left, where she signalled and pulled the car well in, tugging up the handbrake. She switched off the engine then wound down her own and also the passenger-side electric windows. The sound of aircraft could be heard immediately and they had glimpsed the procession of nose-up, low-down airliners ducking out the skeins of cloud, wing tips drawing vapour contrails so white against the grey that Chell had tried to insist it was fire smoke.

Ava calmly said, 'Kay, will you get the documents out the glove compartment?'

Manda mumbled, 'And told yous slow-coach-Kay should have drove.' Then Manda added, glumly, 'Even if we'd have took ten hours to get back at the speed she goes at.'

There was a new order in the back seat. Chell at the rear door behind the passenger seat then Kylah, then Finn, then mud-encrusted Manda, sitting on plastic bags and the outer shell of her leather jacket to protect the car upholstery.

Ava fished into that little leather side bag for her driver's licence at the ready.

The police car had parked up close behind them. Finn folded her arms. One policeman stayed in their vehicle and the other sauntered up ominously, on the passenger side of the Toyota. He bent over and looked in. Chell shrunk down. The policeman wasn't good-looking. He was ancient. He immediately inhaled the

236

fuggy, greenhouse atmosphere of condensation on the windows, of wet clothes and the sharp tinge of car heating which had been turned up full.

'Good evening, ladies.'

'Hello.'

'Hello, sir,' Ava said.

'Now.' The policeman paused. 'You probably think you know why we've asked you to pull over. But it's not for that reason. You were driving a little erratically back there as you came up on to the roundabout, Miss? That's the *first* thing we noticed.'

Ava replied, 'Yes I was, sir. I knew I was. They were all shouting and screaming in here and the radio was turned up at full volume.'

'Now we didn't think we saw what we saw. But here you all are for sure. Off the top of my head, that's not committing an offence, as far as I'm aware. All the same, I think I'll ask my colleague to join me. Hey, Steve, Steve,' he signalled. He bent back down into Kay's passenger window.

Ava spoke. 'I'm very, very sorry. We've been at Hever Castle for the day. We got trapped in the maze when the thunderstorm came and we were soaked wet through. You see the results. We're not out for a Sunday drive in just our bras and knickers for fun. We're not obtaining any pleasure out of this. Far from it.'

The cop nodded soberly.

From the back, Manda rasped flintily, 'Bet yous are all glad I got yous to bikini-wax now.'

The cop nodded. 'Ah. My immediate presumption was that we had a hen party from last night. Still in progress. Could I ask to see your driver's licence please? I notice it's a hired vehicle. You have the documentation. Thank you. Miss . . . Hur Ma Lain En. Ava?'

'Yes, Hurmalainen.'

Steve, the second policeman, had arrived; the older cop nodded and winked down. Steve lowered himself and bent to peer in. He was good-looking.

'Good evening,' he said.

'Good evening!' Everyone replied in unison.

He smiled. 'Going far, were we?'

Manda said, 'As you can see, we go all the way.'

'Just Gatwick. We're flying out.'

'This evening?'

'Tomorrow.'

'It's going to be brilliant, mister.'

A passing boy-racer car, with wheel rims and swivelling base-ball caps inside, bleeped its horn twice playfully, as it slowly passed. Manda couldn't stop herself waving back. Steve had risen up to his full height and he chuckled at his colleague, who bent down in his place.

'Now. Driving as you are isn't an offence but I'm afraid to have four passengers in the back is a road-traffic offence. You only have three seat belts there.'

Ava said, 'I know that, sir. I'm not going to try to pretend I don't know that and I'm sorry. There were six of us. As you see. We were delayed at Gatwick. Since Friday night because one of us mislaid her passport.'

'Aye. Me.' She said it proudly.

'Just shut up, Manda,' Kylah sighed.

'And we only found the passport late last night so we thought we'd take today off and then fly out tomorrow with a last-minute booking, when the flights are cheaper. I thought I'd take the girls for a drive in the English countryside. They're all from Scotland. It seemed an awful, awful shame to have to leave one of us behind. So I wrongly squeezed one more in.'

'Well, the company shouldn't have hired you the car for six. Or they should have rented you a larger vehicle, some of which do have seat-belt provision for four in the back. You should know by now what happens to people when they don't wear a seat belt and they're involved in a vehicle accident?'

'Like Lady Di.'

'Like Lady Di. Exactly, dear. It's me, not you, that has to see a dead young person, just your age, every month, from not wearing seat belts and it annoys me, young ladies like you taking a risk like that.'

Chell had that mortified, alarmed look again.

'I'm very, very sorry. I wouldn't try to insult you by claiming

I was ignorant of that. I'm the driver. They're not qualified drivers so it's my responsibility.'

He nodded slowly. Sizing up Ava, literally. Professionally keeping his eyes on her face.

'You would agree to a brea— Oh my goodness.' The policeman stood up suddenly. He turned to his colleague. 'Hear that, Steve?'

'What?'

'Breath test. I almost said, "breast test".'

Steve laughed. Hilarity came from inside the car.

He leaned back down again. 'You would not object to taking a breath test, here and now?'

Smiling at his good humour, Ava said, 'That would be no problem. Either test.'

The cop laughed too. 'Okay. Thank you. Controlled or illegal substances in the car? I won't say on your persons?'

Ava shook her head. 'We're not into anything like that.'

'For obvious reasons, I'm not going to ask you to step out the vehicle for a search, Miss.'

Everyone giggled.

Now the policeman was looking at Manda in the back seat, at the dried mud on her bare legs, almost like a pair of tights, and even a smear on her cheek. The policeman said, 'Still making it home from Glastonbury, are we?'

Because of the long and spectacular mud slide, Manda had become centre of attention yet again. The actual roots of the conflict with Ava had been discarded from her mind and the occurrence had been turned into a completely positive event for her. This was a curious and praiseworthy trait of Manda: utter and immediate forgiveness for anything that should benefit her in the eyes of others.

'Yes. We've had localised flooding here and there,' the cop ruminated. 'On the slip roads.'

'Yes.'

'Been breathalysed before, Miss?'

'No. Never.'

Steve rustled the plastic which contained the sterilised

239

mouthpiece and fitted it, then he kneeled slightly and placed the machine close to Ava's mouth. 'You need to blow in here.'

Manda said, 'Only blow job *she'll* give on this holiday.'

'I'll pretend I didn't hear that,' the older policeman warned.

'Okay. Blow. Blow. Blow and fine. Thank you very much.' Steve straightened up and waited a moment. The infernal and sinister machine made some contradictory, tender, mouse-like sound. 'And that's a completely negative reading, Miss. I'll just show it to you.' He displayed the readout to Ava, his finger pointing to the readout to ensure she confirmed it. 'Thank you very much.'

Steve walked away but the other policeman remained posted at the passenger window. 'Very good. I'm pleased about that. Now I'm going to give you a verbal warning this time, Miss. And to all of you.'

'We're very sorry, sir.'

'I haven't finished yet. It's illegal to have an unbelted passenger in the rear. Though if I were to issue a ticket, I don't suppose you'd have anywhere to keep it.'

Kylah made an amused noise at the quip.

'I can't allow you to drive on in an illegal configuration . . .'

A tension filled the still car.

'. . . So we are lucky enough to ask that one of you join us in our car, since the airport is a very short distance from here, and we'll drive one of you over there and provide a lead escort.'

'Just like a rock band,' Kylah whispered.

'Okay, Miss. If you could get dressed. If you could all get dressed please.'

Ava said, 'We were looking for somewhere to get dressed. We had to get undressed in a bus shelter by the road, near Hever.'

'Talk about distracting drivers.' The old cop shook his head and sighed.

Steve laughed.

Then the two cops stepped back, allowing the girls time to gyrate back into their wet, adhesive summer dresses inside the car. Arms and even legs were seen to stretch out, heads to pop through necklines, the girls pushing their crowns up against the roof to shuffle dresses down. The cops stood in traditional stance outside, arms folded and impatiently awaiting.

The older cop said, loud enough to tell everybody, 'Wait till I get home and the wife asks what was happening tonight. "Well, first, dear, I had to get six young ladies back into their clothes."'

With Kylah in the back of the police car, driving out ahead, Ava and the other girls followed. When the two cars approached the Europcar office in Gatwick – to the dismay of the staff there – Steve had turned on the flashing lights in response to Kylah's pleading, and she had waved and laughed and blown kisses from the back window of that police car, for the brief journey.

Considering their hair and clothing, Manda's sunglasses and the mud-besmeared, thrusting bra under the Karen Millen dress, the Gatwick Village Pizza Express staff viewed their group with only adequate suspicion.

Manda was equally suspicious of their menu.

'What do you eat here?'

'Pizza, Manda.'

'Aye, but what is the names of them? They don't have a Cheese Feast with extra cheese like in Pizza Hut.'

'They have Quattro Formaggi, don't they?' said Ava, flipping the menu, at least trying to be helpful. 'Same thing, isn't it?'

'Yeah, I think they have that,' Kay nodded.

'What in God's name's that?'

'Four cheeses.'

'Oh. That sounds all right then. On second thoughts. Naw. I'm going have exactly what you or Finn or Kay had yesterday. One of them. I want that. What was that then?'

Manda had an annoying habit of calling the waiter 'Waiter', as she viewed the large card menu with frustrated fury and questioned him. 'Waiter. These are really weird pizzas yous have,' she told him.

'Take your sunglasses off, Manda, you look stupid,' Kylah whispered.

She pretended to ignore this but after a few moments she quietly took them off and was suddenly cheered by noticing the carafes of house wine. She ordered a large red.

Kay asked, 'Anyone want salad? I'm having Niçoise salad with dough balls.'

'I don't eat salad,' Manda called out over the large round table. 'Though I used to. I'd put sugar on it.'

'You put sugar on your salad?' Kay frowned.

'Aye. What's wrong with that?'

'What kind of sugar?'

'Sugar-sugar. That you put in your cuppa, but the Old Man was aye at us, so I stopped eating salad. He told us that was the healthy choice. To stop salad.'

Ava said, 'Actually, most salad dressing is very sweet so that's not so odd.'

'There you go then. So I'm no so daft, am I?'

Chell said, 'Manda. Your boobs is *really* stuck out. And there's muck on your bra.'

'Naw. This is a great dress. Maybe I could borrow this off you again, Ava?'

'You look like you're in some sort of . . . country and western porn movie,' said Kylah.

Because all their cases were still back in left luggage, Manda had borrowed the only clothes that would fit her, straight from Ava's backpack. She had changed round the rear wall of the Europcar offices, in the evening twilight, between two parked vehicles. Then she'd had a pee there as well with the dress not held high enough as Ava pretended not to look.

The Karen Millen was the only dress they could find with buttons up the front which might accommodate Manda, and this, only if the top buttons were left undone. Manda kept repeating, 'It's just good clean mud. It's all just good clean mud,' when the many mud stains on the dress were highlighted. 'This is all your fault anyway,' Manda had pointed out to Ava.

When the pizzas arrived, before the two waiters had even started to place the plates before them, Manda snapped, 'Pizza *Express*. Waiter. That wasn't really so quick, was it?' She took one bite then dropped the pizza slice back on her plate saying, 'I can't eat that.' The waiters had already sped fearfully away.

'What's wrong with it?'

She chewed, waved her hands up and down, leaned over and spat the pizza globule back onto the same plate while making a great show of splashing more wine into her glass, spilling quite a lot on the tablecloth then swallowing almost half a glassful in one go. 'Oh my God. That's spicy.'

'Well, you said you wanted to have what I had last time,' Finn reminded her.

'That's boiling. I don't like boiling spicy food. That could harm you. When I go to Light of India they know fine what I take. I always take the same. They bring me it without my asking.'

'That one is always spicy.'

'How was I to know?'

'Jalapeños is spicy.'

'What penis?'

Kylah sighed, 'Do you want my four-cheeses thing then? I'll swap you.'

Chell yelled, 'But she's gone spat her big-scummy-chewen-gobber-bit on it, Kyles.'

Manda leaned forward, and using her dessert spoon, scooped up the chewed bolus of dough, tomato base and a fraction of a jalapeño from her plate. She splatted it down hard in the only partially empty area: the single space on the plate among Kay's perfectly soft baked dough balls.

'Aye, go on then.'

Manda stood and leaned over, her breasts almost coming free so that Chell turned away, alarmed by their threat. Manda took the Quattro Formaggi from Kylah and then passed her spicy pizza over. As Manda stood, everyone heard but did not comment on the bovine-like free fall of small mud blobs from within, deep underneath Ava's beautiful dress, hitting the carpet at Manda's feet. She sat. And shifted. 'That's better. If that waiter gadge had brought my Coke in time, I could have drunk that.'

'Shush. Here he comes now.'

Manda still took a scoosh of wine from her glass as he

approached. Then she noticed the Coke on the waiter's tray, 'Och, it comes in bottles like in a posh bar. I thought it'd been a big pint with ice out the scoosher. Like in Pizza Hut.'

Manda sat with her hands in her lap till the waiter had almost gone, but too quickly and too loudly she announced, 'Jeezo. This mud up my arse crack isn't half driving me nuts,' and she shifted unappetisingly in her seat. It's possible there was a squelching sound in there, under the dress. 'It's like when you're wee and you've a big fresh plaster of a wet jobby down in there and you're too shy to tell anyone. At primary school. Like Chell was aye doing at primary. Mind, Chell? Mind how you were always plopping in your pants you were so nervousy? Chell used to fart when there was cabbage at lunch and you could smell it was cabbage. You have no innards. I'm telling you.' She turned aggressively to Chell, who flinched.

Manda lifted the first slice of Quattro Formaggi pizza towards her rapidly moving lips and with a glutinous, effortless slide, the cheese sped off the base and plopped down into the lap of the Karen Millen dress. Manda froze with just the glistening, bare base of pizza stranded before her mouth.

Ava had already been casting a troubled eye on the constant strain those buttons seemed to be undergoing, wondering if anyone had needle and thread in those weights of suitcases.

Manda looked across the table meekly. 'Sorry, Ava.' She scraped and picked the slide of melted cheese up from the dress, using the same dessert spoon, and this stringy cheese blob also was slapped into Kay's dough-ball plate, this timing scoring a direct hit upon an uneaten one. Manda took another draw of wine and topped up her glass.

'Maybe it's time to call the hotel and try to sort out tonight,' said Ava and she stood, abandoning her half-eaten salad. Ava hitched up her backpack, grabbed her mobile from the table, which she'd been scrawling through earlier, and she took a slice of pizza from Finn's plate without asking, in a sort of flatmates' familiarity – then she walked away and out of the restaurant saying not a further word.

Once she was out of earshot Manda quietly and sensitively

informed them, 'Ava's that wee bit peeved cos I dropped it on her dress but it'll wash out no bother. And the rest is just good clean mud. Suppose you could say she's a wee bit *cheesed* off at me.' She looked around the table for laughs but there were none. 'Eh? She doesn't eat much that one, does she, Finn? I think she's got a problem there. Hardly eats. She wants to watch that.' Manda burped, though she hadn't managed to consume any food at all herself, by this point. Then she took another drink from her wine glass, looking over the rim at everyone, cautiously.

Ava walked nibbling at the pizza slice from one hand and holding her head a little further back with each bite, until she was outside Tie Rack and had chewed and swallowed the light crust. She wiped one hand on her arse, feeling the damp fabric, and she pushed a dial button on her phone's address book. It rang once. Ava said, 'Hey. Got your texts. Because I've people around me all the time.' There was a long pause. 'I'm still in Gatwick. Honestly. America. Vegas, I hope. A room of my own in a sleazy hookers' motel. I think we'll be booking something for tomorrow afternoon or evening so you need to come in the morning. There's six of us. They all have work up in Scotland, except my best friend. No, she's beautiful. But she wouldn't like you. I never say "please" but I will. On the station platform? Well, text me then. Don't phone. I will reply. The usual. Text me in the morning. You too.' She hung up and dialled again. 'Can you give me the number please for room reservations at the Gatwick Hilton Hotel?'

The Gatwick Hilton Family Room was generously large compared to the ones Ava had been getting used to. A very huge double bed, a smaller double and a single bed, all in one long space. Six coffee cups inverted in their saucers. Large television, PlayStation and games included. Ava threw down her backpack on the largest bed. She stood very quietly within the room, enjoying its stilled sense of self-enrapture. Its perfect purpose-lessness when unoccupied. The auto-brain certainty of its air-con noise which was set surprisingly high. The room held more peace than the corona of precious hush sent out before a famous painting in a grand gallery.

When she checked the bathroom there were plenty of towels but certainly not enough for six young women. Yet she had already heard Manda and Chell boast how they actually brought their own towels with them. She fitted the chain on the main door and stripped completely naked, using a towel in the small of her back and around her body where it felt damp. She enjoyed the feel of curling her toes in the man-made fibres and the activated static of the hard-wearing carpet, then she dressed in dry clothes – old black Levi jeans, and a slip, under her purple top.

She phoned Finn's mobile. 'Right. I got us a thing called a family room. Half the price of what we all paid last night. Two double beds, a big one and a smaller, and a single bed. More threesomes. There's a PlayStation thing too. The front desk weren't interested in who my family was as long as I was using Amex. Do I really look like I might have had four kids or something? Jesus Christ. Yes. But maybe you should still come in pairs rather than a big stampede led by Manda. Is the downhill champion herself coming first or else she'll cry, I suppose? Solo? Okay. I'll prepare her acid bath. Room seven three four two. Seven three four two.'

Ava waited, stretched out on the bed for the fifteen minutes or so, before she heard the squeak and bump of a heavy luggage trolley impacting the door. She arose and looked out the door's spyhole. Manda had her big, mud-smeared cheek – an eye – looking in at her. Ava unchained and opened the door. The first thing she looked at were the two bottom buttons on the dress. They were holding in there. Manda put her finger to her lips and tried to push the trolley in.

'I'll help,' Ava said. She heaved off one suitcase as Manda stood by and gave whispered instructions, then Manda took the case and dragged it on into the room, using two hands, tugging it backwards down the corridor. Ava repeated the operation with the second huge case. It was like a dead body. She pulled it on in.

'Ava,' said Manda as if she was naming her for her own fascination. 'Has it really got a PlayStation? Oh aye. So it has. Kylah's great at PlayStation. She's coming next with scaredy-cat Chell then Kay and Finn. You should hear Chell chattering away like a skeleton that needs oiling. This is just dead brilliant. Look at the size of the place. If only we'd got this last night too.' Suddenly she turned. 'Look, Ava. I'm awful sorry about today.'

'Well, I didn't mean for you to slide away in the mud.'

'Aye, I know, but I was dead brilliant, wasn't I?'

Ava shrugged and smiled. 'You went fast. It looked good.'

'And then us getting escorted back by the Feds. It was a classic.' Manda went quiet and then said, 'It's this wee problem I sometimes have. Finn has talked to me about it. Politely. I think it's to do with my securities.'

'Insecurities.'

'Aye. It's good I can talk about it though, isn't it?'

'We're all insecure.'

'Aye, I know. I'll stop it right now. That's me away to shower then. You're pretty strong for such a skinny bird, eh? I didn't think you could have the strength to shove me down,' she laughed.

'Do you want to sit now and talk while we're both alone?'

'Aye. This is brilliant. Loads of beds, eh?' Manda sat on the very edge of the bed, furthest from Ava.

Ava leaned against the wall.

Manda said, 'Look. I don't think I'm as good as other people so I sort of attack them straight away. It's a way of . . .'

'Defending yourself?'

'Aye. I'm on defensiveness from the first step with folk. Finn says. Course I do know that. I know I'm doing it.' She frowned and suddenly spat out, 'Why do you think this is?'

Ava sighed. 'I think you're proud. I think you've had a hard life.'

247

She shrugged. 'Aye. Ava, though. All I know is struggle and knowing that life is all about other people, keeping their foot on your head and keeping you down. I've already fucked up my life, getting pregnant and having Sean. I love Sean to bits, like nothing on earth.'

'I'm sure you do.'

'But part of my attackness to people comes from being defensive about him.'

'Mmm.'

'My parents split when I was wee. Mum was an alchy basically. Dad got left with me and Catriona and did his best but I know I broke Dad's heart by having another child in the world with no advantages, growing up with just one parent on the scheme like me and my sister did.'

Ava nodded. 'You only understand your parents and realise all they did for you when you're an adult. You'll realise things about your father and also Sean will realise things about you.'

Manda looked straight at Ava and said, 'You find beautiful butterflies in the dungheap as well as among the flower beds. You know? You can be a queen despite all the stuff that's happened to you in life.'

Ava nodded. 'Yes. That's true. But you have a crazy streak. Maybe we're both more alike than we realise?'

'Well, I'm not so sure you have such a crazy streak and you don't have a wee boy either.'

'Kay told me she had an abortion.'

Manda looked surprised. 'Did she tell *you* that? I'm surprised. She fair keeps that under her . . . petticoats. Now there is a girl with a crazy streak.'

'I did too.'

'God. Did you? Never?'

'Yeah. Few years back. Took the easy way out. You were braver, far braver than me, Manda. I'll say that to your face. I didn't have the courage you've had.'

'That's very kind of you to go and says. But it takes braveness to get rid of a baby. When you're a posh Catholic especially. Maybe I just didn't have those guts and you and Kay did. I can

248

be brave but I'd be fibbing if I didn't say that I was scared to death sometimes when I was expecting Sean. Cried myself alone to sleep lots of nights about the future.'

'I'm sorry for what you've been through.'

'Both of us.' Manda shrugged. 'Aye. I suppose it's two sides of the same coin.'

'I suppose it is.'

'So you had an abortion, eh? You could be just like me then. But with the big houses and England and all that?'

'I suppose I could be, yeah.'

'I'll have my shower.'

When Kylah and Chell reached the family room, Manda was wrapped in a towel and had rubbed up her hair into a scarification of blonde spikes.

Ava helped Chell and Kylah into the big room with their cases, and Manda made a show of directing and ordering the best places to put them. Much like the car-park attendant at the castle. Chell jutted about excitedly in the room but when she looked in the bathroom she groaned, 'Oh, Manda.'

'What?'

'Why'd you go wash your skirt in the sink?'

The handbasin almost full with brown water; just the blue edges of a denim hem emerged from it.

Chell said, 'It looks like that stuff you spewed up last night, Manda. Could you no have cleaned it in the bidet thing?'

'I'm no putting my skirt in yon contraption; foreign people clean their arse and fannies in it.'

When Finn and Kay arrived up in the family room, the squad was spread across the beds in long T-shirts and pyjama-bottom variations but with one surprise. Wearing jeans and a top in futile anticipation of going out, Manda was asleep on the far double bed.

Kylah, looking straight ahead, legs crossed in the lotus position, was on the big bed end, with the PlayStation handset gripped and the wire jumping as she hoisted her hands dramatically. She was facing the telly screen and said, 'Leave her. The snoring's better than her actually being awake. And it helps her cut down on her smoking.'

The room had an odd hush punctuated by the pauses and silences, then the subterranean flowing rivers and plonky cave-roof drips of *Tomb Raider*, which Kylah was powering through. The restfulness was often shattered by intense automatic gunfire as Lara Croft selected weaponry and let loose at a foe.

The family room was a no-smoking room with a smoke alarm blinking on the ceiling. A tight purple condom (large) had been stretched over the smoke alarm, but for extra caution, Kylah would smoke leaning out the window – letting in the aircraft noise. There was only room for one smoker there. Chell would go to smoke in the bathroom, standing, one leg on the toilet seat, one on the bath edge, her face almost reaching the extractor fan which she exhaled smoke accurately into, though she didn't quite reach it.

When Kay linked up the laptop, Kylah put *Tomb Raider* on pause while they all gathered round the screen as they yet again considered last-minute bookings, free of Manda's interference as she snored and snuffled behind them.

Chell said, 'So that Faliraki and that Ayia Napa place we was looked at yesterday. That's in the same country?'

'What's it called again: Aye. A Nappy?'

'Ayia Napa.'

'Faliraki is on Rhodes,' said Ava.

'Rhodes; that's in Africa, eh? What we did in Modern Studies?'

'That was Rhod*esia*. Rhodes is a Greek island.'

'Another one? There's too many Greek islands.'

'Rhodesia is an island?'

'It's called Zimbabwe now.'

'Faliraki's on an island called Zimbabwe? Was it formed by a volcano?' Kylah asked.

'Did we do that in Geography with smelly old Mr Eldon, Rachel dear?'

'We could have,' Chell murmured. Finn and Ava had given up.

Kay said, concentrating, 'There's Vegas flights. Package deals too. Let's go for it in the morning.'

'Vegas sounds like it's for us, eh? What a place.'

'Cigarettes is cheaper in America, aren't they?'

'Yes. Cheaper than Britain and you can smoke in all the casinos because they don't want to lose custom.'

'And you can drink for free, Ava was saying this morning, girls.'

'Yes. You just put quarters into the gambling machines and a waitress comes and as long as you tip her really good for the first few drinks, she'll refill you for hours.'

'Anything you want?

'Pretty much. Not champagne but spirits and mixers and good cocktails.'

'Fuck me, that's like paradise.'

'Home of the free.'

'It's amazing you've been there. You've been everywhere.'

Ava shrugged. 'Not everywhere.'

'Free booze, cheap fags and yous might win millions on the old one-armed bandits while you're at it. The jackpot is like fucking millions. Las Vegas is paradise.'

Finn changed in the bathroom but didn't shower. She lounged, yawning in men's thin summer pyjamas, announced, 'I'm going to shower in the morning and let the exfoliating rains of England soothe my bones.'

'What's the shagging arrangements?'

'Three will have to go in the big bed here, one in the single and someone share with fatty. Or two will have to share the single.'

'We're not drawing any more lots.'

Ava said, 'Finn and I should get on the bed and sleep either side of Manda. She's dying for the love of women. It's so obvious.'

'Oh, I dare yous.'

'Right,' Finn said. 'It's unfair Manda gets to sleep alone in a bed just cos she farts, snores and is the devil.'

'She wasn't that bad last night.'

Finn commanded, 'Ava is exempt from sleeping with Manda cos she nursed and shared with her like a true martyr last night. So I votes Ava gets alone in a single bed. Agreed?'

'Agreed,' they all admitted.

The main lights were switched off and Kylah was forced to turn the volume right down as Lara Croft burrowed deeper into the tombs – the glow of Lara's slow then rapid peregrinations lighting the room in steady halo. There was slight tension and amazement while Ava stood by her single bed and stripped down to her knickers, breasts fully bared, before climbing in. Everyone turned to peek or pretended not to turn to look at her but said nothing.

'Three in a bed and the little one said?'

'Who wants Manda then?'

'Nobody.'

'I will,' said Kay.

'You *are* joking?'

'No. I don't mind. But I'm not sharing a room with her if we book Las Vegas.'

'Okay.' Finn and Chell both scrambled in a race for the queen-sized double and got in together.

Kay sighed and went over to Manda. 'Manda, Manda. Wake up. Shove over. Budge over. I need to get inside the covers cos of the air conditioning.'

As if she was in a trance, Manda woke and sat up straight. 'What movie's that? Cartoons? Ya fucking bairns.'

'Get undressed, baby, Kay's coming to get you,' Kylah drawled, her acrylic nails clicking on the PlayStation handset louder than the game volume.

With a bleared-out face, Manda asked, 'Am I sleeping with you, Kay? Och well.'

Manda shuffled to the toilet, bending to get a T-shirt, but

then accidentally kicking one of her own cases. She cursed, 'Och. My pedicure's getting bust now.'

Kay got into the far bed.

The only sounds were Kylah's clicking fingernails and Manda running a tap in the bathroom.

'Give it up, Kyles.'

'I'm almost on the next level. It stops me from wanting to smoke.'

'Listen. Listen.'

'What?'

'All them bloody aeroplanes has stopped. Again.'

Kylah paused her clicking fingers to better appreciate it.

'Right enough. Yet again,' she said, miraculously, impressed by the consistency.

'It's silent as anything.'

Suddenly Kylah jumped forward and killed the PlayStation. Kylah clambered onto and into the big bed so Chell was in the middle and both Finn and Kylah snuggled in simultaneously; they immediately both began attacking and tickling Chell under the arms and on her torso as one would to an infant. Chell screamed and giggled and sucked in breaths until they stopped.

Eventually Manda ambled back through from the bathroom – in the light from the desk lamp that still burned – wearing a childish T-shirt with a cartoon character on it. She looked sideways at the three girls in the bed, opened her mouth to say something but then did not. She climbed in beside Kay and groaned wearily, 'Right, Kay Clarke. Get ready for the sexiest night of your life. You'll have done the whole family soon.'

They all laughed.

'How do you put that light off?'

'It's there.'

A switch clicked. A huge bank of lights came on full power and people moaned.

'No, no it's here. Here.'

'Naw, naw. You have to get up, Kay. You did it; it's that lamp on the desk by your computer.'

'You go. I don't want to stir next to Manda in case I set off her bowels.'

'Fuck off. Right enough though, these beds is big. I'd hardly know you were in here with me. Ya skinny-malinky.'

Everyone laughed, for some reason.

But Kay didn't shift.

'Occhhhhh,' went Kylah and she hauled the sheets aside and stepped out of bed, padded over to the desk between the strewn cases and clicked the desk light off. The room was suddenly in darkness.

Kylah felt her way back to bed. The room was unilluminated yet there were lights and signals and small little red and green beacons everywhere in the black, from the smoke alarm, the charging phones and dormant equipment; the electronic accoutrements of this age – night familiars watching over them.

They all lay silently in the night-timeness until Kylah's voice suddenly spoke out of the black. 'Right. Here we go, girls. A wee tribute to our leader.' She sang in a clear and quite beautiful voice, perfected by her invisibility and all of their concentration being centred on the sound alone with nothing to look at. 'I only know the one verse, I think.'

> 'Everybody's building ships and boats
> Some are building monuments
> Others are jotting down notes . . . eh . . .
> Oh fuck . . . yah de yah deh dah.

'Forgot. Sorry.'

'Doesn't matter.' Manda's low voice went, 'You sound beautiful, Kyles.'

> 'Everybody's building ships and boats
> Some are building monuments
> Others are jotting down notes . . .

'Ah that's it.

'Everybody's in despair, every girl and boy
But when FINN the Eskimo gets here
Everybody's gonna jump for joy'

And all but Ava joined in.

'Come all without, come all within,
You'll not see nothing like the Mighty Finn
Come all without, come all within,
You'll not see nothing like the Mighty Finn'

And now Ava giggled and joined in too.

'Come all without, come all within,
You'll not see nothing like the Mighty Finn'

They were shouting a bit now, banging their legs and arms
on their mattresses, in time.

'Come all without, come all within,
You'll not see nothing like the Mighty Finn'

'Shush it, shush it now. That's too loud. We'll get complaints,'
went Finn's voice, garlanded with laughter.

'Brilliant.'

Ava's voice said, 'My goodness. You all have really beautiful
singing voices. Honestly. Really beautiful.'

'Those is trained voices. That's years of training, Ava,' Manda
called across the room, though Ava lay in the bed next to Manda's.

'And Marlboros.'

They all laughed.

'You were all in the school choir, weren't you?'

'Aye. Aye. Yonks ago we all was. Eh, girls?'

Suddenly Kay called out, 'Kylah. Sing something nice on your
own.'

'Aye.'

'What?'

'Something nice.'

'Something we all know but . . . from old.'

'"Cap in Hand" by the Proclaimers,' Finn's voice insisted.

'Nah, I can't do that. Too shouty, but it's nice, quiet and slowed down. The words is hard, but I mind the melody in the chorus.'

'Nah. Not politics. Older than all that.'

'Like from when we's were right little, aye?'

'Okay. Okay but this is awful cheesy. From primary school.'

There was a long pause then Kylah's clear voice, deliberately quiet and perfectly gorgeous, sang.

> 'Away in a manger
> No crib for a bed
> The little Lord Jesus
> Lay down his sweet head'

The others joined in, but almost just as whispers or perhaps humming the melody, or even just mouthing the words in the dark.

> 'The stars in the bright sky
> Look down where he lay
> The little Lord Jesus
> Asleep in the hay
>
> The cattle are lowing –'

'Moooo,' came from Manda's direction.

'Hush. Don't spoil it.'

> 'The poor baby wakes
> But little Lord Jesus
> No crying he makes
>
> I love thee, Lord Jesus
> Look down from the sky

> And stay by my cradle
> Till morning is nigh.'

There was a stunned, long, nostalgic silence.

'Oh. So sweet.'

'Och, that's nice. That brings back memories galore.'

'Aye. And this feels like them brilliant nights when we's were eleven and twelve and that and we all used to do a sleepover at each other's; doesn't it, girls? Like pyjama parties we've had; eating crisps and talking and talking till you just fell asleep. When we were just wee lassies.'

'Life seemed so. Exciting then. Eh, girls? Everything was still to happen to us, so's it felt tons better.'

'Aye, ach. Nothing ever happens to us any more.'

Kay's voice – over by the window – enquired, 'Is it the stars in the *bright* sky though?'

'What?'

'Is it? The stars in the *bright* sky. It's night-time. Is it not just, "The stars in the sky, Look down from above"? That's what I recall.'

Manda tutted critically, next to Kay's voice.

Kylah said, 'I'm no good at remembering words. Probably is.'

Finn's voice out of the dark said, 'Stars in the bright sky sounds better. Like a poem.'

'But if the sky's bright, what are the stars doing out?'

Kay tried to solve it. 'It could be twilight. When you see the stars first, at that beautiful time?'

Kylah sang, testing it.

> 'The stars in the bright sky
> Look down from above'

There was silence.

'It sounds lovely.'

'You've improved on the original,' Ava's voice wryly insisted.

Chell's smaller voice said, 'But girls. The stars is still there even in the daytimes. Just you can't see them. And it's the night that shows the stars. Like Kylah. She's a star now and we all know it, but one day she'll show up brilliantly. And all of us. I just know it. The stars are still up, shining just for us all girls.' Chell's voice had dropped to a whisper.

There was a long silence and somewhere deep within it, one by one, they were asleep, in dreams and in peace.

Monday

1

It was the soft, busy clicking of fingers upon the keyboard that awoke Finn. She did not have to think where she was. She heard aircraft noise. In a prefab city of capitalism, pancaked out under the low, benign clouds of Sussex.

Finn lifted her head off the pillow – the warm conjunctions of Chell and Kylah's bodies over to her right. She watched how Chell's breath was touching the hairs on the back of Kylah's head, trembling the loosened strands so they quivered like weed in a riverbed, barely shifting. Finn's head wasn't high enough to see Ava's bed. A restrained light came from the closed curtains, enough to operate around in.

With her back to the beds, Kay was sitting at the desk, again in the chair, her bare shoulders fixed in the V-shape of the white vest thing she wore to bed, her legs in pyjama bottoms, drawn up and folded beneath her on the seat. She was certain Kay's shoulders had been broadening a little since they were school-girls. Just perceptible. Finn recalled from their last time together that Kay now played badminton in some sort of team at the university, but missed lots of games due to study and had been threatened with expulsion. Had she not hinted that she'd some-times lifted weights with her awful-sounding sort-of-boyfriend?

Finn gently moved the bed sheet aside; covers seemed to have been stripped back. She moved her legs out and lowered her feet down to the carpet and she stretched her arms up. All silently. She needed to pee. But she stood and looked over at the bed of Ava. Ava was concealed in a long, still, undisturbed tube of covers.

Picking her feet through opened, gutted suitcases, Finn approached Kay undetected, noticing she had small earpiece headphones in her ears and was absorbed in the clear, formal light of the laptop screen. Emails. Updates to the sort-of-boyfriend. Finn didn't want to startle her so she touched the bare shoulder.

Kay turned and smiled calmly. 'Hey.' The earpieces were tugged out and dangled to the desk but no sound came from them.

Finn leaned over, moving her face down near Kay's. 'Did you sleep?' she whispered.

'Yes. Surprisingly.' Again whispered.

She looked over at Manda; one arm was stuck up out the bed and twisted, uncomfortably-looking, on the headrest.

'We have a problem,' Kay whispered.

Finn turned and looked in Kay's face. She whispered, 'You mean, you and me have a problem?'

Kay's eyes recoiled. She grinned oddly. It came sounding to Finn like a reprimand. 'All of us.'

Suddenly Finn dropped her head a little more and quickly pecked a kiss on Kay's jawbone just in front of her ear, in the Continental manner. Like Ava kissed her French father, and like Finn never kissed her own father. 'Morning.'

'Good morning,' Kay replied but she was looking rigidly at the screen of emails.

'What is it?'

'The Vegas flights have all vanished, or worse, doubled in price.'

'Why?'

'No earthly idea. But look at this.' Kay began tapping commands. She quickly wiped the emails away. A minimised screen at the bottom popped up and Kay lifted a finger and pointed to some lettering.

Finn was looking down at the nape of Kay's neck and at her shoulders; that watery perfume which only older women use? Finn whispered academically, 'You've got really nice shoulders. I'm just skinny these days, you're sort of . . . toned but not butchy.'

Kay shifted a little in the seat and looked up at Finn. Still whispering but now it had dropped to almost inaudible, 'That's the badminton but I'm getting awful at it. I'm getting fitter and fitter and worse and worse at baddy, incrementally.' Kay hushedly added, 'Flights included. Five nights at the Alvaro Hotel. A four-star hotel. That's really good. Just off the Strip, six hundred and five pounds each with breakfast. That's incredible.'

As a sort of obscure reward for Kay's morning research, Finn knew she must respect it and suddenly kneeled down beside her to look at the screen, though her head swirled, realising she had no interest. 'Wow. Five nights. That's amazing.'

'A big problem. It only flies tomorrow at four in the afternoon. Not today.'

'Tomorrow. Oh, you're joking me? Oh no.'

'Yup. And I've checked and rechecked and there's bugger all else today like that. Only tomorrow. There's two package deals this afternoon and this evening but one's nine hundred quid and the other one thousand four hundred and both in weird, crappy-looking hotels, no breakfast included and awful flight times back. But this gem only goes tomorrow. Changing once, in New York.'

There was a long pause.

Kay looked down at Finn and raised her forehead hopefully, signalling that this was an acceptable and very attractive concept.

'Don't you want to? Go to Vegas?'

'Vegas would be curious. But . . .' Finn's head nodded back to Manda's bed and she risked a glance at the slumbered bulk. 'There'll be more fights like yesterday.'

Kay leaned, almost to Finn's face, head minutely canted to the ear. 'It could work to our advantage. If they have the death sentence in Nevada?'

Finn smiled.

Kay suddenly went practical as she always did. 'One more night on our cards. Then flights on Tuesday and we'd be out of this money pit. I mean this is madness, living in bloody hotels for days.'

'I know it's madness.'

Kay and Finn looked at each other. Finn felt she was waking up now, dreams falling away from her, harder facts coming in from differing directions. The first one: 'I need to pee.'

Finn went to the bathroom, struggled for the light switch, left the door open and sitting on the pan suddenly groaned a little when she clearly heard, spoken at normal threat level, 'What are *yous* two whispering about then?' in Manda's bass voice.

Kay said something Finn couldn't make out. She flushed the toilet, washed her hands and moved back through to the bedroom. Manda was up, out of bed, her big voice sounding in grumbles and hard vowels.

Kylah too had sat up on her elbows now.

Finn had a shocking and unexpected desire to be somewhere alone with Kay.

At normal volume (which was high), Manda announced, 'Don't forget now, girls, they only serve McMuffins at Mackers till half ten.'

'Morning, Manda. You're up . . . spry,' Finn smiled.

'Aye. That's me. Always up for it. You never know what day'll be your last.'

'Aye. Especially with you about.'

'Morning, Kyles.'

Kylah nodded and yawned. Her sleepy morning face made her look fifteen years old again, Finn thought.

Finn stepped across the room and Manda, standing behind Kay, now watched her every move. 'Hush, Manda. Some are sleeping.'

'No they're no if they want double egg or double sausage McMuffins. I got them told last night to get up for half ten. They won't serve them up afterwards. Jings. I don't know what'll have myself. A double egg or a double sausage McMuffin? I'll just have one of each. And a Coke. I don't like coffee.'

'There's something you need to see, Manda,' said Kay. 'Look.'

'What?'

'There's an amazing package to Vegas. Six hundred quid each for five nights including breakfast and flights.'

'Six hundred. We've spent way more than that in this bloody airport-thing-place in two days.'

'I know.'

Manda leaned down next to Kay, taking the place where Finn had been. Finn grumpily had to sit over on the end of the bed, then after a moment she said, 'I'm going for a shower,' and she went for her toilet bag submerged down in her backpack.

Finn had been in the shower a while when she heard a voice and quickly squinted through the perspex splash shield then wiped a squeaky palm on it to try for visibility.

'Finn?'

'What?'

Chell called, 'Hey, Finn. Can I just come in to fill the kettle? Do you fancy coffee?'

'What?'

'Can I come in?'

'Aye. Course. Come in.'

'I'm sorry, I'm sorry, I won't look. Do you fancy coffee, cos it's a family room there's all six cups and all stuff to make it? It's brilliant. I just have to fill the kettle?'

'Coffee. Sure. That'd be a lifesaver.' Finn stepped out of the spray, grabbed and shoved her hair right back, elbows up. Chell came in through the steam, galaxies of atoms of it, illuminated in a yellowish, drifting intensity up by the spotlights. Finn suddenly thought how earlier philosophers were unburdened by science, still searching for the good life. A lost art. Chell had an unlit cigarette in her mouth and she carried the kettle out in front of her. Chell's other hand shaded the left of her face, making a show of not looking at Finn in the shower.

'Did you sleep, Chell?'

'Aye, thanks. Like a baby with all my friends.'

Finn didn't return beneath the spray. She stood watching Chell lean over the sink and angle the kettle in under the tap to fill it. She looked at her arse. Finn actually stood free of the perspex splash. 'Did Kay explain about the Las Vegas flights?'

'She says something, aye, but says she'll explain it when you're there. You know she loves her big general meeting of the committee thing.'

'You're dying for a smoke, aren't you, pet? You can smoke there if you want?'

'Can I just take one wee gasp? Kylah's at the window.'

'Aye.'

Chell suddenly produced a lighter from the breast pocket of her pyjamas.

Finn stepped back under the water to rinse herself with her eyes closed. When she opened them, Chell was stood high up on the closed toilet seat, her head ducked for the ceiling. Again she had her hand positioned to shield her view of Finn. Finn smiled. 'Watch you don't fall off, Chell. That's all daft. I don't think you need to do that.'

'Kay says there's smoke detectors in these family rooms and then the mannie'll come and see we're not a family and think we're a wild hen party and chuck us all out.' Chell blew smoke towards the extractor fan in the ceiling but most of her smoke missed and pummelled in alongside the steam, missing the suction.

'Well, we've already slept, so let them chuck us out.' Finn could tell Chell was concentrating more on her cigarette than anything else. She jammed the shower off and squeezed out her hair then used her palms to swipe her body down of droplets. Finn saw the cigarette was only halfway down.

'I'm no looking, Finn.'

'I don't care if you look, you've seen me in the scud before,' said Finn.

Chell looked straight down. 'You've a wee tiny tattoo! When did you get that?'

'Way last year.'

'Writing. It's so tiny and nice. What's it say?'

'It's a quote.'

'What's a quote?'

'Something a person's written or said.'

'Oh aye. What's it say?' She craned forward on the toilet seat, squinting, trying to read it.

Quickly, Finn said, '"And yet it sometimes seems to me I did get born and wandered in the towns and tarried by the seas in tears."'

Chell stepped down off the toilet, taking Finn's hand which reached up to steady her, then she turned her back and popped the cigarette butt in under the toilet seat and turned once again, but she bent over daintily at the waist to put her face right up close to Finn's left pelvic bone and examined where the scroll and delicate curlicue lettering began at an angle, moving down in three lines. 'So does that show, above your bikini line?'

'Just a bit. You only see a bit. To read it all, you need to get to know me better.'

Chell sniggered.

'I was scared the girls would spot it yesterday when we's were in the scud in that bloody car. I was trying to hide it. I wanted to show you it in Benidorm or that, when we got there. I'm no sure if we're going on a bikini holiday now.'

'They sunbathe in the mornings in Las Vegas. The power chicks all lie round the pools in the morning after partying. I saw that on telly once. That'd be brilliant cos I'll have new bikinis every day as good as them.' Chell remained down there. Now her lips were moving to the words of the tattoo. When Chell talked, Finn had felt the small puffs of her doubtless smoky breath on her pelvic bone.

Finn offered, 'And it'll keep me from getting a belly, cos it would look awful if I had a belly hanging over it. Even an inch. It makes me do my sit-ups.'

'You do sit-ups?'

'Aye.'

In a hushed, awed voice, Chell said, 'But what does it *mean*? "And yet it sometimes seems to me I did get born." But it's obvious you got borned?'

'I think it's about . . . unreality of life, strangeness. The dreaminess.'

'But it's sad too, Finn.'

'Aye. And it makes me think of you.'

She whispered, 'Cos I tarried by the sea in tears.'

'Aye.'

She straightened up now and looked Finn in her face. 'It's very beautiful. I like it. But it's a wee bit scary. Did it hurt?'

'Nut. But listen. Don't tell Manda this.' Finn whispered, 'A guy was with me. My ex-boyfriend. Our first night in bed together and he was . . . going down on me thing, and he kept stopping, reading a few words at a time. And that was annoying me enough. Then after a minute he stopped and goes, "Tears. Tears?" You know, like rips in your clothes? I'm lied there on my back and in a really bad-tempered voice I goes, "Tears. Tears, you stupid man. Like crying." Right in the middle of it all. That was the beginning of the end for that relationship. At the beginning of it.'

They both burst out laughing, really loud, and Finn took a towel and wrapped herself in it. 'There.'

'Tears. What an idiot. Even I can read it's tears. And he'd be educated as well,' Chell added.

'Aye. Privately of course. Most of them is boneheads with money.'

Finn swiped the mirror clear and studied her face in it. 'I'm getting old.' She took a small towel and rubbed her hair a little but just to get the majority of the water off.

Chell stepped away holding the kettle. 'You're not. You're gorgeous. Coffee, aye?'

'Please, darling.'

'With those wee fake milky things?'

'Aye please. No sugar please. Chell?'

'Aye?'

'Only you know about the tattoo for the now, otherwise, it'll have to be down with my knickers to show Manda and that, in front of everybody.'

Chell nodded and put one straight finger up to her lips and smiled.

When Finn came out the bathroom with her damp hair free and a towel wrapped round her, Kylah was still sitting up in their bed looking not quite with it all. Manda gave Finn a suspicious look.

Ava was sat up in bed too but with the sheet pulled high over her tits, her bare shoulders, freckled by holidays in France as a young girl, luxuriously free. Finn smiled at her. 'Greetings, brave voyager.'

An array of white teacups were organised on the desk, the plugged-in kettle whining a low groan like an aircraft. Finn sat down on the edge of the big bed.

'Right, everyone listen,' Kay said. 'Decision time for real now. All the flights and packages to Vegas are way up in price and the cheapos have vanished. There is an amazing deal in a four-star hotel for five nights. Problem is, it goes tomorrow at five-ish.'

Kylah said, 'Oh come on now. We can't spend our holidays in this airport. We're a laughing stock and we're spending all our next year's holiday money as well at this rate. We've spent gallons stuck here.'

Kay nodded, commiserating. 'All in all I was calculating for each of us it's amounting to about seven hundred including the banjaxed Spanish trip.'

Kylah looked at Kay. 'I owe you and Ava about seven hundred quid?'

'I'll work it out exact but that's how it's looking at the moment then you have to add on another six hundred to book this. Then it's our spending money only, girls. But your spending money is going to be low in Vegas, apart from food in the evening, because breakfast is included here.'

'But we've gotta pay for shows and that. You've got to go to the shows in Vegas. And men strippers,' Manda brayed.

Finn frowned.

Kylah just laughed. 'I'm so sunk. I'll pay yous back but I'm sunk.' She turned to Manda and says, 'That's no Saturday nights out for a year, Manda.' She looked at Finn and nodded.

Kay said, 'Well, the alternative is to abandon Las Vegas. Get on a plane to Spain now and we're off. But I mean six hundred pounds is the price of some five-nighters in Benidorm. Benidorm isn't Las Vegas.'

'No, no, girls,' Manda bellowed. 'We'd agreed. It's got to be Las Vegas.'

'*Las Vegas or Bust*. Ever seen that?' called Kylah. 'Jerry Lewis. Brilliant.'

'So really, everyone. This is Kylah and Chell's call.'

Kylah suddenly seemed intrigued. 'Six hundred?'

'Six hundred and five pounds for flights and five nights. Breakfast included. And don't forget, girls, Ava knows how to get drinks free all day in the casinos, so we'd save hundreds, food is cheap and there's everything there . . . so in a weird way, I think this would work out cheaper than us loose in Benidorm, buying drinks all night.'

There was a group silence.

'Aye. Fuck it,' said Kyles. 'I don't care. Let's go for it.'

'Yes.' Chell punched the air.

Manda went, 'But what are we going do the day . . . ? Hey. Let's go for another wee drive in the country, Ava. That was brilliant yesterday.'

Ava, Finn and Kay laughed dismissively.

Manda leaned over and waved a hand to get Ava's exclusive attention. 'Imagine me being in Las Vegas. I'd love to know how it all works – when I do things – I wouldn't know how it all works.'

The kettle had clicked and Chell had turned and started making the infusions. 'Right, Ava and Kay, you'll share the teapot for a cuppa each?'

'Yes please.'

Chell was pouring the kettle into the single teapot and putting water into individual coffee cups then stirring them chinkingly.

Manda was glaring at Ava. Finn followed her gaze. The sheet had slipped down and one of Ava's small breasts was free.

'You're flashing, Ava.'

'Ooops. Sorry.' She pulled the sheet up to her neck.

'You've got a nice tit there, Ava,' Chell said in her usual brusque but encouraging manner.

'I wish I'd tits like that. That didn't move hardly,' said Kylah. 'Mine were all wet in underneath them yesterday. I'm twenty-one and they're starting to droop a wee bit.' She looked down at her breasts and lifted them both within her pyjama top, her hands letting them fall.

'Are they fuck, lucky besom. At least you've got some compared to me,' said Chell aggressively.

'So much bikini and such little tit,' Manda drawled hurtfully and they all saw Chell's face fall. Angrily Chell said, 'So. Manda. Are you no having a coffee then?'

'Nut. I don't really like coffee. Expressos and that in Glasgow.'

'Espressos,' Ava, quietly but forcefully, said.

'Eh?'

'Espresso. Not ex.'

'Espresso? I thought it was ex-presso; cos it was, like quick?'

'No. Espresso. It means squeezed, crushed. Squeezed coffee beans.'

'Is that right, Ava? Well, thanks very much for the bloody philosophies lesson. I'll get ma Coca-Cola in Mackers with ma McMuffin breakfast, thank you very –'

Ava said, 'With your voice, Kylah, you might have a singing contract at the Sands Hotel on your first night.'

'Oh! Oh. Imagine!' Manda yelled, so they all frowned at the volume.

'Finn, here's your coffee, no sugar, Kyles takes milk and sugar.' There was chinking and clinking as Chell stirred the teaspoons.

Kay had been looking at the return journey. 'You change at JFK on the way back too. Good hours.'

Ava said, 'What's the actual flying time to JFK tomorrow? Make sure we don't go the other way round the bloody world or something. I almost booked a cheap flight like that to the States once and I swear it went the wrong way round the world.'

'Was that the one with your interesting toilet break?' Manda bleated.

Kay looked confident. 'Nope. Seven hours to New York on the same day and the way back.'

Ava said, 'That's a bloody good deal then.'

Chell crossed over with tea in a saucer and handed it to Ava. 'You sure you and Kay don't want milk, just brown tea?'

'No, that's lovely. Thank you, Chell.' The tits came right out again as Ava sat further up to drink and the sheet slipped off then she at last put the tea down carefully on the bedside cabinet and pulled away all the covers. She reached, lifted up her discarded slip from the night before and pulled it on, covering herself. Manda watched all this forensically with a curled lip.

'What's the verdict then?'

'Let's book it big time. Maybe Robbie Williams'll be in Vegas, girls?'

'I like Robbie but I just don't fancy him.'

'Are you mad?' yelled Manda. 'He's gorgeous.'

'Seriously, girls. Will we book it? Because I'm scared of this one vanishing and we can't blow a thousand quid again. There's no changing minds. This is it.'

'How'll we split it? It's so much.'

'We'll split it on Kay and I's credit cards. Again. A grand and a half on each, I guess,' Ava called out over her teacup – she was laying out long upon her bed. Manda was scoping up and down Ava's legs now, trying to detect any blemishes or potential treatments.

Kay said, 'Sorry, girls, but after this, that's it. We're going to have to add up the bills of what everyone owes Ava and I. We'll need a few drinks for that.'

'We's're fucked anyways, aren't we? I mean, we've been bears, haven't we, cos of Manda's passport, so now we might as well go for it big time, and be grizzlies.'

Manda suddenly said, 'We's can put me and someone on mine.'

'What?'

'We can put me and say, one-other-someone-else on my credit card.'

'Do you have a credit card?'

'Of course I do.'

'From the salon?'

'Aye. But I'm allowed to put stuff on it.'

Finn went, 'Manda. Since when? You never told us you had a credit card.'

'It's for emergencies.'

'Fuck sake, Manda, we've been in an emergency since Friday night with Kay and Ava stacking it all up on their credit cards. Near everything. They're going to get heat from their parents. You do understand that, don't you? They are about to put three and a half grand on their cards just so we can go on this holiday. Ava put the hire car on hers and yet she always buys a round. They're doing all that and you've got your arse sat on a credit card. Me, Chell and Kylah can't afford to get credit cards, Manda. You do know that?'

'I bought yous all your Pizza Express stuff last night. Even though I thought it couldn't be ate by humans.'

'Don't you forget it's cos of you, all told, we're hundreds down on the Spanish trip; huge hotel bills on their cards and we've no got anyplace yet. Don't forget that, Manda. And don't dare start cheapskating us. We're all in this mess together, money-wise. Right? We've got to live out each other's pockets, and it's by the grace and generosity of Ava and Kay we are, or else you'd be out on your arse, on the way home. Fuck sake, girl.'

Manda seemed remarkably sanguine despite this attack. It was unnerving. She plainly stated, 'It was not my decision to stay yesterday. That's was all yous decisions. Before I heard about a brill place like Las Vegas, I was all set for cheapo Magaluf. Don't try to lump yesterday's cost on me. I'll pay it, that's no a problem, but don't say it was all my fault like Saturday was. Yous were so sure I'd be ill and no be allowed on a plane and there I was, dashing around the English countryside and sliding down hills, like a hero.'

More calmly and practical, Kay asked, 'Are you serious, Manda? Can we actually put a thousand two hundred on your card?'

Manda growled, 'Aye. Slap it on the plastic, Kay. Slap it on the plastic, love, as Catriona says. That's what they're there for.'

Finn shook her head. 'That's holding out, Manda. You never let on you had a credit card, you bampot.'

She winked infuriatingly. 'Don't you worry, Sinnin' Finn. I'll see yous right.'

There was a thundery silence in which everyone occupied themselves, sipping and drinking their coffees and teas.

'So. Are we going to book it?' Kay asked.

'Let's put it on all the three cards then.'

Kay said, 'Once we book this, there's absolutely no going back. I can't put any more on my card. It *is* Las Vegas or bust, girls.'

Ava said, 'And listen, ladies. We should take out medical

insurance. Only thirty pounds each or something. In America you need it. Break a leg and break the bank.'

'We'll do that. Yes. Good thinking, Ava.'

'Does that cover VD?'

'Giving it or getting it, Manda?' Finn called out.

'Fuck off.'

Kay said, 'Right. Everybody check you've got your bloody passports safe. Make sure your knickers are sewed to your vests, girls, because I shall book it.'

Manda's credit card, for her and Kylah's combined fare, wouldn't work on the first attempt. 'Slap it on the plastic, Manda, eh?' Finn sneered. Everyone looked at one another ominously but not in surprise.

'Och. It can't be maxed out. Though I was doing a wee bit clothes shopping on the catalogue for this hurl,' she revealed, dauntingly. She looked over Kay's shoulder and instantly said, 'Tut. You've got the number wrong, Kay. That's a one, no a seven,' indicating, despite her dizziness, Manda knew her credit card number by heart. On the second attempt it actually worked. They were amazed and passed the credit card around, examining it, looking at Manda's embossed name, not the salon's.

'It's a personal card, is it then?'

'Aye. I mean, Catriona give it me for the salon. I have to make lots of urgent and very important phone orders sometimes. She won't mind me using it in an emergency.'

'I can't believe we've done it,' Kay was repeating, 'And it's gone on all the cards.'

'Well, that's that. Las Vegas here we come. God help it.'

Manda said, 'Right. Aye, come on, we need to start showering and getting our arses in gear. The McMuffins.'

'Well, Ava showers first cos she skipped it last night,' said Finn defensively.

'Minky. Glad I was sleeping with Kay,' Manda drawled.

274

Chell went, 'Well, I'll tell yous this. I'm no showering after Manda. When I come up here last night, she's done this jobby that stunk the toilet out.'

Manda laughed, so the whole bed she was sat on rocked. 'Las Vegas here I come. Oh aye. That was some jobby right enough. It must be the Guinness or that. It was *long*. I've never in my life done such a long jobby. It just went on and on and on. We could of took a photo of it on the disposable camera, Kyles.'

'Don't scum me out.'

Manda laughed. 'Aye. And I flushed the thing two, three times an it just wouldn't go round the bend. I had to come in here, get one of the teaspoons and chop the shit up into bits to get it to flush. Lucky I got none on my fingers, the spoon was so wee.'

That halted the last few leisurely liftings of the coffee and teacups.

'Och, don't worry about that. Just a bit Guinness jobby. I cleaned the spoon after. I ran it under the tap in the bath. The hot-water tap too, not the cold one.'

'And then . . . you put the spoon, back in the drawer?' asked Kylah.

'Aye? Course. What's wrong with that? It was well scalded, girls.'

'For . . . fuck sake, Manda. I used all the spoons for the tea and coffee here.'

Kay said, 'I feel faint.'

Ava had her face in her hands.

Manda chuckled drily but as an isolated echo within the large room which made her mirth sound distant and it soon withered. She stood from the bed and she stretched, guiltily, all eyes uncomfortably upon her. She coughed awkwardly then called, 'Come on, girls. Got to get a shift on if we want to get a big fucking Mackers breakfast. Egg and sausage McMuffin. It's brilliant but only served till half ten. Yous must be gagging for it?' She looked at her watch and frowned. 'Oh, I've put it on upside down again. Las Vegas. It's going to be a classic, girls. Oh, it's going to be a classic okay.'

2

Manda: Pint of Guinness Extra Cold.
Ava: Double straight Stolichnaya vodka with ice.
Kay: Medium-size glass of red wine.
Chell: Bacardi Breezer.
Finn: Tomato juice with vodka, unworthy of title Bloody Mary.
Kylah: Red Bull and vodka.

The young women were located exactly as usual, in the smoking area of the Gatwick Village Inn. Making up for the tobacco restrictions of the night before, Chell, and even Kylah, chain-smoked jumpily.

The suitcases had been returned yet again to the left luggage where Manda had been especially frosty to the poor attendant's familiar but justifiable questions. However, Manda had said to him, 'If you must know that's me off to Las Vegas, mister. But tomorrow. Don't worry, pal. I'll be sending you a postcard.'

Unfortunately for the young women, Manda was in a thoroughly buoyant mood. Between the usual narration of long, familiar and ranging anecdotes, Manda turned frequently and fiercely observed the toings and the froings of clientele in the pub. Especially a table of lads not too far away whom, each time they laughed loudly, Manda craned around towards, desperate to involve herself in their mirth.

While looking over at the lads, she continued in the loud voice, 'Now was this the other holiday? Let me think. No, that was the same holidays. I get mixed up. You know? I've been to Magaluf so much.'

'You've been twice.'

'So we're in this club; ditched Shelly cos she was spilling beer down her legs by then. Legs that needed waxing, by the way.'

Manda gave a cautionary look at Ava. 'I tell you. Me and Cat weren't feeling it in the club. You know? We weren't feeling it. It was a weird atmosphere and then this ancient couple starts talking to Cat. And they buys us drinks – couldn't get Guinness Extra Cold in there, I remember. The music's so loud I can't hear what's being said. But Cat keeps giving me the eye and they gets us up to dance but soon me and Cat go off to the toilet but Cat takes my hand and leads me away and I'm like, "Cat. What's going on, doll?" but we're out the door and away. Cos do yous knows what theys were? Do yous know what that couple were?'

At last, Kylah, who had heard the story umpteen times before, obediently took her cigarette out her mouth and blandly asked, 'What were they?' She put her cigarette straight back in her mouth.

Manda yelled, 'They was swingers! It was a club for swingers and they was swingers trying to get off with Cat for a big brutal swinging session. You knows what swingers is, don't you? Chell?'

'Aye. I know what swingers is.'

'Aye. They was swingers okay. Dirty buggers. Swingers is like people who is so ancient and ugly and they can't let threesomes and brutal gang bangs and all that just happen to them on a normal night out, like they happen to us young folk. Those things just happen, don't they, to normal folk like us? Like that time at Tosh's crap party, Kyles. Life's rich tapestry, as my Nana says. Though obviously, Nana's no talking about swinger sex when she says that. You don't organise your sex life over the computer and in magazines and that unless yous are pretty sick, do you? Nobody would shag swingers, so's swingers have to organise it all among themselves in clubs and societies and magazines and Internets and all that. Like organising Sunday lunch with parents. But they swingers all sit around together and watch, you know, the postie from one town and the wifie of the bank manager from the next having a go at each other. And they all join in! It's like mince, tatties and peas. I like the mince placed on the mashed tatties then the peas on the top. Most normal folk do. But swingers must mash their mince and tatties up into a right old muck. And eat at the same time every night. Where's the fun in that? They're no . . . what's the philosophy word? Spontaneous.

No spontaneousnesses. I mean, these two swingers was ancient. Cat told me they was saying, "Ditch your mate and come with us," and she says, "That's my wee sister," and they were, "We don't have a crèche." Cheeky bastard pervos. They were fucking ancient. Wrinkles and that. They must have been at least thirty. Aye. They was swingers okay. We even left our drinks there. Now, girls.'

The others looked up, fretfully.

'I'm just away a wee minute-ey to phone wee Sean and explain the meaning of Las Vegas to him. I'll tell him all his aunties are thinking of him and yous'll be thinking of him too when Santa comes this year. Watch my drink. I'll be straight back.' Manda paused.

The group of lads at the table behind them burst out laughing at something. One of them – the guy in the beanie hat – had been standing up to emphasise a point. Manda paused, staring at him and turned back to the girls with high contempt. 'A puffa jacket. Who wears a puffa jacket these days, eh? Ya mule. A puffa jacket. Plebs.' She shook her head in commiseration, rammed her chair out and turned to the young women. 'Now don't be going nowhere.' Manda walked off towards the open exit of the Village Inn then halted. She pretended to pause, exactly beside the table of loud lads, to check absolutely no messages on her mobile. Other than one lad giving her the briefest, dismissive glance, none of them looked at Manda. She sensed this quickly and therefore she immediately moved on.

Ava yawned at Finn, not covering her mouth. At least her teeth weren't perfect, she had some fillings at the back, Chell noticed.

'I'm going to get newspapers.' But Ava made no move.

'I might get one too,' Kay added.

In a curiously hollow tone Finn asked, 'What do you feel like doing today, Ava?'

'Drink, magazines and newspapers in a locked hotel room with anyone. Except Manda.'

Finn stared her down. 'You're bored. Aren't you?'

Indifferently, Ava said, 'No.'

'I can tell when you're bored.'

Ava shrugged. 'Okay then. God. Don't be so clingy.'

278

Finn turned aside.

Chell coughed and then there was much talk of Las Vegas and buying guidebooks until Manda returned, sped past the table of lads, without casting them a glance, sat down in her chair and grabbed out at her pint. Everyone was silent. Manda looked around the table. 'God, cheer up why don't you all?' she almost shouted. 'Yous wouldn't think yous were going to Las Vegas in the morrow.' She glanced over to determine if the table of lads had heard this. 'Huh.'

Chell asked, 'How's wee Sean?'

'Fine. You won't believe what I've gone and just found.'

They looked at her.

'Know yon Game Grid place round the corner?'

'Mmm.'

'It didn't have one before but now it does. Guess what's there right now.'

'What?'

'Ezzy Dancer.'

Chell said, 'Oh no. You're joking?'

Kay frowned. 'What is that?'

'This brilliant dancing game.'

'Oh dear.'

'Manda'll never let us off it.'

'Come on. Let's go round for the crack. It'll be brilliant. I swear it wasn't there the other day. It must have been out of order.'

Finn had stood up abruptly and all turned to her, but as their smiling faces rose towards Finn's they saw the rarest of sights. Tears coming down like little costume diamantés. Finn cried without her pale face reddening at all, so the singular tears looked strange, like moving maggots or rice beads.

Chell went, 'Aww,' in shock.

Finn turned and made for the Ladies toilet just over behind them; she pushed the swing door open gently, not aggressively, and vanished within. Chell was on her feet but Ava put out a constraining arm. 'A minute, Chell. Give her a minute.'

Kylah and Chell looked on with amazement at these swirls of conflict and ripened drama developing before them.

Manda was wide-faced. She gasped, 'What was that about? I thought we timed this holiday for no periods. Ezzy Dancer isn't that bad. I won't force her to do it.'

'I don't think it's to do with Ezzy Dancer, Manda.'

'What's up with old iron tits? She's right miserable getting, girls. Oh.' Then she thought she got it, swivelled on the chair. 'Oh. Is she feeling . . . guilty? For having a go about me for having a credit card when she doesn't even have one herself? That'll be it. After all, I've contributed to her having a holiday and all she can do is greet.'

Chell shrugged and said, 'Well, I'm not getting involved but you did snarl at her a wee bit there, Ava, when she just asked if you were bored.'

Ava, whispered, just audibly, 'Jesus Christ.'

Manda was open-mouthed. 'Never? A lovers' tiff? It's going to be tears and whispers on this holidays, girls, I'm telling yous.'

Kylah said, 'What's up with her, Ava?'

Ava coughed. 'It's like yesterday when she didn't want me to drink and drive.'

'But she never cries, except at Orla's funeral.'

'But you never had a drink. Just as well, with they Feds pulling us.'

'I once drove home so drunk I can't recall the journey. Woke up at home. My Mini Cooper had my sickness in the passenger-seat foot space. Yesterday she was worried about me drinking and driving. Sometimes she's a little overprotective.'

'Who's to go in there and see her then? Chell, I votes. She's the nicest of us?' Kylah looked around.

Ava turned quietly. 'Kay. Will you go have a word with her for a few moments?'

Manda announced, 'Jeezo, girls. Tears after lunch and last thing at night, eh? Cos I don't mind admitting I was getting a wee bit teary at Kylah's singing last night, eh? It was like the end of *Titanic*. I'm glad the lights were out.'

Chell nodded. 'Aye, that's true, Manda, my waterworks was groaning into action.'

Manda looked around and clapped her hands. 'Och. Anyway. While we's are waited on greeting face. Another round, girls?'

When Kay came into the Ladies, a cubicle was open with a toilet just flushing in it, a lady was emerging, going over to the sinks. One other cubicle was closed with the red enamel display showing on the lock mechanism.

'Finn. It's Kay.'

'I'm just coming.'

'Okay then.'

'Is it just you?'

'Yes.'

The lock flipped. Kay turned and looked to the lady at the sink who was swivelled round at her, suspicious and disapproving. The hand dryer started. Finn was standing as Kay stepped into the cubicle, a strained smile on Finn's face which seemed pulled downward in upset.

'When I come to write the book, Kay, it'll be called: "Tears in the Toilet Cubicle: Our Social Circle".'

Kay turned and shoved the door behind her, locked it but stood against it, back from Finn who was opposite the toilet paper dispenser, leaning against the partition, a grubby fist of cheap loo paper in her grip.

'What's the matter?'

'I don't know. And all this came gushing up. I remember Orla's dad saying he never cried when they put Orla in the ground, then a year after, the next-door neighbour's cat died and he cried for two days. We hold things in.'

Kay nodded. 'Look, Finn. You don't need to feel guilty going off on Manda about the credit card. It's not as if Manda doesn't give you a hard time, like *all* of the time.' Kay carried on, her mouth moving quickly. 'Manda can be so queer and contradictory. The most selfish person I know can sometimes be the most generous. The biggest bore on earth can be one of the funniest. Who else could compare Internet swingers to mince, tatties and peas?'

They both shook their heads. Finn's face opened into a sort of amazed smile.

'And I suppose a lot of what she said actually had some sort of sound sociological grounding, in a completely mad sense.' She paused. 'Something else bothering you? Something about London or . . . I don't know?'

'Ach, Kay Clarke, from the house on the hill. It's been a long year.'

'Yup. What?' Kay seemed a little unsure.

The hand dryer outside stopped and the Ladies toilet went quiet. Finn whispered, 'Come here.'

A little robotically, Kay stepped forward with her arms held out, but only from the elbows for her usual, cautious, torso-touching contact, rather than a hearty hug.

Kay's stomach sunk so hard she thought its lurch must be visible.

But Finn shook her head and grabbed Kay by both forearms and pulled her forwards. Kay was in confusion for less than a second, unsure what Finn was going to do, then she realised Finn was holding onto her forearms firmly, standing erect in front of her. Preventing her coming any closer. Now Finn put her face towards Kay's face, so their noses were close. The movements of Finn's face were odd. The eyes making no contact, looking over Kay's right shoulder, the mouth held slightly aside. For another split second Kay thought Finn was either going to kiss her on the mouth or she was about to faint. Then Finn whispered, almost silently, and looked in Kay's eyes, 'Kay. Ava is my best pal but she is a legendary, awful cokehead.'

'A cokehead?'

'And worse. She was sniffing heroin for a long time too.'

'Really?'

'Keep your voice down. Just whisper. That family is rich and titled in some obscure way. She's no show-off and she plays it down. They have Renoirs in a place in France not hanging on the wall they're worth so much. For insurance, they're kept in a secret vault and they all go and sit twice a year and drink champagne and look at them. I've never been but I've seen the photos.

Ava was really, really bad on drugs from when she was seventeen till a few years back. She was nearly dead twice with overdoses before I met her, then she was in these posh health farms and all that.'

'Rehabilitation? You're joking me? She has perfect bloody skin.'

'I don't know much about drugs. She was snorting heroin, coke and guzzling booze. But just . . . she did it till she fell over. Frightening.'

'God; using needles?'

'Nah. She's much too vain for that. And too rich. When you're really rich you can snort heroin. You don't need to inject. Says she has a genetically perfect nose for it. I mean, I've seen her snorting coke like she's . . . disgusting. And the money! When she started, it used to last days. Now it's a few hours. Then she quits. She thinks if she just does coke once a month she's an angel.'

'Rich kid. She's a bit of a cliché, Finn. I thought she'd be smarter.'

'I never knew her at Oxford. That's why she got tossed out; apparently she was just wasted all the time. Running wild. Her and her rich pals were just flying round, smashed out their heads. Actually flying, I mean. Once she woke up in Rome when she should have been in a Logic lecture, which is impressive, really. "Where's the logic in that?" she said. She only got that credit card back from her father in January.'

'Were you suffering that all through first year? It could have messed up your study.'

'By second term, yes, but it wasn't me suffering. You should have seen the state of her; she's gained two stone and she's still skinny. I've bad choice in friends, Kay.'

'Not in me.'

'No. Not in you. She's got those pals that'd overdose on camera, if *Vogue* guaranteed them it'd be on the front cover. She's a dazzling mix. The *Critique of Pure Reason* in one hand and a coke bag in the other. I don't want the others to know. I just want you to, cos you're so smart and discreet.'

'Finn. She doesn't have . . .' Kay lowered her voice so she was just mouthing the one word . . . *drugs*, 'with her now, does she?'

'Nah.'

'Cos on this jinxed trip . . .'

Finn chuckled. 'She's not stupid. And she's had nothing around for months. See, she's too posh to use street people. All her connections are just rich users from her Oxford days. They aren't in London.'

At last Finn set free Kay's arms so they stood before each other. The cubicle door adjacent shut and the partition vibrated. A person began to piss in the toilet. At least it added to the absurdity and brought levity.

Kay looked at Finn through the long-drawn scoosh and froth of it and they both smiled. They shrugged. The piss went on a very long time. Then the flush.

Kay made a meaningless face.

The next door unlocked. The sink ran. The hand dryer began. Kay leaned forward so her mouth was next to Finn's ear. 'Let's go.'

Kay turned and unlocked the cubicle. They stepped out. The pisser woman was over by the mirror, checking her make-up. Her dead face examined them in the mirror.

The table of boys behind theirs had been replaced by a young, harassed family. A new round was up. Manda looked at them both immediately and then everyone else did.

'Well. Did yous two meet Elvis in there? Never mind. You will soon. Hey, Finn. I've got the round. The ice is melting in your gin and tonic.'

> Manda: Pint of Guinness Extra Cold.
> Ava: Double straight Stolichnaya vodka with ice.
> Kay: Medium-size glass of red wine.
> Chell: Bacardi Breezer.
> Finn: Gin and tonic with bottled tonic.
> Kylah: Red Bull and vodka.

Kay awkwardly returned to her seat. Finn still stood and said, 'Ta. Give us a fag, Mands.' Manda quickly peeled off two Marlboros and passed one to Finn.

'When all's told there is no end to my brilliantness at all,' Manda told her.

Finn grabbed the new gin and tonic and took a healthy draught from it then fumbled desperately to light the cigarette. 'That's true, Manda.'

Chell leaned over the table, trying to veer all conversation elsewhere. 'What's it like on a plane, Finn? Is it like a bus? Like is it hot or cold?'

Manda turned sharply and intervened. 'Well, I fly often and I would more describe it as cold, cos it has air whoosher things above you, like on the bus down the other night, and cold air comes out. You turn them off. If you can reach them. And we've all got to get seats together, a huge row of us. Oh, it's going to be brilliant. Just think, we'll all be singing and . . . oh, it'll be a classic. It'll be legendary.'

Chell asked, 'So I just need my trackies and runners?'

Manda leaped in authoritatively. 'That's best but you need, like, your-best-T-shirt. You've got to wear your-best-T-shirt cos obviously you're travelling to Vegas now. People will see you all over the world. I'll be wearing my Donna Karan T-shirt and of course I have my Donna Karan trackies too.'

Chell said quickly, 'They're DKNY, not Donna Karan.'

Manda snarled across the table. 'It's the same thing. It's the same thing. Chell. I've already told you.'

'It's not the same thing. Donna Karan is the, like, expensive designer stuff and DKNY is the more high-streety line.'

'DKNY is *still* Donna Karan. You can't say DKNY is not Donna Karan.'

Chell stuck to her guns. 'I'm not. I'm not saying that, amma? I'm saying it is Donna Karan but it's the cheaper line DKNY. Donna Karan is dresses. If you see an actual Donna Karan dress. Well, that's millions.'

'It's no millions. We could get a Donna Karen dress in Las Vegas too – maybe – if we's all chipped in. So?'

'So nothing.'

'Well then. I told you.' Manda thrust out her arm. 'That watch is DKNY, Ava.'

'No. It's YNKD. Cos you got it upside down as per-usual,' Chell laughed.

Manda blanked this. 'So you need your-best-T-shirt, Chell. That Diesel one you have, you should wear. And I'll be wearing my gold runners and then you have to have your tracky top so you can zip it up if you get freezing. Or you need a light jacket. Like that jacket you've got. Calvin Klein. Aye, that's a nice jacket, Ava. I mean, I know you're wearing what you wore last night but it's still nice. Nice boots and all; what are they?'

'These? Mulberry from years ago. I really like boots when they're worn in.'

'Aye. Bit like Finn's cool motorcycle boots. I notice yous both kind of dress the shame. Student shabby chic, I would call it. The boots are a bit on the scruffy side but I could see they were once quality.'

Ava's patience ran out and she shook her head and said, 'Look then. Where are we going to all stay tonight? Or some of us?'

That merest hint of possible apartheid silenced Manda immediately.

'Aye. Aye, right enough, we need to decide that.'

'See, to save money Finn and I could just go back up to London, stay the night at our *tiny, little* place, then come back down for the check-in tomorrow, though the train is quite expensive.'

'Och, that would be a shame,' said Chell. 'To split up the old party.'

Ava said, 'How about that glass-and-steel place with the lifts we went to on . . . Saturday, was it, at the other end of the transit?'

Finn marvelled at how Manda's face changed: Manda's eyes suddenly enlivened with pure wonderment. 'Oh, the Meridian. That would be amazing. Girls. You! Finn. Kay. Yous haven't seen it yet. You really missed yourselfs. It's incredible there. What a hotel, all . . . lifts . . . going up. And . . . everything.'

'Or . . .'

Now Manda looked at Ava as if she held all possibilities.

'. . . we could save a lot of money by going out to that cheap joint we stayed in the first night.'

Manda looked crestfallen. 'Oh aye. Flight Dick thingmy. Suppose. No PlayStation in the rooms for Kylah there, that's for sure.'

Kay said, 'It's so much cheaper than the Hilton. Even the family room. That was a laugh last night but we really need to save the pennies.'

'Suppose.'

'Let's get twin rooms in that cheapo joint then.'

'Okay.' Manda looked at Finn. 'No tears over that?'

Finn shrugged. 'No.'

Kay said, 'We should book. Over the phone in case they run out of three twin rooms.'

Ava said, 'I'll do it. I've got a card.'

There was a tough silence. Nope. Manda wasn't volunteering her card.

Kay said, 'And, Manda, look. Please. I know you'll want to take a suitcase over for tonight but please, girls, leave them in left luggage or just one suitcase each if you really must.'

'Oh aye. My trackies is in just the one case. I know what one. I think.'

Finn spoke up. 'Can you all not just open your bloody cases, take out what you need for the morning and put the cases back, then go change?'

Kylah said, defensively, 'Nut. No you can't. Each time you take the suitcase out, that gadge says you have to pay to put it back in. It's like, that's a new hire of the left luggage starting all over again. We's've spent a fortune there as well.'

'I'm sorry, Manda, but the whole holiday is revolving around the three of you and your suitcases.'

'So? So? We didn't know we's were gonna be stuck here day on day, did we's? Normal you just haul your cases to the hotel in Magaluf and that's it. No need to worry about the bastern things till the night before you go home and you can't get them shut. Yous've been lucky cos we haven't been on a single proper decent night out in bars and clubs – cos we're stuck in this queer joint. Have we? We're no on make-up and big nights out like we'll be every single . . .' She paused and her gaze had followed two guys walking past the entrance to the Village Inn. 'They're bonks,' she declared. 'Bit plebby but the tall one's mine . . . Aye. We haven't been on a big night out every night, like is normal when yous're on your holidays, but imagine we'd needed our cases *every* night for clubbing.'

'Yes. Just imagine.'

Ava's mobile blonged a text-arrival tone and she idly viewed the incoming message. 'Just Mummy.' She added, 'And do you believe you'll wear everything you brought at least once, Manda?'

'Nut, love. Course not. No ways. I never do. But that's no the point, is it? Sometimes you need choices for a night out and you can't be seen wearing the same thing twice. I dunno how you two can travel just with the stuff yous have. It's . . . incredible. I mean. You can't have enough for five nights out in your backpack things. And you haven't hair straightners nor nothing. You can't be yourself without your stuff, girls. It's well known. It's a proven-thing.'

Ava tried, 'Can't you just get changed in an airport toilet in the morning?'

Manda was aghast. 'But we need to do our make-up too. You can't travel to Las Vegas without full make-up. What if you get . . . seen. I've to go get this nail done as well.' She shoved her heavily ringed hand right up in Ava's face, so Ava blinked. 'I see *you* don't do your nails, Ava. You should sort that out. You've a fair pair of pins on you as well, girl, I'll say that. A pedicure to round them off would be my advice. Now. Are we all ready for a good wee session on that fucking Ezzy Dancer?' Manda reached out and sieved down her sluggish, shifting pint.

3

At the back of McDonald's, the Game Grid amusement arcade was empty. The machines within seemed to talk among themselves, like burbling, jungle canopy wildlife. Because it was off-season, no children had been entrusted there and no parents were jubilant just along at the Village Inn – though this was the design and location purpose of the arcade.

The infernal machine, Ezzy Dancer, stood hugely before them, eight feet tall with elevated, embedded disco lights on top of the large speakers. The lights obediently flashed, reminding both Finn and Ava of sad village-hall discos long past. Above the Ezzy Dancer's raised dance floor for two persons, with rubberised supportive back bars and touch-sensitive foot pads, a mania of information scrolled up the large pulsating screen, then disappeared at the very top.

The dance-step arrows were flying upwards on the screen while an urging, wry, male American voice – like a cynical sergeant from the Marine Corps – imprecated and threateningly encouraged from the woofer speakers. '*Excellent.*' '*You could be a professional,*' the voice sneered towards phantom dancers who were not there, tempting observers to insert money, mount the platform and dance.

'They have one in McAdam Square Amusements now but it's always out of order, Finn.'

'Is it?'

Kylah stood aside the Ezzy Dancer machine pondering. Ava, Kay and Finn had taken a stance further back, their impatient body language signalling an unwilling involvement in proceedings.

'Aww brilliant.' Manda marched right on to the dance platform. 'I need to go first. I need to go first.'

Kylah coughed, jumped up beside her and was leaning forward

to the screen. She announced, 'Right. It's got Dance Mix Euro Stage 2 and Euro Stage 1 but I'm way out of practice.' She stepped back and let her almost fatless arse rest casually into the rubber-coated support bars.

Manda stood next to her and said, 'Euro Stage 1 is better music.'

'But it doesn't have "Cotton Eye Joe"!'

'That's on Stage 1.'

'Oh. Is it?'

'But Kylah, "Kung Fu Fighting" is on Stage 2. That's the greatest. And "Word Up".'

'Oh aye, I'd forgot. "Kung Fu Fighting". Aye.'

'How many pound coins you got?'

There was a scuffling and excavation for change.

'Here. Here.' They began assembling three or four coins next to the screen.

Finn and Ava watched. Each player had four arrow pads on the floor, pointing forwards, backwards, left and right. As the crazed music played, the objective was to meet the demand of placing feet correctly upon the weighted pads as instructed by a rushing succession of directional arrows racing on the screen – the required steps becoming faster and more torturous as the difficulty levels of the dances progressed.

'Here we go,' Manda called out seriously.

The music began. Kylah and Manda in synchronisation. Each put their left leg forward, like cats pawing out cautiously to test a substance, then the girls' legs moved to their left for the feet to tap, tap. Depressed, the floor pads lit up in a sickly pink or an electric blue. The legs went right.

Chell looked over at Finn and laughed out loud.

True enough, Finn couldn't help smiling at the robotic absurdity of it, as the two girls lifted their legs awkwardly high, yelled out in exasperation and concentrated with an intensity which held their gaze rigid upon the screen before them. They marched like drunken, goose-stepping soldiers. You could see Kylah was better at it, though Manda ploughed on with surprising dexterity.

If it hadn't been for Cotton-Eye Joe
I'd been married long time ago
Where did you come from where did you go?
Where did you come from Cotton-Eye Joe?

'Excellent.'

'You animals.'

If it hadn't been for Cotton-Eye Joe
I'd been married long time ago
Where did you come from where did you go?
Where did you come from Cotton-Eye Joe?

Manda screamed as she missed a step, paused to try and recover rhythm and then was back in it.

'You suck.'

Manda was red-faced and stopped dancing altogether, leaning down on her knees, laughing, but Kylah turned aside, still obeying her own arrow commands and yelled, 'Manda, keep going or we'll no get the next level, you hoor.'

'Keep up the pace.'

Finn turned to Ava who was laughing too. Finn joined in the laughter.

Manda turned to the screen, concentrated, took a side glance at Kylah's feet movements and was in time once again.

When the dance and applause had finished, Manda abandoned the podium then produced a small bottle of mineral water from her infinite bag and was drinking it without offering a drop round. Finn scrutinised the bottle, sure the identical brand had been stocked in the Flight Deck Hotel hotel minibar – so it came courtesy of Kay's credit card.

'Ooo, I'm right shagged out,' Manda confirmed for anyone in doubt, tugging the fabric of her top away from contact with her skin and blowing air from her mouth.

'You wanting a go then, Chell?' Kylah asked.

Aquatic blurps emanated from the Ezzy Dancer.

'Hey. Are *we* getting onto another level?'

'Looks like it. Took ages.'

Kylah and Chell both turned their bodies.

'What's it doing?' Kylah shrieked in excitement.

'*Are you ready?*'

Chell licked her lips and clapped her hands together. The demanding beat began. Kylah and Chell began to follow the rushing of arrows, lifting their knees high to their thigh level.

> There was funky Billy Chin and little Sammy Chung
> He said, 'Here comes the big boss, let's get it on.'
> We took a bow and made a stand, started swinging
>   with the hand,
> The sudden motion made me skip, now we're into a
>   brand new trip.

> Everybody was kung-fu fighting
> Those cats were fast as lightning
> In fact it was a little bit frightening
> But they did it with expert timing

Ava sidled to Finn and put her lips to her ear. 'What were the tears about, darling?'

'Nothing. I'm just tired.'

'I'll go over to that dump hotel. Book three twins and you can have an early night.' Ava took a breath. 'I might hide in my room and just read the papers for a while.'

'All right.'

'I'll text you or Kay with the room numbers. Don't tell Manda where I'm going.'

'I understand. I'm going to stay with these loonies. I might have another drink.'

'Okay,' Ava nodded casually and she eased out of the amusement arcade.

Manda turned round and yelled with excitement, 'Kay and Ava can have a shot. Oh aye. They won't get past the first dance.

I mean, all respect to Ava and Kay, but Ezzy Dancer is a skill and yous don't have the experience. Hoi. Where is Ava?'

Finn shrugged, smiling sweetly but Manda stepped directly towards her. 'Where's Ava gone?'

Finn shrugged once more.

'Eh? Where's she gone?'

Making a mistake, Finn said, 'The bog, I think,' and she stepped forward to watch the activity on the Ezzy Dancer.

Manda nodded, then said, 'Why'd she take her mingy back-pack thing?' Unsatisfied, troubled and morose, rubbernecking round, Manda was torn between missing nothing on the Ezzy Dancer yet angrily scanning where Ava had gone. Unable to resist, she stepped out of the arcade, looked both ways and could see nothing of Ava. Aggressively she marched towards the toilets.

Manda walked along the promenade opposite McDonald's, the passport photo booth on her left. She walked on then she cautiously scooted out and edged round the corner of the overlit interior of WH Smith. Ava's dark hair shone as she stood in the till queue. Manda hid in by the shutters, intending to jump out and startle Ava on her return to Game Grid, yet astonishingly, when Ava did exit, carrying a stuffed plastic bag of what looked like magazines and newspapers, she moved straight towards the escalators.

Manda gripped her hands in fury. How could Ava do that? How could she walk away from an important tournament of Ezzy Dancer? Sneaking off to read bloody papers full of political-ness. Manda crossed adamantly to the escalators.

Ava's tallness was an advantage for following. When Manda got to the bottom of the escalators she could see her far out, further across the concourse, but she was moving towards the area where they caught that transit to the other terminal. Maybe she was headed for the Meridian Hotel without them? Booking in for herself cos she was so posh? Manda was thinking how difficult it would be to follow Ava at the Meridian as she disappeared into the millions of rooms of the hotel – but she only need witness the treachery of her checking in, then the stream of texts could be sent to taunt her. Something like:

Saw ya are hid in merid in in hotel alone with news papers. Ya SCRAT! Amanda.

Manda richly envisioned these terrifying missives of wrath. It would be as good as the time Manda took Kylah's mobile from her bag while Kyles was in the toilet in Rascals and nosily scrolled through the address book. Manda found a boy's name who – to her fury – she could not identify, so Manda texted: *I want to suck your cock* and sent it, quickly shoving Kylah's mobby back in Kylah's bag. Now that was a classic.

But Manda's idyll evaporated as Ava turned sharp left and vanished. Manda rushed ahead then rising in her memory she saw where Ava had gone. Down to where the railway station was that they'd arrived into in the darkness of the Friday night. The bitch was headed back to London! Manda tried to fathom how she could have offended Ava so she wouldn't say goodbye. She racked her brainbox and rattled the memory banks. No. Not one thing she had done or said could have offended Ava. Nothing since the mud slide anyway. Perhaps it was that comment earlier about her wearing the same clothes as last night, but she was a manky student, so she should be used to that.

Manda descended the escalators no longer intending to conceal herself.

Ava was standing on the platform indicated as expecting the next two Gatwick Express arrivals. Rex had been sloppy enough as usual not to make it clear exactly what train he was on. His text had simply informed her he'd already left Victoria. Rex had again emphasised that he refused to wander further than the station platform. He really thought he was so big time. Ava had walked to the end of the platform and back to await the train. She saw an odd thing over on the electrical substation. A true-to-scale plastic owl decoy was affixed there on one of the transformers. Presumably to scare away tweety birds from the barbecuing electrics?

When Ava had turned and walked a few paces of studying the platform textures, she looked up and her heart plummeted.

Manda was striding up the station platform towards her. Ava looked at her clothes, seemingly for the first time: her too-tight jeans and ratty jean jacket, a top aglitter with strange silver strips. She looked like she'd slept the night face down on a rolled-out strip of baking foil. Ava knew her astonishment showed on her face.

'Don't go off to London. I think you're brilliant.'

'What?'

'I think you're brilliant.'

'I'm not going to London, dear, just taking some air,' she said, glancing up at a huge departing aircraft lifting beyond the Hilton.

Manda also saw the Boeing rise and in a fearful voice, suddenly mumbled, 'Up, you hoor, up.'

'I'm a little faint. Are you following me, Manda?'

'Taking the airs? Are you no away up to London?'

'No, no. The only place you can get fresh air in this airport is down here in this station. Isn't it? I was feeling a bit queasy after the drinks. Off you go and I'll come back to your dance machine thing.'

Manda stood, unmoving, blinking.

'I've got my newspapers here and I'll be back with you in ten minutes for the dance machine thing.'

Manda stood there.

'Look. See the plastic owl over there. Strange, don't you think? Do you think it's a sort of decoy? A scarecrow rather. It's a predator, so I suppose its shape scares away little sparrows and other birds. They must have been getting electrocuted.'

Manda frowned. 'You not feeling well in the head or something?'

'Not really. Give me ten minutes of air and I'll be back in.'

'I'll wait. With you.'

'I think you'll be bored. I'm just going to sit and read the papers.'

'Oh. Right. You got *Heat* there?'

'No. Just newspapers.'

'That's a magazine.' She flipped out a hand coyly.

'What? Oh yes. That's *Vogue*. But it's in French.'

'Aye. But I can look at the pictures.'

'No. Really, Manda. I need a bit of time alone. If you please, thank you.'

'Oh. All right then. I'll wait for you on the seats over there.'

'No. Alone. Alone. I need to be alone.' She tried not to shout.

'Is everything all right between us? Like have I done something to piss you off?'

'You know all this talking is making me feel worse.'

'I'll wait on the bench over there.' Manda walked away towards it but she kept looking back.

Ava watched after her with fury. Was she being punished? It was this mad holiday that had driven her into relapse and still she was harassed. Ava turned her back and hauled her phone out of her jacket. She put down the plastic carrier bag of newspapers, supported between her shins while she rapidly scrolled the address book to 'Lauren'. A false entry, using a minor-character, co-student's name. She knew Finn had checked her phone address book in the past. Ava pushed dial but just as she did so a train was distantly approaching among the wobbled silver strings of trackwork. She turned with the phone to her ear. Manda was lingering down by a lamp post staring at her.

Ava said, 'Fuck.'

The phone began to ring but the train was now rushing in alongside her. She scanned the windows. The ringing phone wasn't being answered. The coach next to her creaked to a halt. Doors hissed aside and people drawing suitcases began to crowd out and move down the platform.

'Hello!'

'Rex. Don't meet me right away.'

'What? I'm behind you.'

Ava spun. Standing almost in front of Manda: little Rex with his hand to his ear, smiling and nodding towards Ava, his dyed hair spiked up now, the horrible, toffee-coloured leather jacket that was rumoured to have cost seven grand.

Manda was looking at them both, observing his mouth moving in actual dialogue, working together in a dramatic conjunction.

Ava fingered off her mobile connection, reached into the back pocket of her worn Levi's and closed her thumb and forefinger on the cash wad of many hundreds. When they came together, Ava stooped to kiss Rex's mouth and while she did, tongue and all, she slipped the wad into the back pocket of his jeans, and turned them both together in a minor, clumsy tango, to conceal the action from Manda.

'Ohhh, I never knew you still cared.'

She looked in his eyes and said, 'That's plus a tip. There's someone here with us I tried to get rid of.'

Now Rex's expression changed and he looked around.

Manda, like some kind of attendant flunkey, had moved forward and stood almost beside them.

'Who's he?' her dull voice demanded.

Rex looked at Manda, his alarmed expression completely bedevilled.

'Who is this?'

'My good comrade Manda.'

Rex stared at Manda, a stiffed displeasure coiled in his nervy frame.

He looked at Ava. 'You look, very well,' he managed. Then he glared at Manda again with the expression he'd once used in a zoo, staring down at a sea cow circling, frustrated, in a huge basin – a creature of whose existence Rex had been previously unaware.

He fished into his side bag, one of those canvas hip bags Soho boys in the film and music industries are never parted from. He took out a package. It was a music CD in its case. As he did so, he angrily hissed, 'Who is she? Who is she? Why'd you fucking bring someone along? She's seen me now.'

'It's cool. Really. It's cool.'

'Fuck you, Ava. How would you know what cool was? This is a fucking airport with CCTV, sniffer dogs, and now you turn up with a freeloader.'

'I'm going to a shithole hotel. It'll be okay.' She put her hand on the CD and took it from him, holding it firm.

'I came all the way down here and you show, strung out and with company. I don't know who . . . you're so street. I don't do it with rude girls. Don't call me again, you fuck-up.' Then he suddenly paused and studied Manda closer. 'Oh God. Oh God! You're rotten show business. You've got yourself a fucking body-guard minder. Wait till people hear.' He yipped a laugh.

And Rex walked away forever. She watched him go. His hand didn't touch to the back pocket, yet he walked past Manda without meeting her stare and on, far down the platform. That's how sure he was of her money. He skipped over to a platform attendant, smiling, lively, like a cheeky chappie. The attendant in black uniform, red piping on a cap, said something. Rex nodded and smiled.

'Is he your boyfriend then? Bit of a midget, is he not? I suppose he's kinda . . . nice jacket.'

Rex crossed then hopped into the waiting train on the opposite platform, vanishing within. Ava turned and retrieved her newspapers which she'd left lying on their side in the plastic bag, grabbed them up, striding away. Manda took up step beside her.

'Who's he? Why are you meeting him all in secret? What was that he give you?'

'That's an ex-boyfriend and we split. Both upset about it and I'm away on holiday and he's jealous. He's returning a CD that had great sentimental value for us.'

Manda looked up at her. Even she was sceptical.

'Let's see it?'

Ava held up the CD to Manda's face but wouldn't part with it. Manda squinted. In cheery, jovial font it read: *Edmundo Ros and his Rumba Band Present: Who Shot the Hole in My Sombrero?* Edmundo himself graced the cover in a colour-tinted photo, grinning triumphantly, his bullet-holed sombrero hoisted aloft.

'Looks pretty shit to me.'

Ava glanced at the cover; even she herself frowned. 'This is brilliant music,' she insisted.

They had both walked rapidly now, back towards the escalators, round and onto them.

'Is that the guy you got pregnant by?' she called loudly. People glanced at them both. 'I'm surprised he could reach you for a snog. Is he a good snogger? He looks it actually.'

'Why are you sniffing around after me?'

'Okay then. I'll go back to the others and tell them what happened.'

'No. Hey, Manda. I want to go over to that hotel we were in on the first night and get really drunk. Never mind the others. Want to come with?'

'Eh? Oh. Aye, sure. That'd be brilliant.'

'Let's not invite anyone for a bit though. Just the two of us.'

'Oh. Brilliant.'

The Hotel Hoppa courtesy bus awaited passengers outside the terminal where Manda and the girls had caught it on Friday night.

To Ava's pleasure, the bus was crowded so Manda had to sit separately from her. Manda slumped with a sour face, next to an older man, and when Ava did glance back at her once, Manda made the regulation and derogatory sneer at the man beside her.

Once again the Hotel Hoppa began to mount road slipways and descend beside gravel-strewn hard shoulders, but the journey seemed shorter. Distance showed the fringed tree line, the flaccid flag and the familiar ochre frontage of the Flight Deck Hotel. The bus circled the roundabout with the grass centre by the petrol station then wheeled left into the go-kart-like loop of the drive and car park.

Manda still forced her way to the front impatiently. 'Away to Las Vegas the morrow,' she nodded at the bus driver, stepping down to light a cigarette immediately upon her right foot striking the ground. But simultaneous with this act she successfully blocked the exit of the bus for a few moments as she halted, leaned and gleered into the fitted wing mirror to check her make-up. It had been caked on earlier at the Hilton room desk mirror, accompanied by a full commentary on her superior techniques.

Manda stepped ahead after the man on the bus behind her ran out of patience and tutted. She gestured to Ava, her arm movements diverting smoke around the other passengers. 'Fair old share of weirdos on this bus, eh? The others'll be really fathoming out where I've got to.' She spun round to survey the hotel. 'Back here again.'

Ava grabbed her backpack and Manda hopped after her, like a ratty minion, jabbering, glancing repeatedly at her face. The hexagon-inspired lobby door slid open and they entered the familiar tardiness of the Flight Deck Hotel. The usual queue for reception. Manda noticed the unreceptive receptionist at the desk, handling the queue. 'It's old himself. He'll be amazed to see me back. Hiya.'

Ava said, 'Maybe I should do the check-in?'

'But I want to write the card thing when you check in. That's brilliant.'

'You don't want to do me a big special favour, do you?'

Manda's rubbery forehead stirred reactively.

'Why doesn't one of us . . . dash over to that supermarket thing across the roundabout and get some drink? Look.' Ava opened her purse and took out two red fifty-pound notes, passing them into Manda's hand.

'A hundred. Are you mental or something?'

'Get three bottles of champagne and some bags of ice.'

'How'll I know what room you're in?'

'I'll text.'

'Won't run out on me, will you?'

'Of course not. I'll book rooms for everybody now as well. You'll get a few Guinness with that if I do run out, won't you?'

'Oh, but that wouldn't make up for your company, lass.'

'Charmer. See if you can get bottles of French champagne, any French champagne. Must be French. Listen, just phone me. I'll be in the room and I'll tell you what to buy.'

'You'll no blow me out? Leave me sat on the grass in the car park there, swigging the carry-out? Cos I will if you blow me out. I'll just sit out there and quaff the fucker. I'm telling you.'

The man in front of them in the queue – in fact the same man who had tutted Manda for blocking the exit from the bus while she checked her make-up – turned round and looked at them.

Both Manda and Ava stared straight back in an intimidating manner.

'Aye? Can I help you?' Manda said in full accent.

And he turned straight back round again.

'I won't blow you out.'

Manda didn't hesitate. She was off.

4

Ava checked in, booking three twins, all smoking rooms, but requesting each of them on different floors as she wanted to get well away from her colleagues. She talked in French with the unreceptive receptionist who became very receptive indeed to her. He was from Toulouse.

Up in the twin room, Ava chained the door behind her, opened her backpack and took out the CD. She did not bother to look at her own surroundings.

There was no CD disc inside the case but the black, circular declension suspended four small, clear plastic bags with an airtight manual sealant strip along the top. Each was held in place by a specially cut half-strip of already thin Scotch tape. Each bag contained white, heart-lifting, fluffy cocaine crystals. Ava still smiled affectionately at Rex's handiwork.

There wasn't time to waste. Others intruded on her need as always. Ironically, Manda – who, single-handed, had virtually driven Ava's desire to get lit up again.

Ava was armed with excuses and carefully freed one bag, ensuring she didn't rip it open. She looked around, checking where the air currents from the creaky air-conditioning grilles above circulated. She reached in her jacket pocket and removed a scrunchie with which she strapped her hair back severely, positioning herself on her knees in front of the mirror of the desk area. She opened the bag and tapped a small pile onto the countertop, her eyes watching it carefully, as if she were just tapping out the exact amount of salt on a piece of fish in a fine restaurant. She didn't make the little heap into a line. She simply lowered her nose, sealed her other nostril with her petite pinkie and inhaled it in a swift, violent nose-suck. It was elevated immediately and vertically, up her nostril, and she kept inhaling, vibrating her face from side to side, ponytail swatting, then holding her head back she gulped and tasted.

She fumbled with the minibar which was opened by a key, craftily inserted – a market-researched psychological carrot on a stick – and pulled the door. Ava lifted out a quarter-bottle, some kind of pseudo-champagne she had never heard of. She twisted off the top without removing the tinfoil, then gulped at the neck cautiously, so it didn't bubble up in her mouth.

She sat still for a while, expertly judging the first familiar psychopathology, assessing the quality, then immediately she tapped out another small heap.

Here her mobile phone went and Ava fumbled for it nervily to read the caller identity. 'Brillient AMANDA'.

An aggressive voice was already there and Ava smiled.

'Is this French champagne?'

Ava said, 'What is it?'

'Ball Ginger.'

'Bollinger?'

'Aye. Ball In Jay. They don't have got nothing else he's saying.'

'Is it chilled?'

Ava heard Manda's voice speak. 'Got this stuff in coldness?' Somehow, even down the phone, Ava perceived the assistant's harassed state.

'And ice, Manda. You can't forget, three bags of ice.'

'Do you want to talk to him? There's something wrong with him? Like he's from another place?'

'Just get three Bollinger and three big bags of ice.'

'What's your room number then, you fly devil?'

'I'll text it.'

'Why?'

'Keep it private. If I say it now you'll repeat it out loud.'

'Repeat it. So?'

'A lesson in life. A lady should never speak her hotel-room number out aloud wherever she is. Down the decades, you'll receive bouquets of flowers. Or unwelcome callers.'

'Eh?'

Ava hung up but texted 3034 to Manda's mobile.

At last Ava felt more herself. And the attendant melancholy, that it took all this to make her feel herself. It was as if a palimpsest of her spirit existed slightly outside her body, down her frozen left side, and this other self could slide in and out of her mundane self with the ease of an ejected CD tray.

When she was high.

Ava had lost touch long ago – was she more herself when she was lit up or when she was sober?

She lowered her other nostril and the small heap of powder was packed up with a sharp, efficient sniff. She leaned against the bottom of the bed a while, pushing her legs out and then drawing them up and taking pulls on the lukewarm miniature. Wiping her unmade-up face clear. She knew she had to quit. But she did every time. And every time was the next time. Then she stood and lunged at the bathroom to wash her face – even the cold-water tap was lukewarm in this feted lab culture, kept at mean temperature. She patted her face with a hand towel and flung the towel into the bath. She looked at herself in the mirror then swayed across the bedroom to the window and pulled the net curtains aside. A car park. Trees on the horizon, the movements of vehicles reflected in a row of windscreens, while slow-moving clouds – their unchanging forms being preserved – moved over this England. All through double-glazed glass.

She wanted to be somewhere the surroundings meant something to a human being. Venice or Toledo. Or Rome, where a human could actually be at rest. She recalled one of her few moments of great peace, being in a cafe next to the Pantheon, drinking very good espressos, serene in the knowledge all human excess and all human modesty had already happened in the square miles around her. In Rome there should be nothing for a person to live up to, because everything had been done. A noble lethargy. She sneered. Her own mind sounded like her pretentious journals:

full of snappy imprecations to herself that hinted at an overall grand project. But each handwritten note and every well-formed thought had one sneaky eye on vulgar immortality. She must chuck her journals in the river the moment she got home. Then she thought of the Vespas, their metallic paint jobs scraping against Bernini fountains. Live six months in Rome. Las Vegas would be a masochistic nightmare again, a fake Venice with chlorine canals; where the languages of capitalism and pornography discovered they really did have everything in common and accepted the marriage gladly. She jerked the curtain closed.

There was an aggressive knock at the door and Ava had a burst of paranoia. She stood and picked up the packet, rubbed at the surface of the desk and returned the CD tray to her back-pack. She held the small pack in her hand.

Through the spyhole: Manda in a reverse telephoto corridor. She had carrier bags. Ava unlocked the chain and opened the door. Manda barged in. It was only then Ava realised this would be a hard person to be high around, and for some reason, she wanted the calming Kay there as well.

'Here's your change. See you're raiding the minibar though I got slagged.'

Ava looked down and realised she was holding the small bottle of bad champagne.

'Well, I got all that you says. Hope you won't mind but I got a six-pack of Draught Guinness for myself. With all this ice I can freeze it up into Extra Cold!' Manda stretched over and lowered all the bags into the middle of the bed. Then she dropped a clutch of notes and coins beside it, the notes screwed into a mutilated ball.

Ava smiled at the six-pack of Guinness, the black flanks of the cans against the plastic as if inside a wet T-shirt. She grabbed two bags of ice and went into the bathroom. Manda followed, watching over her shoulder. Ava put the plug in and half filled the sink from the cold tap, then was ripping the ice bags, tipping them in. Some of the ice cubes had adhered together into chunks, other cubes missed and went skittering along the sink edge then fell, firing across the floor tiles.

'You're spilling it everywhere.' Manda picked up a cube and went to toss it in the sink.

'Don't. These floors are dirty.'

Manda tossed it in the bath where it fell into the towel. She picked up another few fallen cubes then she ambled off and returned with the alcohol. Two bottles of champagne and two cans of Guinness were fitted in the sink.

'That's a grand-looking set-up,' Manda declared.

'Give it a few minutes to cool.'

'Och. I've no pint glasses to drink Guinness from.'

'Have some champagne.'

'Oh, I will please, aye.'

'You could drink your Guinness from the teapot.'

'I suppose if push came to shove but I'll take it out the can, ta very much.'

Ava felt the urge inside her for more already. It wasn't going to be possible like this, repeated visits to a locked toilet all afternoon. Ava just did not care any more with coke in the room.

'Hey, Manda. As well as champagne and Guinness, I'll tell you what's cool, but do you think you can keep a secret from Finn? It'd be a secret just between you and me.'

'What secret?'

'Something I need to trust you about, but if you choose to tell her, that's your choice.'

'What? Are you into girls and that after all, like her? I mean, I can accept that –'

'No no. Want a sniff?'

'What the hell's that?'

'It's like amphetamine. Speed. Like the stuff they gave you when you had wee . . . Sean. But better.'

'Hey. Where'd you get that from?'

'I can't take it on the plane tomorrow, so we have to do some and dump the rest. I'm not into turning people on to stuff. It's your decision, but if you don't want to, I'm going to take a little bit since we have to chuck it. So you can try a tiny amount if you wish.'

'Just a tiny amount? Do you take it a lot?'

'No. I used to.'

Manda looked at Ava and the small bag of drugs. She glanced around the room for the first time. As if someone else might be there. 'I knew you were a dark horse, girl. Oh, I knew something, but I couldn't fathom you out for the life of me. Is that illegal? Aye?'

'Yes.'

'What happens if you get caught?'

'Well . . . a court case or something. I wouldn't worry about it.'

'Aye, but the Feds pulled us yesterday and you had it on you. You're a nutter.'

Ava looked at Manda. 'Actually. That's another thing you can't tell Finn. About our friend, we met in the station.'

'What?' Manda actually smiled, immediately entertained by this intrigue.

'I just got this off the guy at the railway station.'

'Never. You besom. Was he a drug dealer? I never met one before.'

'Well, he sells it. He's just a guy.'

'I'm not so dumb, Ava. I bet you that's –' and dropping her voice – 'Is it coke; cocaine?'

'Yeah. The old devil's dandruff.'

'Oh, Ava. That would be just the stuff you were into. I should of guessed. You ought to watch yourself. That must be dead strong. Can that kill you right now?'

'No. Not unless you did something silly.'

'Like what?'

'Well. Maybe if you had a bad heart or something.'

'My heart is fine, despite the fags. I hear it beating.'

'It's addictive but it's not very toxic.'

'Jesus. Is Finn into the old cocaine in London too?'

'Oh no. She's dead against it.'

'Oh aye. She would be. Mmm.' Manda was weighing up the politics of this. 'She would be, but you want to be careful though, Ava. You can get hooked on that stuff.'

'So what? I can afford it.'

'Suppose you can. That's why you were trying to shake me off. You cheeky besom.'

'Want to try?'

'Ah. Ha, ha, ha? Aye, okay then.'

Ava turned round and tapped out a very small ration on the desk; this time she used the laminated TV instructions card to make it into a faint line.

Now Manda looked at Ava a bit apprehensively. 'Is that guy a criminal? Does he have a gun? I don't want to get mixed up in any of that.'

Ava laughed. 'No. He has no gun and I never saw his dick,' she lied.

Unusually, Manda ignored this comment and got straight down to business. 'Is this all paid for? You're not in some kind of thing in films. Owing money. Maybe they'll kick the door in and machine-gun me?'

'No.'

'This is called doing lines, is it?'

'Yes.'

'Oh brilliant. There's guys back in the town that do this. Lines. DJ plebs.'

'Yes. This is goofy. Great quality. That's why I'm giving you such a mean little portion. Just to see how you like it.'

'And if I do, will that mean I'm addicted?'

'No. You have to take it for a long time and spend a whole lot of money for that and we're just going to do this this one time together.'

'Are you addicted?'

'No. An addict takes it every day. I don't.'

'Will I blast it now?'

'No, no. We'll get a drink. You've not to suck it up your nose; whoosh it up, past your nose. You have to imagine a place way up near your forehead and try to inhale it up to there.'

'I see. Right. This is not shooting up, is it? I'm not into that.'

'No, no. Goodness, no. That's with needles. This is snorting.'

Manda became aggressive now. 'Aye, aye. Snorting coke. Doing lines. I know. I know that.'

'You must suck it up your nose real quick, no hesitation tight up back, or it's a waster. You'll feel it dissolve and a bitter taste, that's why you need a sip of champagne as well, so both hit you together and the champers takes away the taste and gives you the buzz as well.'

Manda held up her hand to stop her. 'It won't kill me?'

'No.'

'And after I've took it then I can go say to people, "Aye, that was me. I was doing lines, doing coke. I do coke sometimes." Can I say that to people, after?'

'Well, not to Finn or anyone on this holiday. You can't tell anyone on this holiday but in future times you can tell others. It's a secret between us for now. Don't tell the others.'

'It's just a wee secret between you and me?' Manda tried out the sound and the glory of it all, in a theatrical tone. 'Aye. I was doing coke with my English friend down in London.' She paused. Contemplated the sound of the sentence in the air. She tried again. 'Aye. I was down in England with my English pal and we's were doing coke at the airport. It was mental. You really missed yourself.' Again she paused to savour the import of the statement. She could hear the background music of Rascals as she imagined it all, her semicircle of underage disciples before her.

While these rehearsals went on, Ava had gone into the bathroom and she came back with a bottle of champagne and a towel, holding the bottle by the neck, curiously trying to peel off the foil.

Manda said, 'See, Ava, I want to be able to say I've done it but I'm no bothered about taking it. Do you know what I mean?'

'Oh yes. I know exactly what you mean. The glamour of it?'

'Aye. The glamour! That's it. Are we having some champagne now?'

'Surely we are. Yes. Certainly. Get the glasses. Normally it's best to drink champagne out the bottle, it stays fizzier, but it's not cold enough yet.'

'Is that right enough?'

Ava shielded the bottle with the towel.

'Are you no going to shoot the cork in the air like we did when we opened the new salon?'

'No, no. Far too undignified.'

'Aye. Right enough, I broke one of the new spotlights in seconds. Ma big sister went mental.'

The cork popped, with a deep report but muffled within the fabric.

Manda had produced two bell-shaped wine glasses and Ava poured into both of them then went back to the bathroom and crunched and shuffled the bottle back into the ice.

'This is nice little party though. Isn't it?' Ava called casually.

'Aye. Gallus. Just the two of us and no them lot. How's that Guinness doing?'

'Splendid.'

Ava used one of her many fifty-pound notes to roll the proverbial tube as Manda watched with devotional interest. 'This is quite a Las Vegas thing to do,' stated Ava encouragingly. She checked inside the rolled note to make sure the end wasn't folded on a corner or frayed and obstructing the tube. 'Right, what's your clearest nostril? Which do you think has the best suction, left or right?'

'That's a queer question,' but Manda sealed each nostril and sniffed testingly.

Ava told her, 'Stronger than that. Sniff. Stronger.'

Manda fairly hissed now.

'That's the way, girl.' Unconsciously, Ava imitated her PE master from school.

'I think this one is clearer.'

Ava nodded. 'The right usually is for some reason.'

'Okay. Ready. Aye.'

'Block the other nostril.'

'Oh, it feels funny.'

'Shove the tube up as far as you can. Right up there.'

'Oh, that's a bit minging. My snots is going to spoil your beautiful fifty-pound note,' she suddenly speculated.

Ava laughed and said, 'I'll go first.' Ava rolled another note, kneeled, laid out a small pile, bent down on it and evaporated it in a quick movement up her nose. She stood up and sipped from the glass, holding her head right back.

'Wow. You're good at it. Here I go, Ava.'

Ava looked down as Manda's bulky head and shoulders stooped over the line, the note in her nose swaying, then there was a silence. Suddenly Manda pounced – it seemed much more substantial than any previous sniffs and she didn't hesitate on the line, she moved the note end along very swiftly, skilfully advancing forward the spout, and she enfiladed the powder away.

Ava, towering above the girl, couldn't deny a feeling of corrupting, powerful domination, almost with a sexual element. 'You're a natural.'

Manda made a noise at the back of her throat and shook her head. She immediately went to touch at her nostril, simultaneously with tipping the champagne glass into her mouth.

Ava looked into Manda's eyes, smiling encouragingly. 'That was good. Now just sit back.'

They both sat on the floor together, sniffing and not talking. There was a long expectant silence. Ava muttered, 'We should call up Kay.'

Manda asked, 'Seriously? Call up Kay?'

'Mmm? Oh yes. We shall just shortly.'

'What do you make of old Kay then, Ava?'

'Kay? Oh, she's very nice. Mmm. Let's talk about this in a minute. Feel good?'

'Eh, aye. I'm grand. It's good that.'

'What, can you feel it?'

'Eh. Aye, the fizzog seems to be going a bit stiff.' She ran a hand across her face and added, 'Might be good for wrinkles this. On older cunts. Take the lines out their face. Oh, wait a minute. Oh aye. Oh aye I can feel that. It *is* like the stuff they give us when I was up the maternity having wee Sean. Great. Quite good that.'

'What?'

'The rush and that. Aye. The buzz. Aye, not bad that.' Manda took another long draw of champagne from the glass and jumped up. 'Might just fix myself a wee Guinness.'

311

'Well, you shouldn't drink too much. Just sip for a while.'

'A Guinness'll do me no harm. Full of iron.'

Ava was surprised. Most of the blow must be stuck up her snout, she presumed.

Manda came back through with a can of Guinness. 'Now what will I drink this out of? These thing glasses'll have to do. Stupid bastern things. I bought a twelve-pack of Guinness once, Ava. Oh.' Manda burped. 'Aye, that's the thing with the champagne. Gives me a bit of indigestion in my gut. Aye, I bought this twelve-pack Guinness once and I got a Guinness pint glass with it. Had a wee . . . what's it called? . . . aye . . . a shamrock on it, that'd be handy the now.'

'How do you feel?'

'Grand, aye.'

'I'll just take another little root de toot.'

'Aye. Be my guest.'

Ava tapped out more powder and sniffed it up her nose then took a swallow of champagne. 'Oh yeah,' Ava groaned.

'So old Kay there. You reckon she's okay? Aye, I'll tell you. The thing with Kay is. She wasn't really part of our gang. We didn't think she was a drinker either but I'll tell you. She can drink whisky like a man. You wouldn't think. Thought she was a bit of a tight arse at first, to be honest. This was in those times before Rascals though. Aye, all this was before Rascals so you know. Huh. I mean, what happened before Rascals doesn't really count. Does it? Does it? Cos it's before Rascals and Rascals is the place, so. And after that, Finn and Kay were dead pally and then we's got pally with Kay. And she turned out great. Like she had the moves, put down the boys and she'd dance and drink. And there were a few boys she was going into bed with too. Imagine that. Kay's that kind of girl that, in fifth year, just blossoms like a fucking flower. And she was coming on nights out with us and that. And wee Orla got iller in the next year and Kay Clarke, the doc's daughter, was a big support. In a nice background way. She didn't try to come in and take control, and tell us what we should be doing and feeling and all that. You know?'

'Mmmm.'

'So there. Aye, and Kay was at the funeral, standing by our sides. I'll say that. And I tell you. That girl was a rock to us. I tease Kay Clarke but I won't forget that. When Orla was ill she was great, then Kay was off to the uni and that stuff, like all yous are, but it's no like Kay Clarke got a pencil right up her arse. She'd come back from the uni and she'd be on the phone to us and Kylah and Chell – as well as a few of her snobbiest friends. Know what I mean? "How are yous, let's go for a drink." She wasn't at all snobby about being at a uni or that, the way most of them from the town get and go on at you. They come out with stuff like: "Oh, you should see Edinburgh and Glasgow nights out, you don't know what you're missing, Amanda, in your wee town." No, no, I says back to them. Nay, nay. You don't know the scenes yous miss down at your university thing and your study books. Back in the good old town, ya hinging skanky wee student hoors. It's still all going on, and so Kay started hanging out with us. Then she nabbed Paddy Matthison that night. One of the bonks of the town. Fucking grabbed him good she did. Those legs of hers, ya hoor. The boys like that cos she was wearing shorter skirts then. It's me said to her, "Kay, wear shorter skirts and better shoes, you hoor, cos you've got good legs," and she did too, and she got laid a few times. Cos of me of course. Aye, she got off with Paddy Matthison and they went to end-of-year dance together, the bams. They looked great. But she dumped poor old Paddy and he was right upset. Married now though. But he was upset. And that was Kay off to the uni and now she's got some archy-tect boy hanging on her tit with its teeth, but I haven't met it. It's too high and mighty to come up the town for a night out with the girls, but Kay still goes out with us when she's back at holidays –'

'Want another line, Manda?'

'Aye, sure. I'll just pour this stuff.' Manda was delicately pouring out the Guinness. Taking more care with it than around the coke, where she was a bit lumbering and jumpy. She placed the glass graciously by the telly and left the drink to settle.

Ava put out a bigger line for Manda this time, to try and get her to shut up, or to lead the speculations on to more general vistas and less specific ones.

Manda took up the fifty-pound-note tube as casually as a straw in Mackers. 'Eh. Whoah. You beezer. Up and in it goes.' Manda grabbed the champagne glass and drained it. 'Oh that's me for the indigestion now. I could drink those wee milk things for coffee, oh, but that was another hotel. I'll see if they have them here.'

Manda jumped up and began shuffling in the cupboard and sure enough there were dairy creamers for the tea and coffee. She plonked back down next to Ava. 'But when Kay was wearing those shorter skirts it was me said to her, "Girl, you really should be waxing not shaving, cos it really is better for the skin long-term." Like I know you shave your legs yourself, Ava, but long-term the skin is better from waxing the whole leg. I'm not just saying that cos I'm in beauty consultation professionally, as a practice manageress. It's a well-proved thing. And another thing . . .'

'Right. Right, I've put the money in,' Chell said. 'Kay, you selects the song. You see here? You choose the song you want to do, Kay.'

'Mmm.'

'Look, Cameo. "Word Up". That's brilliant, "All you sucker DJs, around the world." Too right they're suckers. Aye. He's brilliant that guy Cameo. He's got the thing on his knob.'

'Codpiece,' Finn said.

'Aye, aye.'

Kylah went, 'Aye. The gadge from Cameo is brilliant, and do you know, like, that fashion designer who made that knobpiece for the Cameo guy is the same who made Madonna's spiky tits? He's Jean-Claude Van Damme, his name is.'

Kay quietly corrected, 'Jean Paul Gaultier.'

'Eh?'

'Jean Paul Gaultier. He designed it. Jean-Claude Van Damme's an actor, in those films for lads; Hollywood action movies.'

'Oh aye, oh aye, you're actually right enough, actually. Jean Paul. I don't like his stuff. Too. Weird.' Chell shook her head.
'*Get ready, suckers!*'

> Yo, pretty ladies, around the world
> Got a weird thing to show you

'Pink. The pink, Kay. Move it, rubber legs.'

> So tell all the boys and girls
> Tell your brother, your sister
> And your mama too

'Pink, pink. Blue, Kay. No! The blue. That's it!'
'You're on next, Finn. It's . . . Philisophies versus Architects.'
'*You guys stink!*'
'Keep going, Kay. We're really bad.'

> Wave your hand in the air
> Like you don't care . . .

Obediently, Kylah waved her hand in the air, like she did on the real dance floor as she stepped right. 'Kay. Kay, Finn, yous're no even doing it with the arm!'

'. . . So's I says to wee Sean's daddy, "You get him something good at Christmas," and he goes and says he would. He'd get him some clothes. Now when someone says they're gonna get their wee son clothes, you expect clothes, you know? Proper clothes from Baby Gap where I buy his clothes. Have you been to Baby Gap?'
'Eh, no.'
'Oh, you should go see it, Ava. You'll want kiddies when you see how adorable some of the stuff in there is – like dungarees. I got him some dungarees and he loves them. Gap, it says on the

front. You know? As it would. So's I get him things at Baby Gap and what does Sean's daddy get him at Christmas? Stuff from the market. Crap wrapping paper too. I tell you. I wouldn't be surprised if they're second-hand by the looks of them. Or you know those collections that get made to give clothes to the wee starving African bairns and you put them in dump bins. I wouldn't be surprised if he reached in and pulled some things out of there. Or maybe his new hoory girlfriend-so-called reached in and got them. He'd have been too pished mortal to reach in. So he whines to me when he does his visits, "Sean's not wearing any the clothes I got him," and I'm like, "You bet he's not, buster, cos the clothes you bought are fucking plug. I'm no putting my Sean in those. Never mind them being crappy from a market. I don't know even where them clothes has been, you minkso." I tell you as well, I think that bitch girlfriend of his wrapped up the clothes too, cos they was in crap wrapping paper but it was awful well wrapped for an all-thumbs-fumbler, like him. The cheek of it. His girlfriend wrapping up my son's gifts. I'll tell you this. He didn't get them in Frasers, which as you'll know had a very good wrapping service. Aye, so he has old slack fanny wrapping up the clothes and that's the best he can do at Christmas for his wee son. He's a . . .'

'Mmm.' Ava was profoundly meditating on locking herself in the bathroom, but she imagined Manda simply leaning against the locked door, talking on the other side of it. 'Want another line, Manda?'

'Aye. On you go then.'

Manda mustered up onto her knees from where she'd been slouched and she turned round. Ava put out another line and Manda slightly nudged in, perhaps misunderstanding this first line was actually intended for Ava and was slightly larger, but to no avail. Manda scooped it up her nose and lurched away from the desk. 'Hell, I can fair feel the old ticker hammering away, Ava. You'd think I'd been going all night, on top of a six-foot weightlifter with a ten-inch dick – backwards – while I sucked his toes. That's the way the heart's going. I'll just have another Guinness to calm it down. I think that champagne's a wee bit gassy for now.'

Ava leaned and snorted her line up. She lifted the Bollinger bottle, holding it quite far down the neck for steadiness, and slowly tipped it back, taking a draw.

'One thing about last season's stuff in Baby Gap –'

Ava swung the bottle down away from her mouth unable to be alone with Manda any longer. 'I think perhaps we should text Kay now and invite her over.'

'Kay? Do you think so?'

'Look. Here's my logic. Finn is going to come over soon enough and this stuff needs to go down the toilet before she does. Kay is like heading Finn off at the pass. Finn won't think we're up to anything if Kay's over here.'

'Aye, I see your point. But you might no be able to take this with Kay here.'

'I'll talk her into it.'

'I don't think so. She might be a wee bit freaked by the . . . in fact you need to watch her. She might call the Feds on you, the way she is.'

'She won't take a little toot?'

'Her! No way. She'll scoosh some of your champagne but I think she'd phone her dad and clipe on us in a jiffy. Aye, that's it. She'd want to send her dad up a sample for testing before she'd put it anywhere near her wee stuck-up konk!'

Ava actually laughed at that. 'Well. We. You and I, shall just not tell her.'

'I found her measuring a wall once. Walking along it.' Spitefully with a curled lips, Manda pronounced, 'Archy-tect. Ach, don't get me wrong. I like Kay but she won't approve of this sniffin.'

'And she'll tell Finn?' Ava stated.

'Aye. Too right she'll tell Finn. She can keep secrets but this'll go straight back. Her and Fionnula are tight. Thick as thieves.'

Ava was in a momentary dilemma. A couple more lines then having to flush the coke and call Kay? Or. Continue with the coke and put up with more hours alone with Manda's stimulated monologues? In less than one second, Ava reached for her mobile to text Kay.

In an imitation, Manda reached for hers too. 'Oh look. Look

here. I never heard them come through. There's texts from Kay to me. "Where are you?" Oh. You're phoning Kay now, already?' Manda frowned.

'Kay? Hi. Sorry. Yes. Manda's just with me. We met up and we're drinking over at the Friday-night hotel. I've booked three twin rooms for us all. Yes. We got a deal too. Where are you? Oh. Did you buy a *Guardian*? Shame. I've got one. Yes. Just come on over and drink some champagne in the room with us. I'll text you the room number. Okay. See you. Sorry to take so long. Kay. Are you just coming yourself? Yes. Just leave them dancing and come over for a drink. French champagne. Yes. I'll see you shortly, I hope.'

Ava hung up and began texting in the room number.

Manda said, 'We'll whizzle some of this up us then before Mother Superior comes over. Can I tap it out into lines?'

'Yes. Be careful. No sneezing. You haven't sneezed once. When you first do it you normally sneeze.'

Manda was busy sculpting lines. 'No time for sneezing.'

There was a soft knock at the bedroom door and Ava stood quickly, laughing, and she went up the corridor. When she opened the door inwards, there stood Kay, smiling, with her suitcase in her hand. Ava stood back and swung her arm out to welcome and indicated her to move in.

'Hi Kay,' Manda called.

'Hi.'

'Sorry we took such an age. We had to book in and then we went over to the supermarket across the roundabout to get some drinks.'

'I did,' yelled Manda from the floor. 'I did that on my own. Hi, Kay.'

Kay looked down at the floor. One bottle of champagne on its side and two cans of Guinness and Ava was holding another champagne bottle by the neck.

Ava said, 'And Manda and I were talking.' Ava looked in Kay's eyes and made a critical, secret rising of the eyes.

Kay nodded, said, 'No problem. I wasn't very good at Ezzy Dancer. Kylah and Chell were yelling at me. I was just reading the papers and I had a strange sandwich at one of the coffee places.'

Kay put the case and her calfskin bag and her computer down in the space between the wall and the bed and sat, feeling a bit of an intruder, on the end of the coverlet. Kay shook her head. 'Why are you sitting on the floor?'

'We just sort of, gravitated here.' Ava passed the bottle up to Kay. You could see the slight hesitation at the lack of a glass but Kay mucked in and lifted the neck to her mouth. 'Goodness. It's cold.'

'I got ice,' Manda said. 'It's all in the sink.'

'Oh. Fabulous.' She took a swig and then didn't pass it on. Took a second.

'That's the way, Kay. Good old Kay. I was just saying, you're no a bad sport for such a proper devil.'

Kay turned her eyes down on Manda. Manda seemed unusually cheery. 'We've another bottle yet,' Manda said with wide eyes. 'And I've four Guinness.'

Kay took a longer swig and passed the bottle down to Manda. 'So how have you been, Kay?'

'Eh, fine.' There was a slightly odd atmosphere in the room Kay couldn't quite pinpoint.

Ava had sat back down with her legs crossed at Kay's feet, so she faced the knees on Kay's jeans.

Kay volunteered, 'We drink a lot, don't we? Really. I mean, not just this trip. We do drink a lot. In Edinburgh I can go out sometimes with friends and we don't drink.'

'We're Scottish.'

'But Ava drinks too.'

Manda nodded sombrely between sips from the bottle. 'Birds of a feather. It's a drinking world, isn't it?'

Ava raised her hands. 'The country is flourishing and we're in a constant state of excitation and celebration.'

Manda said, 'Well, this is a stressed holiday so far, isn't it? It's funny.'

'It is a . . . classic, yes.'

'So we're all taking a drink to relax, cos, well, we've not really been relaxed, have we, girls?'

Ava looked up and said, 'So, Kay. Tell us about yourself.'

Manda ground her teeth. She thought Ava had forgotten she'd met Kay before, because Ava seemed fairly distracted on the amount that she'd been hoovering up. But then Ava added, 'And tell us why you think you're so suited to this post?'

Kay laughed. 'Well. What would my duties entail?'

'You would be required to help us consume the rest of this champagne and possibly go out with us on market survey to see how much more champagne the local supermarket actually stocks.'

Kay laughed again. 'Well. I think I'm qualified for the post because my traditional Scottish introversion crumbles under the influence of champagne.'

'Ah, does it? That would be interesting to see. You're our best interview candidate yet.'

'What else?' Manda asked.

Kay mused, 'Well. This is one of those Christmas Eve scenarios. A day that's only justification is that it precedes the significant day after. These days always are a little restless, which's nicely set off by champagne consumption.'

Ava said, 'Top marks.'

Manda nodded. 'Aye. Kill the day and roll on night-time.'

'Well, you have the curtain drawn.'

'It's a horrible view. I want a lovely view. On to the canal at Venice or something in Rome.

'Rome! Ach . . .'

'Or maybe the leg-scratching hazards for the kilt-wearing jaunts across your noble Highland flanks.'

'My noble Highland flanks,' laughed Kay, slapping her denim thighs.

'They are noble flanks, but I was thinking more of . . . Ben Nevis, is it?'

'Ben Nevis is ugly.'

'Big and ugly like me,' said Manda.

'Manda!'

Ava said, 'But you, Manda, have the great gift of personality.'

'Aye. I've got that okay.'

Ava passed the bottle up.

'Do I get the job then?'

'You must be prepared for dissolution in a Kafkaesque milieu.'

'A what?'

Kay used both hands to steadily decant the bottle back into her mouth. Manda and Ava didn't look at Kay. They scanned the carpet and moved their heads, lazily, across the room. As if there were a circling house fly somewhere. Kay slapped her lips. 'There's something dissolute about drinking out the bottle.'

'Good.'

'Want some Guinness, Kay?'

'Ah. No thanks.'

'Right-ho.'

Kay said, 'We could make, what is it, black velvet? Is that Guinness and champagne mixed up?'

'Oh heavens, no,' Ava called. 'Not with good champagne. Sacrilege.'

'Suits me though. Champers gives me indigestion. Look, Kay, I've been tanking these like shooters.' Between two fingers Manda held up a dairy creamer tub. She had put her glass of Guinness down to peel the top off the creamer. Manda held the little tub to her mouth then snapped her head back to swallow the contents.

Kay noticed three other small tubs, their tops peeled back, discarded on the carpet. There was even a spot of milk on the carpet which – even though it was a hotel room – irritated Kay.

'We might have to get down to another room to get more of the little buggers. Give us a swig of champers all the same.'

'You've got milk up your nose,' Kay giggled.

'Eh?'

'You've been slamming back the little milks so much, some has got up your nose.'

Manda rubbed at her nose and sprang up for the mirror. 'Oh aye. Right enough. Some did go up my nose.' Manda unsteadily moved up and forward, putting her hand down on the crown of kneeling Ava's head, in order to move safely past her and onwards to the bathroom.

'I think you've got the job then,' said Ava quickly. 'But don't tell Finn. She could be jealous.' Ava clapped her hands. 'Manda, Manda, go get the other bottle please. Like our army and air force, we too must do our duty.'

Manda came through with the other bottle, twisting at the foil. 'I want to open it this time. Let me have a shot, Ava.' Manda then burped. 'Och, this French gut-rot is coiling my gizzards something awful. Hey, Kay. The Mighty Finn's in a weird mood today. What was she saying to you in your wee toilet conference?'

Kay shrugged. 'She felt guilty for slagging you off about having a credit card.'

'That was it?'

'More or less.'

The cork popped and hit the curtain. The cork just fell vertically, dead. Because they all followed the cork and looked towards the curtain, they all now heard the noise of an aircraft taking off – or landing – but they would not have noticed the sound if their attention hadn't been drawn towards the window. They had become inured to the sound. Manda passed the bottle down to Ava.

'Be my guest.'

'No. I'm thinking I might mix mine with Guinness; at least then my burps'll be nice Guinnessy ones. Not that wine taste.'

'She didn't say as such but maybe she thinks she's a bit heavy on Kylah and Chell as well,' Kay said.

'Heavy? She adores Kylah and Chell. It's me comes in for all the shit.'

'I think she feels she's growing apart a wee bit and that depresses her.'

'It's her own fault. She never comes back to the town to see her folks. She doesn't, Ava. She hasn't been in Rascals yet, even.'

'She's very busy, Manda. There's a heavy workload on our course.'

'Finn's a cold fish to her folks. She always has been. So she was grat about all that, was she?'

'That was about it.' Kay took the bottle, 'Cheers, girls, here's to peace and love.' She raised the full bottle to her lips.

'That was a lot of time just to say that, Kay,' Manda implied, decanting Guinness finely into another glass.

Kay said, 'That was it, girls.'

'Methinks the lady doth protest too much.'

'What do you mean?'

But Ava frowned. 'Is that quote right?'

'What?'

'The quote. Is that from *Hamlet*? My mind. I'm losing it all. And my education was expensive. Is expensive. No secrets?'

'Pardon me?'

'You weren't talking secrets?'

Kay was finding Ava a bit more forward than she'd got used to. More inquisitive, and also her sharp, snappy intelligence was being felt. There was no fooling her. Cleverly, Kay said, 'There's no secrets about with Manda on our team.'

All three of them laughed.

'Hey, Ava. Ava. Let me tip just a little bit into the glass to see how it tastes.'

'Manda. That's quite barbaric. I'll send you out to get more if you're not careful.'

Manda tipped a little champagne into her Guinness glass.

'I could order more on room service,' Kay whispered.

Ava said, 'Kay. You're leading us astray. I don't want waiters up here.'

'Why?'

Manda growled, 'Imagine a really good-looking waiter came up here. And we all three pounced him. It'd be his dream come true. His eyes would be popping out his head. I must admit, I'm dying to get a look at a knob. It's been ages.'

Ava said, 'Put on the porn. There's always porn in hotels these days. Even in really charming, expensive old hotels that I've been in. I was shocked. And depressed.'

'Well, I've been thinking – Oh, oh, that is fucking delicious.

That's great, cos it's like sweet Guinness. I like sweet and I like Guinness so that makes a great mix. Girls! Taste that.'

'No thanks.'

'Come on, Ave.'

Ava took a tiny sip. 'Oh my dear. That's like, sweet Bovril or something.'

'That's good for you, that is. That's the best of life in there. I can think one more thing would make that perfect.'

Ava and Manda burst out laughing.

Kay looked down on their shaking crowns.

'Aye, a nice knob. You know, like some guys are growers no show-ers? You think you've just a wee tiddler in your hands then – Oh michty me!'

'Okay, Manda. We get the picture.'

'Get the porn on.' Ava flicked her head back at the telly. 'You'll see them in that.'

'Men. A hopeless tribe,' declared Kay.

Ava looked at her. 'At least you have a boyfriend. Men are great.'

Manda said, 'It's them causes your wars. Men.'

'Plenty women would, in that position.'

Ava said, 'Yes. It's like drugs. If you give people armies then people are going to use them. Drugs too.'

'Yes, I suppose it is.'

'Do you ever take anything, Kay. To light up?'

'I'm sorry?'

'Do you ever take anything to light up?'

'To lighten up?'

Manda looked on silently. Exactly the same expression as when she used to watch, as other girls bullied younger ones in the playground. Manda had always taunted, but she let others do the really dirty work and looked on.

'Do I take anything? Smoke dope, you mean?'

'Yeah. Like that.'

'No. I'm not into dope.'

'You mean grass.'

'Well, whatever it's called.'

'You've never smoked it?'

'Oh, I tried it, but it makes me . . . discombobulated. I don't like it. I presumed it'd make me thoughtful and able to concentrate but it was awful. I was confused.'

Ava nodded. 'That would be skunk or something. Blows your mind.'

'Yes, probably.'

'Well, talking about secrets and Finn. You can't tell her but we've some stuff here.'

'Grass?'

'Nope!' Manda said proudly.

'Have you been taking something? I thought you seemed a bit . . . . out of it.' She wasn't smiling.

Ava said, 'Just relax.'

'I am, relaxed. It doesn't relax me being told to relax, I should point out.'

'Do you want to try something?'

'What?'

'You're just going to flip out,' Ava shrugged. 'And phone Finn, I guess.'

'Have you got drugs in here? I don't actually believe this.'

'Why not?'

'Ava. I don't know you well. But I know this. That's unbelievably stupid. Have you been giving Manda stuff?'

'I haven't been giving her anything. She's been taking a little of what she wants.'

'You've been manipulating her.'

'I have *not* been manipulised, Kay.'

'Oh shut up, Manda. Shut up. This is actually serious for once.'

Manda lit a cigarette and muttered, 'Don't tell me to shut up,' but she said it in a disinterested way.

'So that's that then,' said Kay, finally.

'Is it?'

'Scratch another holiday.'

'What?' Manda frowned.

'Well, if you think I'm going through airport customs trusting you tomorrow, Ava, you must be insane. Count me out. That's great. That's just amazing, Ava. Top marks.'

'I'm taking a bit now, Kay, so there's none left for the airport tomorrow.'

'Oh yeah. Sure. And she has some on her. You expect Manda to remember what she has on her and what she doesn't? She didn't even know where her passport was, and that was just on drink. That's just great, Ava. Drugs. That's really unselfish and generous of you. Thanks a lot.'

'Woh. Kay. We're not taking anything through customs. I promise.'

'What is it then? Cocaine I'd guess, knowing you?'

Ava shrugged apologetically.

Kay turned to Manda. 'Are you okay?'

'I'm great, lassie. It's nothing special. Makes you feel good. Like when I had wee Sean. It's a singe. Try some.'

'And you've been giving it to my friend?'

'Fuck sake, Kay.' Manda turned to Ava. 'I told you she'd absolutely flip out. She'll probably call the Feds.'

'Well, that's a point, Ava. The police asked you if had anything on you yesterday and you said no, so you were putting everyone in the car at risk without us even knowing and that's one of the most selfish things I've –'

'I didn't have a thing on me yesterday. I swear.'

'She just got it all off a guy at the station.'

'A guy at a station? A guy at a station! How do you know he isn't police or hasn't followed you here?'

Ava looked at Manda and they both laughed together.

'He's a friend. He was in the area and he gave me a hit of gear. I'm going to do it and that's that. I mean, what's wrong with that?'

'Well, where exactly would you like me to begin about what's wrong with that?'

'Actually. In point of fact. I was perfectly happy to take it alone.'

Manda held up the cigarette packet. She could see Kay's stress and Kay sometimes had a fag under stress. 'Want one, Kay?'

'What, a cigarette? Yes please.'

'Kay, I'm not trying to freak you out. I wanted to take a few snorts so I wouldn't get the urge in America and I want to be honest with you. I can't be bothered trying to score over there. It's just something I do every few months. Jesus. The society's run on it.'

'Not our society. And I like the use of the word "urge". We're all at the mercy of your urges, are we?'

'No one's been or is at my mercy. Your issue seems to be just customs, not some overall, arching morality. That's rational. I'm not insane and tomorrow I won't try to take stuff through customs. And had no intention of trying to do so.'

Out of her Calvin Klein jacket Ava took the second little bag that they were on to.

Kay shook her head and looked at Manda. 'And you took that. Just out of the blue? You're stupider than I thought.'

'It's okay, Kay. It's a fair buzz.'

'You are stoned. You daft thing. How much have you had?'

Manda looked at Ava. 'She's going to get up and walk out,' Manda said matter-of-factly, as if Kay couldn't hear her, and she stared at Ava. 'You'd better tell her the room number of her room so she can just go.'

'Don't tell Fionnula then. Please?' said Ava.

Kay smoked her cigarette and leaned over. Manda passed the ashtray up to her and she put it on her lap. A telling hesitation betraying a distant curiosity.

Kay said, 'Well, you've backed me into an impossible situation and you know it. Everything you do has consequences and all that. If I told Finn she would flip out that you'd given Manda some. She would certainly react in a bad way. In fact, Ava, I think you underestimate Finn's concern for her friends. I think Finn would break her friendship with you over this. Now you lay all that in my lap. Like this ashtray. And I can see you get a thrill out of that. So the holiday is ruined for everyone and all that money lost no matter what way I go.'

Ava glowed inwardly. She was surprised but shocked as well that Kay recognised the thrill. And Ava understood this was the next step for her now – she got off on taking away the innocence of others so she could carry on in her decadence and that truly was a surprise to her. She fell thoughtful but only for an instant. Money was a plaything to her – mere counters in the game – so she made a wager with herself and said, 'Okay, Kay. Take a snort with us then go to your room. I'll give you everything I've got on me and you can flush the rest down the loo. You take a snort and you can flush the lot. I swear on my life,' Ava smiled up at her.

'So is that how you get your thrills, Ava? I thought you were too sanguine to be true. Does that get you off? Getting other people into it?'

Manda sneered and turned to Ava, but Ava knew Kay was right. Ava would put people at risk for her own selfishness.

Kay sat smoking, holding the cigarette amateurishly, like a vain Hollywood actress in a movie, who doesn't really smoke and hasn't extended her professionalism to that extreme. Kay took three puffs then furiously stubbed the cigarette back out.

Ava coughed.

Kay said, slowly, 'And if you put the stuff down the toilet, you'll try and get more in America and I'll get a big story over there and have to shit myself through two airports on the way back.'

Ava felt a sexual force, better than any of her afternoon hits, run up from the base of her spine. 'I won't do that if you take some and I'll tell you why. One, I'm thinking of quitting. I had a bad, bad dream. Plus, bad coke is dangerous and this is the best in London. I'm rich. I don't take crap coke. And this is safe. It's like flying is safer than being in a car but we don't believe that when we're in a plane. One snort from you and I'll give the rest to you to do with as you please.'

'Fuck sake, Ava. You don't need to do that.' Manda shook her head as if her wisdom was infinite.

Kay pointed at Manda. 'You've a disciple already.'

'One snort from you and this –' she jiggled the little packet '– and the other packets go to you for the flush.'

Manda chipped in, 'Aye, watch though, it says to don't put things like that down the lavvy pan.'

'You've more than that packet? I've watched movies, Ava. That's a lot.'

'Not really in legal terms. In legal terms it's still more or less personal possession, not dealing. It's just possession.'

'Yeah, yeah, I've seen the movies.' Kay frowned wearily. 'I wish you were a nice selfish cokehead, Ava, not a manipulative sharer. This is the holiday of generosities this. Give us another cigarette.'

As if she were servicing two poker players at a high-roller table, Manda hurriedly fumbled out a cigarette and handed it up to Kay. Kay took the lighter as well and lit the Marlboro. She carefully lay the lighter down on the bed next to her.

Ava took a slug of champagne then she passed the bottle up to Kay who took it amicably enough and bent it back for her mouth, cautiously drinking, deliberate, nothing showy.

Between sips Kay asked, 'Tell us. What other drugs do you take, Ava?'

'Just this.'

'Oh lovely. And in the past?'

Ava stared up at her. 'Everything?'

'You took everything?'

'More or less . . . not crack cocaine. That's for losers.'

'Heroin?'

Kay blew smoke, turned and looked straight at Manda. Manda gave a scowling, disapproving stare at Ava.

'Yes. I smoked and snorted it. I didn't inject it.'

'And how long did you do that for?'

Ava looked a little outside the comfort zone now. 'From when I was seventeen until I was twenty-one.'

'Fuck sake,' went Manda.

'With my older boyfriend who got *me* into it. He wanted a crazy teenage thing with that look in her eyes. Always got what he wanted, he did. He was rich too. I was like the girl in the Neil Young song. Do you know it? "Come On Baby Let's Go Downtown". Know that song?'

Manda frowned. 'What. "The Young Ones"?'

Ava looked at her, disapproving. Kay handed the bottle back

down to Ava in a friendly manner and she took it. 'Ta. I was sick the first day and had a habit in eight days. I recall being quite proud. Like the day I learned I was pregnant. Monkey powder we called it. Until I was twenty-one,' she giggled perversely.

'And you haven't taken it for two years?'

'Have not been near it. I can't be in the same room as it. I've left parties if it's in any room. I never used to leave parties. I assure you of that.'

Manda nodded severely. 'Aye, you're like me.'

Ava said, 'There's no incentives to quit for a person like me. There are two sets of drug laws in this country. One for the rich and famous and one for the people in the housing estates. Anyone disagreeing with that is talking shit. The rich don't bother anybody. The poor do. It's Dickensian. If I got bust with this today, my dad's lawyers would have me off on a first offence. If I was caught with it up in your estate in Scotland, I'd get clobbered.'

Kay pointed out, 'If the police came in here now, all three of us would get done. I see why you don't want room service.'

'No police are coming here. After the second spell in hospital I ditched that older chappie and quit. Well. My parents had hired this ex-army private detective and he escorted me and put me into Barkers. Barkers is expensive. A health farm for rich attention-seekers. Clinic Trolls, I called them. I'd taken heroin every day for four years and it took me four days to get off it and I was shocked. I was actually disappointed. I used to go to the gym. Fuck, do you sweat those toxins out. I looked like I'd jumped in the river. Two months after, I started again in Oxford. That was the danger. Everyone made such a bloody fuss about getting off. It was all too easy. I knew I'd start again the very day I was off. Amex was supplying for me. When you've plenty money, there's no such thing as a drug problem. It's all semantics. What problem? You have a supply, you have no drug problem. You're just using substances the way you use cotton buds, coffee, cigarettes and tea. It gets like that. I wasn't robbing houses for God's sake.

Second time I stopped on cigarettes. None of my good clothes fitted me any more and I couldn't be bothered shopping. You could see my ribs here. I could hide a hardback book, put it down the front of my dress and nobody noticed, my clothes were so baggy. They didn't let you read at Barkers. You were meant to concentrate on your therapy. I was on forty red Marlboros a day to kill the urge. Four weeks under the old tree, reading in the garden. You couldn't smoke in the fucking house. Escaped the monkey powder and nearly died of English hypothermia. Then I said to myself, that's that. I'm sated. I'll quit, if I can do coke every few months as a reward. Here I am two years on.'

Manda went, 'Fuck sake. That's a story. You're mental, Ava. You could be dead. You're worser than Robbie Williams when he left Take That.'

Kay said nothing. She smoked the cigarette and the three of them passed the champagne bottle. The ball was in Kay's court.

'Right,' Kay finally went, 'I'll take one sniff if you promise me not to take anything but booze for a year.'

'Wow. A real truth or dare.' Ava smiled.

'If I hear from Finn you've been at it, I'll tell her you gave it to Manda today.' Kay turned to Manda. 'And if you tell Finn we took it here today, I'll break your back.'

Manda made a face but said nothing.

'I think you know how Finn will react if she finds out you gave it to Manda. She'll drop you dead. Like you were a . . . dirty little junkie.'

Ava nodded, an old nod-out nod, and she held up the bottle. 'Drink to it?'

'I would if I thought you'd half a chance,' Kay said. 'You won't make it. I think you can afford any failure. Nervous already?'

'I'll surprise you. I'll tell you the dream I had the last time I took coke up in London. When I was a little girl I used to walk up the riverbanks with Belinda Trammel. Belinda Trammel with the missing front tooth and the sunflower dress. We'd try to catch dragonflies in jars. I dreamed, I was walking up the river again with Belinda. We were ten. The sky was blue and we each caught a dragonfly in a big pickling jar. She'd always walk me back to the big house and Mummy would make us lemonade and we'd sit in the garden and drink it under the cherry blossom tree. In the dream, when we got to our garden gate, Belinda said, "That wasn't very nice on the river today, Ava. I'll go with you again one day but please, please don't turn up high on stuff again," and in the dream I looked down at my arms and they were the arms of me at that age, of a little girl of ten. I'd forgotten what my arms looked like when I was ten, but I swear, they were exactly real, holding the dragonfly jar. It was so vivid. I was ten years old and high and when I looked in the pickling jar there was a dragonfly but it was drowned. The jar was full of lemonade and I poured it out on the grass, but it wouldn't fly. I woke up filthy with sweat and I felt so sick. Sick. And I thought, I've *got* to quit.'

Kay said, 'Well, you're not making a very good job of it. It's basic psychology, Ava. That's a dream of innocence lost. You feel guilt. Now, to assuage your guilt, you're trying to turn other people on to your weakness – so we seem a bit like you. So you don't feel so lonely. But remember this. Me and Manda are not like you at all. You're not getting your innocence back.'

Ava looked up – stunned. Apart from Finn she was used to Yes people around her. What Kay – the slightly demure Scot – had said to her face seemed pure fact.

'Why don't you just quit and get a life?' Kay asked, seriously. 'Drink on it.'

Kay took the bottle, and keeping her eyes locked aggressively upon Ava's, she slowly tipped the bottle back and swallowed from it then handed it down. Ava took a swig, looking into Kay's eyes. Aroused.

Manda took the bottle off her and drank as well, as if she was somehow included. 'That was brilliant. That was quite tense that was. Maybe I should try to give up the fags for the same time?' She reached out for her pack. 'I've been meaning to quit.'

Kay said, 'I'm warning you, Manda. You've never kept a secret in your life, so I'm expecting the best from you. You won't let me down, will you, cos you'll be letting down Ava's promise as well?'

'You take a snort and I'll keep the old potato hole closed for once.'

'It's serious, Manda. That's a serious truth or dare. One that lasts a year.'

There was a pause, a feel of charged, lethargic danger. Then Manda poured a can of Guinness into two glasses and she poured the bottle of champagne into each glass which it filled neatly until its emptiness.

'Manda. Manda. What *are* you doing?'

'What? We've another bottle.'

'No we don't. That's the last one.'

'Oh, is it? I thought there was another. I'm buzzin here.'

'Oh for fuck sake,' Ava groaned.

'Here, get it down you.'

'Will that be the straw that broke the camel's back, Ava?'

Ava sourly took the buzzing concoction of stout and champagne in the narrow tube glass.

Manda barked a laugh. 'Just not your style, eh, lass?'

Ava drank it with a pudding face. 'Right.' She spun round and started setting up three lines. 'We'll do them tighter, in a race. Show her the tube, Manda.'

Ava took her purse out of her jacket and handed it to Manda then she pulled off her jacket and threw it over the room. She jammed open the minibar with a crash and peered in. 'Oh for fuck sake.' She slammed it shut.

'Oh yes. A fifty note. What else. Keep the clichés coming,' Kay chuckled, but cold and cynically.

'You roll it like that and you make sure it's clear.' Manda aimed her eye down the tube. 'Got to imagine a place way up your nose and try to suck it up there. Up your best nostril.'

'Best nostril?'

As if she was an authority on the matter, Manda pontificated, 'Usually the right and you seal the other like this. But you don't sniff it polite-like. You fire it way up into your brainbox, and yours is big enough. And don't think of your daddy.'

'I don't believe this.' Kay stripped off her jacket and tossed it on the bed.

'You need a drink. You should chase it with a drink.'

'She'll want a bloody G&T.'

'Well, that's okay.' Ava opened the minibar.

'Give me anything.'

Ava beamed. 'Cognac. That's the one for you, Kay.' Ava lifted out a miniature of Martell cognac and gave it to her. Kay screwed off the scratchy cap and nodded.

All three of them kneeled side by side.

'Blast it up, Kay. Absolutely ram the thing.'

'Oh, I shall.'

'One, two . . .'

Kay sighed and said, 'This reminds me of the egg-and-spoon race at primary school, somehow.' But she noted Ava's technique and tried to look past Manda to her.

'Three.'

Kay took half the substance, hesitated, but then inhaled the rest. She was amazed the way it instantly seemed to crackle and dissolve in an occult, magical manner at the top of her sensitivity and it evaporated there, at that imperceptible point it was converted into some strange power. There was a sour taste and perhaps a crackle in her ears, then she was glad of the fiery fumes of the cognac to burn it away, so she sucked at the tiny bottle neck. All three of them slouched back and sat, like after a session of very competitive badminton.

Ava took the Guinness and champagne cocktail then took a long swallow of the drink with its tab of coloured head. 'You did it, Kay.'

Kay sat, breathing nervously. Then she found herself thinking of something without recognising the origin of the thought. A lush of energy went through her and she wasn't sure if she could feel her face, but she was more interested in a new thought that came to mind and didn't bother reaching for her face. Ava said something to her but the voice seemed far, yet Kay answered immediately and wittily and forgot what had been said. Then came a feeling of restlessness and she stood up and took another swig of cognac to steady herself. She sat back down again. She looked down at her breasts, could feel her heart writhing in there a bit. Then she felt focused and confident.

Manda said, 'Do you think they have Baby Gap in Vegas?'

'Oh. Sure they do,' said Kay. 'They'll have a huge one,' and she wondered why she was talking about that at this moment. She tried to be disgruntled. But she wasn't.

'I'm going to get Sean some things there.'

'Yes.'

Kay had slightly forgotten about Ava, then a huge accomplished feeling of satisfaction came over her. She had just done a wonderful thing and she was proud.

She turned round to Ava. 'One year, Ava. I'm sorry you've been through those things, even though you inflicted them on yourself, and I'm sorry for Finn too.'

Ava nodded. 'I'm sorry for Finn. She's helped me. I'm not worth it.'

Kay nodded. 'You're probably not.'

'Lighten it up, crew,' said Manda and she drained her black velvet down. 'The Dare is on. The Dare is *on*. That's it. It's between the three of us now so let's shut up about it. We all know the score.'

Ava and Kay actually nodded.

Ava gulped at her drink a few times and seemed oblivious to it.

Manda looked at Kay and went, 'You've done it all now, lassie. And I used to think you were such a tight-arse square.'

'Hey. What's wrong with me? I'm not square.'

Manda shifted round on her bum to look at Kay. 'Actually Kay. Not much at all is wrong with you. Your arsehole used to be clenched up tighter than a Church of Scotland minister's but you've sucked some pepper up it the day, love. You're a good old egg and today's your . . . gold medal. I was telling Ava how you're a good old egg. Wasn't I, Ava? Wasn't I just? Wearing short skirts and rolling Paddy.'

Kay smiled but frowning. 'Oh yes. Paddy.'

'I give you a Manda gold medal today.'

'Well said,' Ava nodded. 'What do you think?'

Kay admitted, 'Actually, it's really great. But dangerous.'

All three of them shrieked with induced euphoria.

'We need more booze.'

'Yes we do, don't we?'

'How'll we get it?'

'Not room service with this stuff about.'

'We know. We know the ways of a drug fiend now, Ava. Well, I can't make it down the stairs to a supermarket in this state. I'm a virgin on this. I just can't,' said Kay.

'Some virgin you. You need a nail file for your vaginal warts, you skank.'

'Manda. Save that language for your friends in Rascals.'

'Aye. They're all fifteen with shite clothes.'

'That's her wee fan club, Ava.'

'I've heard about that.'

'It's true they all love me. Wee tarts. I do their hair.'

Ava stood up. Manda and Kay slowly lifted their heads.

'It's the Statue of Liberty.' Manda was looking up, seriously.

'I'll go, but just to the bar to see if they'll give me it over the counter.'

'Get us a Guinness?'

'It would be my guess they won't have it in cans.'

'They do in pints.'

'Well, I can't bring a pint up.'

'Why not?'

'I'd spill it.'

'Take a sip. Ask for it an inch low but demand a discount.'

'I'll get champagne.' Ava bent down and grabbed the pile of change on the bed. Kay's sitting position had enticed the bundle of notes to slide in next to her thigh and Ava touched her there as she lifted the money away. Kay looked down blearily.

Ava turned, bent and studied her face in the mirror, sniffed, looked up her nose and rubbed there at her nostrils; she glanced down at the front of her purple top and brushed it, all the little automatic ballets of deception. Ava moved up the corridor and rattled the chain off. 'Don't let anyone in and keep that gear hidden. Put the chain on.'

The door swung shut.

Kay and Manda looked at each other.

Manda said, 'Will we do another line of her stuff?'

'Yes.'

Manda clattered into the minibar, crashing bottles aside with a sweeping hand; something rolled out and across the carpet. A can of Schweppes bitter lemon. 'Want to share voddy and Coke? Coke and coke-a-Cola'

'Yes. Quick before she comes back.'

Manda creaked off a miniature vodka cap and poured it in a streaked Guinness glass then she stood and went through to the bathroom. Kay heard the slide and twirl of ice cubes being dropped in. Manda hurtled back in and slid along the carpet on her knees, pouring the vodka then busting the little can of Coke which she frothed in as well.

Kay frowned setting up the lines. 'Is that too little or too much?'

'Put out a wee bit more. Careful with it though. It fucks up your ticker. You can feel it leaping around.'

Manda snortered up her line and quickly stood, walking round the room in a repeated, short route between the desk and the side of the bed. 'Good arse, good arse, good arse.' The ice clinked in her glass.

'I have a good arse?'

'Aye, you do, but just . . . good-arse stuff. It's a mug's game this though. Lucky cow.'

Kay nozzled her ration. 'Goodness gracious me. Hey, drink.' Manda passed the vodka and Coca-Cola down to her and she took a long swallow. 'Oh, that's a bit sweet. Champagne would be better.'

'It gives me a sore belly. That was some dare you gave the Princess. And I'll tell you this. She's a stubborn bitch. She'll do it.'

'I'm warning you, Manda. Not a word. If Finn found out?'

'Aye, I know. Old iron tits would go catatonic.'

'Mmmm. Well. I can see why people get into it but. Well. It's silly. Actually, I feel really good.'

Demonstrating perhaps the quickest predilection for the distilled alkaloid of the coca shub in history, Manda frantically yabbered, 'She's taking a long time. Think we should tank another?'

'She's only been gone a minute.'

'Has she? Is that right enough? I'm going to have to go and get this nail done now. Well. In a wee while. Jeezo. I feel very. I feel very confident. I'm delighted about my wee Sean. Just that he's sort of. In the world. And I put him here. Aye, I'm starting to miss the wee bugger. Should of brought him with.'

'That could have presented difficulties.'

'Ach, you always look on the bright side. No, I mean, the other side. Oh, I'm dying for a creamy Guinness now. Like I can see why Ava is into it. You know. If you had the money. You slag her off but with the hundreds in her purse that besom could be at this every day.'

'True.'

'Lucky besom. I'm a bit all trembly. Aye. I'm sorry I'm always at you, Kay. I was telling Finn. I'm trying to be a better person, more of a frog and less a scorpion. Well, I look like a frog so that's a start.'

'Ach, you'll weather the storms, Manda.'

'Aye, aye. I will.'

There was a knock at the door.

'Fuck. She was quick.'

'Shit, I forgot to put the chain on. I'll jiggle it round.' Kay strode up the corridor but checked the spyhole. Ava alone. A pint of Guinness in one hand, two bottles of champagne fingered by their necks in the other hand. Kay juggled and clanked the little chain against the door plate, overdramatically. She swung the door open.

Ava walked straight in. 'Ta–da!'

Kay shut and chained the door.

'Ava. You beezer. You're a wonder.'

'I had to take a sip at the bar.'

'Are you getting a taste for the Irish?'

Manda took the pint and slurped at it. 'Did folk look at you walking through the hotel with a pint?'

'The barman said it was okay because it's quiet down there.'

'Aye, that's a boring bar. Not like up here where the action is.'

Ava just wavered back to the bathroom and they heard the bottles enter the more watery consistencies of the sink, lone ice cubes touching the heavy glass, and she returned. 'That all needs to cool.' She slid down on the floor at the bottom of the bed again. 'Well, what have you been saying about me?'

'Nothing. Manda was talking about herself.'

'She's been known to do that.'

'Away. I do not.'

'Manda. When you first took a snort, I got an hour and a half monologue on Baby Gap. It doesn't seem to affect any other part of your body but your mouth.'

'Get out of here. It affects plenty parts of me.'

Ava stood and stretched, hands placed in the small of her back, her flat stomach pushed out so the small silver belly-button piercing showed below her shirt.

'Okay, Kay?'

'I'm cool.'

'I see you haven't flushed the gear.'

'Maybe we should try it one more time?'

Ava laughed, but not too delighted, not too triumphant. She sat on the bed and pointed at the television. 'On with the pornography.'

'Oh no.'

'It's funny to watch. The plots are the funniest thing.' She lunged forward and took the remote.

'Aye, but then the weirdo gadge at the reception will know fine you was watching porno, cos it's your room and it'll say on the bill. Dirty Porno Film For Pervert In Room, whatever. I was looking at the card thing.'

'It just shows as a movie so all the businessmen that stay in these places can whack it off away from their wives and claim the porn as part of their hotel bill. That's the market for it.'

'Oh, gross. Maybe I'll sit on the floor. The bedcover.' Kay waved her finger about confusedly.

'How much does it cost, the porno?'

'Six, seven quid.'

'Fuck sake.'

Ava said, 'I can't enjoy porn though and they say some women do. I find it depressing and a bit rapacious. I don't have a moral problem with it. It just depresses me.'

Kay said, 'It is ridiculous from what I've seen.'

'Huh. And what have you seen?' Manda smiled.

'Just . . . when it's shown in movies. What do you mean you find it depressing? Because it's sordid?'

'No. No. It's not all sordid. Just pornography in general depresses me. The concept and the need for it. It's . . . such a lonely thing and I'll be frank, I sort of feel I'm missing out on all that skilful bonking. I wouldn't mind being in among it. Sometimes.'

'Ha ha. I know what you mean. But you had the chance, Ava. With your chronic threesome.'

'That's true. I did my best. But with porno. With the men you see in them . . . they all look like failed wrestlers. There's never good-looking blokes. I just feel. It's just. People should be having real sex. It's all so . . . I once saw a handsome couple making love in the next apartment building. That was really erotic.'

'Did you watch, you dirty besom?' Manda laughed.

'Of course I did. Porno can't equal that. It's so staged. Sex utilised to make money. They pretend it's all about wild, free sex, celebrating sexuality, but it's all about celebrating money. Screwing for money and being filmed screwing for money and making money from the film. It's not about sexuality at all. Curious really. Yet everywhere in the world people are making love for free. Just to enjoy. I was thinking this earlier. Pornography and capitalism are closely related as ideologies. You'll see in Las Vegas. They should rename that town: Let's Fuck Us. The suggestion of ideal worlds for men that don't exist. Believe me, the language of capitalism and pornography are joining forces. I'm going to write about it.'

Kay said, 'And the women are always subjugated in some way in the imagery. Never the men. I always just feel it's exploitative.

You wonder if they're doing it by choice – or they've lost touch with what choice is. Within that world, the women must crave conventional love just to be different.'

'What are yous two on about? I want knobs to look at.'

'Let's look at the menu. That's choice.' Ava was selecting Movies. Then she scrolled down to Adult. A display of six features was displayed. 'Oh God. Look at all this.'

'Oh.'

'What? What?'

'Look. It's Dorothy with her pigtails. It's a porno spoof.'

Kay spoke slowly, '*Swallow the Yellow Thick Load*. I can't believe they can show this in hotels.'

'Oh that's brilliant,' Manda gurgled and strangled her chuckle in her pint-glass rim.

'We've got to see this.' Ava had selected it with a skilled familiarity, Kay thought, suspiciously, and she laughed.

'Here we go. I'm going to turn the volume right down because it's all groans and moans and things and people in the corridor might hear.'

'Turn it up,' Manda horked.

All three of them sat watching the screen.

Manda sipped noisily at her pint.

'Look.'

They all laughed simultaneously.

'The Scarecrow. The Tin Man.'

'The Lion!'

'Poor Dorothy. She's in for it.'

'That's some set of silicones on her. They've got her dress dead right though.'

They watched longer, but lighting cigarettes, turning and smirking at each other.

'Here we go.'

'They look quite ridiculous.'

'They're gonna leave their masks on.'

'She even has Dorothy's little shoes.'

'Where's Toto?'

'Take care. He could make an entrance yet.'

'I thought the story would be a bit more drawn out and they're at it already.' Ava frowned sadly. 'The set is actually quite good. I like to look at the sets,' Ava said quietly. 'My last boyfriend liked to watch them when we were high. Usually faked-up offices and things with wobbly walls or sometimes it's an actual bedroom and their only concession is a bowl of flowers on a cupboard. The sets fascinate me. In porn mags too. The house backgrounds in Readers' Wives pages interest me more than the women. But this set's quite . . . elaborate.'

'Is that what you call it?'

'Here we go.'

'Why do the guys always look so slimy? With muscles and those big tattoos.'

'There are sometimes cute girls without fake boobs.'

'No her,' Manda pointed out. 'She looks like the twist you used to get on the inner tube of your bike tyre, when your Old Man would sort it.'

Ava laughed.

'Oh for goodness' sake,' said Kay.

'What's wrong with that?' said Manda.

'Oh for goodness' sake!' Kay repeated.

'Seriously, Kay. What is wrong with that?'

'I don't know how she can.'

'They're right at it now. How long does this last?'

'I don't know. Thirty, forty minutes?'

'Poor Dorothy. Look at her now.'

'All the rooms are full tonight. I don't remember this bit in the film. It's the Scarecrow is got the biggest whang on him. I don't know why, but I was guessing it'd be the Lion.'

'Look at them go.'

'Is that champagne done yet?'

'I'll check.'

Ava hopped next door to the bathroom. Manda who was sat with half her pint next to Kay reached over and nudged her. 'Hey, Ave. Are we having another wee doochter on the vim there?'

'Yeah. Sure.'

Kay and Manda made gladful faces at each other and smiled.

In a worried voice Kay said, 'You don't think any Munchkins are going to make an appearance, do you? That might be too much for me.'

Ava came back through, watching the screen as she peeled the foil, thumbed up the cork, wheeled and shot it just over the girls' heads as they sat on the bed.

'Ahhh.'

'Get out of here.'

'You might have give us a black eye.'

'Just you worry about Dorothy getting it in the eye the way this is looking.' Ava took a slow drink from the bottle then she sat on the end of the bed, close to Kay, and passed the bottle. Kay lifted it to her lips and drank.

'It's not really cold enough, I'm afraid. And it's Veuve Clicquot now.'

'Hard life this,' said Manda and she chuckled.

Kay passed the bottle to Manda who poured a grand scoosh into her Guinness, causing a coffee-like reaction, and she passed the bottle back to Kay.

Suddenly Kay said, 'I've got to pee.' She went to the toilet, shut and locked the door.

'She aye locks the door.'

Ava leaned down to her. 'Never lock the door when you're tooting. You might pass out in there.'

'Unlock the door, Kay,' Manda yelled.

There was no response until the flush went.

'What's that noise?'

'The bath tap. She's washing her hands under the bath tap cos the sink is full,' said Ava.

'She's awfy well brought up,' Manda whispered, nodding. 'Likes a toot though. Who would have thought?'

Kay came back through. She clambered onto the bed among them.

'Don't lock the door, you might have passed out.'

'Is there a danger of that? I feel anything but sleepy.'

'No. Let's get more wasted.'

343

'Yes. Let's.' They all abandoned the porn and scuttled towards the space beside the telly. Ava set them up. They held the champagne bottle as if it were the baton in a relay race. They each snorted and the bottle was passed around.

All three of them settled on the bed now, more relaxed, more stretched out, yet each more distracted, Manda tipping her Guinness at odd angles for her visual amusement. Their attentions were refocused back to the edited, seemingly ceaseless energies displayed upon the television screen. They all burst out laughing.

'It's the Wizard. They've found the Wizard himself and he's wanking off behind the curtain. Classic.' Manda was perfectly amused.

'He looks the most evil of them all,' said Kay, horribly entranced.

Ava shivered down her whole body with coiled energy and said, 'Forgive this one. I think I can see what's coming.'

'Ah ha ha ha ha.'

'Aye. Here it goes.'

'Four of them,' Manda whispered, circumspectly.

'And here we go.'

'What a bunch of wankers.'

'Blimey.'

'They must have been saving that up for weeks.'

'Oh my God.'

'I hope they pay her well.'

'The wee hoor hardly spilled a drop. Good on her.'

'Watch it just finish now. Just like men do. The narrative ends after the ejaculation. There's no second acts when it comes to ejaculation.'

'That's it,' Kay announced.

'Well, that was, culturally, fascinating.'

'Prah—'

'It wasn't even yellow.'

They all slouched back on the bed. Feet tapping, hands working on cigarettes. The screen reverted to Menu. 'What else?' Ava shakily hoisted the remote.

'Oh no, not more please. That's Christmas ruined forever for me. I'll never forget that, every Christmas Day. Now it'll be *Little House on the Prairie*.'

'*Little Hoorhouse on the Prairie*. Or *The Railway Child* or whatever. Her waving her bloomers. Bound to be a version of that.'

'Oh please, no.'

'What's this one? Look at the title. That's girls on girls. That small symbol tells you: two crosses.'

'Oh, not girls. I want to see knobs. Ach. Ya lesbo, Ava.'

Kay said, 'Girl on girl will just be a relief after Dorothy's travails.'

'*Two Thousand and Quim: A Space Odyssey*.'

'Oh no. No. There'll be guys jumping around in gorilla suits bashing the ground with big dildos.'

'That sounds better.'

'No, no. It's quite proper. Less liquids. Girl on girl in a spaceship.'

'That's quids and quids you've spent. That's mental. That's four and a half Guinness in these parts, six at home. All for lesbo porn.'

'It's for men, Manda. That's the point.'

After a few minutes Manda honked, 'What happening? Are you on the right channel? I don't get the story. Turn up the sound.'

'They're in space. They're both bored.'

Kay said, 'She's awfully pretty. She looks sweet. What a shame.'

'Best wait till she gets her helmet off.'

Ava wondered, 'Imagine really big silicone tits in space. In zero gravity, I mean. They would look wild, floating about.'

'You're about to find out.'

'Ach, it's just more of them getting bored-er.'

'They've been out there for three years without men.'

'I know the feeling.'

'Do you hell, Kay.'

'And nothing's happened?'

'Probably an alien with a weird knob'll jump them.'

'It doesn't mention an alien.'

345

'This is shite. Can I have some more champers, Kay?'

Kay turned and gave her the bottle. There was the guttery sound of it glushing into her glass then a frying hiss.

'Here we go. Time for bedtime.'

'Undressing for the freezers,' said Ava, in a hushed, captivated voice.

'Oh, she has got a nice figure.'

'Yeah, and her. See, they have nice figures.'

'Aye. Just like you two bastards. There should be room for the curvier girl in outer space.'

'Ah. Nice tattoo. It's so tiny.'

'What's that?'

'That is a ray-gun-shaped small dildo, Manda. Surely you recognise one immediately?'

Ava laughed.

'It's tiny.'

'It's for the bum I'm predicting.'

'As if they carry that on a spaceship, eh?' Manda protested.

'Oh. She's tying her to the captain's chair. Oh, that way.'

'Nice ass.'

'Will we do another line, Kay?'

'Yeah. Sure. Sorry. I'm fascinated.'

'Just a small one to keep the glaze on.'

'Hoi. What about me, Aves? What about me?'

'Sure. Watch it though. We're pushing the boat out a bit. We'll be jumpy later tonight.'

'Oh. Shit.' Manda's mobile went. So did Ava's, just seconds later.

'Christ.' Ava scrutinised the caller identification.

Manda looked at her phone. 'Kylah.'

'This is Chell?' said Ava, puzzled.

'Will we answer?'

The three of them looked at one another. They could all sense they were tempted not to.

Kay hissed, 'You can just hear the sound of them ones moaning; turn it down or Christ knows what Chell might presume.'

Ava reached for the remote.

Kay had now turned to Manda and she held up her finger to her lips.

Manda nodded. 'Eh. Hiya! Kyles, what's doing? Eh? We're over in the hotel of Friday night. Mind? We've booked yous all rooms. Your key's at the reception.'

Ava's phone had stopped ringing.

'No Ava's fine. Now? She's right here with me. Kay's here too, we're just having a bit of a wee bevvy. Oh, right.'

Ava and Kay continued to look wide-eyed at each other.

'The three of us. What are yous doing now? So look, are yous bringing over some cases for the morrow then? Be a darling and get Finn to bring mine, would you? The one with the black mark on it. You can't be yourself without your stuff. All right, cheers. Eh . . . our room number? I'll text it to you. See ya.'

Manda pressed the End Call button and double-checked it was definitely hung up.

'They're over at the left luggage.'

'Well.'

'Shit,' went Kay. 'Oh well. We'd better, eh . . .'

'They'll be here in what, twenty minutes?'

'That's that then. The bloody party's over, coke and porn is banned.'

Ava said, 'We sound more like a bachelors' convention in Vegas than castaways in Gatwick.'

All three of them looked over at the bag lying on the space by the television.

'A last blast-off?'

The three of them tumbled off the bed and kneeled together as if along a Sunday church pew. Ava set them out and they each sniffed, not even trying to do it in synchronisation, each selfishly consuming, then they leaned back, all three of them with their shoulders against the bottom of the bed, looking up at the television screen, squinting at its closeness.

'Ohhhh. I'm fairly flying now. I feel I'm living two days at the same time.'

'Me too, sugar. I'm sweating a bit.'

Manda chuckled, 'I'm sweating like a docker's armpit.'

Ava said, clear-headed, 'Manda, you need to text this room number to Kylah.'

'Oh yeah. Forgot.' She took up her mobile and quickly clicked at it.

'Here comes the ray gun.'

'Whey.'

'Nice.'

Kay said, 'This is giving me all kind of ideas.'

'I'm no sharing a bed with you again the night.'

They said no more, just staring up at this most unlikely of images. Kay turned and looked at Ava. Ava looked up at the screen then felt Kay's gaze and turned to look at her. Kay smiled. Ava just nodded and turned back to the screen. 'There is that,' she said ambiguously.

'Here comes the . . . walkie-talkie space thing now as well. Jeez-oh, girls. She's game.' Manda turned to the other two.

'We can't just sit here stoned. Finn'll be here soon.'

Kay nodded slowly.

'We better do the . . . burial at sea? Before Finn gets here.'

'One more?' Manda suggested.

'No. Let's knock it on the head for good. For all of us now.'

'No, it works both ways.' Kay nodded.

Manda nodded at the screen. 'Like her.'

They started to spring into action, all three crowding into the bathroom with the little bag they'd been using and the CD case.

All the ice was melted so they lifted the bottle of champagne out the sink.

'Do you want to do the honours?'

'Jesus, what a sheer waste,' went Manda.

'Farewell, the white lady of dreams,' said Ava and she opened the small bag and dropped the crystals into the toilet cistern where they adhered on the porcelain curves. Then she handed the CD case to Kay. 'It's all yours. It was your dare.'

Kay said, 'Actually, it's all in your hands, Ava.'

Ava nodded. There was something final about it.

Kay shakily opened each bag, looking more and more daunted at the amount.

Ava shrugged. 'I always order a week's supply.'

Kay shook out each bag, emptying the powder into the toilet.

Mournfully Manda whispered, 'It's like when your Old Man buries the dead goldfish when you're a wee lassie. Sends them down the pipes to the great sea. No. This's much more sadder.'

Ava ran each little emptied bag under the tap to clean them out and then she used a sodden mulch of toilet paper to seal each little plastic pouch within. The toilet was flushed twice to swallow these then two more bags wrapped in toilet paper were sent down.

'That's it. Manda, take a wet towel and wipe down the table thing really clean. It's covered in it.'

Ava and Kay walked nervously around the bedroom, looking for any evidence.

'For goodness' sake, put that porn off.'

'But they haven't finished yet. There's another spaceship coming to dock with them.'

Kay turned off everything she could find on the television then switched it all back on again and selected a running news channel with the volume turned down; the remote jumped out her hands and fell on the carpet twice. 'Jesus, I'm not sure if I can handle this in front of Finn. My nose feels weird.'

'Let me check it.' Ava suddenly placed her fingertips on Kay's jaw and gently forced her whole head back.

'Fine.'

'Am I okay?' Ava snapped her head back.

Kay laughed and looked up Ava's nostrils, frowning. 'Looks okay. What am I looking for?'

'Big blobs of coke crystal hanging there. Don't use nose drops or anything tonight. It can sting like hell and you can't do anything to stop it. Should all be dissolved but you have to watch and not be constantly pulling at and touching your nose, or blowing it.'

Kay started collecting the devastation of scattered champagne bottles and cans, placing them in an upright gathering over by the curtains. For some reason, she suddenly opened the curtains and the window to let in some air. Kay recalled this was a throwback to illicit cigarette smoking in her bedroom. But the curtain knocked the empty Guinness cans onto their sides. She just left them. The sound of an aircraft whine was immediate through the window gap.

'Manda, let me see up your nose?'

'Uh.'

'You've got hairy nostrils.'

'A wee bit, aye. I have a brilliant pencil-shaver thing you could put up them.'

'You're okay, but stop rubbing at your nose. It's all going to be a bit obvious. The three of us sat here, me between you, the biggest hoover nose ever, and the three of us rubbing away at our noses, with Finn asking what we've been doing all afternoon. "Oh, nothing!" Sniff sniff rub rub poke poke.'

Kay held out shaking arms. 'Oh God. Will we tell them we were watching dangerous pornography?'

Ava said, 'Yeah. That'll keep them preoccupied at our dissolution instead of them staring at our nostrils. Maybe we should wash out faces a wee bit? I've got body spray, if anyone wants.'

'I'm okay, I think.'

'Oh dear.'

They all sat nervously.

'Just tell them we've been boozing like hell too.'

'Know what? This is stupid. Scene of the crime. Let's get down to the bar and meet them there.'

'I don't know if I can drink any more.'

'I really think the bar would be best. I feel like a walk.'

'A walk. Round this weird airport joint?'

'Aye, but then we'll need to go through the whole rigmarole of getting the cases up.'

'Yes. Are you sure you can handle it?'

'I might have a shower,' said Kay quietly.

'Right. Here's your room key somewhere. It's here.'

'Aye, brilliant. Aye.'

'You okay, Manda?'

'Aye, okay, aye, brilliant. I am okay brilliant aye. I'm brilliant, aye. I'm okay.'

Now the concept of escape had been evoked, Kay and Manda became frantic.

'Calm down. Big breaths. Just act like we're drunk on the booze.'

'Okay. We're both going to another room. Aye.'

'I'll share with you, Manda. It would be impossible to share with anyone else. My jacket.' Kay began pulling on her jacket. 'Get my case and bag and computer. That's what I'll do. Print out the tickets in the Business Hub thing here.'

'Aye, brilliant, aye, your case, aye. The computer. And the bag. I'll carry the computer, Kay.'

Kay tumbled out with her suitcase and almost fell over. 'Whoops.'

'Right, case. Eh, bag. Room key? Have you got the kay, Key? Key, got the kay? Have you got the kay, Key?'

'Yes, yes. And the number?'

'It's written in the booklet.'

'That was brilliant. Okay, Ava.'

'Hugs, girls,' Manda called, arms out.

The three young women formed a triangle of hugs, their faces close, lips almost against cheeks, breathing on them rapidly.

'Thanks,' Kay whispered. 'This is quite mental.'

'Just take it easy. You'll come down. Don't drink more, just chill.'

With Kay leading, carrying her suitcase and the pannier of her computer, they both moved off up to the door.

'Jesus.' Kay rattled away frantically at the chain.

'See you later?'

'I'll text,' said Manda.

'See you soon, Ava. Aye, we're aye. In our room. Aye. Brilliant.'

Kay and Manda bustled out and slithered through the artificial light of the long, windowless room corridor.

Ava shut the door and was left alone. She laughed and shook her head. She pulled out the newspapers and looked through them roughly but unable to settle. Then she went into the bathroom, washed her face and brushed her hair, hoisted her shirt and blasted on body spay. She watched the BBC news for a while, frowning at the slowness with which the tiptoeing of so-called objectivity, the muddled facts and the half-hearted truth-telling stuttered out.

After twenty minutes or so there was a knock at the door. She walked up the corridor and checked the spyhole. Finn.

Ava opened the door and smiled. 'Greetings, Voyager,'

Finn stepped forward and grabbed Ava under her arms in a hug and lay the side of her face against Ava's mouth just as Manda and Kay had shortly before. Finn was breathing heavily too. 'The dancing machine was horrible but addictive. Had to help bring Manda's suitcase over here. I've ended up Manda's porter, as was my destiny.'

'Proud stevedore. You ask for no reward.'

Finn chuckled and she looked up, straight into Ava's eyes. 'You always say the right things.'

Ava fought to maintain the deception. 'I'm really drunk.' Ava shrugged.

'You don't look it.'

'Oh but I am.'

'Splendid.'

Ava gestured around. 'We've all returned to Ithaca? Come in.'

Finn was smiling. She walked in behind Ava. She didn't look around the room. She looked at Ava. Finn put her backpack down. 'Where are the girls?'

'They just left. You missed them. They are ashamed.'

'Now why would that be?'

'Because we drank so much champagne which Manda insisted on mixing with Guinness and we indulged in the shameless viewing of pornography. We gave ourselves over to the male gaze and its voyeuristic heartlessness.'

'Really, huh.'

'It was hilarious. And Manda was sterling too, with all her comments.'

'I can imagine. She would be criticising the slightest blemish on a girl.'

'Absolutely. Would you like a cup of tea?'

'Yes. The way you make it. All English in the teapot.'

'Polly put the kettle on.'

'I'm glad to see you, Ave.'

Ava walked away past her. 'Well, I'm glad to see you, Mary, Mary, running through the heather.' Ava shouted from the bathroom, filling the kettle, 'Where's Kylah and Chell?'

'Taking showers they danced so much. Their room key was at reception. Thanks. They're away there now conspiring and whispering together like telepathic twins, clambering over their suitcase mountain. Manda's case is there too. It looks like a luggage carousel. I was worried about you. For some reason.'

Ava laughed, but as she walked back through she realised she had deleted Rex's incoming texts and calls, but she hadn't deleted that final call to him which would lie in her records as a mysterious call to *Lauren*, dated that day. 'Why do you think these things, darling? Oops. The kettle isn't full enough. You know the kettle must be full to make a good cup of tea. I can taste it if the kettle was only half full. We'll need to go down to the physics department one day and ask them to discuss this with us. I'm cold. Kay opened the window before she left. Do you know why she did that?'

'Why?'

Ava said, 'She'd been smoking cigarettes. She doesn't normally smoke. She did that as a pure instinct from the days of smoking in her bedroom when she lived with her parents.'

'You're right. She did used to do that.'

Ava had grabbed her jacket, swung it on her shoulders and made for the bathroom.

Finn could be heard standing and moving to the window, kicking through the champagne bottles. 'I see what you were up to with all these bottles; Kay was subconsciously trying to recreate the glory days of Hever Castle in its prime.'

Ava laughed from the bathroom, while entering Call Records and deleting the call to Rex, then she clutched the phone back into her pocket. She walked back through with the kettle and replugged it.

'Ava?'

'Yes?'

'Would you do something for me that I've never asked you to do before?'

'What?'

'Analyse our biographies. The Hollywood and the art-house version of our lives. I've never once said to you to stop it. I've said I don't like it, I said, come back when you're sober, I told you not to borrow my underwear and I chased off your posh cokehead friends through sheer force of Scottishness, but I never once said, Other who watches me watching you. Lay off that crap and stick to booze. At first I thought it was rebellious and an act of freedom. But I prefer you so much on just drink. Now I just want to admit my timidness and ask you to quit it.'

Ava frowned at her. 'Did you think I was up to something today?'

'This morning I woke up in an odd frame of mind. But I did think that. That you were almost on the oblivion express again.'

Ava bunched up her forehead. 'Hey. Did you ever say to Chell?' She threw her jacket on the bed.

'Never. I didn't say anything to her.'

'Really?'

'Nothing. To Chell. Why?'

'Yesterday she said something to me down by that lake. Very odd. Out of the blue she told me to look after myself. That I was too confident. She just came out with it. I was startled. Strange.'

'I told Kay today you used to have a problem.'

Ava turned to look at her. 'Really?'

'Did she ask you about it today?'

'No. Why tell Kay?'

'Well. She's subtle. And not a gossip.'

'That's true.' The kettle had clicked boiled. 'But. I am aware that you never gave me any ultimatums to quit. So. If you're asking me to stop, I will.'

'You will? I thought we were at least going to have a big massive fight. That's why I'm so nervous.'

'You don't seems nervous.'

'You don't seem drunk.'

'Well, aren't we opaque?'

'I'm making the tea now with a warm teapot, so go and empty that please.'

Finn sped off with the teapot with warming hot water in it.

'Breakfast or Earl Grey. That is your hard choice.'

'Breakfast.'

'You really should have milk-free Earl Grey; these dairy creamers are all gone and I'll tell you why. Manda got indigestion after one glass of the champagne and drank the creamers.'

Finn walked towards Ava, her face open and smiling; she handed the warm teapot over. Ava clicked the kettle and reboiled it.

'You take my advice and quit and I'll take yours and go for Earl Grey.'

Ava nodded, oddly weary and wise. 'Okay.'

'You promise?'

'I promise.'

'You look pale now. Have you had anything to eat today?'

Ava had to think. 'Eh, no. I'm not hungry.'

'You're a rock-and-roller, Ava. Maybe we could get room service to feed you up. You go days without food. It's fucking infuriating. I have to do sit-ups.' Finn had produced a packet of cigarettes with a lighter inside and she lit one.

'Of course we could. Let that teapot sit a while.'

Finn crossed and threw herself into the horribly patterned armchair – too big for the room – she smoked with mock elegance, one bare leg with its motorcycle boot canted awkwardly from her short skirt – the very skirt from Monsoon which Ava had titled, That Skirt Of Which No Philosopher Born Has Worn. A single little leaf of grey-blue cigarette ash was on her elongated thigh, like a resting fruit fly. Finally her short, purple fingernail flicked it away.

Ava said, 'You look like a dangerous man's dream.'

'I don't like dangerous men.'

'A dangerous man's dream with a secret, sexy Samuel Beckett tattoo. What a catch you are, my dear.'

Finn smiled. 'Hey. Madam. Let's go all those places you said we would.'

'We will.'

'Will we? You'll ditch me for a Greek heir. Or you'll run off with the richest lesbian in Monaco. Or knowing you, probably the poorest.'

'I thought of the perfect job for you today. You can work in the Campo dei Fiori.'

'What's that?'

'It's the flower market in Rome, every morning but Sundays in a beautiful piazza. I want to share with you, sleep in a bare flat on a mattress. We'll write our philosophy books in Roma. Fuck the lodge at our place; it's off the plan.'

'Will we do that?'

'We'll do that. My Italian's awful, but six months.' Ava shrugged.

Finn smiled. 'We'll become friends with the handsome but gay guy in the cafe downstairs and I'll go down every morning and bring you up an espresso in its saucer. He'll let us. If I didn't feel the obligation, I'd go tomorrow.'

'It's a bit Henry James for us.'

Finn smiled. 'But what a . . . buzz.'

Ava chuckled, looking at Finn dangerously. 'Strange. To fantasise about travel in an airport.'

'Hey, I'm not trying to join the rush of people who want to use you, Ava. I know you have to be careful.'

'I knew that a long time ago, my dear. A long time ago.'

'I've only ever asked you for one thing and that was a few minutes ago.'

Ava nodded. 'I know.'

Tuesday

1

As the sky above them had turned into a milk without feature, the madness of the journeys, necessary or unnecessary, continued in the air avenues above, as if the sky itself was a featureless infinity pool and the aircraft noise was only the constant trickle at its edges.

At around five thirty, slow dawn stirred a building force of light down onto the hundreds of vehicles in the silent car park outside their windows. Manda Tassy and Kay Clarke still lay awake, rigid in each of the beds of their twin room, with all the ease of awaiting a fatal injection. Birds tentatively sounded, then built in foolish confidence, though they chose their habitat among the gaping maws of jet engines.

'I mean, I am excited to be going to Vegas, Kay. But this is ridiculous.'

'Yes. Goodnight. Manda.'

'Goodnight.'

A few moments passed.

Wildly overstimulated, they weren't going to sleep.

The six young women assembled in the Flight Deck Hotel lobby at a time synchronised in a blizzard of cancelling, reconfirming and recancelling texts. Finn and Ava were led to believe much vital, diplomatic toing and froing between rooms and along corridors was taking place, to do with the swapping of cosmetics.

'Chell, I thought I had told you to wear the Diesel T-shirt under your trackie top?'

'What's wrong with this?'

'That's just Adidas, girl. Don't let yourself and us down.'

'Leave it out, Manda. We're just sat on a plane or queuing for the toilets.'

'Anyone could be on that plane. Anyone. The most gorgeous guy in the world. That Reeker Glaciers could be next to us.'

'Who?' Kay raised an eyebrow.

'Reeker Glaciers.'

'She means Enrique Iglesias. The son of that old codger Mum likes. We saw him in a magazine. He's a bonk.'

'Manda. Those kind of peoples is in first classes,' said Kylah. 'Not in the mosh pit with us.'

'Those type of people is me, Kylah.' A thumb was stabbed hard on her three gold necklaces. 'I'm going to go first class after *Big Brother* and the lottery and all that.'

Sunglasses were dropped down from their hair, like visors. There was a morning chill to the outside air, despite the sunglasses – exhaust pipes showed fumbles of smoke at their spouts. The ravaged grass between the pavements looked crispier. They saw a large jet at a nose-up angle appear briefly then vanish behind the distant terminal. As it emerged the noise reached them, a ragged, haked and torn sound of infinite power. The weather had clouded, a dirty grey spread of high altocumulus, like the edges of the white of a huge frying egg, spread out over the sky, silhouetting the aircraft that took off, black, as if they were printed upon identification charts.

Once again the Hotel Hoppa routed through the familiar satellite hotels as if fixed to the ground by a magnet. The girls sat, now familiar with the journey to the terminal and not interested in investing any comment or effort into this mere temporary state.

Ahead, the South Terminal, big as a Nile cataract, spread across the late morning; its architecture of modular expansion gave back no message. Familiarity had now grown into fondness for the young women. When they entered the terminal they repeated the repetitive security messages spoken from the ceilings to themselves, as if following the prayers of their church. They now recognised the heavy electrical presence of the low-level trains and a mix of airline kerosene, axle grease and brake-shoe burn, rising in the cold air up the escalators from the railway station.

They passed the bureau de change on their entrance into the great hall of the South Terminal but now they moved quicker, confident in their paths round and up. From lifts they entered Gatwick Village with their eternal trolleys and backpacks. It seemed now they had been there forever, as they swung swiftly by the Body Shop with its sinister attendants, passed the forever-ignored Unique Gifts.

They came to Garfunkel's Restaurant.

'Waiter. Breakfast. Six. Smoking. Off to Las Vegas,' Manda said and clapped her hands.

The waiter looked around doubtfully. 'Well, there's room for six people over there, but you would need to leave all trolleys at this side, over there.'

'Well, that's okay but you make sure you keep a good eye on our stuff,' Manda threatened. 'I have clothes in there so brilliant you wouldn't believe and you can't be yourself without your stuff.'

The waiter frowned. 'I'm afraid that's not smoking though.'

'Oh?

Kylah said, 'Och, it doesn't matter so much for brekkie. Who smokes during a fry-up?'

'I do.'

'Aye, and I love a coffee with a ciggy at brekkie,' Chell protested. 'That is my brekkie usual; with Coco Pops.'

'Aye. You're gonna have a heart-attack fry-up though, aren't you?'

'Have cigarettes after, in the Village Inn, Chell? I'm sure you'll be having a drink,' Finn shrugged.

'Eh. So what is it to be please?'

Manda had forgotten about the waiter standing there.

Kay stepped in. 'That table is fine. Thank you. For your patience.'

Manda raised her forehead into three arcs. 'Patience? He's here all day. It's us got the plane to Las Vegas to catch.'

361

'This is great.'

'Bags me in the bothy booth thingamy bit.' Manda barged in, knocking the table a bit.

Everyone settled round the table – Manda then Kylah then Chell along the inner banquette – Finn, Ava then Kay on the spindly outer chairs, a little uneasily facing the others with moving customers and waiting staff constantly skimming their shoulders. Manda said, 'Hey, Ava. What was that yous were saying about the time going back in Las Vegas? What does that mean?'

It was left to Ava, who cautiously said, 'Well, a five-hour time difference or something exists, behind our time, in New York and it's another three hours or something, I think, behind that in Las Vegas. So the actual time in Vegas is eight hours behind us right now.'

'What now? It's like eight hours ago in Vegas right now? It's back in time?'

'The time is eight hours behind in Vegas. Yes.'

'But what's happening in Vegas is actually happening now, aye? No like in *Big Brother*, when what's happening, happened hours ago?'

'Eh, no. It'll still be dark in Vegas now. It will be two or three in the morning. People will be partying.'

'Really? Partying right the now. That's mental. Why is that?'

'Cos of the size of the world.'

'The size of the world?'

'When it's light on one side of the world it's dark on the other, Manda. Cos the world is round and the sun shines on one side at a time.'

'Oh, right, I see. So the flight'll really only take two hours or that?'

'No, Manda. The flight time is the same. Just the time when you get to the place is different. Like when you put your watch back an hour in winter and it's dark at four in the afternoon up in the town.'

Manda pursed her lips and held up her wrist to display her watch, upside down, hanging loosely on her wrist. 'Time's not my big thing.'

'Aye, we'd noticed.'

'Right, is it six fucking jumbo fry-ups all round, bonnie lassies?'

'No. I'll have the scrambled eggs with smoked salmon, I think.' Ava nodded.

'What? You're jesting me. That's minging.' Manda furiously scanned the menu, to confirm the existence of such an atrocity.

'It's nice. In the morning, sort of rich and smoothing and exotic.'

'Salmon in the morning. That's disgusting.'

'Why? You have kippers,' Kylah said.

'When I was wee I did. No now. I'm a busy Practice Manageress, I don't have time for picking out the bones in the morn with a hoor of a hangover on me. I mean, only old grannies eat kippers. And salmon.'

Ava shrugged and ignored her.

'Aye, I might just have scrambled eggs on toast,' said Finn.

'Oh, skwambled eggs for you too, copycat.'

'Aye, I might just have that too?'

'Chell, you wee besom. You just says you were gonna have a big fry-up like me.'

'Aye, but thinking of it . . . all that . . . stuff.'

'God. She can eat what she wants, can she not, Manda?' Kylah challenged.

'We're on a big journey now, back into time. So get a good brekkie down you. It's like my Nana says at Hogmanay, "Butter up before the sauce," and we'll aye be having a wee drink to get us on yon big flying contraptions. They look too big to me. It's a full breakfast for you, Chell, and that's that. Your Old Dear would scold me sore if she found I wasn't looking after you proper.'

Ava said, 'It's funny, is it not? Here it's called Full English Breakfast but in Ireland, when I was in Dublin, it was called Full Irish Breakfast.'

'Aye and it's called a Full Scottish Breakfast in the hotels in town too,' Chell told them.

'Everyone fighting over the great invention,' Finn sneered.

'Quite right too.'

'But we have porridge in our Scottish breakfast, Ava. Not cornflakes.'

'Porridge scums me out. Coco Pops any day.'

Manda looked slyly at Ava. 'Aye. I've had porridge for breakfast a few times myself, when I've not got home till dawn. I can remember the boys' names too; know what I mean, Kyles?' She elbowed Kylah repeatedly so Kylah grimaced and vibrated on the spot.

Ava simply said, 'French people are appalled by the great British fry-up. They can't imagine how we can eat all that in the morning.'

'Jeezo, they're ones to talk. Frog's legs.'

'Snails too they eat. Have you ate snails, Ava?'

'Many times. They just taste of garlic.'

'I'd sooner swallow a blow job,' Kylah stated.

Manda roared. 'You always do, you wee hoor.'

'Black puddings. God.'

'Away. Black pudding with ketchup is the greatest,' Kylah maintained.

'Know what it is?'

'What? Black pudding?'

'It's the black sheep of the flock.'

'No it's not. It's pigs' blood.'

'It is. It's pigs' blood in oats all mixed up. That's why it's black.'

'What's white pudding?'

Chell said, 'Maybe that's the white blood corpuscles stuff just?'

Finn and Kay laughed out loud.

'Can we not talk about this? I've a whole huge brekkie to munch through now and I just wanted Coco Pops.'

'Hoi. Here's the gadge. Hoi. Right, mister. It'll be a full English – though you should really be calling it a full Scottish breakfast, cos we invented it . . .'

The waiter smiled, tolerantly.

'So one, two, three full English breakfasts with extra mushrooms and beans on all them.'

'I don't –'

'Shut up, Chell. Kay, what are you having?'

'Actually, I'll have a full English breakfast as well. No beans please.'

'Good on you, Kay. Good old Kay. She'll tack it, she'll tack it will Kay: whisky . . . other things. Boys! The short skirts, she's a trooper is Kay. An example to yous all. I bet she goes on top in Las Vegas too. Eh, Ava here is having . . . some weird shite . . .'

'Scrambled eggs with smoked salmon please. Thank you.'

'The Mighty Finn?'

'Scrambled eggs with toast please. Thank you.'

'You know that each breakfast comes orange juice and toast and choice of tea or coffee?'

'Does it comes orange juice?' Manda sneered. 'I don't want orange juice, mister. It plays havoc with my guts in the mornings. I can tell you that now. You'd need plenty bog paper in that toilet of yours if you jam an orange juice down me. Can I have a Coke?'

'Medium or large?'

'Large of course. With ice, pal. Aye, Coke.' She looked at Ava and Kay who refused to meet her eye.

'Chell?'

'Coffee please?'

'Kyles?'

'I'll have coffee too.'

'So is everyone else having orange juice?'

Others nodded.

'I'll have tea for one in a teapot please. No milk. I need a coffee but later,' Ava smiled.

'Hark at Lara Croft. And the Mighty Finn?'

'I'll have coffee.'

'Toast please? Brown or white bread?'

Manda pointed, 'White, white, white,' and then, culturally perceptive when she wanted to be, she pointed at Ava, Finn and Kay, 'Brown, brown, brown?'

The three girls opposite nodded predictably.

'Come on, girls, this is my treat, is that it? Is that all yous want? Right, that's it, pal. We're off to Las Vegas so make it snappy and you'll get a good tip. Where are you from then?'

'Indonesia.'

'India. Oh aye. Nice there, is it?'

'Indonesia.'

'What's that? India but you're aye partying? Indo Knees Up.'

'Thank you very much,' said the waiter, still smiling amiably and walking away.

Kylah sighed. 'Manda, steady on. You could hurt people's feelings with that. He might think you're insulting him or his country. And don't be teasing him about his English. He speaks good English and you don't speak any languages.'

'Eh, how? How-me? I think he's a bit cute and I can tell he's attracted to me too. I'm just curious. I'm only jesting. Indo Knees Up. The gadge thought it was funny.'

'I don't think he understood you,' Kylah tutted.

'That's funny. I'm in brilliant mood. Off to Las Vegas. It's going to be legendary. What'll we wear out the night then, girls? I think I might go for the three-quarter-length black trousers and my black spaghetti-strapped top with the silver dragon beastie thing on the front. Shoes!' She yelled out as if to another table. 'The black wedges with the white trim. Kyles, what're you wearing?'

'I haven't decided. Let's get there first.'

'Well, I'll tell you now what it is you should. It'd look good. Your maroon flares and your white sequinned shirt. Shoes! Your strappy black ones, no the covered-in black ones, the strappy ones.'

'Mmmm.'

Manda now turned a stormy eye on Kay, Ava and Finn. 'Now don't yous be wearing funny stuff in Las Vegas; none of your gothy studenty ensembles all the time, or yous'll no match up with us and you won't get in the clubs there either. Christ knows, you didn't make the effort to bring much. You'll be in Vegas over there. Vegas! Yous'll maybe need to buy some stuff for nights out and in fact I've been thinking.' Manda pointed over towards the entrance of the restaurant with its shallow mezzanine, where Ava and Finn's backpacks rested casually against the three trolleys, almost as a dossal attached to their sides. 'Yous all have room in there for shopping in your hod carriers. Oh aye. I know fine what a hod carrier is. We could do a wee bit shopping in Las Vegas. Only problem with these sort of strap-on bin liners yous have, is my new stuff would get all creased up if it was in them, so good designer stuff, Donna Karan for instance, would have to get put in Kay's suitcase which

366

I can feel myself by the weight is not nearly full enough. Kay.' She placed a glottal stop after the name. 'Ah mean, yous two.' The pointing finger went out hard at Ava and at Finn. 'Yous might as well of brought two ordinary black bin bags instead of those back-packer things. We're no hitching it round the Highlands like scabby tourists, girls. This is Vegas. *Las* Vegas.'

'Don't let it go to your head, Manda,' Kylah drawled.

'You's'll be left looking right pigs in a poke with no decent togs to wear. Here. Here. I've just had a brilliant idea.'

'Oh no,' went Kylah.

'Now I thought of it first, out loud. We must get a guidebook. Here, I'm off to get one right now . . . Oh. Here comes the brekkies. Right, we got to get a guidebook for the nightclubs and that, girls. See what the nightclubs is and how it works. I hate not knowing how it all works. I like to know how it all works, like what the bouncers are up to with the dress policy and all that and as to getting into the VIP areas –' she turned a challenging look at Finn – 'and all that . . .' she mumbled, rising up off her arse to scan the surface of the arriving plates of food, in anticipation of finding fault.

The waiter swung round with two plates of breakfast, accompanied by another waitress with earrings who Manda scrutinised intensely. He was canny enough to place Manda's plate first.

'Thank you,' repeated Chell and Kylah as their plates went down in front of them.

'And my Coca-Cola, don't forget my Coca-Cola.'

'This looks. Big,' said Kylah.

'Magic. What a slap-up.' Manda pointed around the table with her fork. 'Yours'll just be coming,' she assured them. 'Aye. Guidebook of Las Vegas.'

The waiting staff reapproached. Scrambled eggs were placed before Finn and Ava and another full breakfast for Kay *sans* the baked beans portion. Tube glasses of orange juice now descended. And a few frames of toast were awkwardly forced on the over-crowded table.

Manda was in already, folding bacon on fork, and compressing it down on a knob of severed sausage. And then her mouth was full but a poor barrier to her continuing. 'Here comes all your stupid teas and coffees galore. Jesus. Yous had of thought they'd bring it all at once with a couple more gadgies.' She pivoted her head full round on the stubborn shoulders. 'Look, there's two just stood scratching their fannies over by the till, doing fuck all.' This was in full hearing range of the earringed waitress and the guy from Indonesia. 'You got my Coca-Cola yet, pal?'

'It is just coming.'

'Is it now?' She nodded, chewing violently. 'The proof'll be in the pudding. Won't it?' she assured him, pointing a fork.

There was the scrunch and crush of various young women spreading butter on toast.

'I don't know if I can manage all this,' whispered Chell, prodding at her platter with just a single fork.

'Use your knife, Chell. You're no wee Sean. Do I have to cut it up for you, love? Get stuck in. Look at Kay. Kay Kay the doctor's daughter's going at it like the clappers. The rampant besom. Is you starved, Kay? Why's that? Huh? Are you knackered, Kay? Why's that? You've got bags under your eyes like a pair of wee hoors' droopin black knickers. Me I'm fine. Here's my Coca-Cola too.' She watched the Coca-Cola pint come across the floor towards her, ready to leap over the table, should it stray even slightly to the left or right in direction. 'Thanks,' she nodded sharply to the waitress and then lowered her face down immediately and stared around the glass for any fingerprints. 'Clarty-looking cow,' she whispered as the waitress retreated. The Coca-Cola was snatched up and a large swallow engulfed. But something was not right. The drink with its shuffling ice was sharply replaced on the table and a savage cutlery attack made in the region of the tomato and mushrooms which were duly plunged into yellow yolk. This was transported to the mouth. She announced, 'Know what I fancy, girls? Oh, it would go great with this grease. A nice drappy Guinness Extra Cold gurgling down. Aye. Hold on.' She was rising from the seat already. 'I'll just have a wee word with my boyfriend.' She moved to the side and squeezed by the table, striding towards the Indonesian gentleman. You saw his cheery spirit visibly crash with Manda's imminent approach.

'She's off on one,' Kylah chewed.

'She's dead excited but won't admit it,' confirmed Chell, dividing up a sausage into many segments but not actually eating any.

Ava touched her napkin to her mouth and thoughtfully said, 'At check-in, we should try to get Manda upgraded. Just Manda.'

'What's upgraded?'

'If you are nice at check-in and request an upgrade, just sometimes you get one. I'm a frequent flyer so there's a chance they'll offer it to me. If I could get a business-class seat, I'll give it to Manda.'

Kay laughed. 'Oh, that would be brilliant. What peace.'

'What do you mean, upgraded?'

'You go into business class, or first class, rarely.'

'Really?'

'Oh wow. Really?'

Kylah rattled out, 'Don't tell Manda this or she'll go mental.'

'It depends on your look. If you look businesslike or blingy you often get it.'

'Well, none of us is businesslike-looking.'

'Manda *thinks* she looks blingy.'

'She looks like a Highland rapper girl with herpes on the brain. All that gold.'

'Ava might, with her posh accent.'

Kay said, 'She might sleep. I'm going to try to sleep. Let's pray Manda sleeps.'

'Is that right enough, about upgrading?'

'Yes. Wouldn't it be brilliant to get Manda stuck up there, ruining the flight for all the posh businessmen? She'd drive them insane.'

'Och, it would be sickening. She'll never let us hear the last of it.'

'She'd come down the plane every two minutes with her cocktails or whatever, showing off. We might get more peace from her snoring away next to us.'

'Look. She's off.'

Not glancing back, Manda was striding importantly out of the restaurant making a direct line for the Village Inn.

'Looks like she's bullied that poor guy into letting her bring a bloody Guinness back in here.'

'She'll get more obnoxious after the first sip.'

'She's right though, we should get a guidebook, though it was our idea. Is that good, Ava?'

'Yes. Want to try?'

'No thank you.'

Chell said, 'Anyone want my tomato? I don't know what fried tomato on a breakfast is for. I don't understand it. It seems the odd man out.'

'You dunk your toast in it.'

Finn said, giving the matter a tone reserved for the furthest-thrown speculations, 'That upgrading plan has a lot going for it, Aves.'

'It does, doesn't it?' Kay agreed quickly.

Ava said, 'Let me do the talking for a moment when we check in. Perhaps you could pin Manda down on the ground in the distance with a firm neck lock. I mean, it's just blind chance but you never know. Jesus Christ,' said Ava.

'What?' went Kylah.

'The more I think about it, I might perhaps just pay for a business-class seat for Manda.'

The entire table laughed enthusiastically.

'More money well spent.'

'Yes,' nodded Ava. 'Well, what was it? Fifty pence a minute or something to rid ourselves of her at the castle. What's a few thousand, so as not to sit next to Manda on a plane?'

'The disturbing thing is, if she sleeps on the plane she'll be all set to go out the minute we get there.'

'Sometimes I think she's going to have a heart attack she gets so excited.'

'No her. She's hardy as an ox.'

Cautiously Ava said, 'I'm only joking, girls. I'm learning not to say anything, because she is fascinating. She was really remarkably funny yesterday. She talked non-stop for three hours on champagne. Mainly about baby clothes.'

'Och, we've all heard that lecture.'

Kay laughed. 'And at the porn, she was fascinated by it but putting it down all the time. She *never* shuts up.'

'She talks in the cinema too. Loud. I won't go with her any more.'

'That's it. You've just to let her just rabbit on, you've got to take all the sly insults. If you just ignore them she doesn't have the strength of mind to plug on, so she moves to the next thing.'

They ate in peaceable, thoughtful silence for a while until Manda approached, speedily, and nipped in nimbly behind the table.

'Fucking Indiana Jones wouldn't let me bring in my pint, the bass. Stupid, ugly twat.' Manda started digging into her breakfast again. 'Oooh. It's still good and hot.'

'Where were you then?'

'Och, just went to the bar for one.'

'You tanned a Guinness in a few minutes?'

'Nay. Nay. I just took a good doochter and left it with someone.'

'You left your pint with someone?'

'Aye. A nice old geezer. From . . . ach, a forget where he's from but it's near Scrar-bra-bra. I asked him.'

'Scarborough.'

'Aye, that.'

'He might put something in it.'

'What?'

'Date-rape drug,' Chell frowned.

'He's ancient. Face like a bust couch. Besides, it's like Finn and Ava were saying yon other day. It's not a cruisey place the airport. We've been here days and nay chance of even a decent snog. So if the gadge drugs me, where's he going to get me? He's no on the same plane as me cos I got him told. That's me off to Las Vegas, mister, I tells him. And wasn't he away some no-place-sad-shithole in Greek or wherever, poor old soul. At least if he drugs me I'll sleep on the plane. How's that breakfast slipping down, girls?'

'Grand, aye.'

'Come on, Chell. Get it down you. Oh boy, that Guinness goes exact with an old full brekker fry-up.' The first belch now came.

'Excuse me.' She looked around, beyond their table to others which, true enough, must have surely heard. 'I was meaning to ask they barkeeps there. "Hoi, gadge. What cocktails do they drink in Las Vegas and set us all up one?" Let's do that. It'll be brilliant, girls.'

'What cocktails do they drink in Vegas, Ava?'

'Well, you can get anything. Martinis, margaritas –'

'We was at school with a girl called Margarita. Mind Rita the Greeter?'

'She's married now. To big fat James Bride.'

'But we's just called her Rita. Besides. That's a cool name. Margarita. But those days we didn't know what a margarita was. We didna know much at school.'

Manda spoke around a gob full. 'Aye. But some knew the feel of a wet fanny in the face well enough.'

'Watch you don't choke on your food, Manda,' said Kay quietly after a moment.

'It's okay, Kay. There's no pubes in it.'

This did silence Kay.

Industriously, Manda continued munching at her food through the long and awkward interlude.

Chell tried to break the ice as usual. 'So, what cocktails are you going to drink in Vegas, Manda? Ava was saying there was no sea and beaches in Vegas. It's in desert. So no Sex on the Beach.'

Ava said, 'Pina colada. You know what they say about pineapple juice, Manda? If a man drinks enough, his sperm tastes of it.'

Manda's head snapped up mid-chew. 'Is that right enough?'

Ava smiled seductively.

'That's why your mouth tastes of McEwan's Export every Sunday morning, at Mass, Manda,' Kylah casually said.

'Fuck off. I don't go to Mass.'

They all laughed at this, without grudge.

'Right. Back in a tick.' And Manda was off again. 'Away to see my old pal. Don't let Indiana Jones take this away, I'm no done with it yet.' Manda sped towards the Village Inn, giving a sneer to the waiting staff on the way out.

'Unbelievable.'

Kay said, 'I really don't know if I can take any more. I'm having doubts, girls. Really.'

'Too late now, Kay. You said so yourself. No turning back.'

'It's okay, girls. Only six days to go,' said Kylah.

Ava said, 'I don't know if I can take Manda much more either. Really. It's getting like, any excuse and I'm out of here. I'd go anywhere with you girls but her, she's . . . too much.'

The other girls smiled hard.

When Manda returned, she looked even more pleased with herself than usual. 'Aye, eh, just to let yous know that that's another fresh pint my mate's keeping for me and he bought it for me too.'

'You've scored at last, Mands.'

'Don't get his pension book mixed up with your passport.'

'Fuck off. I've used all my toast. Are you using that toast, Finn?'

'Eh, nah . . .'

'Thanks.' Manda started mopping her plate clean with the piece of dry toast. 'Oh good arse. That was brilliant. Chell, you've no half finished, darling.'

'I'm finished.'

'Never. You're gone be starved halfway round the world time thing and we'll be hitting the bars. Everything in the cases is goan be creased to fuck, stuck in there for however long I've been in this joint.'

'Aye. That's why I've got my iron with me,' Kylah reminded her.

Manda nodded, ultra-cautious. 'Oh aye. You did, didn't you? You'll give us a shot the night, eh? Ach. They'll be bloody irons galore in Las Vegas hotels. Won't there, Ava? And curling tongs too. Yous were all up to high doh and they'll be handing them out to you when you go in.' Her concern evaporated as she noticed something. 'Are you really done with that, Chell?'

'Aye.'

'You've hardly touched it.'

'You've hardly touched the Coke.'

'I wouldn't say that.'

Kay and Ava tried not to grimace.

'Pass it over here then, wee lass. Waste not want not, as my Nana – Oh. Do you really not want any sausage? And you all cut it up like for a wee puppy dog. Sausage is the best thing. You take this empty plate of mine. That's called a good cleaned plate, Chell.'

Manda passed her shining, bare plate to Chell and with both hands hovered Chell's platter down into position before her. She lay her face almost horizontal over the new plate and began hauling the food up.

'That was great,' Kylah stretched.

Kay said, 'I can't believe how much I ate.'

Manda sharply warned, 'Some people are no finished yet.'

'I'm dying for a fag.'

'Wait a wee minute now and we'll all go,' she chewed on.

Everyone patiently waited on Manda's completion. She didn't hurry. At one point, in response to the silent and patient table around her, she stated, 'Oh, I wish I could have my Guinness Extra Cold here by my side.'

Eventually: 'Oh, that was brilliant.'

'That was great,' Chell cautiously said.

'My treat, girls.'

'Aw Manda, we'll split it.'

'No ways. This is my party till the money runs out.' But immediately there were strings attached. 'You.' Manda pointed at Kylah. 'Away and ask that gadge for the bill, I'm no talking to that loser any more.'

'You pay at the till, Manda. Just go up. We'll all go up,' Kay said.

With a big relieved momentum they all started to rise and move towards their luggage trolleys.

The earringed waitress approached. 'Everything is okay for you?'

'Aye, aye, don't worry yourself. I'll pay at the till, hoor,' Manda smiled joyfully.

The waitress squinted. Manda had produced her purse from the voluminous bag and led her to the till. 'That was great, love, but your boss there needs a few lessons on being a good practice manager. There's no gonna be much of a tip left here.'

Manda: Pina colada and pint of Guinness Extra Cold.
Chell: Pina colada.
Kylah: Pina colada.
Kay: Pina colada.
Ava: Pina colada.
Finn: Pina colada.

The trolleys had been fully thrust back into the smoking area of the Village Inn, in as intimidating an advance as possible, but still only a small round table for two was available and other tables stubbornly refused to surrender and move on. In fact, they seemed less likely to move as the smoking community kept examining the party of young women with the slices of over-ripe pineapple and metallised frizzle sticks in their outlandish cocktails. Manda, Chell and Kylah sat at the table smoking steadily, intimidated now by the impending tobacco ban on aircraft. Chell sat on a pulled-up and now requisitioned chair. Kay, Ava and Finn found they could perfectly well sit on the trolleys of suitcases, solid as a stone bench among the stilled statues of the Tuileries. From WH Smith, shaking in Manda's two paws, was *The Unofficial Guide to Las Vegas*, the spine already badly creased at the Nightclub Profiles section.

'It's incredible, girls, it's incredible. There is so many brilliant clubs it's beyond amazing. I knows how it all works. I know. This is the best book ever writ. It tells you all. All. The dress codes and covers; they have cover prices. The most amazing thing is, local women and men sometimes get in places free, so we's have to pretend to be American Yanks a lot of the time. That'll be a crack.'

Ava said, 'They ask for your ID card, Manda, to show you're a Nevada State Resident. You can't fool them.'

'Ach, we'll soon find a way round that. We'll get a local lass in tow with us. A wee hoor or something.'

Kylah suddenly went, 'Hey, look at this, Ava.' From her vanity case Kylah removed a sheet of paper.

'What's that?' Manda looked away from the pages for a split second. 'Oh, just the plaster planner,' and she tutted dismissively then uneasily settled into the pages again, whipping out her arm frequently for swallows of both Guinness and pina colada.

Ava frowned as Kylah passed the sheet of paper. Ava unfolded it. The sheet of A4 lined paper contained a shaky but actual outline in blue biro of two feet.

Arrows pointed to various toes and heels which were flagged up: heel here, upper, bridge there, wee toe, third toe, and a number code was in operation. The numbers referred to a list at the page bottom:

open strapped top black
open strapped top silver
yellow heels
Nine West silver
old heels
black shoes

'What is this?'

'It's a plaster planner. Shows me where I fix what sticking plasters to go on my toes and feet for what heels and what shoes. So's I don't get mixed up and get blisters.'

'Oh, I see. That's quite ingenious.'

Without looking up from the pages, Manda droned, 'That's nothing. I've got two plaster planners. I've got two, I've brought so many shoes with me I have to have two plaster planners. I hope yous have all brought heels at least, you bloody nuns. You'll maybe get in Coyote Ugly to laugh at the hoors dancing on the bars. You might get in there in those bloody motorcycle boots, Finn, but you'll no get in much else. I'm warning you now. It's classy.' Again this was announced without the face moving from study of the book.

Finn said, 'Coyote Ugly. Oh no. That's going to be a club just full of shouting men.'

'Aye. Exactly, Finn. Men. That's what a nightclub is. You'll be ogling the barmaids happily, I know, but some of us are in a club on serious business and don't you forget that and go spoiling it all for the rest of us.'

'Oh fuck off, Manda.'

'So that's it, is it, Finn? Only nightclubs where there's no men that we're . . . destined for?'

Chell quickly said, 'Coyote Ugly. That will be funny.'

'It'll be legendary, girls. We'll be there. Have you brought heels, Kay?'

'Yes, I have, actually.'

'Good on you, girl, always to be relied on, Kay.'

Finn knew she was next for interrogation so just admitted, 'I got my favourites fixed for the holiday. The strap was bust.'

'Good on you. Those ancient ones with the cute heel? Have you not bought nothing new in all London since those ages ago ones? Ava?'

'Yes, I've two pairs,' she reported flintily.

'Two pairs bundled into the bottom of your bin liner. I'm proud of you. What are they?'

'Well, I've heeled boots.'

'Those you're weared?' This was said without looking up at her from the book. Manda had perfectly absorbed and retained what everyone was wearing from the first instant that morning.

'No. I've a more dressy pair for short skirts and under jeans.'

'No-jeans-some-clubs,' came the senatorial dictate.

'And I've a pair of D&G heels.'

This produced a pause. 'You're joking me, you jammy hoor. Have you got Dolce & Gabbana heels?'

'Yes.'

'Holy smoke. Gonna let us see them?'

Ava shrugged and slipped lithely off the cases.

'How much were they then?'

'I've forgotten. Three hundred and something in the sales. Thing about designer shoes is, I'm different sizes in different makes. It's most disconcerting. I'm thirty-eight and a half in Prada but I'm thirty-nine in D&G.'

Manda's eyes snapped up. 'Now is that right enough?'

'Mmm.' Ava's voice had deepened the way she was bent over into her backpack. She came up with a silver fabric shoe bag, knotted tight by its pull strings at the top.

'Is that the left one or the right one?'

Ava felt at the shoe within the glittering cloth, frowning as if trying to guess a Christmas present. 'Left.'

Manda sneered, 'I didn't take my box for *my* pair of . . .' she paused for effect . . . 'Pradas. Though obviously I'd like to. But I'm telling you this now, girl, you're going get your heel broke just stuffing them in that rubbish sack of yours, once they're just flung on the aeroplane by them loading-up gorillas.' All this was said simultaneous to Manda, without asking, tossing the guide-book on the table and jackknifing forward to unknot and remove her left trainer. Manda whispered, 'It's okay, girls. Kay's got ma passport and my cash is in the other sock.'

Ava hesitantly passed over the shoe. Now Manda's white sports sock was off and dropped on the table in a curly, greasy tube. They all watched as Manda tugged impatiently and revealed the shoe from inside the bag then held it up like a rare glass artefact.

'Oh my God. They are beautiful,' said Kylah.

'Wow. They look strong. They're Dolce & Gabbana designer. No D&G,' Chell stated.

Manda was not being drawn into this argument a second time. 'No bad at all,' Manda nodded respectfully.

The shoe had a thick, shapely high heel, embossed with actual metal rococo working, drawing a marbling of dark blue and milky white around the narrow flanks and tracing this texture down onto the open toepiece. Manda took the shoe and fiercely jammed it onto her bare foot then hauled the strap with its metallic studs round her broad, capriped foot. The strap already strained but just connected into the final hole of the buckle. 'Mmmmm. They fit me like they was made for me,' Manda claimed.

Ava winced as Manda rose onto her feet; the shoe violently oscillated from side to side under the strain, then Manda found a sort of stability and took a step forward. 'What about that then? Cinderella will go to the ball.'

Everyone reserved judgement, terrified to contradict her but straining with indignation on Ava's behalf.

With caution Kylah advanced, 'A girl's shoes is a girl's shoes, Manda. It's sacred. I think they would look that bit better on Ava.'

Manda raised her face to Kylah and Kylah actually dropped her gaze.

'What do you mean by that? Since when were you the expert? You stick to the singing, love.'

'Your calves is a wee bit wide to offset the shoe.'

'What? Who the fuck are you, Chell? They're no boots. I don't wear them on my calves. Too wide. My legs is way longer than yours.'

Now the face whipped round on Ava. A sleary expression burst out from left to right, fighting it out among itself to see if it were a sneer or a smile. 'Aye. You'll lend us a wee shot of these in Vegas for a night down the bar or that, Ava?'

'Well, I might wear them most nights myself?' she dared venture.

'Really? Well, we'll just see what happens when you're needing the hair straighteners.' Manda quickly bent over and undid the beautiful shoe from her foot; it was stuck slightly from sweat and weight so she kicked it casually forward where it fell on its side and she went about resocking and shoeing herself.

Kylah bent over and picked up the shoe and handed it back to Ava. Chell reached out towards the guidebook which she herself had bought in WH Smith. Manda snapped the book up back into her own hands. 'Uh-huh, uh-huh. I'm no finished swotting up on this.'

A gloom of sipping cocktails took hold of the table again.

'Do you think we can check in soon?' Chell asked.

Manda announced, 'Now, I've an appointment at British Hairways to get this nail fixed.'

Kay frowned. 'Did you make an appointment?'

'They know me there, girls. I'm almost like a regular, so I'll just stroll over and in and –' the name was quoted with massive portent '– "Katherine", there, will do my nail in just a jiffy. One professional to another.' She let this concept linger in the air for all their benefit.

Ava said, 'To check in and to get rid of the baggage will be great.'

Manda went, 'Aye, okay then. Do that. But you'll need to wait on me.'

'Get a shift on then, Manda, cos we don't want to be hanging around with all this clobber.'

She didn't look away from the page. 'Aye, aye, Finn. Don't get your knickers in a twist. After all, from your backpack, it looks like you didn't take that many.'

3

Finn pushed Manda's brute trolley and they moved out of the front entrance of the Village Inn and past McDonald's, past UK Explorer and Monsoon, beyond Accessorize. They could smell the sausage rolls of Hasty Pastry as they squashed in the lifts and moved downstairs. They rolled by the security gates which led through to Airside and Departures.

They had stood idly for quite some time when, from behind them, towards the security gates, Manda appeared back from the hairdresser and beauty salon.

'Here she is,' Chell said without too much of a triumphant tone.

Kay and Finn looked suspiciously towards her. Manda was waving her finger at them, cunningly combining the display of her new acrylic nail with giving them the finger. Kylah was waving about the disposable camera excitedly.

'Aye, that's my nail done,' was yelled as she approached, the voice not really dropping in volume as she came close. 'Aye. They was quite good but no as good as me and my sister's salon.' Manda turned her attention to her own trolley which Finn leaned against. Manda slapped first one of her pink suitcases then the other. 'Aye. One. Two. They're both here safe.'

'We have to get a photo took, this time for real check-in,' Kylah stated.

Ava took control. 'Right. Listen.'

'What?' Manda crossed her arms.

'There's six of us. I used to use American Airlines and my father uses it all the time. There's the slightest chance, just the slightest, that we might get an upgrade or two, but I doubt it.'

Manda scowled. 'What's upgrade?'

'You get put in business class instead of economy.'

Manda began to visibly tremble and her arms dropped to her sides. 'No. Never?'

'Maybe not. But I think you should let me do the talking.'

'You hearing that, Manda? No butting in.' Finn jutted her head at her.

'So. This time. Passports?'

Everyone produced their passports dutifully and efficiently. Kay still retained Manda's and handed both of them over to Ava.

They joined the queue.

'When'll I take the photo?'

'Not now. Not now.'

'Wait till we're all checked in. We don't want to look too daft and touristy.'

'We go first cos we've got the lighter baggage.'

'Oh. Right,' went Manda, sourly.

'Follow us with the trolleys, eh, Chell then Kylah. Manda, you at the back.'

'Tut.'

There was only a short queue in front of them. Everything seemed vivid under the high ceilings. Objects reflected light. Manda deftly noted how the adjacent business–class check-in had a red carpet, though of dubious cleanliness, reaching the length up to it. Nobody was in this queue and the attendant behind the desk sat still, slightly bored, looking straight ahead, willing customers to materialise just to pass the time.

Manda, angrily cut off at the rear of the short queue, craned from left to right as she had at the hotel check-in, on Friday night, scowling at the sedate progress of the few people who had already reached the check-in counter.

When it was Ava's turn, she casually advanced to the check-in, smiling, with Kay at her side. Ava said, 'Hello. Sorry to bring such a large group, there's six of us checking in as a party.'

'Good morning. Afternoon.'

'We're flying on with you from JFK through to Las Vegas

later today, so we were very hopeful you could book our luggage all the way through.'

'Yes of course, that should be no problem.'

Ava put down the passports and the travel documents.

'I don't mean to be cheeky, but my father and I are frequent flyers with you on American and I wondered if there was the slightest chance of an upgrade today on either sector? I know that probably won't be possible.'

'Well, let me look at that. Are you part of our frequent-flyer programme?'

'Yes. My father is also. Monsieur Hurmalainen.

'Oh, Mr Hurmalainen. I know your father. He does fly with us a lot.'

'You know him? Oh, that's nice.'

'Let me see. You are six today and flying forward on 649 out of JFK to Las Vegas. A holiday, is it?'

'Yes. Just till Saturday, I'm afraid.'

'Lovely though.'

'Yes.'

'Well, Tuesdays are quiet. It's your lucky day. I'm afraid I could only manage . . . eh . . . the upgrade of two passengers to business today or just one to first. I see your colleagues have some luggage so that would spread your burden a little if you have weight there.'

'Let's put one of our party in first. That's very, very generous of you. Thank you.'

'Not at all. Who would be the passenger in first?'

'That would be Amanda Tassy,' Kay quickly said, pointing at the passport.

'Manda? Manda? Bring your trolley up.'

Manda had been bopping around behind them as if she were being buzzed by a vicious wasp, squinting hysterically at each mention of her name.

'Aye. What is it?'

'You can go in first.'

'Me? In first?' said Manda, slowly breaching the enormity of it. 'Aye, aye. Me in first. Aye.'

'Okay,' said the check-in attendant, seemingly unfazed. She leaned over towards her colleague. 'Tasmin. One upgrade to first.'

'Sure, I'll get it on this,' Tasmin replied and covered her mouth to yawn.

Their check-in lady started typing onto her keyboard. 'I can book you on to the second leg now but I'm afraid I can't upgrade on that flight so early. Quiet here today but I can't say how it would be by then.'

'No, that's all right. That's lovely, thank you.'

'Okay, if you could put the cases on here.'

Manda looked as if she had to dive from the highest diving board, so Kay and Ava together lifted the first of her cases onto the weigh belt. Manda's eyes simply followed the large FIRST baggage tag which was enveloped around the handle grip of her first pink Samsonite. Then a HEAVY tag was added. The lady printed out the duplicate security ID tags and attached one to the passport and one to the flank of the case, the sticker designed in a sextant of tearaway segments, so that while one portion of it may be lost in contact, other sections would always remain to identify the case. She buzzed the case a little further back to enable Ava and Finn to lift Manda's second suitcase up and she repeated the process. She printed out a boarding card but placed it flat in front of her, pinned inside Manda's passport. 'And the rest of you will travel economy today?'

'Yes please,' said Ava.

When they had all checked in, Kylah was calling, 'Photo, photo. I'll ask someone.' Kylah stepped quickly over to a rotund American-looking lady with gold cords on her glasses. She removed her glasses, and listening to Kylah's spiel, her face lightened. She took the camera from Kylah as its simple features were pointed out.

Kylah dashed back into them. 'You've got to get the check-in thingmy place behind yous.'

The girls formed a line; Kylah connected in at far right,

kneeling a bit to reveal the check-in queue behind them at which the staff members smiled, momentarily indulgent. Kylah threw out her arm joyously but in a mock manner as she froze it in the air for the camera; her other arm went across Chell's lower back. Chell had an arm around Kay's shoulders and Ava stood in the middle with an arm draped around Finn's and Kay's shoulders, then Manda was out on the edge but with no arm around Finn, though Finn had one around her. This was because, like a lottery winner's cheque, Manda held the specially coloured first-class boarding pass delicately between her ringed fingers for display.

'Well, hi there and do I hear you guys are off to Vegas?'

'Aye, first class some of us is,' Manda bawled out.

'Now how does this camera work?'

Holding her arm and her smile, Kylah called through her teeth, 'The flash should be charged so just take it, missus.'

'Okay then.' The lady lifted the camera and took the photo.

The flash went off, distributing no more than a brief, weak light, seemingly limited to the camera itself, diluted in the large, airy dimensions of that brightly lit hall, yet still reminiscent of the lightning straps on the Sunday.

The young women immediately split apart, bursting out in directions, Manda circling and looking at the first-class boarding pass, all of them in a certain euphoria at having rid themselves of the clinging baggage. Kylah reapproached and thanked the lady who nodded and smiled looking at them all then she moved off in her own modes of distraction.

Manda looked around them. 'I can't believe yous can do anything at all, yous must be so sick jealous that I'm going first class to Vegas.'

Ava smiled, 'You're only going to New York, first class.'

'Oh. Am I? Aye. But to New York is . . . how many hours is that?'

'Seven hours.'

'And I'll be in first class where Victoria Beckham and Reeker Glacier and all famous and rich sit? I'll be next to them. Oh, that is legendary.'

'Yeah. And don't get too drunk or we'll leave you in New York and go on without you.'

Manda gave a vicious eye.

'I think you'll get free drink, won't you?' Finn asked cautiously.

'Will they have Guinness Extra Cold?'

'Don't ask for that, Manda lass, ask for champagne.'

Ava shrugged. 'As far as I remember you get anything you want; a huge seat that sometimes goes back into a bed, very good food, as much to drink as you want, sometimes massage.'

'Massage? By guys?' Manda stiffened.

'Sometimes, I think.'

'And is the food all weird posh stuff? Snails and that?'

'No, no. It'll be good, you'll have a choice of fish and meat.'

'Will they make us a Mackersy burger?'

'Eh, I doubt it.'

'Huh. I thought it was first.' Manda looked at Ava. 'See how your tickets were six hundred including the hotel, how much would a first-class ticket like this cost?'

'One way to New York, five, six, maybe seven thousand.'

Manda looked down at the ticket. 'That's incredible.'

Finn reminded her, 'And don't forget it was Ava that got that for you. They even knew her dad at the check-in.'

Manda looked into Ava's eyes. She smiled, but she said, 'So is this just one-way first class? I don't get to come back first as well?'

'No, Manda. You don't. And if we do get a chance we'll send Chell next turn. You both could have gone in business class this time.'

'Och, I don't mind,' said Chell. 'I'd sooner be with all yous wherever yous are. Hold a hand.'

'Aye, but it would've been nice to make your first journey ever on a plane in business class.'

Chell shrugged. 'Ach, middle class, first class, working class, I don't care where I sit.'

Ava turned to Kay with a weepy face. 'Ooo, she's so cute and adorable.'

'What? What?' asked Chell.

'Right, at least we can wander around without those damn suitcases.'

'Do we's go through to the other bit of the airport? Manda, there's shops through there too.'

'Is there? Cos I'm first class, do I go a special place and a special way?'

'No.'

'There's no point going there too early because sometimes your flight gets delayed and you can be stuck through there for hours.'

'What'll we's do then?'

Manda: Pint of Guinness Extra Cold.
Ava: Double straight Stolichnaya vodka with ice.
Kay: Medium-size glass of red wine.
Chell: Bacardi Breezer.
Finn: Gin and tonic with bottled tonic.
Kylah: Bottle of cider with ice.

'So I've to, eh, phone wee Sean and tell him Mummy's flying first class and that. I knew I'd make him proud one day. Then I'll phone my bloody sister too and tell her, she'll be spewing jealous . . . Oh no, she's beeling at me, isn't she? Bitch. Aye, well. Aye, I'll text Shelly McCrindle and tell her I'm travelling in first, these days. Not that Shelly's a pal or that. I mean, she's popular but she's not what I would call a friend. More an acquaintance. Aye, she's more acquaintance.'

'Okay, Chell?'

'Aye.'

'Are you okay?' said Finn, looking at Kay. 'You're very quiet.'

'Oh, I'm fine. Okay. I'll be honest.' Kay looked at Ava and paused. 'I'm a bit nervy and I'm wondering who'll be sitting next to Manda in first.'

'Robbie Williams.'

'Gordon Blair.'

'The Queen.'

'Nah, she has her own plane, dossy besom.'

'So this is it, girls. Who'd of thought? Off to Vegas first class for five nights. It just shows if you work hard in life you get somewhere. Like those cunts in yon castle. I'm riding with them now. Who'd of thought it? Nobody in Rascals. That's for sure. I'll no be thinking about them on Saturday, out of my mind, in the lushest nightclubs of Las Vegas. Oh I'll no be thinking about them, I can assure you, one and all the now. It's going to be brilliant. It's already a classic. That was brilliant that I lost my passport for yous. What a scream, eh? It worked out for the best. We could all be in smelly old Magaluf if it wasn't for me.'

Finn shrugged, admitting, 'I suppose that's right enough.'

'Too right it is. Yous keep that in mind. I could be in Magaluf with some baldy nonce from Birmingsham or Scar bra bra, full of English, bristly skinheads, panting away, sliding around like my tits was in a curling match. Instead my big bum's sat on a first-class ticket to Las Vegas. I was half thinking, I might get a bit of kip on the plane but no way. I want to be awake. Scoping out the richies on the first class. Their clothes, their shoes, their handbags. The women I'm talking about. Though I'll probably meet a man. You know, Ava-style. Join the mile-high club with my runners still on, in the toilet. It's probably twice the size in first class. There's probably a bath with gold taps in there. The tracky bottoms'll be down and the gorgeous guy'll be . . . Aye. I want to see some fucking bling up there. And I'll be telling them too. If I see any low standards from the women, I'll be telling them straight. "Hi, hoor. Yon handbag's from Nine West, ya fucking hinger, get some Prada on your arm, you dozy slapper. You're in first class!"'

Manda had shouted it so loud, Kay ducked and looked around the Village Inn, thinking someone would believe it was directed at them.

Manda laughed. 'Don't worry, Kay lassie. You're no back in chapel any more. Oh, bonnie lassies, these are the times of our lives and they're only beginning. Only just beginning. Who was that of yous?' The pointed finger went around the circle, in very slow motion. '"Nothing happens to us any more," one of yous says. One of yous,' she snarled. 'Christ. Maybe it was me? '"Nothing happens to us any more," you went! Lassies. Lassies. Wake up and smell the roses. I could write a book I could. Or one of you phila-surfers could . . .'

Kylah turned aside to Chell with a scientific squint on her forehead. 'She's not going throw up, is she?'

'No, no; she's fine,' Chell nodded, confident in the precise pathology of Manda.

Manda hardly even paused for their exchange. 'I'll not be spewing. The Rascals' crew'll be spewing when they hear about this. These are the days of our lives, lassies. You don't even know; spraffin around with your wee worries and talking in toilets for half an hour like old Kay and Finn here. And I love the lot of yous. I'm not afraid to say it. You don't think I do. You think Amanda is sat on her high horse, with no feeling and no thoughts of others. But I do have thoughts of yous. So I do. I love each of yous right down to the dirt under your fingernails. No that you have any, cos most you get your manicures done at our place. Well. You, the Mighty Finn, with those wee scabs on the end of your finger, I can't vouch for you. But don't worry. It doesn't mean I don't love you too; you know I love you all. And you too, long tall Sally the shover, you English ho . . . devil. And I'll tell yous this. You'll stand okay with me. Through your problems, every last damn one of yous.' She nodded now, a bit tearful, combined with lack of sleep; the head wobbled on the neck like a fat thigh.

The others had never seen her in such a state of emotional excitation. It was remarkable that the allure of first class could evoke such finely tuned hysteria – who says the glamour of air travel is lost?

'Aye. I love the every one of yous and want you to know it. Just in case this bastarding plane goes down in the sea. I'll be thinking of yous. Up in first class of course where I belong, and I'll no spill my free drink on the way down either and I'll have my leg over a rich boy too. I'll be thought of us all, knowing these were the days of our lives and plenty more to come. Days of our lives and yous didn't even know it.'

She seemed to be finished.

Finn nodded. 'Well, Manda. I've got my nail brush with me but your sentiments are returned. You're a pain in the arse but we all love you too.'

'So we do, Mands.'

'Drink to it.'

They all raised their glasses.

Miss Tassy's head worryingly fell forward and she nodded in an other-worldly way.

'Are you okay, Manda?'

'Ah'm overcome with emotion. And first class to Vegas. I haven't thanked you, Ava. Thank you.'

'You're welcome,' nodded Ava, pitying all those flying first class this afternoon: the incomprehensible accent, the sudden yells, the burps, the unwanted toasts.

The head went down. 'I love you all,' she mumbled. And there were a few other inaudible mumbles in there which included the phrases: 'first class' and 'legendary' and 'classic'. Then she rallied and the head came back up again, the eyes red-rimmed but lively. 'Right. A last blast on the Ezzy Dancer, girls.'

'Oh no you don't. No way.'

'No, Manda. We'll get all sweaty.'

'Come on. You knows you want to.'

'We need to go in fifteen minutes.'

'Fifteen minutes is fine. Up with yous all. And there's something else too.'

So they were all up and moving out the bar again, gathering their hand luggage.

'Yous go into the Game Grid. There's something else I'm getting for yous.'

The others assembled outside the luring entrance to Game Grid but Manda walked on round the corner. Chell and Finn curiously followed her. They came to the Coral betting shop: a deep narrow space with standard fluorescent lighting, made out in green plastic with form sheets or newspaper betting pages spread along the walls and a counter with protected glass at the far end. Toadstool-like green seats, fitted into the floor as if on a storm-prone cruise ship, ran along the walls. A bookies was an exclusively male domain and the young women peered in, mystified by its obscurities.

Then, on the corner, there stood a fully functioning post office, brightly illuminated inside to show the filing shelves close up behind the shoulders of the two counter clerks seated through safety glass – those small scales for weighing parcels rested upon the shelves outside.

A rotating stand slatted with aviation-themed postcards stood outside, by the serving counters, the postcards mainly showing jet aircraft – in the differing liveries of many airlines – at the point of lifting off from Gatwick's runway. The differing photos caught undercarriages still down or in the semi-retracted angles of just folding away.

'Jings,' said Chell. 'If I'd any money left I could pay an instalment towards the telly licence.'

They watched as Manda chose six postcards and bought stamps. She came back towards them all and handed the postcards out.

'We've got to send these home before we go, girls. You can post them there. I've bought stamps too, *first class* of course. Tell the folks back home we've been stuck in the hoorin airport for donkey's.'

'Manda, Manda.' Kylah's voice called from the entrance. 'It's out of order. The Ezzy Dancer's out of order.'

'Oh, I can't believe it. Och, fuck it. A last Guinness Extra Cold for the road, girls.'

As they reapproached the Village Inn alongside Caffè Nero, Manda straightened up. 'Hey.'

'What's going on?'

A thin scattering of what looked like staff members from different retail outlets were standing on the threshold of the Village Inn but seemingly gazing in or through it. They had abandoned their shops.

'Oh no,' went Kylah. 'Fucking neds is fighting in there.'

'It's not a fire, is it?'

Manda called, joyfully, 'No ways, girls. At last. Brilliant. The Village Inn has a stripper on! Better be a guy.'

In their excitable, curious way, Manda, Kylah and Chell dashed forward and then stopped, looking over the heads of others. They couldn't get a clear look. Finn, Kay and Ava followed up.

It was impossible to enter the bar such a crowd had accumulated, and Manda was frowning furiously. 'Hoi. I'm travelled first class. Let us through.' She was ignored. It was up at the multi-screens in the Village Inn that everyone watched.

Finn came closer in, looking at the screens, and heard Manda's voice. Manda turned to the person next to her. 'What is that? A big fire?'

The woman looked at Manda. 'Plane crash; but strange.'

'Not in Gatwick. That's not in Gatwick. Strange?'

'Look.'

Manda finally looked.

Kay and Ava came up beside her; they actually stood slightly against Manda, as if in a concert audience. Finn put a companionable hand on Manda's shoulder.

'What is it?' Chell's voice spoke from behind.

'I don't know. It's just a big building, smoking.'

'That's New York,' said Ava.

'New York. That's where I'm going,' Manda said. 'I'm going to right there. First class.'

'What's wrong? I can't see,' said Chell.

'I thought it was just on fire,' somebody said.

The girl next to her in the orange T-shirt said, 'A plane. It was a plane.'

'Where's the plane?'

'In it. It's gone right inside it.'

'Bloody nasty,' said Manda but one eye drifted around looking for a way through to the bar. 'I was going have another Guinness.'

Then came a yell, like when men yell in the pub when a shock goal is scored.

Kay, Finn and Ava turned to look at one another. Ava said, 'Did you see that?'

'That's a replay thing. Is it?'

'No. This is live, this is live; that's just happened.'

'Did that happen now or before? Is that to do with the time change?'

'Be quiet, Manda.'

'Will it affect first class?'

'That's two. That's not an accident any more.' A man turned round and looked at them. 'This is not an accident.' He repeated it directly to them as if they were in some way culpable. They were not. Few were, despite what was coming.

'What is it?' Chell said.

The man said, 'That's not an accident. That's another gone in.'

Chell turned round. 'What's he mean?'

Finn said, 'Take Chell over there a wee minute. Take her over to those seats. Away. Or we won't get her on the plane now. Take her over where the smokers' benches outside are.'

Ava herself suddenly took Chell's hand as if she were a small child and moved her away. Kylah stepped in and followed them off, to where you could sit and look down from those armless seats to the Arrivals plaza.

Kay and Finn stood side by side, watching from the entrance. Manda had belligerently pushed in ahead.

'It's . . . I don't know if . . .' But Kay stopped talking then. It was easier not to. Looking was easier. Looking upwards at the screen the way she, Ava and Manda had looked up the afternoon before at another screen and at what things they saw there – as if expecting some final, stunning answer to come over the screen. But no answers came.

Manda said, 'Never mind this stuff, girls. Let's go.'

Finn clicked her tongue. Very slowly Kay's fingers crept down to Finn's hand and gripped it for a moment then let go. Finn seemed almost oblivious; her hand tightened like a crab claw in acknowledgement then hung loose.

They walked to the smoking benches. Chell was there smoking, Kylah crouched beside her mumbling. Ava was standing. She watched them both approach and took a step to them. 'What's happening?'

'It's. Why would people do that?'

They all sat down on the blue seats. The six of them sat

393

together; people were running past and sometimes talking into mobile phones. Yet others passed calm and even laughing. Chell looked spooked and Kylah remained beside her, but still arrival passengers transited, people moved in from the railway station area below as was normal.

Soon actual calls and shouts came from the Village Inn as if something was happening right in there – as if a hunched demon with eyes and claws was moving at leisure over the crammed carpets, slaughtering, and with those shouts, people walked quickly along the promenade talking into mobile phones, attempting to reach some next world. Chell crouched lower into herself.

'It's okay, Chell.'

Manda said, 'Hey. Maybe we should write our postcards now?' Nobody responded. They all waited to see what would happen next.